THE REDEMPTION

of

Caralynne Hayman

Carole Brown

Praise for
The Redemption of Caralynne Hayman

A story that will wrench your heart and show the light of God in the darkest night. Carole Brown is an author to watch!

Roseanna M. White,
Harvest House author of the Culper Ring Series

This novel reads like a winner. From a threatening, ominous opening to the horrors of a creepy religious settlement complete with misguided biblical interpretation and a new pastor who wants to fix things, the life of Caralynne Hayman will grab and keep readers rushing through each page, each chapter, every death, punishment, and rescue attempt. Brown's work reads like an exposé of every parent's worst nightmare and makes you hold your children, and your faith, a little closer

Lisa Lickel,
author of *Healing Grace*: a novel, and *The Last Detail*

Through an unlikely set of circumstances, I was asked to read an early draft of *The Redemption of Caralynne Hayman,* by Carole Brown. I am not a fan of women's fiction, yet I read right through this novel because of Brown's remarkable ability to build tension and suspense. The way Mrs. Brown builds tension reminds me – in technique, not content – of a young Dean Koontz. At times Brown makes you squirm, but you always wonder what's next and never want to put the book down until the end.

Joseph Max Lewis,
practicing attorney and author of *The Diaries of Pontius Pilate,* a thriller,
and *Just Verdicts*

Carole Brown's debut novel, *The Redemption of Caralynne Hayman,* is a riveting novel of a woman caught in a cult that demands complete subjection of women—and girls way too young to be women—to their men in the name of religion. The cult is reminiscent of Wayne Jeffers' sect of fundamentalist Mormons, and shows how a denomination can get out of hand when they substitute the doctrines of men for the Word of God. Carole Brown is passionate about her subject and depicts characters that have human failings but who manage to rise above them. By the time I came to the suspenseful ending, I was turning pages as fast as I could. Brava, Carole Brown! I expect to see lots more from you!

Laurie Kingery,
author of the Brides of Simpson Creek series for Love Inspired
Historicals

Starts with a bang and doesn't let up. Caralynne has a lot on her mind, and revenge in her heart. It's Caralynne against a strong cult, and both are determined to destroy the other.

James R. Callan,
award-winning author of *A Ton of Gold* and other mystery/suspense
novels

Wow, Carole Brown has a stunning debut novel here! When a religious cult distorts God's identity, allowing systematic abuse of the women and children, only one brave woman, Caralynne, is able to see how wrong this is and fight back. No one comes to her aid... until the heir apparent to the cult finds salvation in God's true message of Christianity and stands up to defend her. But can Caralynne forgive those in the group who contributed to her young daughter's death to truly embrace God? Even if she has found love with her defender? I was breathless reading this. Definitely a suspense novel to go for!

Amy Deardon,
scientist and author of *A Lever Long Enough* and *The Story Template*

With her debut novel *The Redemption of Caralynne Hayman*, Carole Brown pens an authentic story. It's as though she knows her characters personally. I became as a fly on the wall in the cult of The Children of Righteous Cain. Intrigued, I followed Caralynne Hayman through the journey of misguided friendships, fear, and distrust. And in the end, I trusted she would learn about our true source of security. Both now and for all eternity.

Sharon A. Lavy,
author of *Dreaming of a Father's Love*

Carole Brown wasted no time in pulling me into Caralynne Hayman's nightmare. This fast-paced novel burrows into the distorted world of Elder Simmons and his cult—The Children of Righteous Cain. Carole did a splendid job of developing characters and scenes that gripped my mind and my heart. As much as I want to believe that Cara's world is pure fiction, I know that such a world exists.

Tom Blubaugh,
author of *Night of the Cossack*

Rarely does a Christian book come along with such raw honesty as Carole Brown's *The Redemption of Caralynne Hayman*. Written with compassion and sensitivity for abused women, Brown speaks to the heart that has been embittered by abuse and the hope that is found in Christ, who died to set the prisoner free. An excellent debut novel. Can't wait for the next one.

Linda Wood Rondeau,
author of *The Other Side of Darkness* and *It Really IS a Wonderful Life*,
and winner of the coveted Selah Award

Carole Brown's *The Redemption of Caralynne Hayman* deals with the heart-wrenching subject of spousal and child abuse within a so-called Christian cult that misuses biblical teaching and veers dangerously into darkness. Although the subject matter is deep and sometimes troubling, the author's elegant prose manages to uplift. This is one of those novels that lets the reader know there indeed can be light at the end of a dark tunnel within the love and mercy of God.

Nike Chillemi,
award-winning murder mystery author, Grace Awards chair

What would you do if freedom and imprisonment were separated by only a breath? Ms. Carole Brown explores the very real question of a battered wife and her choices between right and wrong. She handles some extremely difficult issues with skill and just as the title, *The Redemption of Caralynne Hayman* suggests, Ms. Browne writes a lovely and rich story of redemption.

If you or someone you know has been through abuse in marriage or as a child, this book will offer healing and comfort. You are valuable and this book is one of affirmation for the woman who needs to know she is not alone.

Angela Breidenbach,
author of *A Healing Heart*

THE REDEMPTION OF CARALYNNE HAYMAN
Published by Lighthouse Publishing of the Carolinas
2333 Barton Oaks Dr., Raleigh, NC, 27614

ISBN 978-1-938499-94-4
Copyright © 2013 by Carole Brown
Cover design by The Killion Group, www.TheKillionGroupInc.com
Book design by Reality Info Systems www.realityinfo.com

Available in print from your local bookstore, online, or from the publisher at:
www.lighthousepublishingofthecarolinas.com
For more information on the author, visit: www.carolebrownauthor.com

Brought to you by the creative team at LighthousePublishingoftheCarolinas.com:
Eddie Jones, Christina Miller, Reality Info Systems, Brian Cross, Rowena Kuo

Library of Congress Cataloging-in-Publication Data
Brown, Carole
The Redemption of Caralynne Hayman/ Carole Brown, 1st ed.

Printed in the United States of America

Lighthouse Publishing
of the Carolinas
www.lighthousepublishingofthecarolinas.com

Acknowledgments from the Author

I've always believed in shooting for the stars, and a favorite saying of mine expresses that belief: Dream Big; Work Hard. It's okay to dream big just as long as we work hard to attain those dreams, and in dreaming and working our way to publication, our paths cross with others who influence us. Some of them are memorable in our hearts and lives.

Sharon, you were my first beta reader for this novel but also one of my dearest friends.

To Mary, who's gone from this world but not forgotten. Your friendship and Help were invaluable..

My dear Ohio friends: you've offered suggestions and critiques. You've laughed with me through the good times and encouraged me through the hard ones.

Christina, I value your wisdom and friendship and talent in editing far more than words can express. Thank you.

Jamin, what would I do without you and all your brainstorming ability? You are a treasure in my life.

Kayla and Janeth, who aren't writers, but who are there when I need something done. You believe in my writing and offer your services with a smile. You'll never know how you lighten my load!

Karen D, thank you for what you do to help. You're always a friend and helper when I need you.

Daniel and Jonathan, my two wonderful sons, who never quit asking when my books would be published. Thank you for being there when I had a technical problem or needed you to read a chapter or even brainstorm with me. You've always been the light of my eyes.

Dedication

Without you, Dan—my hero and husband—this novel would not have been written. Your imagination and suggestions and critiques encouraged me to try harder, writer better, and never quit. I love you.

And to God, who is indeed THE HOPE that shines brighter than any darkness. You gave me this precious talent and wouldn't let me ignore it. Bless this book as you will. It's yours.

CHAPTER ONE

Twenty years earlier

The shadow creatures on the wall shook their wings and legs. Heads with horns nodded. Scary, dark faces watched.

The little girl clasped her floppy-eared rabbit against her chest and stared into the dark.

"Mmm …" Mommy's murmur reached to her through the walls, and the giggles from her mother tiptoed in, shooing away the fear.

Whoosh. She blew out a breath and squeezed her rabbit tighter. "Mommy has a friend with her, Ramsey. She loves me just like I love you and will give me hugs in the morning after the man leaves."

Ramsey said nothing. She ran her fingers over his face and could feel his black button eyes staring at her, trusting her to protect him.

"And she'll read to us, and I'll sit on her lap and we'll snuggle—all of us together." She nodded and tugged on Ramsey's left ear.

She rolled over.

Real live whispers and laughter floated into the room.

Opening her mouth in a wide yawn, she patted Ramsey's tummy and whispered again, "Don't be afraid. I'm right here."

"Please. That hurts."

"Mommy?" The little girl frowned but her eyes wouldn't open. Just like when she and Mommy put cucumbers slices on their eyes.

"Stop it—"

Rubbing at her eyes, the little girl sat up. Mommy had never sounded like this before, and neither had any of the men—the men who brought flowers and candy and money. What were they doing? Maybe Mommy was angry at the man and had sent him away.

She slid her feet to the floor and hesitated. Mommy didn't like her to leave her room whenever any man visited.

"Come on, Ramsey. We have to go check on Mommy." She tucked her rabbit under her arm then padded barefoot to her door and edged it open. Mommy's room was the next one, and a second later she'd tiptoed to it and pressed an ear to the crack. Someone grunted and whispered in an angry voice.

"Serves you right, whore."

Horse? The little girl frowned. That wasn't Mommy's name. Was the man calling Mommy a bad name? She touched the door, and it swung open wider.

The man was on top of mommy, leaning over, his hands wrapped around—her neck.

The big eye on his arm glared at her, scaring her, making her want to run back to bed. But she had to help Mommy. Tiptoeing closer—behind the man—she peeked around him at her mother.

Mommy's mouth was open as if she was screaming, but she wasn't. Mommy stared at the man, her eyes wide and blank. Every once in a while he jerked her and said words Mommy always told her not to say.

She whimpered. "Mommy?"

The man's head turned, his eyes scary and mean, and not at all like Mommy's laughing ones. His lips twisted into a snarl. "Who are you? Are you this—is she your mother?"

His hands released their grip on Mommy's neck. He crawled out of the bed, grabbed for a pair of pants, and slid into them, turning his back to her. Then he straightened.

She backed away and raised a fist to her mouth.

"Come here, girl." His voice had softened, but not his eyes.

She backed another two steps and whispered. "Mommy?"

"Your mommy can't talk right now." The man flipped a glance at the still figure in the bed. "You have a pretty barrette in your hair. Come let me see."

She lifted a hand to the barrette. Mommy always let her wear it when she was with a man 'cause it was a special treat for a special girl. "No." She shook her head. "Go away. I don't like you."

The man growled and sprang at her. Ramsey dropped to the floor as she sobbed and dodged the groping hands. "I want my mommy."

The man said a bad word and stopped chasing her. "Come here and let's talk about your mother."

Her mother hadn't moved, hadn't spoken. "Did you hurt her?"

"Of course not."

"What's wrong with her?"

"Your mother's sick."

"You hurt Mommy."

Bad words spilled from his mouth in a steady stream.

She wanted to clap both hands over her ears. Mommy told her over and over she shouldn't say those kinds of words.

He folded his arms across his chest, the big eye rippling on his arm, never blinking, only staring. "You keep your mouth shut. Do you hear me?"

She closed her eyes and opened them—fast. The eye still stared.

"If you talk, your mommy will die. Do you want to kill her? Do you?" His lips spread into a clown's grin.

Her stomach hurt. Her eyes burned.

Go away, you.

All she wanted was to climb on Mommy's lap and have this bad man go away.

"Remember, it'll be your fault if she dies, and everyone will know you killed your mother."

No. She didn't want to kill Mommy.

He eased forward, crept closer, capturing her, holding her tight with his eyes. Like the snake that'd almost bitten her last summer.

Closer.

Closer.

His hand shot out and touched her shoulder.

She screamed.

CHAPTER TWO

Present day, rural West Virginia

Caralynne Hayman froze in her dishwashing. The plate slid from her hand, and the soapy water swallowed it.

What was he doing?

"Cara. Lynne. Get. In. Here." The words grated, causing the hair on her arms to stand up. She squeezed the dishcloth as a loud crash slammed through the house. Was he kicking the furniture? Throwing a lamp? The horror from last night—the slaps and threats—gripped her body again, and she cringed.

Stop it. Don't think about him. Get your mind on something else.

The sights beyond the window drew her attention, his wheezing a background nightmare. She focused on her prized vegetable garden, a refuge to peace.

A curse, and her gaze jerked to the overused graveled path, an escape from the others in their religious group.

When a rasping groan ground into the room, she gripped the edge of the kitchen sink and took in the sight of their small blue car. It desperately needed a paint job but served as a vehicle of retreat when she craved a refuge from her world.

She wanted a refuge right now, but the insane rhythm of sights only swelled the percussion of sounds beating from the other room.

"W-o-m-a-n!"

The calming scenes, the aura of peace she created when troubled, vanished. The single, drawn-out word yanked her from her mental safety zone. Whirling, she faced the doorway to the hall.

Go? Run? Ignore?

The black bruise—her mirror had forced her to acknowledge it early this morning—throbbed, and she rubbed her chin.

Silence. Caralynne held her breath.

Thump.

She dropped her dishcloth and stumbled to the bedroom. Donald Hayman lay on the floor, eyes dull and pain-filled, his lips moving, saliva trickling from one side of his mouth. His hands twitched. One finger on his right hand crooked at her.

She understood that her husband wanted her to come closer, and her whole spirit revolted.

Flee.

Cara pressed her trembling fingers together. Why was he on the floor? Her head swirled, and she clutched the dresser to still the swaying, to give herself minutes to clear her fogged-up head. Then, willing herself to let go of the furniture, she crept a few inches closer, and another few. Her stomach heaved. That smell—his shirt ranked with something vile. Dull, mustard-yellow. Icky olive green and—and brown.

Her throat thickened, and she swallowed back the gag threatening to choke her.

Vomit. Vomit soaked his shirt and dribbled onto the floor. Was he drunk? Her heart leaped at the thought. If so, she'd have three, four hours of glorious freedom.

A belch erupted from him. His pain-filled eyes were bloodshot. The broad, sweaty forehead gleamed.

She slid across the floor, knelt, and whispered, "What's wrong?"

A big hand gripped his chest, pulling at his shirt, and a button released its thready hold and rolled out of sight.

His heart. Was he having a heart attack?

She jumped up, grabbed at her side, and hobbled to the dresser for his seldom-used heart medicine. As if a hand stilled her intention, she stared down at the plastic bottle.

A red flag—a vision of freedom—waved in her mind.

Tempting. Alluring. Promising.

Scary.

Her husband's finger beckoned again, and his eyes pleaded with her as if to help him break free of the elephant stomping on his chest. She squeezed the bottle and debated. When she didn't rush toward him, the flare of rage in his eyes warned her he'd get even. Donald could—and would—beat the hesitation right out of her.

A shaky breath rattled from her throat. Opening her fingers wide, she let the bottle drop onto the dresser, and it rolled to the edge.

She contemplated him, knowing he couldn't touch her. Shaggy hair, too long over his ears and rapidly turning gray. A belly grown large through overeating. And beefy hands.

She hated his hands. Hated the cruel strength in them. Hated that they'd touched her. Squeezed. Fondled. Defiled.

The seething emotion rose inside her like an angry, consuming demon.

She pursed her lips and held back the words hovering on her tongue. Words that clamored for freedom from the place he'd imprisoned her for thirteen torturous, unbearable years. She pressed a hand against her throbbing temple.

The dammed-up emotions pushed against her senses, demanding a release. They surged over the top, seeped around the edges, and finally burst through any restraints fear and time and tradition had built.

"You could have prevented our Lori's death." Her foot twitched from the desire to kick him.

Would he die if he didn't get the pills?

She prayed he would.

But what if she didn't help him, and he recovered?

Her eyes fastened on his very-much-alive eyes, and she inched backward to the door. Every cell in her body, every past hurt and pain she'd endured, screamed at her. Demanded she race away. Begged her never to look back. Her scalp tingled, and she walked out.

Outside to her garden.
Outside to wait.
Outside to hope.

❧❧❧

"Please, God. Please, God." Caralynne kept an eye on the door, but Donald didn't come through it. She recklessly hacked at the weeds in her vegetable garden.

He won't die. I'll never have that kind of luck—he's far too stubborn to give up his cantankerous hold on life this easily.

Her bruised ribs ached where Donald had beaten her last week, and she paused long enough to rub a fingertip over the spot. She swiped at the perspiration dotting her face. The noon sun came and went. She missed lunch, but there was no way she could get food past the lump lodging in her throat. Her stomach rumbled, threatening to send her running to the bathroom, and she gripped her hoe tighter. Willed her mind to meditate on peaceful things.

Strangely, the vision of a young boy who'd been her best friend, and who grew up to be the first and only man she ever loved—years ago—appeared. His warm eyes and ready smile, the hint of shyness and his contrasting strength still had the power to make her smile. His gentleness with her—an orphaned girl with no sense of belonging—stayed strong in her memory. Her champion.

Her childish hopes and dreams were dashed by the single, forced act of marriage to Donald Hayman. She rubbed her hands together as the recent nightmare poured over her again.

She cleaned her hoe, rubbing, scrubbing off the brown dirt, and stored it in the small utility building where she kept all her gardening tools. Her daughters had tossed several of them helter-skelter, and she fiddled with each one, cleaning and hanging them in perfect rows. When no other task remained, she straightened her shoulders. Time to face the grizzly in his den.

She slogged across the yard as if dragging her feet through thick, soggy mud, stumbled as she climbed the steps. Was he biding his time to jump her the moment she entered the house? She paused at the landing and gripped the rail.

Go, and get it over.

Don't go. You know what he's capable of.

Cara cocked her head, listening.

No sound. No demanding words. No moans.

The kitchen screen door squeaked. She slid one foot forward and kicked the door. It banged against the wall, reverberating through the silent house. No answering roars followed.

She cringed and pressed a hand to her ribs.

The silence distorted itself into a specter of doom. Edging sideways, Cara pulled open one of the top cabinets to take down a favorite glass. A board creaked, and she whirled, her chest heaving.

Nothing.

Cara filled the glass with water and drained every drop, but her lips remained parched. She stared into the hallway, but his hulking figure didn't magically appear. Shuddering, she placed the glass upside down in the sink.

She couldn't put it off any longer, so she shuffled toward the bedroom. With a shaking hand on the doorknob, she pushed herself to act.

The house shifted, moaned, as if waiting, in cahoots with Donald, to pounce on her. Touching the wall to steady herself, she breathed in and out to force away the sudden blackness. Beads of sweat dampened her skin as she stood outside the bedroom.

Had he recovered, the heavy belt he enjoyed using now upraised? Was he waiting, ready for the game he played in his cruel version of fun?

No matter. She needed to know. She thrust herself into the room.

Donald lay on his back as he had when she'd left earlier. Only now, death lay heavy across his colorless features. Her body sagged as her legs turned into water-logged spaghetti straws. Her knees hit the floor.

What had his sightless eyes stared at in the final moments of his life? Cara lifted her gaze to see what he had seen. Nothing but the plain plastered ceiling, the bright bulb still burning. No spiders weaving their airy webs to distract a dying man. No fancy swirls on the ceiling for him to lose his thoughts in. Nothing.

He was gone.

Dead.

She knelt near him but didn't touch him.

"You've given me no happiness, not in living, and certainly not in dying. Donald Hayman, I'm *relieved* you're dead."

What did she expect? That he'd move his gaping mouth and speak?

Tears pooled in her eyes and spilled down her cheeks. She'd struggled too many years, buried her sassiness, kept quiet so he'd ignore her. Everything in her screamed rebellion at his sick demands, but she seldom physically fought his harsh will.

Now, at last, freedom from this evil, wicked man for herself and her girls.

Too late for her precious Lori.

Yet the revenge for her oldest daughter's death hung in the air—sweet and cloying. But she'd dreamed for it, longed for it, prayed for it. *His death.*

She crossed her arms and rocked back and forth. Her tears continued to drip, but she raised no hand to wipe them away. She needed this bizarre moment for her own sanity's sake. This victory of sorts, to keep on living. Celebrating his death in some awful ritual of suffering, giving herself new life and strength.

The afternoon shadows crept into the room, and Cara rose like a spring calf, the vitality erasing the aches and pains that had squeezed the energy from her earlier. The pill bottle caught her eye and lured, tempted. With a shaky hand, she twisted the cap and popped it open. A jerky thrust, and the pills scattered, inches from his hand—if he'd been able to reach them.

She tossed the bottle beside his body. The final touch.

At the door, she looked back and whispered, "Dear God, I had to do it. I had to save my girls."

The need to hurry pressed inside her. Lacy and Leila were on their way home from school. They didn't need to see their father like this. Or ever again.

Amen, and amen.

CHAPTER THREE

Dayne MacFarland waited beside the open grave, a worn black Bible held close to his chest. He trailed his fingers through the silky hair of the big collie standing silently beside him, drawing comfort from the animal. He'd made the right decision in bringing his dog, his only real friend in the people he'd known all his life.

Solemn faces studied the new minister in their midst, but interest and curiosity escaped from eyes trained to hide emotions. Women smoothed their best Sunday clothes and chided their wiggliest children in quiet voices. Men nodded at him and crossed their arms, stiff and silent, judging him by who-knew-what standards. He could see the questions almost bleeding into the air: Is the preacher too young to minister to them? Would he follow their previous preacher's guidelines he'd pounded into them Sunday after Sunday? Was he really, truly still a part of the Children of Righteous Cain after all his training?

Levi and Jodie Schrader, an attractive and influential couple in the settlement, stood close to the grave. Unlike most of the other couples, the two were arm in arm, and once, Levi patted her hand gently.

Promising. Dayne searched the man's face, but no expression betrayed Levi's emotions.

Not so with Kenny and Penelope Lewis. She cast hopeful glances at her husband, but the elder, constantly shifting on his feet, ignored his wife. His sultry looks gave him a twenty-year-old Elvis Presley visage. Dayne knew better.

Dayne continued his casual observance of the group. Most of the women avoided his eyes, but the braver ones sent fleeting, tentative smiles his way. The new minister in their midst.

A baby cried, and a loud *shh, shh* echoed around the grave and interrupted his contemplation. Why did they insist on the children being at the burial service unless it was immediate family? Couldn't they at least assign two or three women to oversee the lot of small children? If he lived to be a hundred, he'd never understand.

His attention riveted on the lone figure lingering at the edge of the cemetery.

Cara. In spite of her extreme slenderness, her quiet demeanor and sexuality lit up her body and overrode the dowdiness of her cheap dress. She'd been cute as a precocious child, a promise of what was to come. And now, the promise unfolded into a rare flower.

Dayne moistened his lips. She was lovelier than he'd remembered. Tall, but she carried herself with no self-consciousness. Dayne's heart leaped. He squashed the emotion. His job was to comfort and minister.

She was the last one to gather but, he supposed, the one to grieve the most. No rumors had come to him about her marriage, and he'd never asked.

Where were Cara's children? They'd certainly not walked up with her. After all, Donald Hayman, their father, lay in the wood casket.

Caralynne's face, quiet and sober, held no hint of devastation. She acknowledged those who patted her arms and tried to hug her. Several women pressed close, clung to her, tears pooling in their eyes as a smile flitted across her lips and vanished. Her gaze surfed past the crowd and met his.

His breath caught.

Those eyes—tearless and hollow-rimmed right now—were the same beautiful, blue-green, fathomless eyes he remembered.

Dayne stepped forward and extended a hand.

She walked to him and rested her small one on it. Her eyes riveted on him, studying, searching, contemplating then her gaze dropped to the dog beside him. For an instant, her brow furrowed.

"Cara." His throat threatened to close as he breathed her name.

Her lips moved. Praying? Wanting to speak? No words escaped. At last she bowed her head and faced the grave.

A throat cleared, and resentment stirred inside him. He rubbed a thumb over the leather cover of his Bible, seeking warmth and peace from the book he'd always used to soothe his emotions, steady his body, and clear his mind. Where was the peace today?

Holding his unopened Bible, he quoted the words that had helped him become the man he was today. "'I am the resurrection and the life: he that believes in me, though he were dead, yet shall he live: and whoever lives and believes in me shall never die.'"

Dayne paused. What could he say to open these people's eyes, to accomplish his mission? Caralynne's head bowed.

"Today, we praise God for life, for He is the giver of life and breath …"

A movement to the left of him caught his eye, and even as he continued speaking, he studied Donald Hayman's brother, Emery. His face reflected somberness, yet the man's eyes glinted. Not with sorrow. Snake eyes. Eyes capable of pinning the weaker person to a board until finished with an interrogation.

As if amused at Dayne's study, the elder's lips tilted a fraction, then his gaze seemed to rest on Cara. His blank eyes glistened, his mouth opened, and a moist tongue slithered over his lips.

Revulsion washed through Dayne and stirred an emotion he didn't want to feel.

God help me. Now.

"But through our short lifetime, male and female must learn to focus on God. He only is the true way to happiness, whether we are young or old. He only is the real reason for our existence upon this earth. When we accept God's love in our hearts, we can look beyond this life to an eternal one."

Another urgent clearing of the throat, and Dayne fought back the desire to bark at Elder Simmons. The primary figure itched to get his speech said. The stocky but solid figure led The Children of Righteous Cain with a firm hand and didn't like to share the limelight. Even when the newly appointed minister could have rightfully expected it.

Dayne nodded at the man.

Elder Simmons lifted his arms. His palms faced outward and his short sleeves fell back. The tattoo—a symbol of an elder's full-fledged membership—on the senior elder's upper arm mocked Dayne as if the obscene object surmised his intentions and plans.

Beside the leader, Emery, dressed in an expensive suit that did nothing for him, still leered at Cara. The contrast between Cara's shabby dress and this man's outfit was shameful. The man might not be the slovenly person Donald Hayman had been, but nothing he wore would ever change his personality.

Dayne gritted his teeth.

Elder Simmons's voice thundered out and seemed to hover over the group, a rumbling cloud of fierce power. "Brothers and sisters, we're gathered here today to pay our respects to the memory of our beloved brother who lived a good life, obeyed our traditions, and provided a shining example for our younger men."

More propaganda, keeping these people in darkness.

"Take the words of our prophet, Cain, for an example." Elder Simmons paused and lowered his outstretched arms. Eyes glowing with the same fervor that radiated in his voice, he stepped to the edge of the grave. "I charge you to safeguard, not only your own salvation, but your family also. To ensure them of heaven, sacrifices must be made. Do not let human weakness rob you of this."

The man teetered, the toes of his shoes beyond the rim of dirt. Would he slide into the grave and land on top of the plain casket?

Dayne's lips twitched, but one glance at Cara's solemn, troubled face kept him quiet.

The elder paid no attention to his plight. "Without a doubt, our Brother Hayman bore the forgiving mark of Cain upon his body. He provided for and yearned for the souls of his wife and three beautiful daughters. He feared for their salvation as any good son of Cain does and did his part in assuring they not miss heaven."

Caralynne shifted, but otherwise no one stirred.

Elder Simmons turned in an action belying his body structure and approached Caralynne. Dayne winced as the fat hands gripped her shoulders. Caralynne's head rose, and she glared at the elder. Would she refuse to do his unspoken order?

The rolling anger erupted from deep inside him and sent his feet in her direction. Sabre whined beside him. Elder Simmons shot him a warning glance.

Don't interfere with God's command.

Dayne ignored the elder's unspoken order and stepped closer, his attention locked on the woman in front of him.

Elder Simmons's knuckles whitened as his grip tightened. "Your blood is now demanded of you, Sister Hayman. Will you refuse?"

Dayne's whole spirit revolted.

Would the man squeeze the life from her?

Her body swayed, trembled, and she fell to her knees.

The elder slid his hands upward over her neck, through her hair, and rested on the top of her head.

Get your hands off her. Dayne bit back his objection. His tentative thought to scoop her up and gallop from the scene withered away. It wasn't time. Not yet. And he'd promised the professor to hold off any drastic action as long as he could.

"Sister Hayman, I charge you, a daughter of Cain, to continue to obey our traditions, and until the Lord reveals to me your next husband, be obedient and submissive to your elders as our law demands. Go and grieve for the past, but prepare for the future, so when the time comes, you will be ready."

Head downcast, Cara lifted her left hand. Elder Simmons took it, and from his jacket pocket, retrieved a knife. His thumb caressed the edge. Holding the knife aloft for a second, alert and focused, he inspected faces in the crowd as if judging their loyalty.

Children hushed. No one stirred. No one spoke. A bird warbled an eerily cheerful song overhead.

With a downward, expert slash, Elder Simmons sliced a small, thin line on Cara's wrist and stared at it as the blood seeped from the cut. He slid a forefinger across the cut, lifted it to his mouth, and sucked. He jerked and she was propelled closer to the hole. He held her arm over it, squeezing, squeezing until her blood dripped onto the closed casket. One. Two. Three drops of red blood. The man's eyes closed as if in ecstasy.

Sickening.

"The blood of the testament, which God instructs you to sprinkle upon your gateway to heaven."

"Amen," the people murmured.

Dayne swallowed his revulsion. He drilled as bland an expression as he could muster onto his stiff facial muscles, and stepping forward, held out a hand to help Cara stand. She put her hand in his but refused to acknowledge him when he didn't let go. A moment later, she tugged her hand, and he released it.

Crossing to the head of the grave, he raised his own hands and refocused the congregation's attention to himself.

"Our God in heaven, we ask you to continue to comfort our dear friends here today." Dayne allowed his voice to overflow with love and caring. "Give peace to Cara Hayman, and comfort her. Encourage and strengthen her for the days ahead. Amen."

"Amen," the people chorused. A reverent pause followed then sifted away, and slowly, they filed passed their head elder.

A few of the younger women paused beside Elder Simmons's commanding figure at the edge of the grave, their adoring eyes pleading for an acknowledgement from him. Fathers and mothers pushed their daughters toward the leader, and he patted heads and hugged small figures.

Giggles. Girlish, too-old-for-their-years glances. Provocative prances and struts.

Actions that pasted a fond smile on Elder Simmons's lips.

Older girls—perhaps fifteen, even sixteen—sent demure smiles to the leader, coaxing nods of approval from him.

Dayne lifted his Bible to bellow out a warning, to rebuke the undercurrent of evil eroding a twisted path through the parents and their daughters.

But the crowd shuffled and reshuffled until only four people remained.

Elder Simmons folded his arms, head lowered, dark face a chilling mask when it rested on him.

For a second, Dayne wondered if the senior elder would insist on outstaying him. But the staring contest—if it'd been one—lightened, and with a slight nod, Elder Simmons followed the others. Emery Hayman spoke to Cara in a low murmur as if urging her to some action. Head shaking, she stepped away from him, refusing to speak. He lingered, seemed to be arguing, and gripped her arm. When she jerked from his grasp, he shrugged and left.

Cara hadn't shed tears at Dayne's words earlier, and she shed none now. He wondered if he should address her or let her alone.

Still as grotesque gargoyles, men with shovels waited on the hillside to finish the job.

"God will be with you, Cara."

She raised her eyes. Dark with confusion, moist with sorrow, and tinged with a touch of anger, her eyes begged for understanding. "Will he?"

"Yes, he will." Dayne had no doubts. Hadn't God been with him at college and seminary classes? Hadn't God soothed his aching heart when his parents died? When he'd been forced to leave?

"I wonder."

A breeze fanned his face, and short wisps of hair stroked her cheeks. He wanted to tuck the fluttering strands behind her perfect ears.

"I wonder," she said again. "We've been taught how omnipotent God is. How powerful and mighty. Why would he care about me when he uses a man like Simmons to reign over us?"

Shock rippled through him. But why shouldn't Cara doubt? Hadn't he, at seminary? She'd not left the group, seen the broader vision, learned the truth as he had.

"You don't need to doubt his love for you. Men may fail us, but God will never fail." Dayne hated the patronizing tone in his voice.

A faint smile eased the tight line of her lips. "Do *you* believe, Dayne?

Do you *know*?"

He skirted a pile of dirt and moved up beside her, took her elbow, and guided her away from the gravesite. "Yes. I know because the Bible says so. I know because I've experienced God's love." Better. At least he'd spoken the truth.

Her attitude wasn't hopeful but definitely held a touch of curiosity.

They strolled toward her home, not talking, away from the men who ambled toward the grave.

"Are you all right?"

"You mean this?" She indicated her wrist, and a rueful smile touched her lips. "I hardly noticed. I'm fine."

At least physically, she meant. "Are your girls at home?"

Her body tensed. "Yes."

"How old are they?"

"Leila is ten and Lacy four."

"You didn't bring them."

"No. They are too young to endure one of our funerals, even if it is their father. Even if I'll have to pay the price."

Was she talking about Elder Simmons? He tightened his grip on her arm. "You are right. I'm so sorry about Lori."

She cocked her head while he voiced his sympathy. A shadow-like darkness spread over her face. He glanced at the sky. Not a cloud marred the perfect blue.

"You didn't know her."

"No. I wish I'd been here for you." He breathed the words quietly and thought perhaps she hadn't heard them.

"I do too, Dayne. I'll say good-bye here. Thank you for the lovely service."

She didn't give him a chance to speak but walked straight down the road, not running, but not loitering either. The simple dress she wore clung to her body. The hem swayed around her long legs, her movements smooth and coordinated. She gave no indication of the conflict he'd seen in her. She didn't look back.

❧❧

Dayne hurried toward the Hayman house. Was she as wonderful as she'd seemed this afternoon, or had his star-studded eyes deceived him? Were these emotions seething inside him a new grownup response to seeing a beautiful woman or the buried puppy love of an adolescent boy seeing his first love?

He didn't have to answer his questions. He already knew. He'd never stopped loving Cara. He might have buried his love, suffered silently the agonizing disappointment when he learned she would not be his, might have squashed any hopes and dreams of their future together, but he'd never been able to crush the love.

They'd taught him at seminary to be available for the grieving, holding their hands, listening to their teary-eyed confessions and memories, and offering words of comfort. He'd do all that, but his real agenda was to see if she still harbored any thoughts of him.

Cara's car was parked close to the door. Lights shone from the kitchen and front windows, but the upstairs remained dark. Perhaps she had sent the girls on to bed.

His excitement at seeing Cara—the second time since his return from college and seminary—sent the blood pounding through his veins. He patted Sabre. "Gotta keep my cool. That's why I brought you. If I get out of line, you give me a nudge with that nose of yours, you hear me?" The collie gazed at him, adoration in his eyes, his mouth wide open in a doggy grin.

"Okay, so I'm excited to see Cara again. Do you have to laugh about it?"

The image of Cara working here, her slender hands covered in garden gloves, smudges of dirt on her nose, didn't help his heart rate any.

The horizon showed streaks of red, violet, and purple against the backdrop of an indigo sky, an indication evening was not loitering around for him to make any earth-shattering decisions.

A tyke of a girl thrust open the door before he could knock.

"Hi, I'm—"

Her big eyes, the same color as Cara's, fastened on the dog.

He smiled down at the child. "Do you like my dog?"

A nod.

"His name is Sabre. You can pet him if you want."

She drew back, only a little, but enough to tell him of her fear. "Will he bite?"

Dayne bent over. "Sabre, shake."

The dog obediently held out a paw.

"Look, he wants to shake your hand."

Lacy solemnly took the collie's paw. She looked up at Dayne. "I like your dog."

"I'm Pastor MacFarland. Is your mother here?"

Solemnly the child lifted a finger to her mouth and opened the door wider. He stepped inside, heard the murmurs, and followed the sounds.

Caralynne sat on a plain sofa, an older girl beside her, a child's book in her hands, a long-eared rabbit staring at him from the cover. She looked up as he entered the room and frowned when she spotted the dog.

His enthusiasm waned. Was he intruding? Perhaps time had changed her and she didn't care for a dog in the house. Her brow smoothed, easing away his sudden concern, her slowly-widening smile a balm to ease his questions.

He took the hand she offered. "How are you, Cara? I wanted to stop by and see if you needed anything."

"Thanks." Cara stroked her daughter's hair. "I'm fine. These are my girls, Leila, and my baby, Lacy."

"Sabre and I are very pleased to meet you. Can you give the girls a wave?" The dog waved a paw back and forth.

The girls giggled. Leila tilted her head the way Cara did, and the unconscious move made him smile. The girl must have gotten her dark hair and brown eyes from her father, but her actions were Cara's.

"I'm Lacy." The youngest peeked at him from behind Cara.

"So you are." Dayne pulled out two apples from his jacket pocket. "I don't suppose you like—"

Quick as a frog's tongue, the little girl captured one of the shining fruits, the sauciness in her blue eyes begging for more treats.

But when he glanced at Cara again to share the moment, he caught the confusion in her eyes. What was bothering her?

The next moment her face cleared. Even as she blinked, she answered Leila's questioning look. "Take the apple, Leila."

She gave her daughter a hug but spoke to Dayne. "Would you like some of my fresh raspberry tea?"

At his nod, she said, "Leila, honey, can you bring Reverend MacFarland a glass of tea?"

Leila hurried from the room as Lacy dropped to her knees and held out her apple to the dog.

"Lacy, no. The dog doesn't want your apple. Please sit down, Dayne."

"Am I intruding, Cara? Did I come too soon?"

"No, it's okay."

Sabre trotted to Lacy and sat, his velvet-brown eyes fastened on her as she crooned to him. Leila returned, carrying a tall glass in both hands.

Dayne accepted the tea, sipped, and widened his eyes. "Delicious. Did you make this?"

The older girl smiled. "Mom made it." Her quiet correction didn't hide the pleasure he'd given her at his praise.

"You're as smart as your mother."

Caralynne shooed the girls. "Leila, would you take Lacy to the front porch and keep her occupied? Please play quietly, and don't leave the porch, sweetie."

"Sabre, go with the girls."

Leila guided her sister outside, Sabre following obediently behind them.

"Did you know your husband was sick?"

"Y-e-s. Sort of." She lowered her head. "He'd seen the doctor for the first time about a year ago, and I think he went several times afterward. But Donald ..."

"What did he do?" Dayne lowered his voice, coaxing her confidence.

She bit her lip. "Donald wasn't a man to listen to anyone. He didn't share much with me. What I learned was mostly through observation."

"I see." He'd hoped her marriage—as much as it irked him—had been one of the good ones.

Her fingers interlocked and tightened. "I saw the tablets on the dresser where he kept them, but I never saw him take any. Whether his condition was serious or not, I had no idea."

She was more beautiful than he remembered. Some of the bounce and sparkle he'd loved years ago was missing, but now and then he caught a glimpse of the free spirit from years past.

It wasn't easy to admit he'd been devastated to learn—eons ago, it seemed now—of her and Donald Hayman's marriage. How could he think his love and hers would command different rules? A mystery, yes, but still foolish. They weren't special cases to be looked upon with favor.

"Donald had definite ideas. If he wanted me to know something, he told me. Otherwise, he explained nothing. He spoke and expected to be obeyed. He invited no questions from me."

What kind of relationship was that? "Didn't you have family times? Personal time with each other?"

"What? Are you kidding?" She bit her lip as her cheeks warmed pink. "I stayed as far away from him as I could. Which wasn't far enough."

"Then you weren't happy?"

"Happy? How happy can a woman be who … is married to a man she doesn't love? A man she desp—"

Despises? "Why didn't you leave?"

"Leave? He never would have let me go." She shook her head, her brow wrinkled. For an instant, an emotion stirred deep within her eyes and startled him. It faded and the lively eyes he remembered returned.

"I don't know why I said that." Her face flushed. "He wouldn't be happy if I tried to leave, but I don't know what he'd have done."

Concern for this woman ate at him, but he held it in check and forced his voice into a casual tone. "What are your plans now?" Plans to include him would be nice. Right now he wanted to catch her up in his arms and never let her go.

As if he could. He had a promise to keep.

A girlish squeal echoed from the porch, and Caralynne tilted her head, listening. She gave a slight nod when satisfied all was well, and one shoulder lifted in a nonchalant move. Her eyes sparkled strange blue-green fire. "I have three months before …"

He knew and hated the rule. His determination to change things, to make the elders see the error of their ways continued to bore into his soul.

"Perhaps …" he read the question in her eye and hesitated. *Give no false hope.* "I'm hoping I can influence them enough they'll want a change—"

Her laughter brought him to a halt.

"Are you naïve enough to think any of them would change when they have everything going their way?"

"They see it differently—"

"No. They're sick."

"Many of our couples have good marriages."

"Are you defending them?"

The cold, harsh tone was unlike anything he'd ever heard from her. Stretching out a hand, he took one of hers. "Cara, I came home hoping to make a difference. To prove to our people a better way. Can you trust God he'll help them make the right decisions?"

"I always loved the way you said my name. Your inflection still has an endearing Italian ring."

"I'm not Italian."

"I know, but I used to imagine you were an Italian prince who would someday rescue me from my prison."

Was that accusation in her voice—or longing? Did she blame him for not saving her from an unwanted marriage? "We were kids. I wish I'd been older and wiser. I could have done something."

"Rebel?" Her eyes gentled and reminded him of calm pools hidden in a forest. "No, Dayne. I quit dreaming a long time ago and grew up in a hurry. Reality is my life now."

Definitely not the same girl from years ago. An enormous sense of loss overwhelmed him. "Can I do anything for you? Anything at all?"

"I don't think so. The girls and I will remain here as long as … we can live in peace and until—some things are resolved."

A simple enough statement, and yet a deeper strain of meaning ran through. Or was it a purpose? Her face was serene, her manner quiet. Unwilling to push for her confidence, he decided to head home.

Her light footsteps followed him outside, and at the porch steps he faced her again. The girls' abandoned toys lay scattered across the floor. The smallest one ran to her, but Leila hovered close to him as if she instinctively trusted him. Hugging her youngest, Cara looked at him, the brightness of her eyes disturbing him. Tears?

"I'll check on you in a few days."

She looked angelic, the light from inside shining at her back. An angel guarding the children in her care. "Thank you, Dayne, but you don't have to worry about me. I can take care of myself."

"I know. But I want to. After all, it's my job as pastor of the flock. Come, Sabre."

"Goodnight." Her whispered farewell floated to him as he strode down the path, Sabre trotting beside him. He wished he possessed the power to turn back the clock.

CHAPTER FOUR

Heavenly Monday morning. If only Cara's plan to wreck vengeance on this evil group didn't overshadow the brightness.

The spring sun wove its beams through the overhead tree branches warming her face and shoulders. Cara shrugged off her light sweater, draped it across her arm, and lightly swung the basket she carried. The girls were safe in school with a gentle teacher. One good thing in her life. That, and Donald's death.

Dayne's devastatingly handsome face flashed in her mind. His dark blue eyes shone with sincerity and keen wit. He had nice hands, and his hair was cut an inch too short to be stylish. Not like the shaggy locks many of their group favored.

The sympathy in his voice had almost been her undoing. She'd like to shovel this heavy load onto his broad shoulders and be rid of it, but she couldn't trust him. Dayne wouldn't understand. After all, he'd been raised from babyhood here. So ... not yet. And probably never.

She pulled her thoughts away from Dayne. Today she wanted to forget everything but Lori's death and the burning coals she planned to heap on the head of every elder in the group. Satisfaction at the thought expanded inside her until she thought she'd burst. She didn't want to feel it, didn't want any personal gratification from her plans. But the emotion surrounded her and gave her a giddy feeling of invincibility.

Guilt nibbled at her conscience, but she shook it off. Her agenda demanded fulfillment. No time for second-guessing her plans.

The country lane to the Lewis home was full of life today. She wished she could fly. She wouldn't flutter around on the ground like the grouse, as darling as they were. No, she'd soar as high as the eagles. Nothing to stop her. Nothing to hold her back.

For three blessed months, she was free. Cara spread her arms in sheer giddiness. Never again would she live under matrimonial bondage. She shivered and dropped her arms as the thought of what she might have to face washed over her. So be it. She wouldn't think those things now.

She took in the scenery along the country lane, and when she finally opened the sagging picket gate of her friend's home, any wayward thoughts of trouble had been vanquished.

Climbing the steps desperately needing some repair, she paused, muffled voices intruding upon her thoughts. Her heart sank.

She'd hoped Felicia Farmer would be alone. She should have been, given the time of the day, but judging from the sounds emanating from the barn, her friend's husband was home. And angry.

Cara set the basket on the porch and checked to make sure Felicia's cat was nowhere around. Half-eaten bread wouldn't make a very nice gift. She slipped down the bare path and paused at the barn door to listen.

"The store in our settlement isn't good enough for you, is it? How many times do I have to tell you? I don't want you going into town, wasting your hours."

"I've used only two of my hours this month. I haven't gone anywhere else." Felicia's soft words were barely audible. "I was out of milk. Michael needs it. I told you last night."

"Are you sassing me, you tramp? I know why you tear into town every chance you get, using up your hours before half the month is gone. Flaunting yourself in front of Mr. Grocery Man who thinks he's hot, aren't you?"

Cara cringed. The generous owner of the store had more than once passed on special deals to Felicia. And Felicia, grateful and ashamed of her need, had returned the kindness in the only way she had. Pies and homemade bread. Cara had known and hoped Mike would never learn of it.

"No. No. It's not true. I would never do that."

The stinging ring of a slap crowded into the day. Cara dared to peek through a crack in the wall. Mike, his skinny frame stiff, thrust his wife against the slats of the wall, held her in position, his hand around her neck, his face red. "You couldn't get the milk at our community store?"

"I—I—they—said—"

He ignored her stumbling words and only stalked away.

Cara held her breath, hoping he was at end of his tirade, but when he turned he held the horsewhip he used unmercifully on his poor animals. She stuffed a fist to her mouth.

Surely he wouldn't. Or would he?

Felicia shrank against the wall, trepidation bleeding from every pore. "Mike, plea-se don't. I promise I'll never go into town again without yo-u." Felicia fell to her knees, her body shaking, her dark eyes full of terror.

Mike's laugh echoed through the barn. Maniacal. Cruel.

"I'm going to teach you a lesson you'll not forget. Won't be so quick to run away."

"I won't, Mike, I won't."

Mike advanced toward her friend, raised the whip, and brought the leather strap down across Felicia's left shoulder. She screamed and sagged sideways.

"Stop, you devil—" Crying, Cara rushed across the barn and beat his back, screaming her words, gasping, choking on the tears.

The look of surprise on Mike's face twisted into an outraged snarl. He swung around and jerked the whip up to lash out at her.

She didn't give him a chance. Grabbing the ax leaning against a block of wood, she raised it a couple feet. "Don't you dare. I won't take your abuse."

"You witch. I should have forbidden your visits a long time ago. You killed Brother Don. Now you want to encourage Felicia's rebellion." The venom-words spilled from between his lips.

"I haven't done anything. If he'd listened to his doctor, he wouldn't be dead."

"Get off my property. I need to teach submission to this woman of mine."

His sneering grin sent her anger soaring again. "Don't touch her or I'll ..."

"You'll what? I could take you on as a second wife. You two can argue and talk all you want. Besides, you've got two daughters I wouldn't mind having around. By the time I raise them, they'll be good, submissive girls for the right man."

He had his eyes on her girls? Never. Over her dead body, and then she'd come back and haunt him until he went mad.

She eyed him, backing away. She'd be no match for his strength. Though he had a slight built, he was wiry. She had the ax, but could she use it? She swung the unwieldy tool upward, both hands gripping the handle.

With a flick of his wrist, the whip curled around the ax. It flew from her grasp and landed much too far away for her to retrieve it. Cara staggered back.

He leaped and knocked her down, landing on top of her, pinning her to the dusty ground. His hands fought to stay her punches as she kicked and squirmed, and he slapped her, knocking her head to the side.

Cara clawed the dirt, searching for anything she could use as a weapon. She strained and ignored Mike's grappling efforts to still her. Her fingers grazed the handle of something, but Mike dragged her hand above her head. When she broke free of his grip, she used her nails to claw and scratch, and he yelped.

"You she-devil. Be quiet." He sprang to his feet and pulled her up.

"Felicia, get the ax. Kill him. Now." Cara screamed at her friend and brought her knee up as hard as she could. When he groaned, satisfaction edged out her terror. The adrenaline rush didn't last.

With a curse, he flung her at the wall, banging her head.

Cara sagged, her fingers splayed against the rough boards. Slowly, she turned and saw the blade descending, Felicia's white, peaked face strained, her colorless lips set.

And Cara realized she couldn't let her do it.

With strength she hadn't realized she had, Cara shoved Mike away and fell beside him. The double-bladed ax dug deep into the dirt inches from where he'd been standing.

Cara lay still, panting, and from the corner of her eye, saw Mike lumber to his feet. He scooped up the whip again and swung it at his wife and again at Cara.

The raw pain nearly knocked her unconscious. She glimpsed his raised arm, saw him stride closer, the leer on his face taunting and ugly.

He flicked the whip across her body again, and she knew if she didn't stop him now, she wouldn't have the strength.

Bending over her, he sneered. "Now, I'll teach you what real submission is, since Donald Hayman failed to."

His voice grated her shaky nerves as painfully as the whip had abused her body.

"Mike, no!" Felicia screamed at her husband, and Mike's feet shifted toward his wife. He lifted the whip. "Shut up."

Unthinking, Cara pulled up both legs and kicked as viciously as she could. *Please, God. Please, God …*

In the longest moment of her life, he staggered back, arms flailing. His fingers released their grip on the whip. Surprise rippled across his face as he fell. From the borderline of her unconsciousness, Mike's nightmarish scream went on and on.

A gurgling moan echoed in her ears as Cara sank into the swirling blackness.

❧❦❧

"Caralynne. Please wake up."

The anxiety in the voice brought her to her senses quicker than the soft pats on her cheeks. She rolled her head from side to side and groaned. "I'm awake, Felicia."

The wispy girl sank back on her heels. Her voice trembled, bordering on hysteria. "I thought you were dead too."

Cara's eyes flew open. "What did you say?"

Felicia's eyes were wide, the pupils dilated, and she whispered. "He's dead."

"Who's dead?"

"M-ike. He f-fell on the ax."

The nightmare returned. Cara sat up and slid a glance at the man lying awkwardly on his back, his mouth still twisted in agony. She shivered and bit her lip.

Don't. The man had it coming. He deserved to die.

But the glow of accomplishment failed to light. Her stomach churned.

Felicia's clothing hung in ribbons from her shoulders, her fragile skin marked with ugly welts the whip created. Cara fingered the strips of material from her own clothing, gingerly touched one of the red, raised welts on her chest, and winced.

"Come here."

Her friend scooted closer, and Cara gathered her in a careful hug. Hot tears scalded the raw places. "You're free, Felicia. Don't cry."

"But—"

"But what?"

The wail pulsed through the barn. "If I'd listened to him—obeyed him like he wanted me to, he wouldn't be dead. What am I going to do? How will I live? I've ruined my chance of getting into heaven. And what if they send me away?"

Cara had heard the rumors too. "Nonsense. God won't hold you accountable for what Mike did to himself."

At least she hoped not. A just God would surely have more compassion than that, wouldn't he? Cara gripped her friend's hands and shook them. "You did not kill your husband. He died from his own evil actions, and don't you forget it. Understand?"

The woman's eyes pled with Cara. "What are we going to do?"

Do? That would take some pondering. The elders would be down their throats when they learned yet another of their esteemed men was dead. She'd caught their askance glances, and Head Elder Simmons sent a note yesterday, requesting her presence in his office Thursday. Which meant a serious talk loomed.

They were unhappy with her reaction over Donald's death, but too bad. She'd tried her best to blend in, to go unnoticed, but to show grief and untamed wailing and tears was a sham. No such grief lurked in her heart, and she wouldn't fake it. Definitely not to please them.

Whatever Elder Simmons wished to say—and she could guess what it might be—she would never succumb to their marriage laws again. If they left her alone, she would stay at least until she'd accomplished her plan. Otherwise, she'd get out. Somehow.

"Brother Farmer."

Cara heard the faint call. She opened her mouth but no sound came out.

Another call.

"In here." The words rasped from her throat.

Trotting feet headed their way. Dayne MacFarland and Levi Schrader burst into the barn.

"Where is every—" Dayne stopped and stared down at the figure of Mike awkwardly sprawled on the barn floor.

"What on earth happened?" Levi knelt beside Mike and rolled the body halfway over.

Felicia burst into a fresh storm of sobs.

Dayne turned to the women, and shock blossomed across his face. His raw emotion sent a wave of warmth through Cara's body. He dropped to his knees beside them, his face a horrified mask as he looked between her welts and Felicia's.

"Did Brother Mike do this?" Anger tightened his lips. Dayne and Levi exchanged glances.

"He's one of the meaner ones, with a bad temper and jealous streak a mile long," Levi murmured.

Cara's body shook, her limbs limp as wilted lettuce. "He whipped Felicia, and when I tried to intervene, he decided I needed some discipline too."

"You need a doctor." Dayne's fingers hovered over the ugly slash on her arm.

"No, help me get Felicia to the house, and I'll see about her. Afterward, I can go home and take care of my injuries."

The men supported the woman between them, and Cara limped up the path to the Farmer home. Inside, while Dayne made tea, Cara helped Felicia remove her clothes, bathed her wounds, and settled her on the sofa. She draped a colorful quilt over her, collected the rags, and stuffed them into the wastebasket.

While Levi called the settlement police, Dayne poured two cups of tea and handed one to Cara. "You need to drink something warm too."

Accepting the tea, Cara sipped and set it down.

Felicia lay back against the pillows, her eyes closed, but she opened them when Dayne touched her hand.

Cara smoothed the quilt. "Will you sip some tea?"

"I can't." Felicia turned her head away.

"Then try to sleep, dear. Someone will stay with you until the doctor comes."

"Could you sleep if your husband lay dead in his own barn?" Her friend's eyes drilled into her own.

Depended on who the husband was. Donald? She'd sleep like a baby.

Dayne drew a small table close to the sofa and set the tea on it. "Levi, could you call Mattie to come sit with Felicia and ask the doctor to drop by? He can make the arrangements for Brother Mike after the police finish. Make sure you tell him he can reach us later. Cara needs to go home."

"Sure thing." Levi pulled out his cell phone. "You go ahead. I'll stay here till Mattie and the doctor get here then catch a ride home with Doc."

Dayne held out his hand to Cara. "Let me get you home." He led her to his car and helped her inside. "Why did Brother Mike go after you?"

Cara shivered. What she wanted to say wouldn't do at all. Too demeaning. Humiliating. Disgraceful. Actions no wife should have to go through. Tears pressed against her lids, and she blinked to hold them back. "I couldn't stand it. He lashed Felicia with the whip, so I jumped him, and he came after me."

"What were you thinking? You know the men here use discipline on their wives. You shouldn't have interfered. What if you'd been killed?"

"But I wasn't, and I kept him from focusing on Felicia." She swiped at the escaping tear on her cheek. "I would rather have died than see her struck again."

Dayne pulled into her driveway and sent a gentle reproving smile her way. "You've still got the same trouble-making loyalty, don't you? Never outgrew it, even when the blame shifted your direction. You didn't deserve it most times, but no one else braved the elders' wrath like you."

He couldn't be too angry with her. How could she explain? No easy way. "You don't have to stay. I'll be fine after a long soak in the tub."

He went around to her side of the car and opened the door. "You shouldn't be alone."

"I don't want to put you—"

"Let me at least stay long enough to make fresh tea for you again."

She didn't look at him, didn't want him to leave. If only she could give in to this longing for his company. "I'm okay. I know you have work. Thanks for helping Felicia."

Dayne's car disappeared around the curve, and Cara burst into tears.

❧❦❧

Much too stubborn and independent for her own good. He pounded the steering wheel. But better let her be for a while. He'd check on her later in the day.

Right now, Dayne wanted to confront Elder Simmons about these out-of-control situations. He wouldn't condone women beaten with whips, and the sooner the leader and the rest realized it, the better they'd all be.

He tore down the road, his rage driving him, and slowed only when he caught a glimpse of Elder Simmons outside his house, water hose in hand. Dayne pulled behind the other man's vehicle.

"Reverend MacFarland, beautiful day of God's creation." The man bent over and gently caressed a rosebud. "Lovely, isn't it?"

The man's comment only deepened Dayne's depression. "Depends on what you see."

The other man was smart, Dayne had to give him credit. Without another word, Elder Simmons shut off the spray and wound the hose on the storage wheel in measured moves. "Come in, Reverend. Wife's gone to her sister's, so I'm all alone. Think she's got some of her carrot cake left."

The thought of food sickened him. "None for me, thanks, although I'm sure it's delicious."

"You don't mind if I water my African violets while you talk, do you?" The elder motioned for Dayne to take a seat and picked up a watering can. "What's the problem? This impromptu visit makes me assume something's bothering you."

"I came from the Farmer place. Mike's dead. He used a horsewhip on his wife and then fell on his own double-bladed ax." Blunt, yes, but right now, he couldn't care less.

Elder Simmons set down the can and grunted. "Why would the man leave an ax where he could trip over it?"

"You're missing the point. Why use a whip on his wife?" Dayne jumped to his feet. As if he were walking on hot needles, he paced. Could he get arrested if he shook the man until common sense cleared the elder's brain?

"Some of the men are hardheaded. They insist stronger measures are the only ways that work. Besides, I hate to point this out, but it's hardly your business."

"As our leader, you should put a limit on any corrections needed."

"You think I should interfere in how a man disciplines his family?"

"When he uses whips, yes."

Elder Simmons's face reddened. The tic beneath his left eye pulsed steadily. "Don't be so melodramatic. You know the Bible declares a man should rule his own house. Some homes do need harsher methods. By using the correct method, I'm sure once is enough to bring submission and honor back to the home and to the man, where it belongs."

"The Bible also says for a man to love his wife as he does himself. If you allow them to whip their wives, you ought to require they whip themselves."

"Well, it's good to see you know the Bible so well."

"That's what I was sent to seminary for, wasn't it?" Dayne didn't try to hide the bitterness he'd battled for years at having no choice in the matter.

"And a fine minister you became. Don't ruin it, MacFarland." The man's pale gray eyes fixed on him. The glint there proved why he'd remained head elder for so many years. "I told your father I had things all worked out, and seminary was the best thing for you."

"You talked to my father about me studying for ministry?"

Something in the man's voice didn't ring true.

"He didn't quite agree, but if he saw you today, he'd realize I spoke the truth."

"My father didn't want me to study for ministry? What did he want for me?"

"I'm afraid he never got the opportunity to express his wishes." A smirk plastered the other man's lips.

"Why?"

Elder Simmons gave him a strange look. Curious? Sly?

"When your father died, it fell to me to make the right choice for you."

His father would never have chosen Elder Simmons for his son's guardian. He remembered his father's encouragement to make his own choice. "We've gotten off track. I came here to talk about how our men abuse their wives."

"Have you forgotten what you've been raised to believe? What our ancestor set down for us to live by? Man is to rule his house." Elder Simmons rocked back on his heels, his hands behind his back.

"No. But neither do I swallow everything I'm fed. I believe in checking my actions with, and taking my guidance from, the Bible." Dayne placed both hands flat on the table and leaned on it. "In seminary, we were encouraged to ask questions. We vented our disbelief at certain things and dug in God's word for answers."

"Rubbish. Is this the kind of nonsense they taught you?"

As a kid, Dayne had been terrified of this man. He'd seemed strong, stern, and unsmiling. Spoken to like this, Dayne would have trembled. Today, the man seemed old and very much used to having his way. No one on the grounds fought against Elder Simmons's orders. "It's the kind of freedom I learned. I thought for myself instead of following blindly."

Elder Simmons stared at him for a long time, and an odd expression crossed his face.

A smile.

"You're young and eager to make your presence known. I wouldn't have sent you to seminary if I hadn't thought you the one God chose to serve as our next minister. You understand what I'm saying?"

Dayne inclined his head.

"We need a man like you, Dayne. Strong. Smart and capable of giving us spiritual food." He eyed Dayne. "Just remember, the elders are *your* spiritual mentors. What has been handed down to us from God is relevant today. I've been given the interpretation. My rules are a necessary part of our group. If we go against them, we are defying God's plan for the family and his people."

"God's plan is for a man to beat his wife?" He wanted to respect this man, but for the life of him, the contempt inside him refused to be tamped down.

"God has an orderly plan for the family. Man answers to God, and he is responsible for his family. Wife and children answer to him. According to God's word, woman is to be in subjection to her husband. When a man allows his wife to become independent or bossy, he is endangering her soul. Total opposition to God's plan. Surely you can see that, my son?"

"I understand God's perfect plan for the family, but I still see no reason why such harsh punishment as I saw today needs to come into play. The Bible does demand a man love his wife as himself."

"What makes you so sure Brother Mike didn't love his wife?" Elder Simmons's voice lowered a notch.

"You don't use a horsewhip on someone you love."

"Perhaps extreme. Perhaps not. It has come to my attention Felicia has a tendency to … stray."

Could he be right? She seemed such a gentle woman. He would ask Cara about her. "And what would have been his intent at taking a whip to Caralynne Hayman?"

"Sister Hayman was there?" The man's face froze into a frown.

Too late, Dayne realized perhaps he shouldn't have brought her into the conversation.

"She should have been home mourning her own loss."

"She is forbidden to visit a friend in her time of grief?"

"I will speak to her."

Not exactly what Dayne wanted, but it was all he'd get for now.

He left the Simmonses' house. On the steps, he paused and looked back at the closed door. He didn't remember battling this kind of frustration as a child. But he hadn't understood quite a few things back then. Well, he couldn't do anything about Elder Simmons at the moment.

He'd better get home. God had given him the message for Sunday, and it would either awaken a few hearts or break his.

CHAPTER FIVE

The man grinned at Cara and pointed.

Long, black leeches clung to her, but when she looked down they vanished and became the fingers of the girls clustered around her—fingers digging into her flesh. Their mouths opened in a silent scream, begging, crying, but no tears pooled in their eyes.

The man's voice snarled at her, the volume developing into a volcanic roar. His red hair bushed out like a clown's. Mike Farmer? A dead Mike Farmer, with no eyeballs in the orb of his face. The skinny neck gave way to a broad chest and bulging belly. Cara stared horrified at the body of Elder Simmons.

"They're mine. Give them over to my protection before everyone realizes you killed them."

Cara's gaze jerked upward, but instead of a face, a bird sat perched on top of the neck. Its beak opened, and the squawk melted into a squeak.

She straightened and clasped the girls closer. "Never. You will not get these girls. Never. Never. Never . . ."

His hands stretched out, his fingers bent into claws, as if to latch onto one of the girls. The claws lifted toward her.

The twittering voice grew softer . . . lighter . . . gentler.

Cara's eyes flew open. The birds outside her open window twittered happily. The warmth from the late spring morning streamed in and enclosed her like a cozy blanket.

The dream receded, slithering back into the shadowy box of her consciousness to wait for the next opportunity to terrorize her. Cara raised her arm to block out the rays of light and to hold back the fear eating her insides. Whatever she did, it would never pay for Lori's death. She could never do enough to save the others, to rescue the girls from fates worse than death, to save her friends who'd never known anything better.

Jerking herself to a sitting position, she opened her mouth to hurl insults into the face of her terror and saw her girls peering into the room. She forced a smile. "What are my sleepyheads up to this morning?"

The two ran to her, scrambling into the bed, each maneuvering to outdo the other for attention. Cara cuddled Lacy close and giggled at her youngest daughter's delight at being tickled. "Mommy, read," Lacy demanded.

"I thought you asked to go to Sunday school today." Cara smoothed the child's tangled blonde curls.

Leila snuggled against Cara's arm but twisted to frown at her sister. "That's right, stupid. I want to go to Sunday school."

Cara slipped an arm around Leila and gave her a gentle squeeze. "Sweetie, don't call your sister names. It's not nice." She gave a gentle shove to both girls. "Scram. Leila, choose your own clothes. I'll help Lacy decide."

"May I wear your special barrette today?" Leila asked.

"You may." Cara hugged her daughter.

Leila ran for the door and tossed back her teasing words. "I'm picking my clothes first."

Lacy frowned, and her lip trembled. "I want to pick first."

Cara climbed out of the bed and squatted in front of her daughter. "And you shall. Leila picks her clothes, and you may pick yours. Run along, and no more fussing."

Smile recovered, Lacy skipped out of the room.

Her old rocker beckoned like a loving grandmother, and Cara settled into it. Her newfound sense of freedom, even if it was temporary, sent delicious shivers of delight up her arms. She pulled up one knee and hugged it. The day promised to be a good one.

Yesterday, when the girls begged her to let them go to Sunday school the next morning, she'd acquiesced, not wanting to deny them a simple pleasure. Cassie, their teacher and occasional babysitter, was a good woman. Cara trusted her.

She did have a problem attending the morning services though. Of course, Dayne would be preaching, and she'd yet to attend since he returned to serve as their minister. He'd be interesting and unafraid to speak what he believed. She liked that.

Perhaps she *could* block out enough memories and her own vendetta against the group to go.

Who am I? What have I become besides a mother who adores her daughters? Cara pressed her forehead against her knee and rocked. *A woman with a mission through no fault of mine, if that's possible. Am I at fault for not being more submissive? Am I to be blamed for not protecting Lori enough? For letting the anger in my heart fuel my mission?*

Am I a stronger person because I've determined to stop the abuse from happening again?

Cara jumped to her feet and sent the rocker out of control. She paced for a moment then stopped at the window, her gardens calling her. *Or would the outside world call me a victim of circumstances—someone pushed into acting in a way I had no idea I would?*

Cara swiped the sleeve of her robe across her wet cheeks. Time for a shower. Besides, she had no answers for the myriad of questions tumbling around inside her mind.

❧❧❧

Dayne gripped the open Bible in his hand. He rose early every day, and today was no exception. Five o'clock gave him time for a last glance through his notes before the morning service. He was thankful for peace over the message he'd prepared at God's prompting, but the list of names on his desk tugged on his troubled mind. A list of men he hoped would be possible candidates to help when the time came, but who could he trust? Would any betray him?

He had high hopes for Levi Schrader. Older than Dayne, he had impressive wisdom and gentleness. Many of the men played follow-the-leader, but not Levi. And many of the elders envied Levi, Dayne was sure, and admired his strength of character. But most were not brave enough to stand by themselves against Elder Simmons. Levi would make an excellent leader if given the chance.

But would he be interested in promoting Dayne's plan of change for the group?

"God, I'm here to help these people. I need your help." Dayne paused, thinking. "I know you gave me this message. Help me say something to comfort and encourage the women, and the knowledge to strike a note of conviction in the hearts of the men."

Would Caralynne attend church? He bowed his head yet again. "And, Lord, will you draw Cara to yourself?"

Like a fleeting screen image, Cara's face flashed through his mind. Precious. Endearing. Haunting.

❧❧❧

Passing the Farmer house marred Cara's walk to church. She hadn't seen Felicia since the fatal Tuesday when Mike died. After dropping the girls at school the next day, she took the woods path in hopes of not being seen, and she knocked on Felicia's door. No one answered. She circled the locked-up-tight house, explored the property but saw no signs of habitation.

Had Elder Simmons given Felicity permission to go to her parents'? How deserted and forlorn the place looked. If Felicia and her son had escaped, Cara hoped she didn't return.

Caralynne approached the edge of the churchyard, her girls' small hands tucked into hers. The people filed into the church, a few stopped to talk to neighbors, and some shook hands and backslapped each other.

She admired the structure of the building. It was built of stone, with solid oak doors and vibrant, stained windows. Sunday school rooms were added as needed. Now a separate structure for meals on bad-weather days and for meetings stood just behind the sanctuary. The congregation, ranging from seventy-five to a hundred adult members, lived within a loosely connected settlement. For outsiders looking on, they appeared a normal, well-adjusted group.

Unless you happened to know better by being a part of the Children of Righteous Cain.

Cara tightened her lips. Leila looked up at her. "Mom, that hurts. You're squeezing my hand *hard*."

"I'm sorry, sweetheart. Are you girls ready for your class?"

Lacy bobbed her head and with skirt flouncing, she skipped the rest of the way. Leila strolled behind her sister, her head swiveling to catch a glimpse of her friends. The pearl-covered barrette held back a lock of her daughter's dark blonde hair and shone in the morning sunshine.

Cara tagged behind. Inside, she checked to make sure Lacy was safely ensconced in Cassie's room. Leila joined Mary Ann's daughter and another girl and tossed a wave at her as she disappeared into a larger room.

Grinning, Cara entered the main sanctuary and came face to face with Elder Simmons.

In spite of her resolve, she jumped. "Elder Simmons."

"Sister Hayman."

"Yes?" She hoped her voice didn't sound as weak as she felt.

"I believe you missed your appointment with me."

"I sent a note—"

"You did." Elder Simmons stared at her, no nonsense in his glare. "I'm an understanding person."

Cara wanted to howl. That was so not true.

"I can see you Tuesday at two. Don't be late."

Lacy's class shouted something in unison through the Sunday school doorway as Elder Simmons walked away. If it wasn't for her daughters' obvious enjoyment, she would grab them and bolt from the building. Instead, she bit her lip and proceeded to the last pew.

She sat and closed her eyes as the crooning of the ladies' choir floated toward her. She always loved their sweet voices and at one time thought about joining them.

Marriage and life ripped the desire out of her.

She enjoyed the group singing, especially when Dayne rose to lead them in a special song. His strong voice stirred her emotions. She fought back the urge to stand and sing along, but she couldn't carry a tune. What a laugh. She gripped the edge of the seat to keep still.

When Elder Simmons approached the platform, she readied herself to blank out his loud admonitions.

"My brothers and sisters, God has given me a new commandment."

A chorus of amens approved his words.

Cara averted her gaze from his fat-lipped smile. His self-righteous tone sickened her.

"The scriptures declare all things are to be under subjection in one way or another. Therefore, to assure myself each family is administering the proper training, I will summon a chosen one to my study."

She pressed her lips together to check the gasp threatening to escape.

"Beginning next week, according to God's orders, the family selected will present themselves to me. During this period, I will review each member's performance, satisfy myself of their dedication, or prepare a judgment to correct any errant methods I discern. During our regular weekly meeting, I will present special instructions for the husband."

An applause of lukewarm approval met his declaration. The man up front spread his arms. "Yes, I can sense your hesitation. I can smell your suspicion."

Well, why on earth not? Did this stupid new commandment include widows? She sincerely hoped not, because she had no intention of going anywhere alone with this madman.

"My friends, never fear God's commands. He never gives them without our good in mind. A simple leader like myself is humbled to be the instrument through which God works to assure us of heaven."

I bet.

Angus Tobert looked around at the uneasy faces and raised his hands. "Praise God. Praise God for His new commandment to us."

Hands raised from the more devout, fanatic men, at first five, then seven and ten. Others lifted until a third of the elders joined in the praising.

Angus' screeching was enough reason to cover her ears, let alone the hypocritical rejoicing.

Elder Simmons posed before them, a benign expression highlighting his shiny features. No doubt the sweat covering him was from the oration he inflicted on the congregation.

What a bunch of lunatics. Cara tried to keep from curling her lips.

Elder Simmons gripped the sides of the podium and lowered his voice. "I believe I have God's direction on the first family to be chosen." He flicked another glance toward his second-in-command.

Angus obediently flapped his arms again. "Rise up, brothers. Give God the praise for His love to us."

Reluctant hands lifted. Voices raised. Someone began clapping until most of the men joined in false enthusiasm.

The boisterous wave of zeal swept the room. Dayne sat straight and silent, eyeing the room and the two men on the platform. Once he closed his eyes, and Cara wished she could read his lips. Praying for this whole miserable scene, no doubt. Fat lot of good it would do.

As the noise subsided, Angus Tobert stepped to the pulpit and read the selection of scriptures in a monotone.

Cara hid her yawn behind a hand.

When the man's oration was finally over, Dayne strode to the pulpit.

With a jerk, she straightened in her seat.

Clean-cut and dignified, yet friendly, he presented himself as an impressive person. His black suit, contrasting nicely with a white shirt, darkened his already-tanned skin. He didn't speak right away, at ease with himself and all those staring back.

He swept the congregation again with his hawk eyes and seemed to pause and rest on her. Had his eyes picked her out from the others? Cara slid down in her seat, her heart's beat quickening.

"I want to read from 1 John chapter four. Please listen as I read these verses. '*Beloved, let us love one another: for love is of God, for everyone who loves is born of God and knows God.*'" The resonance of his voice, the words spoken, was soothing and confident. His natural speaking voice was beautiful, full and deep, dramatic without being melodramatic. Cara closed her eyes and allowed his voice to wash over her.

"'*... because God sent his only Son into the world so we might live ...*'"

When he finished reading, he paused, and Cara peeked from beneath her lashes.

"Today, I'd like to speak to you about love. What is love?" He paused. "Let's first define what it's not."

Where was Dayne going?

"Love is not a conditional emotion. We can't pick and choose who or how much we love. We either love or we don't. We either open our hearts or keep them under lock and key. In this book …" Dayne lifted his Bible and tapped a finger on the cover. "… we find God's divine words, 'There is no fear in love,' so we can conclude a fearful love is no love at all."

A ripple spread through the congregation.

"God wants our love to be a perfect love. That means an unconditional love. A love that looks beyond faults and failures. A love full of empathy for others. Does love scorn the poor and insist they help themselves? Does a husband love when he trusts his wife to return his love, and he delights in making her happy? Is a wife loving her husband when she craves his touch and chooses to do love tasks for him? What do you think?"

Cara shivered. Where had Dayne learned such things? She'd been raised to believe God wanted submission and obedience from females. Love didn't come into play.

Thirty minutes later the choir began their benediction hymn while the people stood with bowed heads. Elder Simmons, on the platform, looked as if he'd eaten a lemon as he scanned the congregation. Before his searing look fell on her, she lowered her eyes.

Once the last amen was spoken, Cara left the sanctuary, gathered her girls, and headed outside.

"Mom, I didn't get a chance to talk to Sissy McCoy. May I?"

Sissy was three years older than her daughter and her current role model. She was too forward for Cara's taste. Not exactly the person she wanted Leila to follow. Yet if she fussed too much, Leila would all the more want to be with the girl. "Yes, dear. I'll be at the oak tree. Fifteen minutes."

Leila ran across the lawn, legs pumping, her occasional attempts of preteen maturity forgotten. Cara's heart swelled at how little it took to make her daughter happy. Lacy plumped onto the grass, and Cara ignored thoughts of grass stain. When four of her friends headed her way, she waved.

Mary Ann Denuit swept the area with a glance then lowered her voice. "What did you think about Reverend MacFarland's message?"

"Strange. Old Reverend Thacker never preached about love." Penelope lifted her hair off her skinny neck and rotated her head. "Mostly about honoring our husbands."

Cara wanted to throw up.

"He preached about us doing our duties." Abby looked at Jodie and offered a smile as if entreating her for approval.

Mary Ann swiveled her head before speaking. "And submission. He was emphatic about that."

Jodie Schrader snorted, her shapely straight nose wrinkled. "Reverend MacFarland probably got those new ideas from that fancy school our elders sent him to. He'd better be careful. Elder Simmons won't put up with any nonsense from him."

"Reverend MacFarland needs to preach what he thinks is right and not listen to Elder Simmons." Sounded a little self-righteous. Good thing she wasn't talking about herself.

"What?" Penelope's thin face widened with the grin. "You're criticizing Elder Simmons?"

"Shut up, Penelope." Jodie studied her design-painted nails. "You know better. We're close to the Simmonses. I might tell him how funny you think this is."

"Don't do that." Penelope's face lost its laughter. "You know I was kidding."

"Elder Simmons doesn't care much for kidding." Jodie's smirky remark morphed her charismatic face into anything but friendliness.

Cara wanted to wipe off the smirk. If Jodie only knew what those smart-aleck expressions did to her lovely face.

"What do you think about Elder Simmons's new commandment?" Mary Ann's baby cried, and she mouthed soothing sounds. "Who'll be first, do you think?"

"Not me, and I think it's a horrid idea." Just the thought of it made Cara want to vomit.

"I'm sure you'll let Elder Simmons know." The seriousness in Mary Ann's eyes outshone the twinkle of mischievousness.

"I might." Cara bit her lip. Did her friend expect her to cause another ruckus?

"You know I love you, Caralynne." Jodie eyed her. "But sometimes you're too mouthy for your own good. If God spoke to Elder Simmons, why buck it?"

Cara opened her mouth to refute Jodie's statement.

"How is Felicia doing, Caralynne?" Abby pulled out a baby bottle and inserted it into her baby's mouth.

"I haven't seen her." Cara met Abby's eyes and bit her lip. "I know she's wanted to see her parents for a long time. They've never seen baby Michael."

"Will Elder Simmons give her permission?" Abby asked.

Jodie shrugged. "You know he'll do what's best for her."

He wouldn't let her go.

"There's always *That Place*." Jodie emphasized the two words in a hushed, spooky voice.

"Jodie, don't. How can you even joke about it?" Unease bounced to the surface of Cara's mind, clattering for attention. Where was Felicia? Could the rumors she and her friends whispered about be true? Did The Children of Righteous Cain have a secret place where women—certain women—were sent?

But why would Felicia be sent to such a place? Her one child, a boy, proved her fertility. Docile and quiet, she rarely received untoward attention from anyone, even her friends. Cara winced. Had she neglected the backward woman and failed to encourage her friend enough to keep her alive?

Stop it. She had no reason whatsoever to think such foolishness.

❦ 47 ❦

She didn't want to think about such an awful place or of unwanted women who for one reason or another lived to serve men who never seemed satisfied to stay home. Women with no hope of marrying again. Or so the rumors reported. True? Or the vivid imagination of others?

Cara picked up where she'd left off. "Besides, she could get pregnant if she marries again. She and Mike were married only a year and a half."

"You could be right, but Levi came home whiter than a ghost the other night. He wouldn't tell me what happened, but I know the meeting concerned Felicia."

"Why so soon?" Mary Ann asked.

Would they punish her, send her away? Cara blinked to hold back sudden tears.

"Enough morbid talk. We'll find out soon enough where Felicia is. I'd say she went to her parents'. Inner Sanctum approved, of course."

Of course.

"I've got juicier news," Jodie crowed. "Did you hear who Elder Simmons's new favorite is?"

"No." Mary Ann craned her neck to check on her twins again. "Tell us quick."

Jodie mouthed the name. "It's Sissy McCoy."

Sissy? The thirteen-year-old daughter of Tommy and Susan McCoy? Jodie could have stomped on her foot, and it wouldn't have hurt any more.

Mary Ann's face paled. "What? Surely not. Sissy's only thirteen."

The breaking-in. The preparatory stage for the marital ritual. The period of time when the girls were taught what married life would be about.

Aching heart about burst, Cara cried out, "How can he do that? Why is he changing it from fourteen?"

"Didn't you hear me? Sissy has caught *Elder Simmons's* eye."

"So it's okay to take a thirteen-year-old because Elder Simmons wants her?" If only she could crunch a railroad spike in two. Perhaps then her rage would abate. Or not.

Jodie held up both manicured hands. "Whoa. Don't take it out on me. I'm passing on the news to my best friends. I thought you, Mary Ann, especially would want to know, since Valerie is Sissy's friend."

The nerves in Mary Ann's neck throbbed. "What if he—"

"Chooses Valerie next?" Jodie lifted her shaped brows. "So what if he does? You have been preparing her, haven't you?"

"She's too young. We celebrated her thirteenth birthday last month. I—I—"

"You're not doubting Elder Simmons's orders from God, are you?"

"Doubt has nothing to do with it. I agree, Mary Ann. Fifteen's too early. He dropped it to fourteen, and now *thirteen*? Why does he have to be so—so greedy?" Cara frowned at Jodie. Her husband might be one of the inner-circled elders, but that didn't give Jodie any right to bark at Mary Ann.

Jodie flounced away. "I wanted to help, but if you both want to be hateful, I won't tell you anything else I learn."

She wasn't ready to forgive Jodie for agreeing with their leader. Still, Jodie was her friend, though a smart aleck at times. She loved them all and always trusted them enough to share the latest news.

"Come on, Jodie, I haven't talked to you for a long time. Let's lighten up." Cara couldn't stand any more talk about Elder Simmons.

"You're right, Caralynne." Mary Ann drew in a deep breath. "I'm sorry for snapping, Jodie."

Jodie slipped an arm around the penitent woman. "Don't worry about it. Caralynne, have you heard yet who they've picked for you?"

Her face warmed, not from embarrassment, but anger. "No. I don't want to know."

Penelope Lewis gasped. "Are you kidding? Why on earth not? At least you could get prepared if you knew."

"I haven't talked to Elder Simmons yet."

"You haven't?"

"He wanted me to come Thursday, but I cancelled."

"You *cancelled*?" Mary Ann's already-round eyes grew bigger. "Caralynne, how did you dare?"

"He gave me *The Lecture* about his great ability of understanding, this morning," Cara drawled her answer.

"I don't see how you have the nerve to do stuff like that." Abby Melton bit her bottom lip. "Richard's occasional slaps are enough. I don't care if he wants me to crawl on my knees, I'll do it. I hate the pain."

Cara looked at the young woman who cradled her baby against her shoulder, and her heart melted. "I'm not brave and I don't like pain either, but I can stand only so much. Anyhow, I'm not getting married to any of their choices. If and when—and I doubt it'll happen—I'll do the choosing."

"Caralynne, you can't get away with that. The elders will punish you." Jodie scowled.

"Let them. What are they going to do?" Cara shrugged.

Four pairs of eyes gleamed with wariness and varying degrees of questioning.

"What if they send *you* away?" Jodie Schrader snapped.

Cara fought to keep from reacting. Jodie manipulated her friends with her mild threats to get results. She would not give her the satisfaction.

Jodie pursed her lips. "Cara, you know very well rebellion isn't allowed. You have to submit. God doesn't approve—"

"I don't believe it anymore."

"You'd better be careful Elder Simmons doesn't hear you." Jodie's eyes flashed.

"What about God? Doesn't it matter if he hears me?" Pushing the limits, yes, but she'd strained her own limit.

Jodie's lips pursed. "God selected the elders to lead us. It's not our right to question their judgment. You are in danger spouting blasphemy."

"Are you spouting *your* beliefs, Jodie? Or what you've been taught all your life? Have any of us thought for ourselves? Ever? This is a free country."

"Do you think we're *wrong*?" Abby's eyes begged for hope even as she stroked her baby's hair.

"No way." But even as she said it, Mary Ann's eyes sparkled. Even-tempered, nothing ever disturbed her. She motioned, and her twins ambled up to her. "I mean, Josh is decent to me and doesn't beat me. But if I told him I was going to get a job in town, he wouldn't want me to."

Cara shrugged, but the images of Donald and Mike lying on their backs, dead and gone, flicked into her mind. She'd like to think God helped her and Felicia rid the community of those blights on humanity. Had she caused their deaths, or were they really accidents, as the group sheriff had ruled? Would he have ruled differently had he known she'd been at both places?

She bade the women good-bye. Abby Melton, her baby hugged close to her breast, hurried toward her husband standing impatiently at his car. The cuff her friend received on the side of the head dimmed the day for Cara. Tightening her lips, she frowned at the skinny man, even though he couldn't see her.

Richard wouldn't have cared if he had.

❦❦❦

Dayne hoped Cara would still be outside by the time he finished speaking with the members of the church. But by the looks of the long line moving past him, he doubted it.

Kenny Lewis, Penelope hanging behind him, pumped his hand, but his eyes rested on the curvy figure of the girl in front of him.

"Did you like the message, Brother Lewis?"

"Sure." Lewis jiggled his feet as if stepping in time to some inner music. "Great message. See ya at the next meeting. Come on, Penelope. Stop dawdling."

Penelope shrugged and gave Dayne a half-shamed smile. "Thanks for the message. I've got to go, or I'll be walking home. Wish I had the time to ask you some questions," she whispered. Waving, she hurried after her departing husband.

Dayne's heart warmed at her words. The crowd of people shifted, undulating before him. No Cara.

❦ 51 ❦

"I say, our blood pounded this morning." Richard Melton cackled as if he'd told a joke. His hand drummed a steady, silent beat on his leg. Abby hugged their baby close to her chest and looked down as if too bashful to meet his eyes.

"I hope it did more than get your blood moving, brother," Dayne searched the other man's eyes.

"Didn't understand it, but no matter. You sure have a way with words."

Dayne opened his mouth to assure the man it did matter whether he understood it, but instead, Elder Simmons approached and the Melton couple moved on.

Might as well take the bull by the horns. "I hoped to have a chance to talk. This new commandment troubles me."

Elder Simmons huffed out a huge puff of air. "You doubt God's wisdom?"

"Never. But I doubt the reasoning for this. It's hard for me to believe God commanded one—" As much as he disliked this man, there was still no need in causing strife between them.

"Meaning me? You have no faith in my leadership?"

"That's not the point. I fail to see why God would ask anyone—even you—to check up on another man's family. I can't agree."

"So you've said. I expected your uneasiness." Elder Simmons tapped his fingers together. "What if I promise to think on your objection? I will diligently seek God's face about this."

It was a start. Dayne changed the subject. "How did you like the sermon this morning?"

"Could give some of our women ideas." Elder Simmons crossed his arms.

Not a bad thing. "Like they should be loved instead of berated?"

"Discipline is good for the soul."

"So is love," Dayne countered. "What does it hurt for a couple to fall in love? Why must a marriage be such a mundane thing?"

"What do you say about the arranged marriages in the Bible? History indicates such couples do well together. Do you not realize God ordained them?"

"That's the key. God's ordination."

Elder Simmons opened his mouth to speak, but Dayne cut him off. "I'm sure many marriages began as arranged. Even without love, some have eventually proven to be right for the couples involved. But modern day dictates other ways for marriage."

"We are sheltering our young girls from heartache and trouble. At least this way they have no worries and are taken care of for life. For what more could they ask?"

Dayne remained silent, his heart heavy. He'd been raised in the Children of Righteous Caine group and never known another way. His fear as a youngster caused him never to question their doctrines and beliefs. Only during his second year at seminary when doubts flooded his mind did he voice his questions.

True, some of the marriages did end up all right. Few of the women complained, but neither did they seem happy, although most of them adored Elder Simmons.

In spite of his intense study of the Bible and their doctrinal manual, he could find no peace in his soul for two of their prevalent practices.

Elder Simmons's large hand patted Dayne's shoulder, and he wanted to shrug it off.

"Son, men have stronger needs than women. God made us the head of the home and women the weaker part of the union. He knew what he was doing. Through our ancestor Cain, we have the key to perfect happiness on earth if we follow what God revealed to him. Strong men to lead the home and secure heaven for the family. Weaker women to fulfill their duty in childbearing and obedience."

"At what price?"

"Careful. You don't want to end up like your father."

Sounded like a warning. "What do you mean?"

"Nothing more than a bit of fatherly advice." Elder Simmons steepled his fingers. "Your father let stress and trouble get to him and died an early demise because of it. Don't let that happen to you. Let us, my son, make the decisions. Your job is to encourage and instruct our people to follow."

Was this his real intent or did some deeper, subtle meaning lurk behind the words? He must have waited a fraction of a second too long, because Elder Simmons pursed his lips. "Would it help to sit in a couple of our sessions? We could reserve a set period to help you put these doubts aside."

He seriously doubted sitting in any of their sessions would do the job for him. Once having seen the light, he had no desire re-enter the darkness. Still, it could be another opportunity to get in some words about the truth. "Let me pray about it, and I'll let you know."

"You are young yet. It's normal for you to be beset like this. As much as we wanted the best in studies for you, I regret you came home to us worried. You need total faith. God shows me the way we are to go. We must not falter. You have to yield to our leadership."

Or else? Could the cagey elder be threatening to dismiss him?

"I'll tell you what. What if I bring you in to help me inventory the families?"

Was he kidding?

"You know, I have to follow God's direction. It's not my fault God chose me to do this."

It was easy to bring God in for justification of one's own wishes. Dayne declined an answer.

"I will check with you in a few days." Elder Simmons clasped his hands together. "There's another matter we need to discuss."

"What is that?"

"It's time for you to marry."

Very funny. He didn't need anyone to tell him when to marry. "I think I'll know when I want to marry."

"The elders and I have evaluated the prospective candidates. We want the best for you and narrowed down the choices to three different girls two years ago."

Wow. What a special privilege. "Who would these girls be?"

Elder Simmons actually smacked his lips. "I personally—uh, oversaw their preparation myself, although many wanted to do it. I know they'll be excellent choices for you."

A surge of distaste rolled up from Dayne's insides and tightened his throat. Cara's face smiled at him from his mind.

"Michele Baker. Suzanna Moses. Ashley Gardner. Ripe and ready."

"Isn't Michele the fifteen-year-old daughter of Jacob Baker?"

"Brother Jacob has been hoping she would be your choice. The other girls are excellent choices too. Say the word, and I'll make sure she's yours."

"How old are these other two?" This sickened him. "I can't consider such a thing. Surely you have more mature selections. You do know if the authorities find out what we do here, we'll be in serious trouble."

The devious glint in the head elder's eyes belied his innocence. Obviously, a few aces hid in his sleeve. "That's why it pays to have the perfect man serving as our own police chief. He's able to foist off any unnecessary and problematic inquiries."

"The chief? Are you bribing the man?"

"Reverend MacFarland, do you really think I'd stoop to such a thing? No, the good chief accepts a favor from one of our more accommodating women. Keeps him happy, and it's well worth giving him the favors for the return of peace."

Dayne faced Elder Simmons. "On second thought, I think I'd better accept your offer to meet the other elders. We need to address these issues."

"Wonderful. I like a decisive man. What about the girls? The sooner you make your choice, the sooner you can be initiated into our group as a full elder."

The bitter lump in his abdomen stirred.

"It's not like you'll have to limit yourself to one wife, you know. You of all people should never have to yearn for sexual satisfaction."

"I need to get going. Let me get back to you on your noble suggestion." He bit off his sarcasm and refused to look back. If he didn't leave now, the consequences of his actions would be serious.

Dayne locked the doors of the sanctuary and started down the steps before he saw the figure of Levi Schrader at the bottom.

Dayne allowed himself an internal groan. He was in no mood to deal with another elder. Especially if he had a bone to pick with his sermon this morning. Or worse, more urging to take a wife he didn't want.

"I appreciated the message this morning. It was different than we're used to, but it gave me something to think about."

This was pleasant news. "Glad you enjoyed it."

"Oh, I didn't say I enjoyed it." Levi waved a hand toward the SUV still parked in the church lot. "I need to go. Jodie's in the car."

"Sure. We'll get together again sometime."

"I'd like that. Next time, be prepared." Levi chuckled, and it was a friendly sound. "I've got a ton of questions I want to ask you."

At least one promising thing, which meant the morning wasn't a total washout. Perhaps Levi would be the specific help he needed.

CHAPTER SIX

Cara sealed the plastic bag of chocolate chip cookies she'd made yesterday. She cut the pepper-jack cheese into cubes and tucked her girls' milk and juice into the cooler. Her daughters pranced around the table, delirious at the prospect of another picnic, and chanted silly dillies. Leila, out of sight from her peers, was as carefree as her sister.

The elders would prefer Cara staying home for at least a month, avoiding outside activities, but she saw no reason for their stupid rules to cause Leila and Lacy to suffer. Besides, no one would ever learn about a private picnic. No one would even see them.

The knock on the door gave her pause. Leila ran for the door before she could stop her, and reluctantly, Cara followed. Dayne MacFarland leaned against a porch rail, ankles crossed as if he had not a care in the world. He must have made a quick change. The blue and yellow plaid shirt and jeans fit him well.

She averted her gaze but didn't bother hiding her grin. "Hi. Where are you headed?"

He responded with his own grin. "Wanted to see my favorite parishioner."

"Meaning me?" He was teasing, but she liked it. "I'm sure."

Lacy tugged on his hand. "We're going on a picnic."

"You are?" Dayne squatted. "What fun. I wish I had a picnic today."

"Mommy, Revern' Mac—MacFarlan wants a picnic." Lacy's eyes were liquid sapphires.

Her child's entrancing eyes captured her admiration for a moment before she took in Dayne's teasing ones. "Not fair. Weaseling sympathy from a child."

"All's fair in love and war."

"Sounds serious."

"Right now I think I'm warring for both."

The twinkles in his eyes teased her, but the tone in his voice put her on alert. He meant—no, she wouldn't think it.

Cara propped both hands on her hips and looked down at Lacy. "I suppose we'd better give him something to take his mind off his problems. What do you think, girls? Should we invite Reverend MacFarland to our picnic?"

Her girls' eyes sparkled and both heads bobbed in answer.

"Consider yourself a part of this picnic brigade. You're in time to help work. Come on into the kitchen and help me finish packing up."

Dayne hefted the picnic basket and eyed the cooler. "How were you going to carry both of these?"

She nodded to the back door. "Take a peek."

He strolled to the door. "I see."

"Our red wagon has been lots of help. The girls can even snuggle in it if they get too tired on the way home, although Leila's beginning to think she's too old for such a thing."

"Mom." Leila pulled a face and swiveled away.

"Do we have far to walk?" Dayne tucked two different types of pickles into the basket.

"Close to a mile. A private place I found one day when I needed some quiet time away from everything." Cara picked up the cooler and followed Dayne down the porch steps to where her daughters romped. "I shared it—"

The thought of her older daughter leaped into her mind. Never again would she share anything with Lori.

When she would have taken the wagon handle, Dayne gripped it and started off. Her girls giggled and squealed, excitement in every bound of their healthy bodies as they pranced across the yard, Leila as skittish as Lacy. When Lacy lost a flip-flop and hopped on one foot, Cara hurried to help her.

"I wanna go barefoot, Mommy."

"Not here, sweetie. There're too many briars. You can kick those off after we get to our secret area."

She straightened. Lacy took off after Leila, screaming for her sister to wait on her. "I don't want to pick briars out of her feet all evening."

"Do they fight?"

"Between themselves? No. Well, not much. I've tried to instill loyalty to each other and the family into them."

"You've done a fine job raising them."

Her throat threatened to close. "I've tried to. Even if I didn't want to be a good mother—which I do—I love my girls fiercely. Sometimes I think I'm a mother tiger."

"That makes me admire you even more."

Her heart fluttered. Was he being sincere? She eyed him and loved the casual good looks clinging to him like a second skin. His jeans—the perfect fit—and the linen material of his shirt. The healthy glow from his hair. His clear, unjaded eyes. How had he escaped becoming what the other men in the group were? Had his seminary years given him a distance from their corruptness?

Her girls' giggles drifted back to her even though she couldn't see them. The forest quiet surrounded them, and the sun peeked through the leafy boughs overhead. "I don't remember you singing like you did this morning."

"I didn't have training, but when I'm asked I try to use what talent I have." He shrugged. "Some seem to like it."

"Some? Your girlfriends?"

"Just friends."

But the tell-tale blush in his cheeks told her different.

"You don't mind sharing this special spot?"

"Are you going to tell everyone about it?" She tossed the question in his direction as she took the right-hand fork in the path.

"No, but I might like it so well, I'll want to come again."

"We'll worry about that when it happens." She pushed aside a dangling branch and made a mental note to bring hedge clippers the next time to trim it back. "I hear the girls. They're already in the pool."

"You allow them to swim without supervision?"

"Of course not. Come on." She motioned and hurried to where her girls splashed in the water.

Dayne joined her. At the sight of the foot of water, a stream swirling gently to form a perfect shallow pool, Dayne was tempted to pull Cara in after him.

"They know this is the only place they're allowed, and both of them are old enough to wade here."

"Anything deeper anywhere? Let's join the fun."

"Farther up the stream it gets deeper, but we don't usually venture far away. I've waded here occasionally when it's really hot, but I'm like a mother hippo alongside her babies."

"You're anything but that."

Cara took the wagon handle from Dayne and pulled it to a level spot close to the stream. She shook the quilt she'd tucked in earlier, but Dayne drew it from her hands and spread it on the ground. "Do we eat first or relax?"

"We usually eat first. The girls play or we take a walk. I read to them, we do puzzles, talk, or sometimes take a nap." Cara pulled out a pitcher and two paper cups. "Looks like today, we'll eat last."

"Sounds like a plan. Did Brother Hayman ever come here?"

"No." The one-word answer spurted from her. Afraid she'd been too abrupt, she offered an explanation. "Donald always did his thing on Sundays after church and dinner. Sometimes fished, sometimes hung with his friends. We never saw him until late that night."

"Would he have cared that you had an outing?"

She shrugged. "Probably on principle, but he never knew. It was another instance of choosing my girls' innocent pleasures over stupid rules."

"It's funny." Dayne settled on the other side of the quilt.

"What is?"

"When I was younger, I never wanted things to change. I never thought I'd disagree with the elders."

"You have doubts too?"

"Yes."

"I've had doubts for a long time. Ever since I—I had to marry Donald Hayman. No, that's not true. I suppose that bothered me. I was scared and young and confused, but my real doubts surfaced much later. I didn't even let Donald's occasional beatings bother me. I guess I assumed I deserved them. It was only when—when—"

For one moment, the nightmarish blackness she'd lived in for six months swirled around her, threatening to draw her back into the horrid pain she'd experienced. She blinked and shook her head.

Dayne stared at her, the concern on his face almost her undoing. "Lori's death."

Afraid if she spoke it would all come out, she nodded.

"She was something like you, I imagine."

The warmth in his eyes soothed the ache.

"Sounds as if she was a strong person."

Her chest hurt. She blinked back tears. "She was full of vibrant life. She loved animals and wanted to become a veterinarian."

"Would it help to talk about what happened?" His gentle voice soothed her raw nerves.

"I've never talked about it to anyone."

"I'd like to know."

She twisted her clenched hands in her lap. "I went to help a sick friend. Took her some homemade tomato soup and fresh bread. When I got home four hours later, Lori wasn't home. I didn't think much of it at first. She loved the woods and knew them almost as well as I but never strayed too far. When it started to get dark, the worry set in. I was frantic and searched everywhere, even here."

"What did you do?"

"I begged Donald to help, but he laughed, and stupid me, I never thought about Emery." The strain of tension threatened to choke her, and she moaned with the effort to not cry.

"Emery?"

Cara pressed her hands against her eyes. "I should have known. He'd been hanging around, throwing hints and making lewd remarks about Lori, but I thought Donald would keep him in line."

"Perhaps he didn't know Emery was interested."

"I know he could have stopped it. It wasn't important enough to him." Cara crossed her arms. "When he came home drunk later, he slapped me around and told me if she was in trouble, it was my fault. I shouldn't have been running around the neighborhood. By the time I found her, it was too late."

Cara focused on a bruise on one hand, rubbing a finger over the discoloration, the pressure building behind her eyes. "I blame myself for not seeing it coming. For not protecting her. I can't imagine what she went through, what Emery did to her."

"Back in Boston, I heard she injured herself and died from the infection."

Cara stared at him as the anger inside her bubbled to the surface. "She injured herself fighting off the evil man abusing her."

"But she was only, what, thirteen?" The shock in his voice was satisfying.

"Twelve. She was a child fighting a man. There was no way she could win that fight."

"Had the elders decided she would marry him someday? Or someone else?" Dayne's voice gentled. "Were you fighting it? Didn't you suspect—?"

"Of course I knew some day it would come up. But she was only twelve, Dayne. Twelve. A child. Much too young for any breaking-in."

"The breaking-in. It used to start when the girls were sixteen, or even fifteen." Dayne's face paled. "When did the elders begin lowering the age?"

"Elder Simmons is the leader. The others mostly agree with whatever he wants, whenever he wants it."

"I tried to forget this ritual while I was gone." Dayne scrubbed his face. "I have my dad to thank for my feelings about it. He hated the ritual and his thoughts affected the way I looked at it. Besides, I couldn't wait to get away, even if I had to concede to Elder Simmons's wishes for my life work." Dayne strode toward the creek bed.

"I thought you were running away—"

"I was. It wasn't that I was immune to the temptation, but the revulsion Dad felt for its initiation here bothered me so badly I knew something was wrong."

"How can it not be wrong? Trained by their parents to give in to the desires of men, then taken by the men for sex? What choice do we have when all we've been taught tells us we must be submissive and willing?"

"I know. I know. I wish I could have stayed away, regardless of what the elders wanted, but God wouldn't let me. He brought me back."

"And I accepted my early marriage as a normal event. Only afterward did I wonder why I didn't experience the breaking-in. I thought it wiser not to ask. That doesn't excuse my ignorance in not protecting Lori. How could I have been so stupid?" Cara wrapped arms around her waist and rocked. "Donald treated me with contempt, but he never hurt the girls. Never paid much attention to them, but didn't abuse them either. I thought of Lori's marriage as years away. I figured I'd somehow come up with a reason to postpone it even further."

"How could you know it would happen? Don't blame yourself."

"I was fifteen before they made a decision concerning me."

Dayne shook his head. "No, Cara, that was when you heard the decision."

A premonition of evil brooded over her. "What do you mean?"

"I remember you were on the list. I cared about you, so my parents tried to arrange for us to eventually marry, thinking it would be better than what might happen otherwise. For six months it dragged on, and Dad fought to gain that end. They hoped our group would make an exception."

"Ha. That never happens."

"But it does. Very rarely, but still it can happen if the elders see the wisdom of it."

"Wasn't your father pretty close to Elder Simmons? Surely they would have listened to him."

Dayne shrugged. "You'd think. I don't know what happened. I know Dad pushed pretty hard, but then he died from a heart attack, and I was sent away to school."

For a long moment, Cara stared at her girls splashing in the stream, their tanned arms and legs gleaming, their childish laughter ringing out. The dark depression inside her thickened and threatened to smother her.

The suspicious thought waved like a fire-engine-red banner. Had Dayne's father died a natural death, or had he become a nuisance to get rid of?

Did Dayne wonder?

His eyes gave her the answer.

"Were you able to get an autopsy?"

"No. I was too young. They wouldn't have listened to me, and Mother—well, after Dad's death, she had no spirit left to fight them."

Cara smoothed the quilt she sat on, drawing comfort from it. Her memory of Mrs. MacFarland's devastation still smarted. Had she suspected someone in the group of murdering her husband but been unable to prove it? A young seventeen-year-old Dayne had gone along with Elder Simmons's plans for his future, lonesome without his dad, eager to get away.

She pulled the basket close. "I hope you like chicken."

"My favorite." He tried to snitch a leg, but she smacked at his hand. "Cara, don't despair. We'll figure something out."

"Sure." Her response came automatically, but her heart closed to the encouragement he offered. He'd run away before. She no longer trusted anyone or anything but her own strength and determination. As much as the man attracted her, she couldn't afford to trust him either.

❧❦❧

Monday morning Cara sorted through her girls' clothes, filled the washer with the colored ones, added detergent, and closed the lid. She hummed "Rock of Ages" as she checked the dryer.

Tight-fisted as Donald had been with casual spending money, he'd provided up-to-date necessities for the home. He'd been a slovenly, fat bully with a mean streak as blatant as a mad bull, but at least their home was decent.

She could have tolerated him if it hadn't been for his distasteful lusts. He held no respectful thought for her. To him, she was only another piece of his property to be shoved around as the mood hit him. That and his slobbery, disgusting delight in breaking in the girls of the group.

Cara jumped at the knock on her door.

Donald's here. The thought struck her with the force of a baseball slamming into her forehead. She cast the thought aside.

Abby Melton stood outside, her baby clasped close in her arms, eyes red, and a bruise the size of a small apple on her cheekbone.

"Abby, come in."

"You're not too busy? I know today's your cleaning day." Her eyes begged for admittance, but Abby hesitated, shrinking back.

"I'm never too busy for you. I've put in another load of clothes. It's time for a break anyway. Would you like some iced tea?"

Abby's head jerked up, then down. Her teeth chewed her bottom lip. "You know I love your sweet tea. I never get enough at home."

Cara poured both of them a glass of tea, slipped a slice of lemon on the rim, and layered peanut butter cookies on a small dish. When she sat down, she scooted the plate toward her friend.

The purple bruise on her friend's cheek told Cara a story she didn't like. "Richard hit you. Again."

Abby's head drooped lower.

Cara laid a hand on her friend's. "Abby, let me talk to him. I can get him to stop. Please."

"No." Abby lifted a cookie but laid it back on her napkin. Tears filled her eyes, rolled down her cheeks. "Last night he threatened to bring in another, younger girl."

"Why?"

"He said I'm not performing my wifely duties enough."

"I don't believe it."

Abby rested her cheek on her palm. "I'm exhausted and nervous as a wild animal. I've been nauseated for the last two weeks. I'm afraid I might be—"

"Pregnant? Oh, no. Does Richard know?"

"No, but what does it matter? My feelings mean nothing to him."

"Have you seen the doctor?"

"Are you kidding? Richard doesn't believe in wasting money on a doctor until necessary. I was six months along before Doctor Hammond saw me when I carried baby Joseph."

The two-month-old baby whimpered, and the young girl patted him. "Shh. Shh."

Cara reached for the baby, cradled him against her shoulder and patted his back. "You know how angry this makes me. Why did you come to me?"

"I need your—your …"

Cara's encouragement. Her advice. Her strength.

Abby closed her eyes. "Richard's fiftieth birthday was last month. I think it's why he's been so irritable."

Crazy was more like it. The man didn't deserve this girl. "Abby, why don't I bring over some supper for Richard tonight? I'll come early so he need not know. You won't have to cook."

"Oh, Cara, you're the best friend a person could have."

Cara filled a baggie full of cookies. "Isn't cabbage soup his favorite?"

"He loves it." Abby flushed. "I'm afraid I won't be able to eat any, but at least he'll enjoy his supper."

"Perfect."

Her friend hurried down the road. As Abby's short—still girlish—figure disappeared from view, Cara took in the pinks, yellows, and purples of her flower gardens. It was a gorgeous day. Too bad so many corrupt men had to be alive enjoying it.

God, why? Why do you let evil exist? If you really exist, can't you stop it?

Cara brushed at her tears, pulled on her gardening gloves, and headed toward her bed of purple larkspurs. Time to get to work if she wanted to prepare soup for Abby to feed her husband when he got home.

Time to teach an elder a lesson.

CHAPTER SEVEN

That night Cara tucked Leila's left foot under the cover and stared down at her daughters. If only the faith she'd once had still lived inside her. A faith her girls innocently believed. Sighing, she knelt, but her eyes fixed on the sliver of a moon peeking into her girls' room.

She couldn't afford to relax. Not yet. They weren't out of the woods and might never be. The upcoming meeting with Elder Simmons on Tuesday would be here long before she wished it. Plenty of men still needed to pay for their sins. Cara clasped her hands as cold hatred seeped into every pore of her body, stiffened her joints, froze her emotions. Her nature struggled against the paralyzing emotion. Fought for the innocence she'd once assumed as real life.

Fought and lost.

Her palms ached where her fingernails dug into her flesh, creating bloody gashes across her hand, but she relished the pain. How could she live with herself if her scheme succeeded? Could she live with herself if it didn't succeed?

If only they would forget about her and her girls. Let her be the outcast to raise her daughters in peace.

I need more time. The kitty-cat clock on Leila's nightstand ticked away—too fast. Could she stop the time? Three weeks had passed since her husband's death.

But with Jodie's news about Sissy the other day, it could mean only one thing. If Elder Simmons wanted the age of the girls to be broken in lowered, he'd do it. What if he decided to drop it even further? Leila was ten.

I'm taking a terrible risk in staying.

She'd have to sneak out, and the daunting task loomed before her, a specter in flowing dark clothes. Driving in plain sight wouldn't do the trick. Packing necessities, sorting what would be taken, what left behind, and Lacy—could she handle the trip?

Run! The command was almost overpowering.

The desire for revenge reared its head. Someone had to pay for Lori's death. Someone needed to open the men's eyes so her friends' lives could be made better. She'd have to guard Leila more diligently. Not let her spend any nights away from home and not let her go anywhere without keeping an eye on her. Leila wouldn't like it, but Cara would talk to her.

She let her head drop to her hands and whispered, "I don't believe in you, God, but if by chance you are there, will you look down on these two children and protect them?"

She waited, but no sense of relief soothed her spirit. No lightness of heart. No assurance he'd grant her any favors.

The sound of a car's wheels crunching the gravel on her driveway interrupted her thoughts. Cara jumped to her feet and stumbled into one of their chairs. With a cry, she shoved it aside and hurried to the door. Who on earth could it be?

Dayne had a hand raised to knock again, his brow puckered, worry dulling his eyes. "Will you go with me?"

Cara gripped the door edge. "What's wrong?"

"Richard Melton's in the hospital."

"Richard?" she choked out and lifted a hand to her throat. "What happened?"

"He almost died this evening."

What had she done? Too much of the larkspur would kill. She'd only wanted to scare him.

Hadn't she?

She'd measured it out carefully. Had she blacked out, lost her senses, and added a touch too much? Her mouth was as dry as the apples she prepared for winter. "He's alive?"

"Yes, but Sister Melton is near collapse. I thought your presence might calm her." Dayne peered at her. "She is a friend of yours?"

"Yes, she is." Cara brushed a stray hair from her eyes and caught sight of her shaking hand. "Of course, I'll go. I'll have to call Cassie to stay with the girls till I get home."

"She's in the car." Dayne waved, and Cara's usual child-sitter hurried to the house.

"You'll stay till I get home, Cassie?"

The woman's nod reassured her. Cara said to Dayne, "Then I'm ready."

Out in Dayne's car, Cara settled back in the seat and closed her eyes as he pulled from her driveway. The spring breezes whooshed in Dayne's open windows and cooled her hot cheeks but did nothing for the burning inside her. What if Richard died?

Murderer!

Cara shook her head and moaned. Too late to worry about it now. Playing a female Robin Hood, trying to better the other women's situations, was the role she'd accepted.

Liar. She wanted the men to pay. To suffer. She had no excuse.

The darkness hid her troubled spirit. At night, she could pretend all was well and nothing bad ever happened. The black evenings softened the harsh truth sunlight brought every day.

"Are you okay?"

She mumbled a sound to keep from lying.

"How is the relationship between Richard and Abby?"

Dayne's voice registered a troubled note, but Cara ignored it. "Relationship? The normal for a couple in The Children of Righteous Cain."

"Meaning?"

Swift anger surged through her body. Her hands trembled, and she clenched them together. "Richard doesn't beat Abby with whips or belts, but he does cuff her face enough to bruise her and belittles her constantly. I've seen him insult her in front of other people, and when she goes away hurt, he smiles as if he's accomplished something admirable."

She wanted to punch something. Why did she think she could change things? "What on earth is the matter with the men of our group? What's wrong with kindness and love? If what you said Sunday is true, why don't they believe you? Practice what you're preaching?"

"I don't have all the answers, Cara."

"You're supposed to know. Don't you talk to God?" She bit her lip. It wasn't fair to attack Dayne. He wasn't responsible for the evilness in the group.

For a minute Dayne didn't speak. "You know, when I went away to study, I had a professor who went on and on about a real relationship with God. I had no idea what he was talking about."

His words caught her attention. "A relationship? What did he mean?"

"I struggled with Professor Moore's concept of God for two years before I could accept what he tried to explain."

Cara shifted in her seat. Dayne had doubts? "You don't believe what we've been taught all our lives?"

"I believe what Professor Moore showed me." He used the car's signal and made a left turn onto the driveway of the small group hospital. "I want to see things changed too. Our people don't know, and I plan to work on what I believe needs changing."

"Like what?" The first stirrings of hope fluttered inside her.

"Like teaching everyone Jesus can be our Lord and Savior—"

"I don't care about that."

"Let me finish. I want to show them our girls and women need to be shown respect and love. They are not objects to disdain, but to cherish."

The car filled with warmth. That was more like it. "Dayne. How lovely. Do you really think that?"

"Yes, I do."

Cara gripped his arm. "Can you help them? Will they listen?"

Dayne guided the car into a parking spot and shut off the ignition. "I have no idea. But I'm going to give it my best shot. I have planned a meeting session with the elders soon."

Cara and Dayne walked inside their spotless but minuscule hospital. Her soaring spirits dipped, stalled, and spiraled downward, the depression hammering at her soul again. Words wouldn't do the trick. Dayne should know that. The men in the group were steeped in their beliefs and treated Elder Simmons like a god. Only radical measures would open their eyes.

Cara didn't care what their spiritual tendencies were. Religion meant little to her. All she wanted was for her girls to have a chance at a good and happy life. Whatever it took, she would do it.

Right or wrong.

❦❦❦

Abby's white, thin arms tightened around Cara, and she patted the other woman's back. She wished she could murmur the words Abby wanted—needed—to hear. The slim man in the hospital bed lay inert. The man who'd created hell on earth for Abby, her friend. Eyes stinging, she straightened and took Abby by the shoulders. "You need a break."

She clasped Dayne's arm. "Would you take Abby to the snack room?"

"Come on, Sister Melton. Let's go get some coffee." Dayne placed a hand on Abby's back.

After the two left, Cara settled into the chair beside the bed. "Richard. Wake up, Richard. I want to talk to you."

He stirred, groaned, and shook his head.

Gripping his shoulder, she shook him gently. "Richard, can you hear me?"

His eyelids popped open and he stared at her, the confusion in his eyes fading to recognition.

"Cara? Where's Ab-by? S-she should be here."

Tough. She was here now and could care less what he thought. If he thought he could bully her, he could think again. "Richard, listen to me. God—if there is one—allowed you to live tonight, but I doubt he'll have mercy on you the next time. You may not tease death, you may taste it."

❦ 71 ❦

Realization metamorphed into a brief flash of fear.

Good.

"You'd better change your ways. God wants you to treat Abby with respect, not abuse."

He closed his eyes, and Cara shook him again. "No, you don't. Answer me."

"Don't spout your ideas at me. I'm sick. Go away." Anger strengthened his voice.

She narrowed her eyes at him. "Abby's taking a break, and I'm wasting time sitting with you."

"I don't abuse her. A slap or two is nothing. I'm not like insane Mike Farmer."

"You do abuse her. Don't you realize what you're doing to her?" She waited a second to let him digest her meaning. "I don't care about you or even what happens to you, but I do care about Abby."

His head slowly shook. "You're a crazy woman."

"I'm not the crazy person here."

"Elder Simmons will deal with you when he hears how you threatened me."

"I wouldn't say a thing, Richard. God wouldn't like you talking."

He stared into her eyes, the pupils enlarging, alarm like a live thing peeping from them. "All right. All right. No more slaps. Now, get out. I don't have to put up with you just because Abby's not here."

"Oh, but you do, Richard. Abby will be upset if I don't stay here until she returns." She let her eyes smile, her voice drip sweetness. "Go to sleep again. I'll be here by your side."

❦❦❦

Dayne settled Abby at a table. Timid and quiet, she'd ignored his efforts at small talk on the trip down here. Her trembling fingers circling the Styrofoam cup gave little hint what thoughts hid behind her strained features.

She glanced at him when he sat. "It smells delicious. Thanks, Reverend MacFarland."

"You can call me Dayne."

Abby shook her head. "Richard wouldn't like for me to be familiar."

Dayne took a quick gulp of his own coffee. Abby was a pretty woman, her speech quiet and careful, like a budding flower never coming to a full bloom.

"I can't understand what happened to Richard. He came home in a bad mood, but the soup helped." Abby's fingers circled the steaming cup as if drawing warmth from it.

"Soup?"

"His favorite. Cabbage." The corners of Abby's eyes crinkled.

"I'm sure it was delicious."

Abby slid a shy glance his direction. "I don't really know. I—I can't eat cabbage right now. I'm expecting, and the taste makes me nauseous."

"Another child? Are you happy?"

"Yes." Her smile confirmed the answer.

"Richard enjoyed the soup, did he?"

"He ate two big bowls."

She's like an eager kid trying to please. "I imagine you're a good cook."

"Not really. I've never been able to cook well." She sipped. "I didn't make the soup. Caralynne did."

The words didn't register at first. Cara's suddenly white face flashed in his mind. He'd told her the news about Richard as soon as she'd opened the door. The tears in her lovely eyes when she'd shooed Abby and him down here. The anguish peeking through those same eyes into his. Was she blaming herself? Had the soup somehow caused Richard's sickness? If so, why? Had she been careless in preparing the soup?

Was she that upset over Abby's worry?

No.

"Will the doctor do tests to find out what happened?"

A frown appeared between Abby's eyes. Her shoulders lifted in a shrug. "He said Richard had a severe stomach virus or food poisoning. He did some cursory testing and couldn't find anything significant."

Odd.

Abby twirled her half-full cup. "Richard complained and accused the doctor of being unconcerned. When Elder Simmons stopped in, he ordered Richard to stop whining. The doctor has far more important cases to work on. He told Richard he should be grateful God willed Richard to live. Elder Simmons chewed me out for not being more careful. I didn't dare tell him Cara prepared the soup."

Thank God. "That's too bad he scolded you."

"Doesn't matter." Her shoulders reared back as if determined to face the facts in her life. "Richard doesn't handle pain well. He's not the most popular of elders."

True, but no need to agree with this woman's low assessment of their worth now. "All men aren't macho types."

Her shy glance barely skimmed his face. "I'm not smart like Caralynne, but I know Richard isn't liked by very many of the men. He doesn't notice. Tells his stupid jokes and laughs as if everyone hasn't heard them a dozen times."

"He does enjoy a good joke." What else could he say?

Abby lifted the cup and drained it. "I know he isn't much, but sometimes I can see something behind his eyes—something craving attention. Some kind of hunger."

Dayne patted her hand. "I understand. Perhaps after this scare, Richard will realize what a jewel he has in you."

Abby's tight smile cued Dayne. She didn't believe him.

"I doubt it, and because I'm sorry for him, doesn't mean I love him. I don't, Reverend MacFarland. If he changed, I might grow to respect him. But I'll never love him like a woman should."

Dayne sat still, stunned at her perception. *How could I have been so blind? I'm as bad as the rest of the men here. Just because they get the right treatment from a man doesn't mean there's love in the relationship.*

❧❦❧

The midnight air cooled. Dayne pressed the button to roll up both windows in his car. Cara shivered and snuggled deeper into the plush seat.

Conflicting emotions tore her insides. Richard wouldn't die because of her well-meaning intent at punishment. Would he change or go back to his old habits?

She'd almost killed the man tonight. Scare him, force him to eat some bitter medicine was one thing. He deserved every bite. Cara rubbed at her burning eyes, a faint residue of her earlier shakes. She could put on a brave face, but fear gnawed at her all the time. After Lori's death, part of her heart died.

Determination to carry out her plans wouldn't be enough. So *was* she strong enough? She didn't know.

"Are you asleep?"

Dayne's soft whisper rolled over her like a silk blanket. "No. Thinking."

"A penny for them."

The urge to share almost overwhelmed her. How wonderful to place some of this depressing burden on Dayne's wide, strong shoulders. She let the wish—the weakness—drift away.

"Worrying about Abby. Wondering if she'll be okay."

"You're a friend anyone would be glad to have, Cara. I see the caring, loyal, and responsible person you are, the one you show everyone." Dayne steered around a slower-moving car. "But sometimes I'd like a glimpse of the part you keep hidden."

The heaviness in her heart lifted, and for a moment, she envisioned herself as a carefree young person experiencing life to the full.

"I don't know what that would be." She closed her eyes. "I'm a foolish romantic."

"A romantic is foolish?"

"Dreaming impossible dreams, wishing for fables, is unrealistic and foolish. I've always had a tendency to imagine what could be, what could happen. I suppose because I like beautiful things." She chuckled. "See the moon and the star-studded sky? Instead of ignoring its beauty,

I get the shivers. I wonder if a different world lives in another universe. A colony of people who know only goodness and peace and happiness."

"Don't know about any other worlds, but the New Testament indicates if we don't praise God—show emotion—the rocks will shout out for us," he quoted. "Showing emotion is never wrong. It's human and vastly satisfying. A wonderful gift from God."

She didn't want it to, but her body shrank away. Why did he have to bring God into every conversation?

"I think this side of you is beautiful, and I love it."

Relieved at the turn of subject, she flashed a grin. "You don't love all sides of me?"

"I love—now you're fishing." He cleared his throat. "How's your garden doing?"

"We've been eating lettuce for days now. Another couple weeks, and I'll have to can the early vegetables."

"You like to harvest the vegetables?"

Cara shrugged. "I like seeing the rows of colorful canned food on my cellar shelves. Like having the healthy food for my girls."

"Don't you get tired of all the work?"

"Sometimes, but I'm strong. I want to provide for my girls, so I do whatever I can."

Dayne's hand slid across the space between them and touched hers. "You're beautiful."

Cara pulled her hand from his. Too much danger for her. "Tell me about some of the things you experienced while you were gone. Were your studies hard? Did you like living in the city?"

"In some ways, but I missed the country. When I arrived home, I think I took the first deep breath I'd had in six years."

"Did you meet many girls?"

She felt his quick glance. Felt the question hover in the air between them. *What have I done? He's not under obligation to answer my nosy questions. And what difference does it make anyhow?*

"Do you mean did I date while away?"

At his words, the tension lessened. "You don't have to answer the question. It's none of my business."

But I want to know.

Dayne pulled into her driveway and shut off the car. He slipped his arm on the back of the seat. "When is your meeting?"

Cara blinked but answered, "Tomorrow afternoon."

"Want me to pick you up?"

"Thanks, but I'll walk. It'll give me time to reflect on how to behave while in the presence of such an august figure." A hand flew up to cover her mouth. "Sorry. I didn't mean to be so flip."

"No problem. The fact is I came home carrying a bunch of my own questions."

"You?"

"Me. More questions than answers."

"How do we find the answers, Dayne? You graduated with honors in ministry, so if you don't know the answers, how is someone like me who's uneducated supposed to get answers?"

He gripped her hand again as if he would never let go. She heard his long drawn intake of breath. "We've got to search the scriptures. Find the answers in God. Depend on God to guide us every step."

She shook her head. "I don't know. He hasn't done much for me. If he's—" She broke off. No need to air her horrid doubts.

"He's kept you alive."

She didn't bother answering. Her own efforts had done that.

"What would you have done if you'd had the chance to choose something else?"

"Are you serious? I've never taken time to think about could-be's and would-be's. As I said, there's not much sense in wishing for what will never happen."

"But if you could have …"

"I don't know. I'd mountain climb. Probably fly. Own my own private plane. Do rescue work."

"What else?" His interest spurred her on. How long had it been since she'd had someone to share nonsense with?

"I'd learn to parachute and hang glide for fun and anything else to get me off the ground and into the air."

"You crazy girl. Mind if I join you?"

Richard had called her crazy too. Cara rested her head against the back of the seat.

His hand stirred beside her.

"I am crazy, aren't I?"

He slipped his arm around her and tugged lightly until she gave in and rested her head on his shoulder.

"You know it's not too late to experience your dreams."

"What do you mean? Elder Simmons would never allow me to do that."

A pause. Dayne stroked her hand with one finger. "Do it anyway."

"I had a hard enough time accepting Donald's beatings. I couldn't take them from the elders. Don't encourage me, Dayne. Please. You don't know—" With a sob, she straightened and flung open the door.

Dayne ran from his side of the car and grabbed her shoulders. "Cara. Cara, don't cry. I'm doing my best to work on the elders. Trust me." He cupped her chin, tilted it, and stared into her eyes.

She gave a shaky nod. "I do."

Mostly.

With a thumb he wiped away the tears from her cheeks. "I wish—"

For me?

"What do you wish?" Cara held her breath.

He took her shoulders for a moment, his grip tight, and then let his hands drop. "Nothing. Go on."

She moved as if in a daze toward the lighted porch. She'd barely reached the steps when Dayne's voice stopped her again.

"Cara?"

She stopped moving, her back still toward him.

"You asked me if I met any girls while away. I did. Several. But every time I tried to get romantic or think about girlfriends, all I could see were the beautiful blue-green eyes of someone back home. A very effective deterrent for romance."

Was she hearing him correctly? Interpreting his words the way he meant them? Her body warmed, the frozenness melting as surely as if the sun was ridding the earth of a winter avalanche. Slowly she turned.

He lifted a hand and returned to his car.

She stared after him, depression gone.

CHAPTER EIGHT

Time to go.

Cara stared at herself in the mirror and smoothed her blouse. Mouth dry, she licked her lips, swallowed. Nothing helped. She slapped at her cheeks, trying to drive some color into her ghost-like face. She might be scared to death, but she sure didn't want the elders to know it.

She still had two months before they forced her to remarry. Or tried to.

So did they want to crack down on her activities? Confine her to her home? Surely they wouldn't punish her for some trumped-up sin, would they?

The scattered whispers, the floating rumors abounded throughout the group. Shivers of apprehension climbed up bare arms at the news of a sudden death. Husbands changed into solemn men, and wives became battered wretches after appearing with bruises, swollen faces, and broken bones. Quiet and mute. The disappearance of a widow who supposedly had gone to visit relatives yet never returning. Too many incidences that raised questions in wondering minds.

Like Rita Davenport. When she'd disappeared, rumors claimed she was at her parents' home. She'd never returned. Never been heard from.

Cara's pulse fluttered, and the lightheadedness sent her collapsing onto the edge of her bed. Once at the sanctuary, she'd have no chance of escape. Pleading wouldn't help. They'd laugh. Her pitiful protest would only increase their assurance they were doing the right thing.

She examined the closet. She'd have to do a major cleaning there soon. The window reflected the sunlight and sent a wild gypsy-like feeling through her. If only she was outside enjoying it instead of—

Cowering here wouldn't help. They'd send elders to collect her trembling body. Panic stampeded over her. She should grab her girls and run.

No. No. No. She couldn't go yet. A few more days to finish her plans should do it. Besides, Donald's insurance money wasn't hers yet, and she needed money to get started somewhere else.

If the elders refused to give it to her …

Cara jumped to her feet and checked herself again in the mirror. Satisfied she'd done all she could to improve her looks, she slipped into her sandals and picked up the car keys. She'd much rather walk, but she wouldn't have time now. Best to drive.

At the door of the room, the small ornamental chest sitting on her dresser called to her. She crossed the floor and lifted the pearl-covered barrette from it. Her finger traced the scrolls and swirls, and as if by magic, a fuzzy-warm shawl of comfort slipped around her shoulders. Smiling, she replaced the barrette.

Fifteen minutes later, Cara pulled into the tabernacle's parking lot. The cars lined up didn't bolster her courage. The whole bunch of hypocrites must be out for her blood. For a minute she gripped the steering wheel and glanced up at the roof of her car. *Could I get some help here?*

No voice assuring her he'd defend her. No lifting of her ground-dragging spirits. Well, what was new? She squared her shoulders and climbed from the car. On the seemingly mile-long walk to the door, she tilted her head a fraction higher.

Before she could shove at the double doors, they whooshed open, and a serious-eyed Dayne greeted her. "I didn't think you would make it."

Her heart picked up its pace. "Are you here to sit in?"

"No, thought I'd show up to lend some support."

"For a minute, I figured you'd decided to join them in the lynching."

"Hardly. Are you okay?"

"As good as one can be when about to face a pack of snarling wolves."

His smile widened. "Don't let them get you down. They need to realize our women have feelings. You might be the one who can force them to face the facts."

"I don't want to be a crusader." She couldn't push things too much. There was the insurance money and the plan. Her work had to be undercover.

"Most people don't like making waves, but someone's got to do it. You'll be fine."

"Well ... we'll see." She walked away.

"I'll be praying."

The words struck her in the back, the force of a hammer pounding into her spine. Dayne and his God. Dayne and his belief. She retraced her steps then touched him on the arm. "Dayne, I—I don't think I believe anymore. How can I? Where was God when I—when my little girl needed him?"

Frown lines formed above his shapely nose, the camaraderie smile gone. "Don't talk like that. I can't bear to hear so much doubt in you."

Cara patted his arm. "I'm not a saint, Dayne. Don't think of me as some kind of Joan of Arc, 'cause I'm not. I hated Donald, and I hate these men here. I'm still angry over Lori's death. I'm grieving and want—"

She broke off and lowered her head, afraid to speak of what raged inside her for so long. Shame swept through her. She'd never be the person, the woman, Dayne wanted.

Her hand slipped off his arm, but a microsecond later, his hand caught hers and drew her closer. "Cara."

His voice caressed her name. She swallowed and blinked back the sudden wetness in her eyes.

"Cara. I'm sorry. I didn't mean to hurt you. I want to hear about anything that's troubling you." His fingers tightened. "You have a right to be angry at the man who hurt Lori. I don't begrudge you that. But don't be angry at God. Perhaps he needed—"

She choked on the bile rising in her throat. "If you say he needed a flower like Lori, I'll be angry at you."

He didn't answer her comment but his head nodded as if in

agreement. "Try to find a mustard seed of belief deep within your heart. Don't be afraid. God and I'll be waiting when you're done talking with them. And if they try anything too harsh, I'll storm the fort."

❧❦❧

Cara shut the door behind her but held onto the handle while she surveyed the room. Elder Simmons sat at the far end of a long table, facing her, but didn't look at her. He continued to study the paper he held in his hands.

That didn't hold true with the other eleven men. Every head swiveled toward her. Every eye fixed on her, pinning her to the door.

The inner circle of goons.

Cara gripped the door handle tighter. She could not do this. Every nerve in her body screamed, "flee." She willed her muscles to move. Her feet shuffled obediently toward the one empty chair. So she wasn't as terrified as her mind claimed. Or else Dayne's prayers were working.

She cut off the thought. No time to dwell upon Dayne or his God. She trained her eyes on Elder Simmons and hoped he'd get his remonstrations over.

When he didn't, and the rest ignored her, she cleared her throat and earned a reproachful glare from Angus Tobert, Elder Simmons's second-in-command.

A giggle of nervousness bubbled up. Who did these pompous idiots think they were? She opened her mouth to speak when Elder Simmons lifted his head.

Clamping her lips together, she lowered her head instinctually and dared to peek at the sober-faced man as a shiver inched up her back.

Stories about Elder Simmons and his insatiable appetite for the opposite sex went the rounds through the years, even though he had a wife who was both lovely and industrious. Rumors insisted she knew on which side her bread was buttered and kept a discreet tongue when it came to Elder Simmons's practices.

A wise policy, no doubt. But one Cara hadn't pursued in her own marriage. It wouldn't have done any good. Donald neither asked nor listened to anything she'd said. She'd been no more to him than another piece of property.

Cara jerked her thoughts back to the present. She needed to curb the tendency to allow her mind to wander whenever she was under stress.

"Sister Hayman, we're glad you decided to join us."

A sarcastic remark coming from between his fat lips? Ha. I mean, did I have a choice?

"Yes." What to say? She didn't want to be here. She'd obeyed the command but dragged her mental feet all the way. And wasn't the man even going to invite her to sit? She debated the wisdom of making her own choice. Better not. Why push her luck?

"I see by my records a month has passed since Brother Hayman went to heaven."

Right. If Donald was there, she definitely wasn't going.

He laid the paper onto the tabletop. "I want to address your frivolous attitude."

"Frivolous?"

He frowned, lowered his head, and peered at her over his dark-rimmed glasses. "I'd say too much chattiness with other women, picnics on Sunday, and your lack of piety relay the truth. Wouldn't you?"

How had he known she took her girls on picnics? Did he have someone spying on her? Someone who blabbed her activities to this man? Could it be *Dayne*? No.

"My girls shouldn't be forced to grieve forever."

"Your girls need to learn submissiveness. If you can't handle their training, perhaps one of our other women can teach them proper conduct."

She wanted to cover her ears at his roar. "No, I will work with them. The discipline won't be necessary."

This was not going the way she'd planned.

The slightest smirk edged his lips. "How old are they?"

For the life of her she couldn't answer.

"S-sssister Hayman—" The hissing in Brother Tobert's high-pitched voice was like fingernails on a blackboard to her overworked nerves.

A sharp movement from Elder Simmons stopped him. The head elder sat forward and rested his elbows on the table, relaxed and in control. "We have come to an agreement on your future."

"Already?"

"In your best interests, we believe the best match for you will be Emery Hayman. He can provide for you in a way Brother Hayman would have wanted. And be a father figure for your girls."

Cara clutched the edge of the table. For a moment, the room swirled, the men's faces blurred into one long stream of pale color. Emery's lecherous grin grew into a monster of its own. The picture of a woman's hand—hers—stabbing a knife deep into his black heart blazed across her mind. Even that would never pay for what he'd done to her Lori. Not in a million years.

Never. Never. Never.

Her mind screamed the words, and whether she spoke them aloud or not, she had no idea. And didn't care. If they wanted to mess with her—well, she was a big girl and could handle it. But not a man of them would ever get near her two youngest. She would—

"Sister Hayman, are you listening?"

"No. Yes. He's too old."

"He's the right age to—uh—keep you in line—and your girls. We expect you to be ready."

"I need more time."

The temperature in the room dropped several degrees.

"There is no more time for you."

She stared down at the empty seat she'd not been invited to sit in. Now or never. If she didn't speak up now, she would regret it. Even with the insurance dollar signs floating in front of her mind, she couldn't let this opportunity pass.

"I won't marry Emery Hayman. I won't marry any man here."

Stunned silence. Silence pregnant with threats.

"What did you say?"

"I said—"

"I know what you said. I'm not sure you realize what you've insinuated. You are near blasphemy, Sister."

"I don't think so." Cara shook her head. "I'm thinking of what's best for everyone. I would be better off living by myself and don't need a husband."

"You'd rather be put away and have someone else raise your girls?"

Mad. She was stark, raving mad.

"You have nothing to say?" Elder Simmons smirked at her. "Fortunately for you, God doesn't command such a thing. You'll come under submission and be the proper wife he ordains for womanhood. Or suffer the consequences."

"I can't."

"We won't allow this anarchy you're hatching. It's too much of a bad influence on our other women. There would be total chaos."

Exactly.

She gasped out the words. "I won't marry Emery Hayman."

"You are rebelling against The Children of Righteous Cain's rule?" he hissed. Streaks of lightning flashed in his eyes. "Who will you have, you—"

Cara sucked in a breath. What would he do? The elder's methods of persuasion veered toward anything but the pleasant. Beatings. Abuse. She suspected—murder.

Beyond the glassed door Dayne hovered, leaning against the far wall with arms crossed but unable to hear. His keen eyes watched the occupants, understanding the pressure building inside the room. She wanted to burst into a nervous chortle.

As if a kaleidoscope twisted, Elder Simmons's voice softened. "I'll tell you what we'll do."

Cara jumped at the close proximity of Elder Simmons's voice. He'd skirted the table and closed in on her while she gazed at the minister.

"We'll give you an extra month to get yourself in order, since obviously you're not finished grieving for your husband."

The words slapped at her, taunting, laughing, mocking.

"Pray, sister. Reflect on our manual, the right way, the good way for you—for our women. Security and peace will reign only when we are submissive." He lifted a hand and trailed his fingers up her cheek, stopping at her earlobe. He squeezed, pinching, his lips pulled into a mock smile.

Cara jerked her head back.

Pompous idiot. Easy for him to say. He didn't have to put up with the subservience, the humiliation, the abuse.

"Perhaps a counseling session for you and Brother Hayman would help."

Right. She'd puke if she got near him. Or something worse.

Elder Simmons took her elbow and ushered her to the door. The door gave a decided click as it shut behind her, and she realized the ordeal was over. Fruitless efforts. Unsatisfactory results. But over.

"How did it go?"

She followed Dayne's gaze back into the room and stared at the men seated at the long oak table. The urge to get away swept over her. Her body stiffened at the sight of Emery Hayman laughing like a lunatic. Did he find her reactions funny? "'Bout like I figured." She rubbed her ear.

"Rome wasn't taken overnight."

"Rome was a lot easier." She turned her back and headed outside.

Dayne chuckled and paced beside her. His shoes tap-tapped on the hard surface, a pleasant, reassuring sound.

"What did they say?"

"I'm to marry Emery Hayman in a month."

"Donald's brother. And will you?"

"Never."

I'll kill him first.

CHAPTER NINE

Dayne paced. It was time to do more, and a call to his old friend might help.

He reached for his cell phone and dialed Professor Moore's number. When the man's gruff but not unkind voice answered, Dayne stated, "I'm in a dilemma."

"Good morning to you, Dayne MacFarland. I'm delighted you decided to get in touch."

A guffaw exploded across the airwaves, and Dayne jerked the phone from his ear. When his old friend's laughter melted into mild snorts, he cautiously pressed it against his ear again.

"How can I help you?" Professor Moore choked out.

How to go about this?

"Do you remember the girl you tried to hook me up with?"

"Of course. I still think you should have asked her out."

"I wasn't interested in her or anyone else."

A pause. "Another girl?"

"I didn't speak about a girl from here, did I?"

"No, you didn't. I knew there had to be a reason all those girls who cast dewy-eyed glances your way never got far with the best-looking guy around."

"I've known this girl for most of my life and have always loved her. But after I was in college, I learned she was no longer free to accept attention from me."

Silence. Digesting the information, obviously.

"Her husband was chosen."

"And you are still interested in her, considering such a pertinent piece of information?"

"I told you my church's thoughts on marriage, but what I didn't tell you is we—they—"

Professor's voice gentled. "What is it, Dayne?"

How could he have been such a coward? No, that wasn't it. Once his eyes opened, he'd been ashamed. Ashamed he was part of the Children of Righteous Cain. "They believe our girls should forgo careers and marry."

"You told me."

"It's worse. The girls are very young when they marry."

"Seventeen? Eighteen?"

"Younger. Sixteen, sometimes fifteen." And now fourteen. Dayne winced.

"And how do your people hide this from the law?"

"You already know what an unusual situation it is here. But since I've returned, I've learned more and see things I never realized before I left. We are a—how can I say this? The outside world seldom interferes. The elders deal with any problems popping up. When I left, we had a mini-store. Now we have three."

"A cult?" Interest sparked the voice coming through the receiver.

Leave it to the prof to get right down to the nitty-gritty. "Yeah, I think so. I didn't recognize our group for what it is until now. And I didn't understand all the details of how the elders run things until now."

Like the marriages.

"Still, wouldn't the police suspect what was going on?" Caution edged the professor's voice.

Dayne ran a hand over his head. The drumbeat of a headache pounded louder. "We have our own police chief, and I suspect he and the deputy are on the take."

"Worse and worse. I wish you'd told me earlier. My research could have been deeper."

"Like I said, some of this I'm learning."

"Right. I understand."

"The thing is, Elder Simmons made an announcement Sunday about reviewing families to make sure they're performing their duties correctly." Would the headache ease if he gave his head a solid whap? "It's the most disgusting thing I've ever heard."

"But quite in the nature of a cult. The leader expands his power, and the need to prove his sovereignty over his followers grows the more his desires are fulfilled."

"What can I do?"

"Right now, keep on doing what we planned," Professor Moore encouraged. "Tell me, Dayne, do you still accept some of the group's practices? What's your response to them on Sundays and when in discussion? Are the people receptive to the things you've learned?"

"I'm afraid I haven't made much progress." Dayne tapped a tuneless song on his desk. "I'm not sure how long I can remain civil."

"I would be interested in studying your group in more depth, Dayne. We talked about possible actions—"

"I know." Dayne heaved a sigh. This is why he'd called. Why hesitate now? Because he'd wanted to handle it himself. He didn't want to bring in outsiders—even as good a friend as Professor Moore. "I think I may need you before long."

"Whenever you say. Call me later."

"I definitely need your prayers."

"You've got them. Now back to this girl."

"That's what happened to this girl."

"I see. She was married off while still a child."

"At fifteen."

"Effectively separating the two of you."

"Exactly. I thought I'd never get over the heartache. The first I saw her was at her husband's funeral."

"I see."

"Will you stop saying, 'I see'?"

Another raucous chuckle. "Go on. This is the most interesting thing I've heard all day. I suffer through such boring students year after year."

"She seems to—attract trouble."

"In what way?"

"Her husband died from a heart attack while she was outside in the garden. Her friend's husband died a horrible death while she was at their home. Another friend's husband almost died from what looked like food poisoning."

"Freak happenstances?"

"That's what I'm hoping. But are they?" Dayne scrubbed at his face. "How can I know for sure?"

"Have you asked her about any of this?"

"Not really. She confided her husband didn't speak of his heart problems. She was visiting the second friend and had given the third family homemade soup when the food poisoning occurred. Nothing obvious, but the timing makes me uneasy."

"Hmm. If this bothers you, I suggest you ask some questions."

"I don't want to stir up trouble for her. Elder Simmons already disapproves of her—her independence. All he needs is a good reason to punish her."

"Punish?"

Dayne could see the prof's ears literally stand on end. Shame rolled through him. "Yes. Severe, at times."

"You don't want to open a can of worms, for sure. I'm surprised the local authorities don't get involved."

"The group has a chief who's sanctioned by the county sheriff." He hesitated. "As long as the chief okays accidents, no one's going to call in anyone else."

"I'd suggest you keep your eyes open. If Simmons doesn't like her, she could be in danger."

He didn't need more confirmation of what could happen. "Worse, she's lost her faith, and I don't know how to bring her back. She's struggling over the death of her oldest daughter."

"Perhaps she's never had any."

"But—"

"Remember what we talked about? Faith in Christ? You came to me totally ignorant. I thought the truth would never sink into your heart. How can she know what she's never heard? How can she believe when she's never seen real faith in action?"

"Could be you're right."

"I know I am. Got to go. I'm late for my next class. Be faithful to her with the truth. That and prayer will bring the results you want."

Dayne hit the off button, slid the phone to his desk, and ambled to his window. The trees bordering the property waved at him.

What Prof said made sense. So what was his next move?

Keep talking to Elder Simmons. Make it plain he wanted changes.

Continue to preach God's love, which would keep new ideas in his congregation's heads.

Talk to his selected list of elders.

Find out what was going on in Cara's intelligent brain. A challenge, but doable.

He'd start with the most attractive item on the list—a trip to the Hayman home.

❧❧❧

Dayne knocked again and listened, but no sound of small, hurrying feet reached his ears. Cara and her girls must be gone. The rush of disappointment dampened the enthusiasm driving him since talking with Professor Moore.

He headed to the main road and stopped as a pickup sped past. It slowed, backed up, and pulled over to the side of the road. The window rolled down and a head thrust itself out. Angus Tobert.

He should have kept going. Tobert's constant hovering and simpering around Elder Simmons drove him nuts. Still, who knew what effect he might make on the man? Dayne put his car in park, swung open his door, and approached the truck.

"Brother Tobert."

The man's smirk sobered him. What did he have on his mind?

"Reverend MacFarland. What are you doing at Sister Hayman's house?"

Was his good-intentioned action bothering the man?

"Pastoral call." He felt no obligation to give account for his actions, but if it shut the man up, he would explain.

"She's quite a looker, isn't she? Her streak of independence makes a man want to conquer the spirit, huh?"

Rage flared inside him, hot enough he couldn't see to rearrange Tobert's features. "Not what I had in mind."

"Of course, she's used around the edges but good enough for the likes of Emery Hayman."

Dayne clenched his fists.

The man peered intently at him. "Don't you wish she was one of the choices we'd given you?"

Would God forgive him if he knocked the smirk off Second-in-Command Tobert's face?

Better not chance it if he wanted to prove God's love to these people, although the man begged for a pounding. He didn't realize how close he was to getting it.

"What are you doing out this way?"

"Don't tell me you've forgotten about our church dinner tonight."

A faint memory of Elder Simmons's wife mentioning the dinner on Sunday stirred his brain. He'd been preoccupied with catching Cara before she left and let the information slip right out of his mind.

"Right. I'll head to our social building next. Need to make a quick stop at the parsonage." Dayne strode away, glad to get away from the unpleasant man.

"See you, Reverend. I'm sure Cara *and* her girls will be there. Triple delight."

Dayne stopped his rapid pace, but when the man's engine gunned and he roared on down the road, Dayne continued to his car and did his own gunning all the way home.

❦❦❦

Cara sat where she could keep an eye on her girls as they played on the church playground equipment. She scanned the crowd, but Dayne hadn't shown up yet.

"I'm glad you came."

"I'm glad I came too. How are you and Richard doing?"

❦ 93 ❦

Abby jiggled her baby to shush him and whispered, "He's different since he almost died. I wonder if God spoke to him or something."

"Maybe he did." But doubtful.

Lacy ran up to complain about another child's unfair action, and Cara planted a kiss on her daughter's tousled hair.

Jodie sat at the other end of the table. She and her husband, Levi Schrader, had driven up in their top-of-the-line SUV earlier, but she'd hardly spoken two sentences since she'd sat down.

"Is something wrong, Jodie?"

The woman's usual tart attitude softened to a brooding ambivalence.

"What do you mean? There's nothing wrong." Jodie frowned and tossed her stylish blonde hair.

"You seem preoccupied tonight." To put it mildly.

Penelope Lewis settled her skinny arms on the picnic table, her sharp features radiant. "Well, I'm not preoccupied. I'm bubbling. I've got big news."

"What?" Abby gaped at her.

"Guess."

"Oh, come on, Penelope, don't play games. Give us the news." Mary Ann scooped up her last bite of pie and closed her eyes. "Ruby Simmons can bake the best pies."

"I'm pregnant," Penelope crowed.

Mary Ann dropped her fork and clapped chubby hands. "That ought to make Kenny happy."

"Yeah. He threatened to take another wife if I didn't give him a child soon." She patted her still-flat tummy. "But now he says he'll see how my pregnancy goes. He's going to celebrate this weekend. He's getting a special treat at breaking-in."

Revulsion, thick and heavy, stirred in Cara's stomach. Another precious child forced into adulthood before her time. Didn't her friends see how horrid this was?

Jodie flinched, hurt rippling across her face.

Cara poured fresh lemonade from a nearby pitcher into her glass. But instead of taking her seat, she went to the other end of the table and lightly bumped Penelope with her hip. "Scoot. I want to talk with Jodie."

The woman scooted down the bench, her chatter never stopping, and Cara took the empty seat. She looked across the table at Jodie. Her friend had a full plate of food, untouched. She held a plastic fork and shoved the food around on her plate.

"What's wrong, Jodie? You've been preoccupied ever since you got here." Cara searched her friend's features. "You know you can tell me."

"Why would I need to tell you anything?" Jodie snapped.

"Is it Levi?"

"No." Jodie bit the one word from between her lips.

The dark-circled eyes, the twitching lids and finger twisting gave away her internal conflict. Jodie was troubled. "Are you sick?"

"No." Jodie stared at her, her mouth set in a mulish line, anger flaring from the depths of her eyes. As if a gate crashed open, she crumpled. "It's me. I—I ..."

"You? What a laugh. You're perfect."

Stark misery blazed from her friend's eyes and sobered Cara's laughter. She reached across the table and took Jodie's hand. "Has something happened? You and Levi are one couple I admire. He's a good husband."

"I know." Jodie stared down at her plate. Her body quivered.

What could possibly be so wrong her unflappable friend had fallen apart like this?

Jodie looked up and whispered, "I found out yesterday I have a problem."

Did her friend have a serious illness? Cancer?

"I can't get pregnant."

Oh, no. Poor Jodie. She'd been trying for years. "Jodie, dear, Levi loves you. He's not going to be angry for something you can't help."

"But he is." Jodie swallowed. "I mean, kind of. The elders are pushing him to take another wife. One who can give him the fruit rightfully his."

"No way. He won't listen."

Jodie's eyes told her differently. "He doesn't want to, he says, but what can he do? They're insisting, and he does want children. He deserves children."

Cara bit her lip. The elders—specifically, Elder Simmons—had the last say, regardless of what a couple might wish. "What about you? Doesn't he care what you want?"

"And now this. When they find out I'm physically unable to bear children, Levi will have to get a wife who can do what she's meant to do. I'll be lucky if he allows me to stay. What if they send me to the house I'm always mocking?" The words tumbled out, and Cara realized Jodie hadn't heard her questions. Strain rode her friend's facial features. The blank eyes spoke of a mind focused on one thing. Her failure. Her disgrace. Her humiliation.

What could she say to comfort her? Levi would have no choice if he wanted to stay in good standing with Elder Simmons. What she thought, how angry it made his wife, made no difference. Levi would do the elders' bidding.

❧❧

Lacy's high-pitched screech interrupted Cara's concentration, and she hurried to check on her youngest. Her child slumped on the ground. Tears streaked down her soft cheeks, and her bottom lip trembled.

"I wanna go home, Mommy."

"We will, sweetie. We need to get Leila first." She settled her in their wagon, tucked her favorite doll beside her, and drew the wagon behind her as she started for the swimming area. Ten minutes ago, Leila begged to go with Mary Ann and her children, and though she trusted Mary Ann, she did not trust the men. She shouldn't have let her go but, focused on Jodie, she'd allowed herself to be persuaded.

She paused at the edge of the clearing but couldn't see her daughter. She started forward and saw Mary Ann beside the pool.

"Mary Ann, where's Leila?"

Mary Ann looked around, surprise playing across her face. "She went with Valerie and her friend, Rachel, to pick some wild flowers. I told them they had ten minutes and not a second more."

Not good enough. She shouldn't have let Leila go. "How could you? Don't you remember what Jodie told us?"

Mary Ann called after her. "Of course I remember. Not much can happen in ten minutes. Don't be such a worrywart. They'll be fine. "

Cara ignored her, although she wanted to screech at her friend much as Lacy had done earlier in her frustration. The sound of her feet slap-slapping on the ground and the rattle of the wagon rolling behind her magnified in her ears as she fought the terror exploding inside her. She rounded a bend, stopped to catch her breath, and listened for Leila's voice.

Silence. Cara frowned. Was that …

She took a few steps forward, listened again. Yes. It was a voice. She hurried forward and caught sight of a small, skinny figure trudging down the path, kicking at the wood chips, singing in a monotone one of the more popular songs preteen kids loved.

Cara pressed a hand against one of the tall maples lining the pathway. Her legs shook like watered-down pudding, threatening to send her pitching toward the ground.

The thought of her daughter in the hands of Elder Simmons …

Leila looked up. "Mom. Are you lost?"

Cara dropped the wagon's handle and ran forward to gather Leila in her arms. "No, sweetheart." She kept her voice soft, not wanting to startle her daughter. "I missed you terribly. Where are Valerie and Rachel?"

The girl squirmed. "They're with Elder Simmons."

"What?" The path lay open and empty, and Cara loosened her grip "What do you mean?"

"We were picking flowers, and he was there." Leila shrugged.

He'd slipped up on them without the girls realizing it. Sounded like the slippery weasel he was.

"What did he do?"

"Nothing."

"You mean he watched you."

"Uh-huh. He told me to scoot back to you. He wanted to talk to

Valerie and Rachel, and I wasn't old enough yet, he said. As if I'm a child." Leila's bottom lip trembled.

Thank God. Cara gripped the girl's arms tighter.

"It's not fair. Valerie is only two years older than me. Why couldn't I stay?"

"Three years, dear." Cara gathered her in her arms. *I cannot endure any more.* "You don't want to stay with Elder Simmons. You know what I've told you."

"What's wrong, Mom?" Leila pulled away and stared into Cara's face.

She smoothed back the girl's hair. "Tell me, sweetie, did Elder Simmons touch you?"

Leila's eyes widened. "I know what you're thinking, but you told me to kick anyone in the—"

"Right." Cara coughed out a nervous giggle at the accusing eyes and determination in her daughter. "I'm glad you remembered."

"I would scream if he tried anything."

"Good girl. I need you to stay with Lacy and keep her quiet while I go check on Valerie and Rachel."

"Can't we come with you?"

"Not this time." Cara pulled the wagon behind a massive oak. "Be very quiet and don't leave until I come for you. Understand?"

Leila's face screwed into disgruntled patience. "Okay."

If Elder Simmons had any evil plans, she would be too late to help the girls, but maybe, maybe …

Cara trotted down the path until she caught a glimpse of red through the brush. Was it Valerie's red shirt? Cara drew in a breath and tiptoed closer.

Elder Simmons was down on one knee, his arms around the girls' shoulders. Their faces were wreathed in smiles. The man slid his hands downward—lower than they should have gone. He swatted each girl—gently, and they giggled.

As if she was being smothered, Cara's mind whirled. Nothing too serious had happened, but who knew what the old goat had in mind. She stepped forward. "Valerie. Rachel. Your mothers are looking for you."

Elder Simmons's features froze into a mask of anger. "What are you doing here?" he snarled.

"I came for them." Cara took another step closer and nodded at the girls. "Girls, come here."

The two looked up at the man beside them. Elder Simmons glared at her. "They are fine, aren't you, Valerie?" He drew each girl close to his side.

Mary Ann's daughter giggled. "We like Elder Simmons."

"Go back, Sister Hayman, and mind your own business. You'd better check on your own children." His words mocked her concern.

"I already have. They're all right."

His smile bordered on devilish. "Are you sure?"

"What do you mean?"

"What do you think I mean?" His eyes glazed with malice. "Bears, snakes, and rabid animals inhabit our woods."

He's trying to scare me. The only kind of animal she feared was the two-legged, human variety. "Girls?"

Elder Simmons clasped a hand from each girl in his and headed her way. "We'll be right behind you."

No. She'd follow them. Cara sagged against the trunk of a maple until they passed her. As the trio reached the bend in the path, Elder Simmons twisted around and stared back down the path straight at her. His eyes gleamed, and a small, sly smile touched his lips.

Did he think he'd deceived her? What were his plans for these two? He was up to evil for certain. He'd begun his work on these two precious innocents. Gaining their trust. Building up their girlish, teenage pride. Ugh.

At least, it didn't look as if the man had hurt either of them. Yet. The plans hatching in his wicked brain were another matter.

The poor, poor girls. She wanted to gather all of them and hide them forever from such sex-craved men. But Mary Ann—and most of the other women—wouldn't thank her. In their deluded minds, obedient women and girls pleased Elder Simmons, and he, God.

Her tears pushed to escape, and she rubbed them away. Something more drastic was needed to wake these people up.

It would have to come from her.

CHAPTER TEN

Dayne didn't make it to the supper. By the time he spun into the driveway, his anger simmered into mild irritation at Tobert's nasty insinuations.

He wanted to take a piece out of Tobert. If God would give a nod of approval, he'd be at the head of the line. But so far, the approval wasn't there. It seemed wiser for him to play it cool, to preach and live love. The more he tried and the longer he lived at home, the more he learned, and the harder it got.

A knock on the door echoed through the house as he tucked his shirt ends into his jeans. He flicked a look in the mirror and headed for the front door. Could be Angus Tobert had come back to taunt him some more. Or not.

"Come on in, Levi. Glad you stopped by."

Levi Schrader's uneasiness was plain. Restless feet crossed, uncrossed, hands thrust into jean pockets withdrew. The man's eyes were filled with questions.

"You're not going to the supper?"

"I wanted to but got held up. Have a seat," Dayne offered as he led Levi into his study.

Levi shook his head. "Can't stay. Have a question for you."

"Go ahead."

"I'm not sure I should be complaining about this." Levi threaded his fingers through his hair.

"If you can't talk with your pastor, who can you talk to?"

When Levi didn't continue, Dayne added, "Talking with me doesn't mean you have to make a decision now, Levi. Only means you're getting something off your chest."

"You're right." Levi drew in a breath. "Jodie found out yesterday she can't have children."

"I see. That's no sin."

Levi shrugged out of his thin jacket and tossed it over his shoulder. "It is in Elder Simmons's eyes. You know our group doesn't condone childlessness."

"And you?"

"I don't know." Levi swung away. "It didn't bother me until Jodie told me this. Now I'm torn."

"This should be your decision, Levi. You have plenty of optional ways to parent," Dayne said. "They're pressuring you?"

"Yeah. I'm not ready to take another wife. I never thought I'd have to make this decision."

"You love Jodie?"

"Yeah, I do."

"I'll be praying for you."

Shoulders slumped, his new friend walked away.

※※※

Richard Melton. The one man he'd never thought to see standing on his front porch, lifted his hand to knock a third time as Dayne opened the door.

How many more of the elders would decide tonight was the right time to call on the preacher? "Richard? Is something wrong?"

"Nope." The man looked ready to flee at a wrong word from Dayne. "Uh, I could use some advice."

"Come in. I was getting ready to head to the picnic."

"I can come back."

Dayne grabbed his arm. "It's all right. One of the ladies dropped off a gallon of mint tea this morning. Want some?"

Richard followed Dayne into the house and took the chair he indicated.

"How are you doing?" Dayne called from the kitchen as he piled a stack of cookies on a small plate and grabbed a jar of nuts. "No after-effects from your virus?"

"I'll make it."

Dayne set the cookies and nuts on a side table and went back to the kitchen for their drinks. "How come you're not at the dinner?"

"Wanted to talk to you."

He handed a glass of tea to the other man and settled into his favorite wing chair. "Have a cookie."

"Thanks." Richard gulped down a cookie and reached for another.

The clock on his mantel, one of the few things he'd kept since his parents' death, ticked away the minutes. If the man didn't get on with it, he could kiss his plans for tonight good-bye.

"Anything specific you wanted to talk about?" A prod in the right direction should get him talking. A thought struck him. What if the man wanted to talk about *salvation*? Dayne straightened and set his glass on a coaster.

"Yes."

Dayne started. Had the man read his mind and answered his question?

"I'm here about Sister Hayman."

What? Better approach this one with caution. "What's the problem?"

"I think she deliberately poisoned me."

He chuckled but regretted his action immediately.

Richard flushed. "I should have gone to Elder Simmons."

"Why didn't you?" Was Richard making up this ridiculous statement? But his heart pounded.

He hated the doubt threading its way through his mind.

"Remember when you both visited me in the hospital?"

Dayne nodded.

"She woke me and spouted some nonsense about God warning me."

"About what?" His throat tightened. His own words to Professor Moore came back to mock him. *Too many unexplained episodes happening when she's around.*

Richard half-rose, resettled in his seat, and for the first time, looked

103

embarrassed. "Said God didn't want me to slap Abby. She wouldn't hush until I promised to treat Abby better."

"Why do her words make you think she poisoned you? Why would she? She's a loyal friend, and I can see her getting angry over mistreatment, but poison?"

"You tell me. Seems pretty clear." Richard drained his glass of tea. "Anyhow, I'm not like some of the men. I never really hurt Abby. A smack now and then doesn't mean anything."

Says you. Dayne kept his voice gentle when he rebuked the other man. "It means something to someone who has a meek personality like Abby. Respecting and loving our wives, Richard, is a positive action. God wants respect and love in a marriage."

Richard snapped a quick glance toward Dayne. "Sounds like one of your messages. It's not the kind of stuff our old minister preached. And Elder Simmons encouraged us to look beyond emotions."

"Doesn't make the gospel untrue, Richard."

Richard crossed and recrossed his legs as the red crept up his neck. "I shouldn't care what they think. I'm not stupid. I know most of the elders didn't want to accept me as an elder."

"Why did they?"

"I guess they ran out of excuses."

"How do you feel about Abby?" Dayne challenged.

"I don't know."

"What would you do if she was suddenly taken from you?"

The man halted the ascent of the cookie to his mouth. "I never thought about that. She never causes me trouble. Is always willing to do whatever I want. I mean, I—I—"

"What?"

Shame pushed the blankness from his face. "You're worse than a woman to nag a man, preacher."

Dayne wasn't ready to give up on forcing the man to face his own feelings. "I think you need to express what's hidden inside of you."

"I'm not used to this." Richard wiped a hand across his forehead. "But I guess I do care for Abby. I have no interest in another wife, even though I take my share of the breaking-ins. I mean, she's given me the cutest baby on earth."

And another one's on the way. Dayne almost said the words but refrained. Abby should have the privilege of telling the news. Not him.

"Good. Now remember what a blessing Abby is and all she's done for you. Treat her with respect. She's a person too, you know."

"Seems strange, but I guess you could be right."

"I know I'm right."

Richard settled back in his seat and picked up another cookie. "These are good."

"Caralynne made them."

Richard blanched and dropped the cookie onto the table. "I think I'm going to be sick."

"Nonsense. Those cookies are fine." He wasn't about to let this man malign Cara.

"I'm telling you. She gave me the willies, coming into the room like a vengeful angel sent from God. Why would she talk like that unless she felt guilty?"

A picture of Cara, her arms around her girls, sparked his memory. "What did the doctor think was wrong?"

"Nothing much. Thought I had a stomach virus." Richard shook his head. "I didn't. I'd not been around anyone ill to catch a virus."

"Hmm. You haven't told me any concrete evidence she's involved."

"She warned me the next time, I wouldn't tease death. God may let me taste it.'"

Dayne's heart sank. Could he be right? Could she have gone off the deep end in trying to help Abby? "Doesn't sound like evidence to me. How did she know you hit Abby? Was she angry at you?"

The man's sheepish face told him the truth. "I suppose Abby whined to her friends."

"She was trying to scare you. I doubt she did anything to make you sick."

"You think not?" Richard looked anything but sure.

Cara's face as a child—six, seven years old and younger than Dayne—

peeking at him from under the huge bush at his home. A child no one claimed, and one the law—Elder Simmons—wanted to raise in his home. Thankfully, Dayne's father prevailed, and Cara joined their family.

Cara, crying, after being teased at school.

Cara, finding out the elders wouldn't listen to his father.

No, not his Cara. She didn't have it in her to hurt someone like this. Unless …

The day of Donald Hayman's funeral when he'd faintly mentioned Lori, Cara's shadowy face had seared its way into his memory. In the light of Richard's story, Cara's anger at the man shook Dayne's confidence in her. For a second.

"What exactly did the doctor say about the virus?"

Richard's sulk wasn't a pretty thing. "Said I picked up the bug from someone. But I've not heard of one case."

"You don't believe him."

"He was lying. I'm telling you, I think she poisoned me."

"Why would he go along with Cara's plan?" It didn't make sense. "What gave you the idea about Cara?"

"Abby. She let it slip Cara made the cabbage soup. She creeped me out talking like she did at the hospital, but when I realized Cara made the soup, I figured she'd schemed to pay me back for the imaginary harm I did." Richard slapped his hands together as if dusting them. "I threatened my woman I'd beat her senseless. She'll think twice before keeping stuff from me again."

To give him credit, embarrassment filled Richard's eyes at his own brash words.

Poor Abby. Dayne eyed the other man, dislike swarming through him like a hundred angry bees. Would the man change his habits or continue his abuse?

What to do? He wasn't about to make trouble for Cara with no more to go on than Richard's word. If this reached the elders' ears, and they believed Richard, they would punish her severely. And he wouldn't stand by to let that happen.

"Richard, I think it's best if we keep this between us. Give me time to check things out."

"I'm uneasy hiding this from Elder Simmons, but you're handpicked by him, so I guess it'll be okay. I did tell Abby I didn't want her around Cara."

Dayne placed a hand on his shoulder. "I'm praying for you."

After one questioning glance, the man left. Dayne sat in his chair until the darkness crept into the room, shadow by shadow, praying he would find out the truth about Cara. God would have to give him the strength to fight the demonic power brooding through the group.

❧❧❧❧

Cara sped back to the wagon. Leila was on the ground next to the wagon, crooning softly and patting Lacy's head. Her heart melted at Leila's sisterly love. She adjusted Lacy's sleeping body and took Leila's hand. Singing Lacy's favorite nursery rhyme, she headed back to the picnic area. "Hush, my babies, don't you cry, Mama's gonna love her precious girls."

When the voices grew louder, she slowed. The elders didn't need to notice her and perhaps wonder what she'd been up to. She scanned the immediate area, but no one paid any attention to her. Slipping behind a couple trees, she angled toward the playground swings but joined a couple of the women who were clearing one of the tables.

"Where have you been all evening, Sister Hayman?"

"I've enjoyed the fellowship of my sisters."

Ha. And finding out more news to fuel the fire of revenge.

"Good." One of the ladies nodded. The other one eyed her, and Cara's heart sank to the bottom of her feet. Of all the women, this one—Kathy Raymond—gossiped with an intensity bordering on a second religion. Not counting the unwanted advice she disposed to those whom she assumed needed it. She and Sister Simmons were thick as the proverbial thieves.

Better walk easy and get away as quickly as possible. Otherwise, the woman would tattle everything Cara said and some things she hadn't.

Cara chanced a glance at her and caught the increased glow in her eyes. She actually smacked her lips.

"My dear, Sister Simmons told me the good news for you. Considering."

"What would that be?" Why make inane comments? If Kathy Raymond thought it was good, she'd think it horrid.

Kathy slid a look her way. "Why, the elders' decision for your marriage. Emery Hayman will be the perfect mate for you."

Cara gagged.

"I mean, he is your poor, dead husband's brother, so he should know how Donald handled you. And those girls of yours. He'll have a job taming them down." Her gray eyes peered into Cara's.

Too close for comfort.

The woman sprayed a stream of spittle Cara's direction. "How old is your oldest? Pretty near time for her, isn't it?"

Cara's hand twitched from the desire to slap the woman. "She's ten years old and far too young to be tamed by the likes of Emery Hayman, if he ever had the opportunity, which he never will."

Kathy pressed thin lips together, while the other woman—Tiffany Kisser—tched, tched.

"Well, you seem pretty rebellious to me. Elder Simmons will hear about this."

Cara shrugged, although she wanted to stomp the ground. "Don't bother. I already let him know I wouldn't marry Emery."

"You told him that?" Shock flared in both ladies' eyes.

Lacy stirred in her sleep, and Cara stroked her soft hair. She checked on Leila, who had wandered over to the next table. "Why not? I will die before I'll marry another Hayman."

For the first time, Tiffany spoke up. "Who'd care for your girls?"

A flicker of sympathy twinkled in the other woman's eyes. So she was human, after all. Too bad the people with whom she associated weren't.

"Looks like you would have learned your lesson." The spite spewing out of Kathy's mouth was like volcanic lava.

"What are you talking about?" Unease nibbled at her nerve endings.

"If you'd kept a rein on Lori, she'd have been more submissive. When she died, it was your fault for not teaching her the right way."

Cara staggered back. Even Donald—and the elders—hadn't been that harsh. How could this pasty-faced witch make such accusations?

Piety dripped from Kathy's lips. "Her breaking-in time had come. A good mother would have taught her daughter submission and eagerness to do God's will."

Numb, she bent to pick up the wagon handle and motioned to Leila. Grief sludged through her like muddy water—heavy, thick, and deep. The loneliness for her oldest, the self-guilt she battled for not rescuing her precious daughter sickened her.

She wanted to hate this despicable being, but the weakness in her refused to relinquish its grip. She didn't have the strength. She didn't care what they thought of her parental abilities, but for the likes of her to breathe Lori's name …

Cara lifted one heavy foot after the other. The shrill sound of Kathy's laughter followed her like the raucous crows that circled over the gardens.

❧❦❧

"Psst."

Cara jumped and almost dropped Lacy but placed her sleepy child in the backseat of the car and strapped her in. She faced the woman hovering close by. "Abby, why are you hiding?"

Abby searched the surrounding dusky area. "I wanted to tell you something."

What now?

"I think Richard went to Reverend MacFarland's," she whispered.

Could be why Dayne never showed up. Cara propped herself against the side of the car. "What does this have to do with me?"

"Why would he do that?" Abby bit her lip and refused to meet Cara's eyes.

Was she hiding something? Afraid? "What aren't you telling me?

Did Richard say why he wanted to talk with Dayne?"

When Abby fiddled with her baby's light blanket and didn't speak, Cara went on, "Well, this means nothing to me." She opened her door. "Leila, is your seatbelt fastened?"

"Richard ordered me to stay away from you." Abby grabbed her arm and gave it a gentle shake. "I don't want to do that."

Light dawned. Her prediction at the hospital must have put some dismay into the man. "I see. What did he say?"

"That you were a bad influence. That you would be punished, and that I might be too if I insisted on being friends."

"What do you want me to do?"

Abby's eyes radiated her concern. "Nothing, I guess. Cara, I don't want him stirring up trouble for you. Please be careful. What would I do without you?"

"I will, and thanks. Don't worry. I don't think Dayne would do anything to harm me."

Or would he?

CHAPTER ELEVEN

Dayne read the list on his notepad. Again. Three names. Three potential partners for his plan of action. Tossing his pen to the table, he bowed his head and stared at nothing. Would these men listen? A conglomeration of faces—all elders—swirled through his mind's eye, but none jumped out except the ones he'd already tentatively chosen.

Levi. In his fifties, kind to Jodie, well-liked and friendly. Being childless could very well be the catapult to push Levi to his side. Dayne was sure some of the group's rules didn't sit well with the man. The interested questions Levi posed about God pointed to an intelligent mind. He'd shown interest in the subjects Dayne preached. A troubled man meant a real possibility for an ally.

Josh Denuit. Younger than most of the other elders, energetic and happy-go-lucky, he seemed to have a good marriage. The man praised his messages almost every time Dayne spoke. Josh's face during the services and his expressive features displayed how much he enjoyed them. Whether he understood the messages was another matter. More important, had Dayne influenced him enough to pull him in?

Kenneth Lewis. Dayne frowned at the name. Kenny was always friendly to him. Sought him out as if ulterior motives simmered beneath the surface. Bee-lined toward him after every service. But his enthusiasm for females other than his wife lay like soured milk on Dayne's stomach. Still, his friendliness indicated a redeemable trait buried within the man. It was the only reason his name was on the list.

That, and the brevity of the list.

At the bottom of the page, Dayne had scribbled one other name, but it was such a ridiculous thought he'd also scratched it out. Richard Melton. He was a small man, filled with himself and definitely cruel to

Abby, yet Dayne couldn't let go of Richard's glance before he'd left last night. Questioning, but perhaps a bit of yearning or hunger in him. His honest reception of Dayne's encouragement seemed to hint of a man who could change if led in the proper direction. Hmmm, remained to be seen.

He heard the knock and dragged his thoughts back to the present. Who now?

Dayne stuck his head into the hallway. Elder Simmons and Angus Tobert waited side by side on his porch.

He ducked back into the study. His desk, covered with notes for Sunday's message, beckoned. But if he climbed out the window, he could avoid them. Should he go with the irreverent idea? The next second, he headed to the door.

"Elder Simmons. Angus." He motioned for the two men to follow him and led them to his study. "What brings you here this time of the day?"

The senior elder settled his belly-heavy frame into one of Dayne's antique wing-backed chairs. The chair creaked, and Dayne winced. He should have taken the men to his living room. He dragged his gaze from the suffering chair and aimed it at the group's leader.

"What can I do for you gentlemen this morning? I assume you have business here."

Elder Simmons propped elbows on the chair arms and tapped stubby fingers together. "We do. Sister Hayman is troubling us."

He paused and probed Dayne's face with his beady eyes.

Dayne pasted an enigmatic expression on his face and loosened fingers gripping the chair's arm. Now was not the time for these two to accuse Cara of anything.

"I'm sure you've perceived her rebellious spirit."

This time there was no getting out of answering. What this man called rebellious, Dayne referred to as independent and carefree. "God made us all different."

The senior elder chuckled and spoke to Angus Tobert. "This is why God revealed to me what an outstanding minister Dayne MacFarland would be to us. He is a pastor with heart and has a quick mind."

The elder resumed speaking to Dayne. "Ah, the beauty of God's plan. Though different, our women must submit. In doing so, their real beauty is revealed. We cannot conscientiously ignore Sister Hayman's actions. We would be doing a disservice to Brother Hayman and to our women. God, himself, would frown upon us."

"God declared man is the head," Angus whined.

Elder Simmons frowned at him and wiggled to a more comfortable position in his chair. The curved legs of the chair moaned in distress.

Dayne wanted to moan in harmony with his chair. "I believe—"

Elder Simmons spoke to Angus Tobert. "See? What did I tell you?"

"I believe the husband is the head of the home." Dayne lifted a hand. "But I also see in God's word that he allowed women to be used in capable positions. They are to be rewarded with respect and love, treated with care and tenderness. They are invaluable as helpmates in a family and can input important information with intelligence. We're foolhardy to think otherwise."

Whoa. Simmons's simper disappeared faster than it took ice to melt on a hot July day. No matter. Dayne wouldn't be this man's figurehead.

Elder Simmons's demeanor sobered. "I hope you aren't being influenced by the devil in this woman."

"What woman? No, I'm not being influenced."

He pointed at Dayne. "We want your help when we deal with her."

As if. "How are you going to do that? What has she done to deserve being reprehended?"

"Never mind. Be at the church Friday evening, and you'll find out." Elder Simmons marched to the door, his henchman following.

Dayne shut the door behind them and stared out the side windows. What did these two malicious elders have up their sleeve?

He'd better warn Cara before Friday.

❧❦❧

Grocery shopping had never been his thing. Yet here he was pushing the cart up one aisle and down the next. Why? Just part of his excuse to see Cara again.

He strolled into another aisle and met Levi pushing his own cart.

"Fancy meeting you here."

"Your wife talked you into doing the weekly shopping?"

"Afraid so. Never been able to tell her no." The good-looking man smiled before drawing in a breath. "I've been wanting to speak with you. Your messages are bothering me."

Interesting. "Why?"

"Well, they certainly make me think."

Perfect. "That's always a good thing."

"You've talked a lot about God's love for us, which intrigues me, and anything that intrigues me makes me inquisitive. I know Elder Simmons is disturbed."

Aha.

"What I've spoken about comes from the Bible. There is nothing wrong with stretching our brains, thinking beyond what we know. Studying God's word always leads us into a deeper relationship."

"That makes sense. I suppose I'm so used to leaving spiritual matters to Elder Simmons, I've been lazy in thinking for myself along those lines."

"That's easily enough corrected," Dayne encouraged. "What can I do to help?"

"Say a prayer or two for me. Keep preaching the same sort of stuff. I know one thing for sure— Preacher Crabtree never gave us much to think about. Sunday morning sermon naps never appealed to me much. I skipped Sunday services as much as I could."

This man was as open and honest as a person could want. Dayne straightened when Levi did. "I'll be praying. You can count on it."

"One other thing. I got word Cara Hayman will be the subject of our meeting Friday evening.

Supposedly, some of the elders are concerned about her lack of meekness."

"What do you think about Cara?"

"She's a favorite with Jodie. But Jodie has a tendency to be outspoken herself. I don't have a problem with Cara. Thought I'd give you a heads-up."

Why had he thought it important to Dayne? Did he sense Dayne's feelings concerning the woman?

Levi gave his cart a shove. "Talk to you later."

Dayne called after him. "Thanks for the heads-up."

❧❧❧

He lifted the sack and peeked in the door he'd cracked open. "I come bearing gifts. Anyone hungry for pizza tonight?"

Both girls dropped their toys and ran toward the door. His decision to come with pizza was a winner.

"Can you help me make these and give your mommy a break?" Dayne loved the happiness radiating from Cara's face as she watched her girls.

"I can," Leila bragged, "but Lacy can't cook very well."

Dayne hid his grin. "Well, you and I'll have to teach her. Are you game?"

Leila ran for the kitchen, Lacy trotting behind.

"I didn't know you could cook."

"There are a lot of things you don't know about me. Do you mind?" He indicated the bag with a nod of his head.

"Of course not. We haven't eaten yet and were going to finish up leftovers. Pizza will be a treat."

"Great. Show me where you keep everything, and the girls and I'll do the rest. Tonight's your night to relax."

"I don't get much of that." She led the way to the kitchen and opened cabinet doors to point out bowls, pans, and utensils. Filling a glass full of water, she sipped, her eyes peering at him over the rim. When he smiled at her, she settled at the table and rested her chin on her fists.

Dayne wished he'd brought his camera. She would make a lovely picture of a mother relaxing in her kitchen. *A Study of Relaxation.*

She squirmed. "Is something wrong?"

"No, admiring the view."

A light pink colored her cheeks.

Dayne pulled out green peppers, onions, broccoli, and tomatoes, giving her a moment to recover. "I thought a veggie pizza, but if you want meat—"

"That's fine. Fortunately, the girls are rabbits when it comes to green stuff. They love healthy foods."

"No sweets?"

She shook her head. "We have homemade goodies, but I've brought them up to view them as treats for special times. Leila and Lacy are usually easy to please. So far."

"Wise as well as beautiful." Dayne guided Lacy to the sink and boosted her onto a chair. "Can you wash these vegetables for me?"

"I want to do that. She's not big enough." Leila crossed her arms and frowned at her sister.

"This dough needs strong hands." Dayne winked at the young girl and lowered his voice. "Do you think you can help me mix it?"

Leila's eyes twinkled. "Of course. I'm a better cook than mom."

"Of course you are." Dayne pulled out the ingredients.

Cara's soft laughter filled his ears.

After measuring the liquid into the dry, he handed over the spoon. "Here you go. See what you can do."

With both hands, the girl gripped the wooden spoon and stirred the mixture, her tongue between her teeth as if she was determined not to fail the job given her.

Soap dripped from Lacy's arms, and the front of her shirt was soaked. Dayne lifted her from the sink, wiped up the water running down the cabinet, and ran water over the vegetables. He placed the metal basket on the table. "Okay, partner, I'm going to chop these veggies. Can you put them in these four bowls? After Leila gets the dough ready, you can help me drop the veggies on it."

He checked on Leila's efforts and wondered if the lumpy mess could be saved. "Good job, Leila. I can see you're going to cook as well as your mom."

He heard Cara's quiet chuckle. What a woman. How could anyone accuse her of rebellion? Her interaction with her girls showed planning and work on the part of the mother. The thought of Elder Simmons and Angus and the promised meeting about Cara sprang to his mind.

Don't think of that right now. Later, when the girls were busy or in bed, he'd have to tell Cara. He made sure his face revealed nothing but carefree happiness when he looked at her.

"You didn't answer my question."

Cara flipped a lock of hair from her shoulder and gave him a coy look. "What question would that be?"

Was she flirting? Nothing he'd said was the least bit amusing, yet her eyes twinkled, her mouth twitched. Dayne gave the lumpy dough a stir, pulled the round, greased pizza pan close, plopped the dough in the middle, and pushed it in front of Leila. "Okay, kiddo, have at it."

He faced Cara. "I suppose you think it's comical to see a man in the kitchen."

"Well, I've never seen a man so at home in one, that's true."

"Dad cooked once a week for Mother. You haven't forgotten the meals he prepared, have you?"

"How could I? I admired him so much and couldn't understand why he didn't broadcast the fact to the other men. He and your mother were the best parents in the world. No wonder you turned out so well."

"You didn't do so badly yourself."

Her face sobered. "I miss them so much, I can't imagine how you feel."

"I miss them every day." He scowled at Cara. "You didn't answer me."

"Uh-huh. I know." She gave him a sideways look. "You look like a little boy with a white streak across your nose. Very becoming for a dignified minister." Dayne swiped at the offending flour. Cara threw back her head, her laughter a sound so delightful he wanted to swoop her into his arms.

"Oh, you look like a ghost now." She reached for a cloth. "Here. Let me help."

She circled the table and dabbed at Dayne's nose and cheek. Her face was close to his, her skin soft and pink, her lashes heavy on her cheeks. The desire to cup her cheek expanded until all he wanted was to gather her close in his arms. "Cara?" He couldn't hide the love thickening his voice.

Her smile dimmed. The pulse in her throat beat in rapid response to his pounding heart. Her mouth opened, and she swayed.

"Mommy?"

Cara jerked back, her head swiveling toward her youngest daughter. She struggled to slow her breathing. "What do you need, Lacy?"

"Leila won't let me help her."

Cara moved toward her daughter, her face averted, one vein in her slender neck still beating a tell-tale confession. What was she thinking?

Cara felt something, and that was good enough for now. He didn't want to push her into a relationship under the circumstances.

"Looks like you did a good job in placing the vegetables in their bowls, Lacy." Dayne inspected the items, and as he'd hoped, she bee-lined to him, her grievance forgotten.

When Cara took her seat again, Dayne avoided staring at her. He shoved the pizza into the hot oven and caught her sneaking glances at him.

She looked away.

Making her self-conscious around him wasn't in his plans. "How is Abby doing?"

For a moment she didn't answer. "Richard seems to have mellowed, so Abby's in seventh heaven."

"What?"

"I didn't say anything."

"I can tell you want to say more."

"Abby's not stupid. She realizes and accepts what he is." Cara stared out the window, and a troubled look rolled across her face. The same expression she'd worn the day of her husband's funeral. "She doesn't love him, so a peaceful day with no abuse is cause for happiness."

"Maybe he's changed."

"That's hard for me to believe. I've never liked Richard. He's small-minded and petty."

"I believe he's never had the encouragement—the motivation to push him into being more than what he is. If someone could point him in the right direction, he might improve."

"It would never be enough for me."

Her decisiveness prompted Dayne to gentle his voice even more. "It might be enough for Abby, who has to live with him."

Cara's face registered puzzlement at his suggestion. The thought Abby could, and would, accept any improvement in Richard as a blessing had never occurred to her. And he saw immediately she not only realized the fact but accepted it. Good.

Dayne lifted Lacy up onto a chair so she could help him wash the dishes. He pulled out drawers to locate a dishcloth, and when Leila frowned, said, "Only those who help clean up get ice cream after pizza."

"My mother's not helping." Leila eyed Dayne.

"Your mother's excused tonight. She's getting a vacation," Dayne answered in a no-nonsense tone.

Lacy splashed more soapsuds down the front of her shirt. "What's 'cation?"

"It's—never mind. Let's finish these so you and Leila can go play after we eat." Dayne guided Lacy's hand holding the rolling pin to the drainer. He left her at the sink and returned to the table with Cara. "I know how Abby feels. We talked at the hospital."

"I see."

What did she see?

"I've been working on Richard. I'm seeing some definite good responses to my encouragement."

"Don't hold your breath for anything permanent." The sound she emitted was as close to a snort as he'd ever heard.

"You don't believe it could happen?"

"Truth?"

He allowed a sliver of a smile to cross his lips.

"Nope. I don't believe any of these men are redeemable. Unless …"

"Aha. So you do have reservations."

"No. But I think Levi Schrader really does love Jodie. He never abuses her and sometimes something's in his eyes ..."

Her voice trailed off again. Had she caught a glimpse of real love and wondered about it? An emotion she'd never experienced in her own marriage?

"I mean, I've seen him tilt his head as if he's really listening when she's talking. And he treats her—well, I guess you could call it respect. Is that love?"

Was she serious?

"Sometimes, Cara. It can be. Love is also like a river that rushes through you, exposing your heart for all the world to see. The next minute it's disguised as a shallow brook, shady, calm, and collected."

"You're poetic."

Watch it, guy. You'll be blushing, and what will Cara think?

"You don't like poetry?"

"I love it and don't get enough chances to read all I want."

"Would you like to borrow some of my books?"

Her eyes brightened. "Could I?"

"Come by and pick what you want."

A cloud of doubt darkened her eyes. "Do you think that's wise?"

"Why not? I'm here at your home."

"Yes, but you're the minister visiting parishioners. I could be perceived as a female piranha after a man."

"Let me worry about the piranhas. Come by next week. Okay?"

"All right."

"Do I smell pizza calling for us to eat it?" he sing-songed to the girls, and they dropped their cloths and rushed toward him.

Dayne lifted the pizza from the oven and settled it on two hot pads in the middle of the table. He deftly sliced and slid a piece onto each plate, poured drinks of raspberry tea, and settled across from Cara. He held out both hands and took the girls' hands in his.

Cara clasped her daughters' hands and ordered, "Lacy, shut your eyes while Reverend MacFarland prays—and no nibbling."

"Father, we thank you for the food we are about to enjoy. Thank you for this family and this special time together. Bless Cara, Leila, and Lacy, and give them your protection and love. Amen."

More than once throughout the evening, Dayne sensed Cara was troubled, but he knew the burden she carried inside her was bound tightly. Questioning and pushing her for answers would only send her spiraling away from him. She wondered about his motive, he was positive. Did she also doubt his belief in God?

He didn't know, but he had all evening to ponder it.

❧❦❧

Cara munched on the last delicious bite of her second slice of pizza. Her awareness of Dayne scared her. He'd shaken her tonight, even though she'd tried to hide it. That look in his eyes when she'd wiped off his cheek—she'd almost given in to the crazy impulse to, uh, kiss him. What would he have thought?

And his prayer. What did he mean when he prayed she would feel God's protection and love? God. He hadn't looked kindly on her since she could remember.

She wanted to trust Dayne. He'd been such a wonderful friend when they'd been kids, always easy to talk to. He'd listened to a girl six years younger. Listened while she'd droned on and on. No one would have guessed how bored he must have been.

He *seemed* to be as wonderful now as then but was he? Had the look in his eyes been what she'd thought or lust for her body? She wanted him to consider her mind and heart, unlike most of the other men. Elder Simmons could have sent him to spy on her, but she hoped not.

Worse, had he duped her for reasons unknown to her?

Her throat closed. No way would he do that to her. She didn't want it to be so.

What would he think if he knew—understood what she was doing? Would he support her and back her up or condemn her and align himself beside the elders?

Her girls were smiling, enjoying themselves, and Dayne's equally happy, expressive face was just as endearing. She couldn't believe he'd escaped Elder Simmons's push for marriage. Her eyes narrowed, but she dismissed the thought. Dayne was too much his own person.

He'd make good husband material—if he didn't resort to the group's practices. She hoped he didn't. He wasn't for her. Elder Simmons would never permit it. Women like her, who'd birthed children, were good for one thing only: to supplement men whose wives failed to give them children, and especially male children. Men like Dayne would have the pick of whomever he wanted.

She hated the burning tears forcing their way from behind her eyes. They clouded her vision of the only man she would ever love.

CHAPTER TWELVE

H̲e wasn't ready to go home yet. Cara's eyes bothered him, kept him seated as he listened to the murmur of the girls' sleepy voices and her crooning one as she sang to them. He could imagine her tucking them in, smoothing back their hair, love shining in her eyes.

She started down the stairs, Sabre's soft padding alongside hers, and his pulse galloped into high gear. He *really* should get home, but he didn't want to. Besides, he hadn't yet explained Elder Simmons's plans.

Her feet hit the floor, and seconds later, she appeared in the doorway, Sabre beside her.

"He's a lovely dog. The girls adore him." She patted the dog's head, who gave her a doggy grin as if to say, "I know."

"He's the son of my first Sabre." Dayne ruffled his dog's hair. "Remember?"

Cara frowned but asked, "Thirsty?"

"I'm fine. Come and sit down. Let's talk." He patted the seat beside him.

She sat on the opposite end of the sofa. "What about? By the way, you're a good cook."

"That's nothing. You ought to taste my barbecue."

"Chicken?"

"And ribs. I hate to brag." He grinned, belying the words. "But you ain't tasted anything until you've eaten my ribs."

"When did you learn to cook?"

"Well, Dad gave me the love for creating good food. But at college, I developed the knack. I had this fantastic professor who became a friend and spiritual mentor. I spent many weekends at his home. He taught me to cook."

"Did you like school? Being away?"

"Not at first. Homesick and miserable, I questioned everything and made myself out to be a regular jerk. Because I was so blatantly obnoxious, I caught Professor Moore's attention." He'd still be ashamed at his behavior if Prof hadn't cared so much. "I obnoxiously sported a superior attitude, determined to prove the theories I'd been raised to believe."

Cara's eyes darkened. "And did you?"

"Nope. All my unskilled arguing rolled right over him. His influence and prayers were too intense. I couldn't break him down."

"So he broke you?"

"Sort of. He was the instrument God worked through to get to me. Took awhile, but my hard-headedness finally softened. I'm a baby yet. Still have a lot to learn. After that, I liked being away. Didn't want to come back. Made plans not to."

Her eyes questioned him.

"I had to come back. Six months before I graduated, I ignored any communication from Elder Simmons, inviting me to take their current minister's place. I went to Boston and accepted a pastorate. But I couldn't get away from God's call for me to serve my people here. I didn't want to, argued for another year, but eventually gave in."

Her eyes widened. Gorgeous eyes. He could drown in them.

She tilted her head. "But why? Why would any God want someone to be here in this place?"

"I think he wanted me to try to make a change. To bring his truth to our people." He opened his mouth to say more, to give her a glimpse inside his heart.

"Well, all I can say is, God's given you a hopeless task." She pulled her legs up and hugged them. "Is this what you wanted to talk about?"

She was done talking about religion. Better to move on. "No. Sorry, I got sidetracked."

"I asked too many questions." Her mouth quirked up in a mischievous smile.

"You always were a curious brat," he teased.

"I was not," she shot back.

Dayne remembered all the times they'd argued in the past. *Was not. Was too. Did not. Did too.* Whoever took the one side, the other argued for the opposite. Both of them stubborn and determined to have their own way. "Remember?"

"Yeah."

"You were a sweet one, but a brat all at the same." He sobered. "Cara, Elder Simmons and Angus Tobert stopped by my house last night. Elder Simmons is calling a special meeting about you Friday night."

"I see."

"Have you done something to catch his attention?"

"Other than refuse to marry Emery Hayman?" She straightened. "Or, no, taking my girls on Sunday picnics did it."

She struck a thoughtful pose, but her stiff body, her angry, jerking gestures belied her words.

"No. I know what it is. I'm a super-bad influence on the other women of this group and can't be tolerated because everyone knows we're brainless, weak, and incapable of fending for ourselves. It's a real good thing God made men." Her voice simmered contempt, but something deeper edged her words.

"Cara." He'd probably never be able to realize what hurt she'd gone through, and wishing he could wouldn't help a thing.

"Don't. Don't try to soothe it all away." She jumped to her feet and stomped around the room. "I hate, hate, hate him. I hate his hypocrisy and all those jerks who follow him as if he's God. I'd like to—to—"

"Punch him in the nose?"

Cara stopped her pacing and turned to him, her face blank. "That's not what I was going to say." Her voice was nervous, high-pitched, but filled with relief.

"I didn't think so." He was glad to see she'd relaxed. "I wasn't going to try to soothe you."

"Then what?"

"I won't let them hurt you."

"How?"

"I don't know, but together we can find the solution." If he only knew the right solution. "Cara, did my father ever hurt you in any way?"

She thrust a puzzled look at him. "What are you talking about? You know very well he spoiled me rotten. I never got into any trouble as long as you were around to blame."

"You scoundrel."

"You should have told on me." Her head tilted back, her throat contracting as she swallowed. "I miss him so much. Him and your mother. I wish they were still here."

"Me, too." So much for that idea. Had his father lost his sensibility before he died? He might never know. "Come here, Cara. Take my hand."

The expression on her face flickered from confusion to longing. With something akin to diffidence, she sat beside him.

Dayne turned over her hand and rubbed a finger over the small tattoo marking her wrist. The evidence she was a Child of Righteous Cain. A proper woman and wife willing to be submissive and obedient. Would they have given her the tattoo if they'd known of her rebellion against their rules?

When he finished his prayer, Cara sat still, the oddest expression playing across her features, the pulse in her wrist throbbing in a silent drumbeat.

❧❧❧

The moon brightened Cara's room. Each object in the room loomed like a prehistoric monster, ready to pounce.

He was here. His presence. She could imagine Donald's hawking frame ... *stumbling into the room after a night of the elders' monthly celebration. Muttering. His heavy rear end settling on his side of the bed, stripping off the ugly shoes he wore when working. The awkward moving as he pulled off his clothes.*

In her mind, his harsh voice filled her ears, and she lifted both hands to cover them.

"Woman, you asleep? Get over here. I need you."

Her breath came in gasps as she fought the panic.

His awful, grubby hands fondling, squeezing, hurting her body. Night after night.

Cara cried out, the shivers running up her spine. She jerked the sheet up to cover her mouth so the girls wouldn't hear. Rolling to her side, she pulled her legs up and wrapped her arms around them. Cold, she was so cold.

He had been her husband, so why did she feel filthy?

Abruptly, she sat up and blinked, trying to get rid of the memory. When that didn't work, she clambered from the bed. Leaning her head against the windowpane, she breathed in and out, calming her screaming nerves.

Something moved halfway across her lawn. She squinted and made out the form. Emery Hayman stared back at her, making no attempt at hiding. She could imagine the smirk on his thick lips, the daunting confidence in his pea brain: she was his.

Her nerve endings sizzled, and backing away, she let the curtain drop over the window again. How could he? The bold-faced pig. Couldn't he at least wait the one month? Obviously not.

She snatched up a quilt and settled on the sofa in the living room. Lumpy it might be, but far more comforting than the bed she hated. If she had the money to get another one, she would burn the despicable thing. A request Elder Simmons would not like.

Enough. She didn't want to think about him or Donald. Or Emery. Dayne.

Like a clean stream of gentle water, she suddenly felt like a new person. A clean person. That was ridiculous, of course. He'd be embarrassed, even laugh, at her stupid thoughts. But what to do when a girl was desperate for relief from her own thoughts?

Cara tugged on the patchwork quilt Dayne's mother had given her years ago, her favorite of any she'd ever seen. Old, worn, and not especially fancy, but endearing. She smoothed the coverlet, her fingers tracing the squares of color, and her heart warmed.

Fuzzy, happy memories.

The quilt spread on the floor, with her and toddler Lori sitting on it, giggling and reading books.

The quilt covering her firstborn when she'd had the flu so badly at five.

The quilt pulled tight around her and her three girls, the heat on the blink several winters ago. Lori had insisted on holding newborn Lacy so Cara could cuddle whiney Leila, who refused to leave her mother's lap.

Lori with her skinny, small frame. Lori, who'd mothered the baby rabbit whose mother some hunter killed. Lori, her big, brown eyes dripping tears when Cara'd cried after a beating. Lori, whom Cara tried to shield from growing up too soon. She'd failed. Lori saw the abuse, the hurt, the terror, and grew old with the knowledge. She should have enjoyed childhood much, much longer.

Cara covered her eyes and let the tears come again.

Someone needed to pay.

❧❧❧

Cara re-read the note Sister Simmons dropped off.

The Elders are calling on all of us to meet at the Lewis home on Wednesday. Their roof is leaking and the house needs siding. Brother Simmons reminds us we are our brother's keeper and calls on you to do the Lord's work in helping them get their home in proper shape. We want to be perfect examples of the community.

Oh, yeah. What a bunch of lunatics.

Ladies, we'll expect each of you to bring two dishes of food, a drink, and dessert. Please be prompt as we'll need plenty of hands to set up tables, and perhaps some of us can even be of help to the men in carrying items for them.

May the God of our ancestor, Brother Cain, rest on each of us. Sister Ruby Simmons

Cara grimaced. *Wonder how a dish of bitter herbs would be enjoyed?*

She headed to the kitchen and took out a bag of her frozen cherries. Her special cherry mountain pie would do for the dessert. She'd make a corn casserole from her plentiful supply of frozen corn. Peach-flavored tea to drink. Easy and quick and filling. Far better than any of those men deserved. If she did her preparations tonight, she could rise early enough in the morning to finish up and still arrive at a respectable hour, although she'd dearly love to go late to see the look on the resident criticizer's face. She could see Kathy Raymond trotting off to advise Ruby Simmons what to tell her husband about the rebellious Hayman woman.

She was still chuckling to herself when she finished cleaning up her cooking mess. She heard the knock on her door. Couldn't be the girls, unless one of them was sick.

Abby stood at the door, her hair disheveled, her baby whimpering at her shoulder. "Cara, have you heard?"

What else could possibly happen? "What? Come in, Abby. Tell me."

"Penelope. She fell down her basement steps last night."

Cara motioned for Abby to take a seat at the table and sank into a chair. "How on earth did she do that? Is she hurt badly? Oh, no, what about the baby?"

Abby shook her head. "I don't know. Kenny was home and found her. The last I heard she was still unconscious."

"I'll need to go to her."

Abby patted her baby's back even as her anxious eyes questioned Cara. "Do you still have time?"

"I haven't used my allotted time for this month. I never do. I'll be okay."

Cara shut the door behind Abby's retreating back and collapsed into a chair, her heart sinking. What would happen if Penelope lost her baby?

CHAPTER THIRTEEN

Forty minutes later, Cara stepped inside Penelope's room at the compound hospital. The whiteness of the room—walls, sheets, curtains—emphasized Penelope's sharp features. The only contrast was the dark hair spread across the pillow. She lay quiet, a lump the size of a ping-pong ball adorning the left side of her head.

The thin lids fluttered. Her head swayed backward and forward in the tiniest of motions. "Caralynne?"

"I'm here."

"They said—they said I lost my baby."

Tears pierced Cara's eyes like miniature daggers. What to say? "I'm so sorry, dearest friend."

The tear-filled eyes rested on Cara. "How can I endure this? I don't want to live."

Cara squeezed her hand. "Don't talk nonsense. You have a lot to live for. You were pregnant once, surely you'll—"

Penelope's head shook. "No, the doctor said I suffered too much damage. I'll never get to hold my baby in my arms. Oh, Cara, my heart's breaking. I can't face—"

Her arm rose to cover her eyes, and Cara had no words of comfort. Penelope's prospects of another baby didn't look good. Cara had experienced the heartache of losing a child she'd held and loved. Penelope would never have that opportunity.

"What about adoption?"

Penelope didn't bother moving her arm, but her head shook. "You know the group's policy on adoption. *Nonexistent.* If I can't give Kenny a boy, Elder Simmons will find a woman who can. I'll never get another chance to birth my own child."

Cara's heart thumped, blocking her breathing until she thought she'd not be able to draw another breath. The hurt inside expanded, squeezing until she could hardly bear her friend's tragedy. How Penelope managed to hang on was beyond her.

When Penelope dropped off to sleep, Cara stepped out of the room and found a telephone to call Cassie, her occasional child-sitter. Replacing the receiver, she heard low voices coming from around the corner.

"I didn't mean to hit her. She nagged me not to do my duty last night until I thought I'd lose my mind. Crazy woman. Worthless, that's what she is."

"Good for one thing only, women are, if you get what I mean," the second man chuckled. "Don't worry, Lewis. I'm not going after you. If she'd kept her place, this wouldn't have happened. Gotta keep them in their place."

Kenny Lewis was talking about his wife. Who was he talking to? Elder Simmons? Or another so-called friend?

Had he somehow caused Penelope's fall?

"I'm tired of her. Tired of the constant fuss. Tired of being clung to every time I want to do something. Women are a pain, chief."

The voices drew closer. Cara's lips tightened, and she kept her back to them as the man and their chief of police walked by, still talking and paying her no mind.

She glared at their backs. Even if she'd wanted to, going to the chief would be pointless. He was as bad as the rest.

She hurried back to Penelope's room and settled into a chair beside the bed. Penelope's eyes opened.

"Did you have a good rest?"

Penelope ignored the question and gripped Cara's arm. "I don't want the doctor to take any special measures. If I'm going to die, I don't want them to prolong my agony. Promise me you'll make them do as I want."

"Penelope, they won't listen to me. They've taken an oath and have to do their best for you." Cara stroked her friend's hand. "Besides, you're not going to die."

"No. If I live, I'll live on my own. If I don't, I won't have all kinds of procedures done." Her lips pressed together. "I'm paralyzed from the waist down, and the doctor's unsure if it's temporary and whether I'll ever walk again. What kind of life will I have? For a woman?"

"What happened? How did you fall?"

Penelope's restless hands plucked at the sheet. Her head shook in frustrated denial. "I don't know. Kenny and I argued. He said he was going out, and I knew what he meant."

Hanging with the other elders? Or taking time with some other female?

"I begged him not to go. I pushed too hard, because I saw the anger flare in his eyes and thought he'd hit me."

"He didn't?"

"I clung to him, crying, when he went downstairs, and—and I tripped over something on the floor. I was falling and woke up here. They said Kenny brought me in."

"Did Kenny shove you?"

Bewilderment clouded her eyes. "I don't know. I can't remember. I'm all mixed up in my head."

"I don't want to lose you." Cara struggled to control her shaking voice.

Penelope patted her hand, and a rueful smile flitted across her lips. "Of all our friends, you've always been my favorite. You want to know why?"

Cara blinked away the moisture in her eyes and shook her head. "I mean, yes, I want to know."

"Because you're your own person. No one ever made you believe anything you didn't want to. You fought for what you wanted or thought was right, even when you were punished afterward. I wanted to be like you but wasn't strong enough. None of us were."

"Stubbornness and my natural-born rebellion came out any time I felt restrained unjustly." Cara grimaced.

"Probably a distinct possibility." Penelope's voice softened and grew drowsy. "Mary Ann is an adoring, lazy, but happy woman. I'm glad she has Josh. He's a good man, and I like him. Their relationship will last."

Cara opened her mouth to give her own input, but Penelope motioned her to keep quiet. "I'm feeling stronger. Let me talk for a while. Afterward, I'll tell you what I want you to do."

"I'll do whatever you want."

"Abby, on the other hand, is the sweetest, most timid person I've ever seen. It's too bad she's married to such a jerk. In another, better world, Richard might have been able to overcome his smallness." She stopped and drew in several long breaths.

Cara frowned. Should she stop Penelope's rambling?

"I don't know if he'll ever change, but Abby will never be happy married to someone like him. Wouldn't it have been wonderful seeing her with a good man, someone who loved and cherished her? She would have been a beautiful example of a perfect mother and wife."

"I didn't know you were such a philosopher."

"I'd make a good one, huh?"

"Have you ever thought what might have been if we weren't in our group?" Cara whispered.

"Not much. I've always tried not to because I've been convinced we were doing God's will." She closed her eyes. "It's only the last couple of months I've had these—indecent thoughts."

"Indecent because we want to be loved and respected?" How brainwashed does a person have to be to believe this nonsense? She couldn't blame Penelope. Hadn't she gone along with the doctrine of the Children of Righteous Cain? Not because of her own belief but because of the gentle MacFarland couple who'd taken in an orphaned child and loved her like their own.

Penelope's eyes opened, pain-filled. "I think I must be a bad person, Caralynne. I've tried to accept God's will. Kenny is an elder and as such is responsible to help our girls understand our teachings. But I can't. I get so angry I don't want him around anyone but me. Am I the most selfish person in our group?"

"No, you're not. I think you're reacting normally." Her chest ached as she fought back the tears.

"How would you know what normal is? That's hardly your forte."

"Kenny?" How had he gotten in the room without her hearing him? How much had he heard?

He thrust his face inches from hers, and Cara pulled back.

"Why are you bothering my wife?"

Penelope whimpered. "She's not—bothering me. Please let her stay."

"You don't know what you want." He flipped a glance at the pale woman on the bed then riveted Cara with an accusing glare. "I never did like you. I saw rebellion in you as a sassy child. Donald had his hands full."

How much rage filled the man? "Why do you hate me? I haven't ever done anything to you." Cara gaped at the man.

He propped one hand on the back of her chair. "Hate you? I don't hate you. I don't like you. I've always wanted to wipe the perpetual smirk off your lips."

"I don't have a smirk on my face." How dare the man?

He chuckled, an unfriendly sound. "Not right now, but only because you're afraid."

Too true. Fear enveloped her when she dealt with the elders. But being nervous about catching their unwanted attention didn't mean she wouldn't fight. She bit back the stutter of denial trying to escape.

"Kenny?" Penelope reached for him.

Kenny ignored his wife's plea. "It'd take a strong hand to break your will. If I'd had my way back then, you'd be different now. Reverend MacFarland's father stood in the way. Well, he's not here now. I'll—"

Cara ducked under his arm to stand at the bottom of the bed. Black rings circled Penelope's pain-filled eyes. Her friend tried to shift her position.

"Are you all right, Penelope? Should I call a nurse?" How could she be all right when her husband talked like Kenny did?

"No." Penelope winced. "I'll be okay. Kenny, please hold my hand."

Kenny straightened and looked at Penelope. "You need to sleep."

"I need you."

He'd refuse. She knew it.

He flipped a hand at Cara. "Sure thing. You can leave us now. I want to tend to my wife."

Cara hated to, but when her friend's eyes brightened, she left. Perhaps, in spite of his earlier words, Kenny would try to do his best for her.

❦❦❦

Cara wrapped the leftover fish filets in a baggie and tucked them into the fridge. Donald had caught them earlier in the spring. If he'd owned any redeeming quality, his provision for them had been the one. They'd never gone hungry. Her appetite had been gone many a time, but not for lack of food.

The fish and the corn casserole she'd made for the postponed workday at the Lewises' had made a delicious supper. Leila and Lacy giggled from the front porch, and love expanded Cara's heart for these two creatures of hers. They might not have been conceived in love, but her love couldn't have been greater for them. She was eternally grateful for her girls.

She wondered how Penelope was doing and wished she could slip back to the hospital after the girls were in bed. Cassie refused to make another trip out here today. She'd have to switch to Plan B.

Cara stepped out onto the porch, and Leila looked up. "What's wrong?"

How had the child known she was bothered?

"Nothing, sweetie. Want to take a walk?"

Toys scattered as the two bounded to their feet.

"We'll have to be very quiet." Cara knelt in front of them. "Can you do that for mommy? Lacy, promise."

Lacy jumped up and down, her head bobbing. Leila frowned. "Aren't we walking on our path?"

"Not tonight. I want to check on some things. We'll have fun though. Remember, quiet."

"Do we get a reward for being good?" Lacy's eyes—the image of her own—widened.

"Don't coax." Cara laughed and tweaked her daughter's nose. "Run and get your shoes on."

The moon was bright again tonight, which would make for easy walking. She'd have to make sure the girls didn't talk while she did her surveying.

One hand from each girl held onto hers. Cara thrilled again at the pleasure these two babies gave her. How fast they grew up. Too fast.

Only a few houses lined her lane, and the Lewises' was one of them. She'd like to see what Kenny was up to while Penelope lay in the hospital. She tightened her lips even as she answered one of Lacy's never-ending questions.

"Listen, Mommy, do you hear a willie will?"

"It's whippoorwill, sweetie."

"That's what I said." Lacy tugged on Cara's hand. "I wanna go to our pond."

"Not tonight. We're going a different direction. We'll go soon though, I promise."

The lights from the two-story house blazed into the yard. Cara paused fifty feet away and stared. The faint sound of laughter barely reached her ears. Was Kenny entertaining company?

She'd love to get a closer look, but she wouldn't leave the girls. Not in the dark. She'd not be able to get anywhere near the place. If she learned anything, it would have to come from observation. Another ten feet or so shouldn't hurt anything, though.

Beside a large oak at the edge of the yard, she settled Leila and Lacy beside her.

"Leila, will you help Lacy count the stars? Keep her quiet, will you?" Cara touched Leila's shoulder and patted her youngest daughter's head. "Lacy, be very quiet for Mommy, okay?"

Two young heads tilted to view the starlit sky.

A burst of female giggles jerked her attention back to the Lewis house. Silhouetted against the front window, two people, arms wrapped around each other, clung together. Cara squinted, trying to make out who. Kenny, for sure, but the other one?

She stepped around the tree, hoping to see better.

"What are you doing here?"

Cara thought she jumped two feet off the ground. She squealed but clapped a hand mid-scream over her mouth. Jerking around, she glared at Dayne.

"Why are you sneaking up on me? Surely you're not following me. You scared me."

"Sorry, no." Dayne spoke in a low voice. "Didn't mean to frighten you. I saw you from the road and wanted to make sure you were all right."

She still couldn't quite forgive him for scaring her. "Why wouldn't I be? I can take care of myself."

"I know." He knelt and whispered, "How are the girls tonight?"

"I counted ten stars," Lacy whispered in a voice meant to be quiet.

"I counted a hundred." Leila cast a glance of superiority toward her sister. "But I'm helping Lacy count more."

"Very good," Dayne agreed and held a finger to his lips. "Shh."

When he rose to his feet again, Cara demanded, "Why are you here?"

"Getting in the jogging I've been neglecting and thought I might stop at Kenny's. See if he needed anything."

Cara jerked her head toward the Lewis house. "Doesn't look like he needs anything from us. Seems to be fending very well, considering his wife is suffering in the hospital."

"He could have company cavorting there. It doesn't have to be the man with another woman. Sure it's Kenny?"

"Who else could it be?" Cara glared at the house. "Will you go check?"

"I don't know. Too much like eavesdropping."

Who cared? "Will you stay here for a couple minutes while I check?"

"Cara, no. What if he sees you?"

"I'll tell him I stopped by to see how Penelope's doing."

"Why must you know?" Dayne rubbed a day's worth of beard on his chin. "What difference does it make tonight?"

"Dayne, please." Cara touched his arm. "I care very much for Penelope and hurt when I know Kenny doesn't really love her. Don't make me leave the girls by themselves." Unfair threat, because she wasn't about to leave her girls alone. But Dayne didn't know that.

"Go, but be careful and hurry."

Cara didn't give him a chance to change his mind. She ran lightly across the lawn until she was beneath the window but standing in the shadow of a bush. She had no problem identifying the people who obviously didn't care about being seen.

Kenny Lewis. Tabitha Tobert, the fifteen-year-old daughter of Angus Tobert. Through the open window, Cara could hear the disgusting moans and murmurs. Was he staking his claim for his next wife?

She should knock on the window. Call out to Kenny. Disturb his tryst. Would he care? Probably not.

She stepped away from the bush as a dark maroon sedan pulled into the driveway, the lights sweeping over the front of the house. Cara drew back into the bush, cowering. Who on earth was this?

Two men stepped from the car, and Cara's heart threatened to sink to her stomach.

Elder Simmons and his right-hand man, Angus Tobert. Coming to check up on the girl? Or other business? Whatever, she was in a fine fix. She hoped Dayne stayed put and kept the girls quiet. If Lacy started crying, the die would be cast. That young lady didn't quit until her mother fixed whatever bothered her.

Cara strained her ears to catch any sounds of discomfort coming from the edge of the lawn, but nothing disturbed the night air except the conversation of the two men approaching. They paused beside the bush, and Cara shrank even farther behind it.

"He didn't waste any time." The smug satisfaction in Elder Simmons's voice grated on Cara's nerves.

"Why should he? Tabitha's been trained very well. She'll make a good wife for Kenny."

Elder Simmons rubbed his fat hands together. "I think I made the right choice for him. He's been restless, and she's young enough to keep him interested for a long time. We'll need to set the date for his marriage in the next few days."

Meaning, *he* would. Cara clenched her fists. She didn't know Tabitha well, but what she'd observed, she didn't like. The girl was too filled with her own importance.

A whimper reached her ears, and Cara wanted to pass out from nervousness. Was Lacy ready to launch a full-blast wail?

Breath held, she settled her attention on the men again.

"What about Sister Lewis?"

Elder Simmons snorted. "What about her? A nagging, infertile woman is never a benefit to anyone. The Lord's will shall be done."

Yeah, that's right, blame it on God. The self-righteous tone sent her ire somewhere around the nearest star.

"Sister Lewis has already served any possible usefulness." Elder Simmons peered at Angus. "It's time for Brother Lewis to move on."

What did he mean?

Angus chuckled. "I'm sure you've got all the details worked out."

"The Lord revealed to me this afternoon what path Brother Lewis should follow to terminate their marriage and keep down any suspicion."

Even through the moonlight, the glow of fanaticism flared in Angus's narrow-set eyes. He licked his lips. "What path?"

"You need to cultivate patience, Angus Tobert. You'll know soon enough. But I will say this: accidents are a blessing from God."

Elder Simmons stomped onto the porch, motioning for Tobert to keep up. He lifted a heavy hand and pounded on the door, and seconds later, Kenny appeared in the doorway.

"Elder Simmons. Brother Tobert." Kenny must not have been expecting company, judging from the surprise in his breathless voice.

"Brother Lewis." Elder Simmons wiped a hand across his forehead. "How's your evening progressing?"

The self-satisfied smirk smeared across Kenny's face sickened Cara.

"Good, good. The best in a long time."

The uncaring beast. Cara tensed, ready to spring forth in defense of her friend.

"We need to talk."

"Not now, Elder Simmons." Kenny tilted his head in the direction of the girl who lurked right behind him. "I hope not about Penelope."

"Of course. We've come about Penelope."

Kenny sagged. "She's better?"

"Brother Lewis, inside. Tobert, you and Tabitha stay on the porch—"

Time to vamoose before they saw her. Cara backed away, her eyes on the men. She skirted the low bushes and dodged a small flowerbed. Bending low, she checked to see if anyone noticed. When no alarm sounded, she gulped in a huge breath and took off, trotting across the yard, intent on getting to the woods as quickly as she could.

And tripped over something. A startled oomph spilled from her when she landed face down on the wet grass. Water splattered her back and legs as the water hose wiggled around like a snake gone crazy, spraying any object or person within its range. A bellow of rage tore through the air. A wet Elder Simmons descended the porch steps and headed her way. Did she have time to dig a hole big enough to hide in?

She unwound the sprinkling hose entangling her and struggled to her feet. Elder Simmons and his sidekick sloshed through the wet grass and the still-spraying hose while a shriek of rapidly escalating unhappiness pierced the air.

Her heart hit the bottom of her feet at the speed of a racecar. Lacy was making her unhappiness known to the world at large, and specifically her mother. Unfortunately, Elder Simmons and his unpleasant henchman were getting an earful.

The men turned as one and stared in the direction of the childish crying.

She hoped Dayne would hightail it out of here, but no such luck. His tall figure even now strode toward her, Lacy—hiccupping her heart-wrenching sobs—held in his arms, and Leila skipping along beside him, chattering as if it was the most normal thing in the world.

Cara cringed and wished a magical door would appear for escape. Would God forgive her if she ran?

She stepped forward as Dayne approached, and she gathered her youngest close. Her shushing noises drowned out the grunts of disapproval coming from the vicinity of her elders.

"Are you all right?" Dayne spoke in a low voice.

Time for a rapid getaway. Cara, patting her child's back, edged away.

"What are you doing here?" Elder Simmons's voice stopped her as effectively as a suddenly built wall.

"Going home?" Cara wished she couldn't see his expression, the fat lips pressed together. But the moon, in a twisted comedic trick, spotlighted his face, every nuance of his features revealed. He obviously did *not* appreciate her attempt at humor.

"I will ask you one more time. What are you doing here?" He motioned at Leila, who gripped Dayne's shirt with one hand, interest glowing from her big eyes. "Exposing these children to the elements. Shame. Have you no sense of propriety?"

Elements? What was the fool talking about? Did he consider the water hose an element? Cara bit her lip and wanted to take up the howling where Lacy left off. If only.

"I think I can explain," Dayne offered. "Let me hold her again for you, Cara."

No way. For whatever foolish reason, she assumed Elder Simmons wouldn't strike her while she held a child. No way would she release her.

"You." Elder Simmons twisted toward Dayne and snapped, "Are you in the habit of meeting *this* woman at *this* time of the night?"

This woman? What kind of woman was he talking about? Cara eased her chin skyward.

Dayne's face reflected his distaste. "I'm used to jogging this time of the night. Cara, the girls, and I stopped to check out the stars. We both wanted to see how Sister Lewis is doing."

Another grunt. Disbelief? Or disgust?

Was it bad luck or God's sense of humor to allow Kenny Lewis, Tabitha in tow, to show up at that minute? His incoherent sputters made little sense.

Elder Simmons raised a hand. "Slow down, Brother Lewis. Reverend MacFarland merely wanted to speak about your wife."

"What about her?" He pointed as he spat out the words, contempt in every word. "She's spying on me. Was at the hospital today spouting nonsense about independence to my wife."

"I see." A knowing glance her way.

"Talking about adoption and stirring her up. I don't want to adopt some other man's child. I want my own."

"What were you thinking?" Elder Simmons hissed at her. "There's absolutely no need to use artificial means of attaining children. You know our policy."

"But I wanted to comfort her. She's bleeding inside from the loss of her child. I wanted to give her hope that she might someday hold a child of her own."

Elder Simmons lowered his head like a bull ready to charge. "God's plan will prevail. If he'd wanted, she would have carried a healthy child to birth. Women are to accept his judgments without murmur or complaint."

"It's too harsh. Our women can't bear childlessness. Holding a child is the one bright spot in their lives," Cara cried out, willing these men to hear. If women couldn't bear children, they were nothing. Useless. Old relics to be tossed aside.

"Another form of rebellion. A lie the devil uses to cause strife between a husband and his wife." The fervor burning inside Elder Simmons turned his eyes to glowing orbs of fanaticism.

No. No. No. How could anyone be so deceived?

"But—"

"Deal with her, Elder Simmons. We don't want her interfering in our plans. She's an insubordinate wretch who's a bad influence on the other women. Penelope is enough of a handful." Kenny stepped closer and glared at Cara. "Give her to me. I'll kill that streak right out of her."

"Brother Lewis." Dayne stepped in front of the man and one hand rose. Cara saw the balled fist, the clenched muscles in his jaw.

The preacher was going to knock Kenny down. Cara's heart leaped to her throat. He'd championed her, but the uncertainty for the consequences was too much too bear. What would Elder Simmons do if Dayne knocked the obnoxious Lewis on his hind end? Uncertainty won. "Dayne, could you hold Lacy now?"

For another second, he stared at the man who'd insulted her. Then fists unclenched and a firm jaw relaxed. With a quiet mutter, he scooped Lacy from Cara's arms.

The breath left Cara's body in a whoosh.

Elder Simmons straightened and made another swipe across his forehead, obviously on edge as much as she.

Cara stared at the man's glistening face.

"Things are looking up for you, aren't they? Trust God and your leader, Brother Lewis," Elder Simmons blustered.

A weak response. He tugged Tabitha closer. "You're right."

"Now. You." Elder Simmons tapped his lips. "I have about reached my limit of patience, Sister Hayman. I think we won't wait until Friday. I'd better deal with you tonight. I'll have Sister Raymond pick up your girls at my house while we're—uh, communing."

"No. Cassie will care for them." Fear pierced like an arrow. No way did she want Kathy Raymond anywhere near her girls.

His eyes narrowed at her protest. "I think not. I have our departed Brother Hayman to think of, and he would want his girls' souls protected. Sister Raymond will be good for them."

"Please—"

Dayne stepped closer, his voice full of determination. "They need to be in their own bed. I'll look after them."

Cara swallowed. Dayne could be a lifeline for her while Elder Simmons and whomever he dragged from their beds did their worst. But not at the risk of Leila and Lacy in Kathy Raymond's hands. As much as she'd like Dayne to go along, Leila and Lacy were first.

The man nodded, but not as if he agreed. For once Cara could read him like a book. A hint of a subtle idea played inside his evil mind. He slapped a hand on Dayne's shoulder. "I thought you might like to be in on this, but I can see where these children should be more of a concern for you. Good thinking, Reverend."

"Cara?" Dayne lowered his voice. "Do you have somewhere else you'd rather the girls stay? Jodie? Mary Ann?"

What to do? She stared down into Leila's anxious eyes and touched Lacy's back, her hands shaking. Her friends would never harm the children, but what would they do if commanded to give them up? Did trust go that far?

"No, watch over them until I get home. I'll be all right."

Dayne whispered, "Sure? You might need me."

She gripped his hand. "Don't leave them."

"I'm worried for you. I should be there." He squeezed her hand.

For a long moment she stared at her sleeping child, her throat closed. She knelt and pulled Leila in close for a hug and whispered in her ear. "Will you be a good girl for Mommy and mind Dayne? Remember all I've taught you, Leila, and help Lacy to behave. Promise me."

"Can I go too? I'll be very quiet." Leila's troubled eyes begged her for permission.

"You can't, my precious. But you can help me by doing what I ask. You like Dayne, don't you?"

A hesitant nod.

"He'll not leave you until I get home. Elder Simmons and I need to talk for a bit. When you wake in the morning, I'll be there. Okay?"

Leila frowned. "Mommy—"

"Let's go, Sister Hayman. Now." Elder Simmons poked a finger in her back.

Cara ignored the pain from the poke and squeezed her daughter tighter. She should grab her girls and run for the farthest state. Better yet—another country. Leave. Hide.

They would catch her. The thoughts of Renee Holderfield—a runaway wife—enveloped her mind, and she shivered. The woman disappeared. No one ever spoke of her or confessed any knowledge of her. No, she couldn't take a chance.

Her shoulders sagged, and she loosened her grip on her daughter. "I love you."

"Mommy? Don't leave me. I'm afraid."

Angus Tobias grabbed Cara's arm and jerked. "Time to go."

"Easy. You don't have to tear her arm off," Dayne snapped. He called after her as Angus pulled her along. "I'll either come pick you up or send someone in a half hour."

Cara's heart leaped.

"No need. I'll make sure she gets home all right." Elder Simmons motioned for Angus to go on.

The two white faces staring after the maroon sedan were the last thing Cara saw before the tears spilled down her face.

CHAPTER FOURTEEN

Dayne had not the slightest clue what was involved in putting a child to bed, let alone two. The sleeping girl in his arms didn't stir. Surely it wouldn't hurt for her to sleep in her clothes one night. He struggled to pull down the covers enough to deposit Lacy onto the bed. The child stirred but didn't wake while he removed her shoes and pulled the covers over her.

Leila, sitting cross-legged by the doorway, spoke. "Mommy doesn't do it that way."

Great. Now she told him.

"How does Mommy put Lacy to bed?" If he wasn't mistaken, the girl had called her mother 'mom' on other occasions. Why the more childlike term now?

"She always lets us pick out our jammies, and she tucks Sassy in Lacy's bed too." Leila's voice bordered on accusation.

"Well, Lacy's already asleep, and I don't think we'd better wake her. Who's Sassy?" He eyed the small room for the doll.

"Sassy is Lacy's favorite." Leila picked up a worn, spotted puppy. "She can't sleep without him."

"How about if we tuck Sassy right beside her?" He lifted the cover enough to lay the stuffed animal beside Lacy. He took Leila's hand. "Well, what say we let Lacy sleep as she is while you and I go raid the fridge?"

Leila's eyes widened. "Can we?"

"I don't think your mother will mind too much tonight."

Leila's face sobered. "When's Mommy coming home?"

Dayne pulled her close to his side as they walked into the kitchen. "Soon. Don't you worry about your mother. She's a tough lady."

"Mommy taught me how to be tough." Leila's head bobbed.

"She did? What did she teach you?" Dayne opened the fridge to check out the contents.

"She told me to kick a man in his crotch if he touched me."

His gaze flew to Leila's face.

The child settled at the table and rested her chin on her fist. Her brown eyes were filled with perfect innocence.

"Uh, good." He faced the fridge again and reached inside to lift the cover from a casserole dish. "What have we here?"

"Mommy's cherry mountain pie. It's good."

Dayne sniffed. Hmm. Smelled delicious. Leila would enjoy a few bites as a treat and maybe take her mind off her mother.

In spite of his assurances to Leila, he wasn't at all sure Cara would be all right. He didn't trust the elders, specifically Elder Simmons. They wouldn't hurt her, would they, knowing he might show up? But they counted on him being stuck at Cara's home. They'd hope he'd be out of the way.

Dayne set a bowl on the table. "Leila, could you spoon yourself some pie into this bowl while I make a phone call?"

While Leila was busy, he pulled out his phone and walked into the front room. If he could get hold of Cassie, he'd hightail it down to the sanctuary and get Cara as soon as he could.

The darkened front room cloaked his worry as he stared into the night, his finger punching in the number by memory. The ringing phone was the only sound in the silence. The moon slid from behind a cloud, and Dayne saw movement at the wood line toward the edge of the property. A deer?

He strained his eyes. To the left, in his peripheral vision he caught another quick movement.

Dayne slapped shut his cell as a sleepy voice mumbled a hello at the other end. He turned and trotted to the kitchen. "Leila, I want you to go to your bedroom now. Go, child."

Her eyes questioned him but she did as he asked.

"Keep quiet, and I'll check on you in a few minutes. Good girl."

He heard her climbing the stairs, the door of her room open and shut. Flipping off the kitchen light, Dayne counted to ten then slid out the back door. He hesitated for a second. Lock it or leave it unlocked? If he needed back in quickly ...

He wouldn't go out of sight of the house. He'd leave it unlocked.

Dayne slipped across the dark porch and down the two steps. Pausing, he listened. Brush crackled, a few night birds hooted, but no voices reached him. Had his imagination played tricks on him through his worry for Cara?

The woods brooded dark and heavy. Dayne gave his eyes time to adjust to the black of the night. When he could make out objects, he ducked toward the closest tree, kept his breathing even and quiet, and listened again.

The noise of scuffling feet—whoever they were—unused to walking in the woods at night, floated toward him. To an experienced woodsman, their movements were as clumsy as an ox treading through a well-tended garden. Dayne shifted slightly until he faced the sounds and saw him coming.

When the man stopped beside the tree, Dayne grabbed him in a headlock, jerked him close, and asked, "What are you doing?"

The man choked out a moan, and Dayne swung him around to be identified.

The moonlight revealed Glenn Leonard, one of the newer elders in the group. Dayne gave the man a shake. "Answer me."

Glenn rubbed a hand across his mouth and cowered when Dayne grabbed his shirt front. "Talk."

"What do you mean, jumping me?" he whined.

"Why are you skulking around Cara Hayman's property?"

Dayne saw the quick sly grin come and go on the man's face. His sulky answer followed. "Elder Simmons sent me to keep an eye on the place."

"On me?"

Glenn held up his cell phone. "Yeah, I was to call if you took off and—"

"What? Glenn, I want to know all."

"If you left, we were to grab the girls."

"I wouldn't leave them alone."

"I know."

The tone, the hint of knowing something he wasn't telling angered Dayne. He gave the man another shake. "What?"

"I don't know anything else."

The dark forest hid the wild creatures' rustling but fed his imagination as he wondered at Elder Simmons and his crooked reasoning. He pulled the man closer and demanded, "Who else is here? Who's the other snoop?"

"Marshall Biggs."

"Where is he?"

"He said he was going to look around. Told me to stay here."

Dayne debated. He had half a notion to lock the two up until morning, but he couldn't blame them. Elder Simmons gave the orders, and men like Glenn and Marshall did the dirty work. "Go home and don't you ever step foot on this property again."

"But Elder—"

"Forget him for now. I'll take care of Elder Simmons. I want you out of here, do you hear me?"

The man stumbled backward and disappeared into the night. Dayne stayed where he was until he heard the distant sound of a car engine. A childish scream rent the air and drowned out the car sound.

The girls. Marshall Biggs must have sneaked into the house while he was occupied.

He sprinted back to Cara's home.

The lights were still out, but Leila's screams and Lacy's loud crying split the air in a continual rhythm—not terror, but anger. He took the two porch steps in one leap as the man slammed open the door and struggled out. He held Lacy under his left arm, and his right hand gripped the back of Leila's top.

It could have been a funny scene, the sight of Leila kicking and flailing her arms, beating at him, and screeching her frightened protest.

If he hadn't been so angry.

"Shut up. I'm not going to hurt you," Marshall hissed.

"You let go of my sister," Leila ordered.

Dayne chopped the man's right arm, slid Lacy out from under his other arm, and gave both girls a gentle shove toward the door. "In the house, Leila."

The man swung a fist and connected with Dayne's eye. Staggering back, Dayne shook his head, fighting off the stars in his vision. He blocked the next jab and sent a left-handed punch into Marshall's gut. The man bent double and offered a half-hearted swing at Dayne's head again, but Dayne ducked the punch and flipped the man backward over his hip and out into the yard.

The man yelped as he hit the ground and rolled over. Dayne jumped over the low porch rail and landed beside Marshall. He knelt down, grabbed his shirtfront, and pulled him up until he stared into his face. "I know why you're here, and I want you off this property."

"Elder Simmons—"

"Elder Simmons, what?" Dayne bit back the rage bubbling inside him.

"He ordered me to take the girls to his house."

The rage rumbled. "Why? Answer me, Biggs."

"I don't know."

"Yes, you do. Don't lie to me."

"He said Cara needed to suffer in a way that will bring her rebellion under control."

Dayne leaped to his feet, dragging the man up. "You leave and don't ever come back here. *That* is an order from me. If I ever see you around here again, so help me, God and I will punish you. Do you understand?"

The man's nod was convincing.

Dayne watched as he trotted off, not looking back. Elder Simmons was determined to mete out punishment on Cara. How far would he go?

But the more important question was: how far would Dayne himself go to rescue his love?

The stars in the sky were cold and mute. No answers there.

❧❦❧

Cara rode in the back of Elder Simmons's car. Going to prison couldn't be any scarier than this. The head elder ignored both his driver and Cara as he barked orders into his cell phone.

"We'll meet in fifteen minutes. Be prepared for disciplinary session one."

Disciplinary session one? Didn't sound inviting. Her stomach tightened as if being twisted into two balloon knots. Her head thumped at Angus' erratic driving.

When they pulled into the sanctuary parking lot, she counted cars. One, two, five, ten cars. Ten elders waited for her arrival.

The car doors slammed. Angus' faded eyes peered in the back passenger window, and Cara shrank back from his look of malicious delight. He jerked open the door and motioned for her to exit. She slid her feet to the blacktop pavement, but before she could straighten, Angus yanked on her arm. Cara half-screamed at the pain shooting through her shoulder and stumbled forward.

"Stand up."

Fighting the urge to sink to her knees, Cara gritted her teeth, drew back a leg, and kicked. Her foot landed with a satisfying thud.

Angus screamed and bent over.

Elder Simmons—halfway up the sidewalk, jerked around, took in the scene, and snarled. "Can't you do anything right? Get her in here. Now."

Face twisted, he gripped her arm in a bruise-producing crush. She kept pace beside Angus as he fast-trotted after Elder Simmons.

He rushed her down the corridor toward the back of the sanctuary and hustled her down the stairs. Cara caught the rail to guide her descent. She wouldn't put it past the old goat to push her to her death.

They stepped into the basement, and a light flashed on, blinding her. She lifted a hand to block out the worst as Angus disappeared beyond the brightness.

"Sister Hayman."

Elder Simmons. Did these baboons think this stupidity a game? If they were trying to scare the pee out of her, they were succeeding.

She shivered, from not only the chill in the basement, but from the thought of what was in store.

"You are charged with blasphemy of God's orders."

"I haven't—"

"You have defied God, your elders, and the group's rules. We demand you now accept your punishment in good faith, proving you are willing to be guided by God's men and that your attitude and heart have repented."

She closed her eyes. Did they expect her to scream, "Goody"? Prostrate herself before them? In that case, they might as well use the ancient sword hanging in the worship center to slay her.

The light switched off, and dazzled by the sudden darkness, she swayed. Rough hands pushed her to her knees. Outraged voices—deep and loud—bellowed in her ears.

"Repent!" For what?

"Punish her!" Threatening.

"Evil woman!" A lie.

The shouts were screams of outrage. She strained her ears to hear whose voices spoke. Elder Simmons's roar for sure, and she recognized Angus' usual whining tone. The third one—a ripple of pure terror curled her fingers. The voice from her own personal hell rumbled in her ear.

Donald Hayman. He'd come back to life. Someone else had been buried in that cheap casket thirty-five days ago to foist the idea of his death. God was playing another cruel trick on her.

Cara jerked her head to the left to catch a glimpse of the figure, but he was too quick. Twisting, she screamed his name. "What are you doing here? You're dead."

The Donald Hayman she'd known for thirteen years had never been that fast.

"When we're done with you, you'll be begging for marriage, you wench."

Elder Simmons, for sure. A hand reached from the darkness, gripped a handful of hair, and jerked her head back. Another hand wrapped around her throat, and as quickly the owners sifted into the dark again.

Black silhouettes pranced. Cara's vision blurred, and she blinked. The crack of a whip streaked by her in a rapid rush of air, and Cara screamed. Fear tore at her lungs and stole the breath from her body. Her mind spun faster and faster. Total blackness washed over her and tumbled her head over heels into blessed quiet, away from the dreadful whip and the men who enjoyed using it.

❧❀☙

"Hey, Will. I'm calling in that favor you owe me." Dayne held his cell against his shoulder.

"Who is this?"

The voice was deeper, older, but it was the same boyhood friend he'd known years ago.

"See what happens when a person goes away for a few years. Even best friends forget them," Dayne prodded.

"Dayne? Dayne MacFarland, is that you? Are you back in this neck of the woods?"

"Yeah, and I need your help. Are you busy?"

"I'm on duty, driving down Route 35 right now."

"Good. I don't suppose you remember about the church group my parents were in."

A hesitation. "I remember. Rumors float around now and then. What's up?"

If he carried this out, there might be more repercussions than he'd bargained for. Yet Cara was in a den of—he had to take the chance. Whatever the consequences.

"I need a favor. Can you meet me at the sanctuary?"

"Is something wrong?" Will's voice sharpened.

Here was the tricky part. "I'm not sure I can't handle the situation, but I want your authority to back me up, in case—"

"I get you. I'll call in the troops."

"No, not unless you have to."

"I need to know what's going on. I can't go in blindsided."

"Can you trust me this once? I'd rather not go into it. If the trouble doesn't warrant your attention, then all the better. But just in case I'd like you there."

"I'm on duty, Dayne. If I see something illegal …"

"I know that, and I don't expect anything less."

"Good. You want a quiet, low-profile approach or should I come in sirens blaring?"

"Let's try the siren approach. Might make more impact."

"One other thing. Will they come out to see what's going on—or should I storm the fort? Sorry, I mean church." Will snickered.

"Let them come to you."

"Okay. So when they come out, what am I to say? Stopped by to see how everyone was doing?"

That was Will. Always the jokester. "Tell them you received a call to check out the sanctuary, and you wanted to make sure everything was all right."

"Gotcha." Silence bled through the air. "It's good to hear from you, even if I have to pay the favor I've already returned a half-dozen times."

"Yeah, right."

"Sure nothing illegal is going on I should know about?"

"If I need help, believe me, I'll holler." Not exactly an answer to Will's question.

"See you in a few minutes."

After he turned onto the sanctuary road, Dayne pulled into the parking lot and headed inside. He listened at the top of the stairs. Angry voices. The crack of a whip. Not reassuring.

He slipped down the steps and headed for the basement conference room from where the sounds came. Dayne paused beside the only open door. A spotlight revealed moving figures, and on the floor lay a body.

Cara. Gaze never leaving the weaving men, he slid his hand across the wall and flipped on the lights.

Eight, ten elders stilled as if they were mechanical toys whose batteries suddenly died. Dayne scorched them with a disdainful look. Cara made no movement. No slow lifting of her head. Was she unconscious? *Dead?* He was too late. Too slow in his rescue.

"What are you doing?" He didn't raise his voice, didn't scream, but if his voice was as cold as the ice lodged somewhere close to his heart, it had to be bleeding from his vocal cords. He pressed his fingers against her neck and felt her pulse beating steadily. Relief beat an even thrum through his veins.

"If you can't fulfill your responsibility, then stay out of this, MacFarland," Elder Simmons snarled.

Where had all the goodwill gone? A week ago the man called him "son."

"This woman must learn submission, or all our beliefs are in danger of becoming a mockery. I've been far more patient than usual."

"What have you done to her?" Dayne dropped to his knees and bent over Cara. "I didn't come back here to encourage terror and beatings."

"Why did you come?"

Dayne flicked a glance upward at the man, but his mind made a note of those present. Ten to fifteen in number. More than he'd hoped. Thank God neither Levi nor Josh was present. "You know why."

"You let Sister Hayman influence you. Can't you see what trouble she causes in our midst? If you want to promote love, do it with justice." Elder Simmons's head tilted. The faint sound of a siren penetrated the thick basement walls. "What is that?"

Dayne shrugged. "Sounds like a state police car coming this way. Someone ought to check it out."

"What?" Elder Simmons's eyes flashed fire. "Why are they here?"

He wasn't about to answer. Let Will handle them.

"Brother Tobert, come. If I find out—" His irate voice faded as he trooped up the stairs, Angus at his heels. The rest shifted on their feet, glanced at one another, and eased their way to the stairs.

Good riddance. Dayne gathered Cara into his arms and stared down into her pale face. Smudges beneath her eyes showed the strain in her overtaxed slim body. Thank God the elders left. He didn't want to be responsible for his actions. A few cracked skulls wouldn't bode well for his reputation.

But the longer he watched Cara lying there on the floor, the less he cared about his reputation.

❧❧❧

Cara moaned and struggled away from the gentle, cool hand patting her face. "No. No. Go away. Let me alone."

"Cara, dearest." The caressing voice, the gentle tone stilled her fight. Not Donald. Not Elder Simmons.

No. She jerked away. A wonderful black world lured. Away from the—she focused on the tunnel beckoning her back like a ghostly finger in a mist.

"Cara, come on. Wake up."

Dayne.

Dayne? What was he doing here?

The terror flooded her body again. Her eyes opened, and Dayne's handsome face stared down at her, worry clouding his dazzling blue eyes. Worry for her? He wouldn't have been with that bunch of lunatics, would he? And what was he doing sporting a black eye?

She cast a quick glance around and noted the emptiness of the room. Relief seeped into every pore. Her second glance took in her still-damp clothes. Had the watering hose at Kenny's soaked Elder Simmons as badly? At least no one would know if she had wet herself. A hysterical giggle tickled her insides, but she didn't have the strength to carry it through.

Clutching his shirt, she whispered, "Where are they?"

"Gone. I sent them packing." His breath fanned her cheeks. "This has gone far enough. I can't risk your life to give the elders time to change the way they believe."

She swallowed and sat up but didn't pull away from his arms. He adjusted his hold on her.

"How did you send them packing?"

"My friend, Will, of the state police, showed up at the most opportune time." His lips pressed into a narrow line.

"The—the chief is in on their dirty dealings. I heard him talking to Kenny. If you expect him to help—"

Dayne eyes radiated disturbance. "I didn't. I went beyond him. I wanted a threat of outside cops."

"It took you long enough to get here." Her voice shook.

Dayne tightened his arms. "I came as fast as I could. I took care of some things first and made sure the girls were okay."

The girls. She clutched his arm. "Where are they? You promised to protect them, Dayne."

"Easy. They're fine."

"But—"

"Do you think I'd actually leave them by themselves? I called Cassie."

"She came?"

"No, I dropped them off at her house. I didn't give her a choice."

Cara relaxed back into his arms. "What happened?"

"Exactly what I meant to ask you."

Dayne's muscles rippled beneath her, and in spite of her weakness, Cara's heartbeat jumped into high gear. "They dragged me down here, used a spotlight to blind me, threats and a whip to scare me."

Dayne's frown deepened. "Did they hit you?"

"I guess not. There's no stinging." She touched his arm. "I think they would have. They were very, very angry."

"I'm afraid so." His head sank lower, and his throat constricted as he swallowed. "What if I hadn't come? What if I hadn't come in time?"

"But you did." Cara shrugged and remembered. "Dayne. Donald was here."

"What? What are you talking about?"

"My husband. Donald Hayman."

"Couldn't have been." His eyes searched her face. "Are you sure you're okay?"

"I'm all right. Stressed. Limp as a dead fish. Worried. Scared. But, sure, I'm all right."

This mess wasn't his fault. Why take her nervousness out on him? "I know what I heard. How could I ever forget his voice?"

"Someone's playing tricks on you. I didn't see Donald when I arrived."

Cara rubbed a finger on the crease between her brows. "He slipped out."

"I would have seen. They made so much racket, I'm sure they didn't hear me when I entered. I flipped the light switch and every one of them froze. No one moved."

"You don't believe me."

"I think you're confused. It's easy for your imagination to run wild, given the events tonight."

"I am not imagining Donald." She pushed herself to her feet and stumbled to the stairs. How could he?

"Maybe you dreamed his face."

She tossed a furious glance over her shoulder, pulled herself up the stairs, and when he called after her, she ignored him. He could take his stupid thoughts about her back home and enjoy them. She wouldn't listen anymore.

"What if the elders are still outside?"

Her steps faltered. Were they? What if they tried to drag her back to the basement? She peeked out the exterior doors. Darkness. No sign of anyone. She gave them a push, but the heavy doors refused to open, and when she slammed a fist at them, a hand grabbed her arm. Cara pulled, but Dayne didn't let go even when she glared at him and tilted her head a fraction of an inch higher.

"You silly girl. Stop acting like you're ten years old again."

He peered into her face, but she would not relent.

"Are you going to walk to Cassie's and carry the girls home?"

Cara blinked. The girls. He had her, but she didn't have to let him know it.

"I didn't mean to seem so insensitive."

Well, that was something, but not enough. She held her expression. "I want to believe you."

Better. Cara crossed her arms. "I'm listening."

He cupped her chin. "Can we talk about it again?"

"Do you believe me?"

"I don't know, but I'm willing to be convinced."

His lopsided smile drew her attention. Her breath caught even as she fought to control it. "How can I convince you?"

"Have you thought of this?" Dayne counted off on his fingers. "They may have used a recording of his voice to spook you. If so, we could look around."

Sounded good. "They spooked me—I won't deny it. What else?"

"Did you think the person could have been Emery? Do their voices sound similar?"

Cara laid her forehead on his shoulder. "Why didn't I think of him?"

"See?" Dayne's lips tilted up in a teasing grin. "You need me. He was here."

"Don't get a big head." She propped a shaky hand on her hip. "You haven't proven your worth yet."

"How about this? What about our resident joker?"

"Richard? Was he here?" Doubt squeezed her heart. "He's not good enough to pass for someone else."

"Sure? He's done several decent imitations."

She supposed someone might think Richard's imitations funny, even good. But she didn't. She loathed him.

"And, yes, he was in the back of the group, not participating but watching."

Probably too much of a coward. "Let's look for a recorder."

She headed back down the hall. When she stopped abruptly, Dayne ran into her, and she slid a glance his way, but the question she'd thought to pop already skulked into her sea of forgetfulness. His mirth-ringed eyes were on her, his blue irises dark and intense. Her heart beat like a tom-tom. She grabbed at the wall, swiveled from him, and hurried on.

Bad. This can't keep up. Not if I want to make the elders pay. Priorities, Caralynne, priorities. I can't focus on lo—Dayne, not yet.

"We'll have to skip the office rooms. I'm sure they're locked up tight." Dayne's voice was right behind her, his steady footsteps a pleasing sound.

"We could—"

"Don't even think it."

"Then where?" Cara paused.

"Let's check out the sound room."

Fifteen minutes later, Cara lifted her hands. "I quit. I see nothing. No tapes, no discs."

"Doesn't mean they didn't use a recorder. We haven't found it," Dayne reasoned. "We can check one more place tonight."

Cara followed Dayne down the basement stairs and asked as they stepped onto the carpeted cement floor, "Why are we back down here?"

He held up a hand. "Which way did the voice come from?"

She frowned and thought. "I think it came from there."

Dayne headed toward the file cabinets lined along the nearest wall.

"Elder Simmons's voice came from that direction too."

"So you heard Elder Simmons's voice and Donald's over here?" He reached to the side of one of the file cabinets, pulled something off, and held up a slender black object. "Aha."

"What is it?"

"This, my dear lady, is one of the newest recorders of our day."

"How do you know?"

"I saw some at a technology show in Boston."

"Is this the one they used?"

"It would seem so. Shall I play it?"

Her nerves screamed a protest, but she ignored them and twined her fingers together. "Yes."

Dayne fiddled with the recorder, pressed buttons, and Donald's voice filled her ears.

"You wicked woman!"

She pressed a trembling hand to her mouth. Dayne's hand gripped her arm. His voice came from another world away. "Cara. Are you all right?"

"The voice I heard," she whispered. "That's the one."

Dayne stared down at the black recorder. "I think I'll take this along. Are you ready to go?"

Outside, he tucked her into the passenger seat, moved to his side of the car, and twisted the switch. Shifting into drive, he asked, "Cara, why don't you go away? Why risk this happening again?"

I can't. Not yet. Someone has to pay. Donald's death isn't enough. She stared straight ahead as a knot of bitterness stirred.

"I have friends. I know they'll take you and the girls in until you know what you want to do."

"I couldn't. I won't be dependent on anyone." The monster fist twisting her insides punched deeper.

"You're risking your life, and what about Leila and Lacy? You think you can keep them safe?"

"I can."

"You're a strong woman, but you're no match for a whole bunch of the elders. You'll have no power against their strength. Don't be foolish. How well did you do tonight?"

He was right. She sagged into the back of the seat. Stared into the dark. "I can't go yet. I need a few more days."

"I guess now's the time to tell you what happened earlier this evening."

"Earlier? What are you talking about?"

"Elder Simmons sent Glenn Leonard and Marshall Biggs to your house tonight."

"Why?"

"What do you think? They wanted to scare you by taking the girls."

Cara wrapped her arms around her body and whimpered. What was she going to do? If only—

"Is that how you got the black eye?"

"Yes, but don't worry about me. You need to leave."

She raised a hand and stroked his cheek, touched the skin around his eyes. "Those men hit you while you protected my girls?" He'd done this for her, for her girls. There was no way he could be working against her. Not and suffer a hit like this. "It gives you a roguish look."

"Listen to me." When she didn't answer, he spoke again. Slowly. "Why do you insist on staying? Your reasoning is crazy. In fact, you never give me a good reason. Ever."

Cara's bottom lip quivered and she sucked in her breath.

Steady. I can't let his persuasion influence me. But, oh, how she wanted to.

"Cara, at least promise me you'll think about what I've said. I couldn't stand it if something serious happened to you."

A strong statement. What did he mean? Because … The thought Dayne might care melted the hard lump residing somewhere inside her chest.

"Do you need money? I could—"

"No, thanks. I have Donald's life insurance money coming."

She sensed the questions bubbling inside him. Wondering, probably. She fought back the urge to tell him too much. Saint Dayne versus Sinner Cara. Nope. Wouldn't work. The sooner she forgot him—the sooner she got away from him—the better.

For her.

For him.

CHAPTER FIFTEEN

Cara eyed her perfectly straight rows of early peas. Her mouth watered as her memory recreated the tempting sensation for her: sweet and crisp. The way she liked them. Adding a few of her pearl onions topped the dish. Not everyone cared for peas, but the garden variety was one of her favorites and well worth the work. Too bad June wasn't here.

The handle of her hoe warmed from the sun and her hands. The smooth, round wood comforted her, gave her a sense of satisfying accomplishment. Yet a niggling worm of futility worried her. Would she even be here to enjoy her garden harvest? Maybe. Maybe not.

The horrid scene at the tabernacle the other night scared her. She knew some of the men would have let slip what had happened. Surely one of her friends would have been by to sympathize.

But no calls. No visits.

Warned away?

Dayne's words—his urging—from two nights ago worried her. If he was concerned, shouldn't she be? Pushing the elders, fighting, making them pay—was it worth the risks? What kind of mother was she to risk harm to her girls?

Cara slashed at the tiniest of weeds. Again and again. How dare they invade her garden? Halfway down the row of staked tomato plants, she stopped long enough to gasp for air. This kind of behavior wouldn't work. She needed to stay calm. *Don't think about the danger. Focus. Carry through.*

The pounding from the back porch thumped its way to her. A short, dumpy figure paced on her porch.

"Mary Ann?"

Mary Ann Denuit flew off the porch and ran to her, her mouth open, the sobs erupting from her throat in giant spasms.

"Cara, I'm so glad you're home."

Dropping her hoe, she met Mary Ann at the edge of the garden. Her friend threw herself at Cara and forced her to plant her feet firmly on the soil to keep from being bowled over. Cara wrapped her arms around the woman. "What on earth is the matter? Come on, let's go inside."

Whatever was the matter, a hot cup of tea, regardless of the heat, would do Mary Ann good. Along with a listening ear.

Mary Ann followed Cara's lead, but her hands wrung, tears dripped from her chin.

Cara searched the outlying property and saw no one who could have frightened the woman.

Ensconced on one of her kitchen chairs, a hot cup of tea steaming its fragrance upward toward Mary Ann's worried face, the woman wrapped fingers around the cup. Her sobs eased.

Cara settled across from her. When minutes passed and Mary Ann said nothing, Cara prompted, "Can you talk now? I can't help you if you don't tell me what's wrong."

"I know." Mary Ann lifted her cup, but her hands shook so much, the spoon inside rattled. The cup settled back onto the table.

"I don't know what to do."

That was helpful. "About—?"

Tears pooled in Mary Ann's red-rimmed eyes then created ribbons of moisture down her cheeks. "Valerie."

Mary Ann's precocious daughter. Barely in her teen years, the young girl had a knack at flirting way beyond her years. "Is she sick?"

"No-o-o." The wail wrenched from Mary Ann.

"Was she disobedient? Did Josh have to punish her?"

"No, of course not. Valerie is always obedient. Too much so." Mary Ann shoved away the cup and bent over the table. "It's Elder S—"

Shivers of premonition crept up Cara's back. Mary Ann wasn't upset; she was in agony. What could have reduced this happy-go-lucky woman to a broken mass of humanity?

Elder Simmons. The name slapped at her consciousness. Elder Simmons, his fat hand slithering over Valerie's back, down …

Cara drew back, the horrible image wrapping its icy arms around her body. She sneaked another glance out the window. "Did Elder Simmons hurt her?"

Mary Ann lifted her head, her face blotched red as raw meat. "Not yet. But Valerie's been summoned."

"Summoned?" Cara circled the table, dropped to her knees in front of her friend, and wrapped her arms around her. "You mean—"

Mary Ann jerked erect and her hands clenched together. "I won't let it happen. She's too young. *She's* not ready. I'm not ready."

Her voice wobbled, and Cara patted her arm.

"I am right, aren't I, Cara?"

The plea in Mary Ann's voice tore her heart to shreds. "You are very much right."

"I knew you'd agree." Mary Ann sagged in relief. "When we got the notice Valerie had been placed on the list to be broken in, Josh and I were heartbroken. She's only thirteen. How can they do this? We thought we had at least two years to prepare her."

Much too young. Thirteen-, fifteen-, and sixteen-year-old girls should still be in school, flirting with boys their age, and having fun. At least, in the real world—the outside one—they did.

"I will never be prepared for Leila or Lacy to be married, even at fifteen. Never."

"What should I do?"

"What does Josh think? Does he agree? Does he think you should obey the summons?"

"No. Well, sort of. I mean, he knows he should. He's an elder, he says. He shouldn't have any questions or doubts."

"But he does."

Mary Ann pressed trembling fingers against her forehead. "I think he's more torn up than I am."

Hmm. Josh must not be quite as brainwashed by Elder Simmons as the older ones. "What do you want me to do?"

"Josh thought you …"

She choked. "What?" Did they know her plans? Had someone heard her talking to Richard? Did they want her to—to kill someone? Did Josh have blackmail plans in mind? For her?

"Would you take Valerie? Hide her?"

Cara blinked. Hide her? Is *that* what they wanted? A giggle of relief bubbled up.

"Why would you want me to hide her?" How could she hide a teenage girl?

"You're the only one we trust. Please."

"Honey, you'll have no choice, no time. Once Elder Simmons finds out Valerie's gone …"

The other woman rocked. "I know. We'll be the target of his wrath."

"What about your son? They might grab him." Another idea rebelliously insisted on being spoken. "They might even stoop to torturing Josh, or you. You've heard the rumors."

"But what should I do?" Mary Ann whispered. "I can't give her up to them. Not yet. I would rather die."

"Does Josh know you're asking me to hide Valerie?"

"He suggested it."

Cara wove her fingers together, drew them apart, then splayed them across her thighs. She could be in a lot more trouble if Elder Simmons found out.

No matter. If she could save Valerie, or any other girl in the group, she'd do what she could. Cara refocused on her friend. "I can't do what you ask, Mary Ann. I wish I could, but I'm sure someone is watching me. But, yes, I think my idea might work."

"What?" Mary Ann's eyes brightened.

"I need a copy of the summons. Can you or Josh drop it off this evening?"

"Yes."

"I may need a few days, so make whatever excuse you can to stall the summons."

"How?"

"Say she has the flu or you need her help. I don't know. Do it."

Cara walked her friend to the door.

"Thanks."

"Don't thank me yet."

The door closed behind her friend. Cara stared out the window as her friend hurried down the path.

From the other side of the yard, she caught a glimpse of a man. After Mary Ann vanished down the path, he glared at her house again, and Cara drew back from the window.

Who was it?

❧⌘❧

"Want to go see Reverend MacFarland?" Cara wiped Lacy's face but looked at Leila. Ever since Elder Simmons forced her to go to the sanctuary—two days ago—Leila had clung to her, would have refused to go to school, but Cara didn't give her a chance to protest. Now her daughter needed a happy outing. A school night, but they wouldn't stay long.

She'd seen no more signs of the man she'd spotted earlier. The paper Josh dropped off an hour ago lay hidden safe and sound, she hoped, inside the book she'd been reading.

Leila's face wreathed in a smile, and Lacy jumped from sheer energy.

Cara propped her fists on her hips. "Why are you still here? Go change and let's get going."

Lacy scampered from the room, but Leila's eyes were round. Worry filled them.

"What's the matter, sweetie? Don't you want to go?" Cara pulled her daughter close.

"Do we have to stay?"

"What do you mean?" Was she frightened of Dayne? "I don't want you going off to talk to Elder Simmons tonight and leaving us."

So that was behind Leila's unusual behavior.

"Not tonight. You and Lacy and I will be together the whole time. No one talks to me tonight without you there." Cara mock-frowned to coax a laugh from her daughter. She wanted her always-confident daughter back.

Leila didn't laugh, but her lips tipped up in a small smile. "Okay. I'm going to wear my pink shirt."

"Perfect."

Thirty minutes later, Cara pulled behind Dayne's car and unbuckled her belt. The neighborhood was quiet. No one loitered nearby, but to be safe, she'd keep the girls in sight. "Sit still, and I'll check to make sure he's not busy." She really didn't care whether he was or not. He needed to see what she had to show him.

The door burst open almost before she finished knocking. Surprise flared in Dayne's eyes, but the next second the warmth in them welcomed her. "Cara. Come in."

She waved to the girls and they popped out of the car like corks out of two bottles. Lacy pranced to the door and gazed up at Dayne. "We've come for a visit. Do you have cookies?"

"Lacy!"

"I think I could find some if you promise to stay for a while."

"Mr. Dayne wants us to stay all night." Lacy tugged on her mother's hand.

"Lacy!" Cara's cheeks grew as hot as sunburn. Kids.

Dayne took the youngster's hand. "Do you think Leila will want some, or can you eat them all?"

The little girl eyed her sister. "I can eat bunches, but she can have one."

"You girls want to eat your cookies on my sun porch?"

Leila's gaze shot straight to her mother.

"Your decision, sweetie. Dayne and I'll be right here in the kitchen."

After Dayne settled the girls with glasses of milk and two homemade sugar cookies on each napkin, he and Cara sat at the table. He asked, "Did you come for those poetry books I promised to lend you?"

"No, but since I'm here, I wouldn't mind borrowing one."

"Sure. Did you hear they've reset the Lewis home repairs for tomorrow?"

"I got the note this morning. I don't want to go, but I suppose I'll have to. Why can't they do these after Penelope gets home?"

"She wasn't doing very well when I stopped in last night." Dayne's face remained sober as he reported on the woman's physical progress. "Her depression and refusal to eat didn't help her any."

"I should go see her again."

"You've been busy."

"Yes, but I can't use busyness for an excuse." She pulled out the letter. "I've come because of this."

"What is it?"

She flapped the letter in front of his face. "This will show you how depraved Elder Simmons is."

The lines on Dayne's face tightened. The teasing smile vanished as he scanned the document. His eyes drifted downward, flitted to the top of the letter, and he read the words again. At last he folded the paper and laid it down. Rubbing his eyes, he said, "I see what you mean. Is this the first episode of this type?"

"No. Lately, Elder Simmons gets his eye on a certain girl every once in a while, and—"

"He takes what he wants." He shoved away his own half-eaten cookie.

"Josh sent Mary Ann to me after they got this. She's a nervous wreck and said Josh is worse. They're not ready for their daughter to be summoned and wanted me to hide Valerie, but I refused—only because it's a fruitless plan."

"How do you know?" Dayne picked up the letter as if he'd read again but then slapped it down.

"As Mary Ann left today, a man was standing at the edge of the woods, staring at my house."

"Watching you or the Denuits?"

"Both, I figure. What can we do about Valerie?"

"I may know of a way to intervene." Dayne lifted the paper. "Can I keep this?"

"I don't want the thing. Tell me your plans."

"Not now. Give me some time."

Cara wrinkled her nose.

"Hey, don't you trust me?"

He'd asked her the same thing before. "Do I have a choice?"

"Yes, you do."

Cara called to her girls. "Time to go."

"Here, let me bag up the rest of these cookies."

"I don't want to take your cookies."

"Sure you do. I stacked a few books of poetry on my desk in the study. Want to grab them?"

Cara walked down the hallway, admiring the masculine simplicity of Dayne's home. She paused at the doorway to his study and took in the black and crimson décor. Books lined one wall. A huge picture of Dayne's father and mother dominated another.

She stared up at the couple who'd given her a home, loved her, and cared for her as a daughter. "I know you wouldn't be pleased, but what else can I do? Please forgive me," she whispered.

Their eyes stared at her, neither condemning nor approving, but sad, as if—as if her sins troubled them. A picture of Dayne's father, his strong but gentle voice circling the room as he read the Bible to the family during the evenings. He'd been such a gentle man, full of love for his wife and Dayne. And her. He and Mrs. MacFarland had opened their hearts and home to a homeless young girl. No one would have suspected she'd not been their own daughter.

Why did God take such a good man and woman? Surely he knew the earth—this group—needed men like him.

If only the God they'd served had been present for her. For Lori.

Enough sentiment. The stack of books on the edge of the desk would be the ones. She started to sort through them, but a framed picture caught her eyes.

A young girl, her hair blowing in the wind, her arms spread wide as if to grasp the whole world, her smile at the camera-man wide and radiant. A teenaged Cara. Why did Dayne have her picture on his desk?

Cara ran a finger along the edge of the costly-looking frame. One possible answer blazed like a neon sign in her mind, but she couldn't allow herself to think it.

What will he think if he finds out what I've done? What I'm doing?

She couldn't hold back the tears seeping from her eyes. They wet her lashes, loosened their hold on her bottom lashes, and trickled down her cheek. She rubbed at her damp cheeks. The sound of Dayne's and the girls' voices came from his front room, and Cara walked to them. Dayne, on one knee, pointed at a fish in his gigantic aquarium. Lacy's giggles and Leila's big eyes testified to their entrancement.

Lacy leaned against Dayne in perfect trust, and even Leila kept close, listening to every word as he explained in simple details about the fish inhabiting the tank. Cara's heart warmed at the sight of their interaction. *This is what life should be about.*

Dayne must have caught her reflection in the glass because he gave her a huge grin from over his shoulder. "I wanted the girls to see my aquarium."

"He calls it his special therapy tank," Leila confided.

"I'm sure it's lots of fun." She held up the books but didn't quite meet his smiling eyes.

"Thanks, Dayne. I'll take care of them."

The picture of her he kept in his study pantomimed across her mind, tossing one pertinent question at her. Why? She'd loved the MacFarlands like parents. Dayne was the big brother she'd never had. He was such a masculine image of strength and beauty.

Her? She shivered. A shameful specimen of failure.

He waved a hand. "Keep them as long as you wish. Enjoy." Cara tucked her girls into the car and headed home. Their chatter and childish happiness surrounded her in a cocoon all the way. But like a disturbed moth, her heart refused to be comforted by their innocent moment of security.

Dayne's favorite parishioners disappeared down the two-lane road. He hurried to his study, picked up his cell, and dialed a number. When Professor Moore answered, Dayne got to the point. "Did you mean it when you told me you'd come if I needed you?"

"Of course, but I thought you wanted to handle the group your way."

"I did, but Elder Simmons is getting worse, and I seem to be making no impression at all."

"What's he doing now?"

The interest in his old professor-friend's voice didn't camouflage the seriousness.

"They took Cara two nights ago, and I'm afraid if I hadn't intervened, they would have whipped her. Now she gave me a letter summoning a thirteen-year-old girl."

"Up to his old tricks, is he?"

The sound of Professor's Moore sipping some kind of drink came through the phone.

"And much more. I've tried talking, and I preach God's love every Sunday. I even confronted Elder Simmons, but nothing's working." He'd come back determined to make a difference, and now the only difference he saw was in himself. Weary and discouraged.

"I'll give my substitutes a call. I should be able to leave day after tomorrow. Can you pick me up?"

All of a sudden, Dayne felt alive again. What a morale-builder his old mentor was. "I can. I thought you didn't know Simmons."

"I thought so too, but when I dug deeper I realized the man was the same one—different alias—as the one I've studied for years."

"I see. Are you sure you won't tell me what you know?"

"Not yet. You're better off not knowing for now."

Dayne didn't push him. With all Prof's studies, the man would have a brilliant plan in mind. It was too bad things weren't going the way Dayne had planned them. "I'll see you in two days." Dayne set down his phone.

He had a suspicion things were beginning to cement.

Cara tucked her apple pie beside the meatloaf. Dread like a haunted figure stirred the cauldron in her stomach and mingled with the delicious aromas wafting from her food. If only she could escape the ordeal. She'd much prefer visiting Penelope or even staying home. But Ruby Simmons or even Kathy Raymond would check to see why she was neglecting her duty.

Besides, she'd have a chance to speak with Dayne. See if he'd found a way to help Valerie. And she hoped someone would have word about Penelope. Elder Simmons had reduced her monthly hours, so she'd have no chance to stop in this week. Not unless she could sneak it in.

Fifteen minutes later, Cara walked toward the women gathered around the tables they set up. She skirted Ruby and Kathy's table and headed to where Jodie and Abby were arranging the food.

"Sister Hayman."

An invisible wall suddenly sprouted high and effectively stopped her advance toward her friends. Could she ignore the imperative voice? Probably not. Not without repercussions. Cara faced Sister Simmons, a pleasant look plastered on her face. "Can I help you?"

"Come here."

Great. Cara lugged her picnic basket toward the figure.

A no-nonsense finger wagged in her face. "You're late."

Five minutes?

"I want you to work with the men, carry things for them, take them drinks when needed. We have enough help at the tables." Sister Simmons eyed her as if expecting a protest.

"Let her help Marshall. He'll keep her straight."

Kathy's malicious suggestion stung Cara, even though she could hope for nothing better from the woman.

"Fine," Sister Simmons agreed.

"Okay." Cara loved the triumph that trumpeted inside her when Kathy's mouth dropped at her agreeableness.

"What shall I do with this?"

Kathy Raymond popped from behind her friend and sniffed. "What did you bring?"

"Meatloaf."

Another indignant sniff. "Common."

"And apple pie," Cara offered. Nothing she did ever pleased Kathy Raymond.

"Ruby brought apple pie. Two of them. You know very well our men love her pies. You should have brought something else."

"Can you ever have too much apple pie?" Cara ordered herself to smile. Sticking out her tongue seemed way too childish and improper and let them know she was miffed. "My pie is different. The preacher liked it."

"Liked what?" Dayne stepped up beside her.

"My apple pie." Cara allowed her eyes to twinkle at him.

Dayne strolled away but tossed over his shoulder, "Delicious stuff. Best I've ever eaten."

Ruby Simmons sniffed, her face grim. "He's not much of a pie judge, is he?"

"Obviously not." Kathy glared.

The senior elder's wife laid a hand on Kathy's arm. "Don't fret, friend. We must be willing to share the praise, even when it's ill-deserved."

Thank you for nothing. Cara bit harder on her tongue.

Sister Simmons waved a hand. "Deposit your—your donations at the next table. Go, and try to be useful someplace else."

Cara whipped away, anger stirring.

She set down her basket—a little too hard—and spoke as cordially as she could to the two women pouring drinks into foam cups as she walked away. The men working on different jobs around the house paid her no mind. Who would be the least despicable to help? She had no intention of working with Marshall, if only because he was related to Kathy. Besides, he'd dared to follow Elder Simmons's command to grab her girls, and getting close to him would be like placing him in the den of an angry and hungry mother lion.

Disgust rolled over her like a bulldozer, flattening any warm emotions. What did it matter? Marshall hefted a sheet of plywood and grunted at his companion. "Get up and help me."

She barely recognized the other person. One of the Leonards? Cara headed toward them, slipped around the stack of sheeting, and started to speak.

"Did you hear Penelope Lewis took her own life last night? Took a whole bottle of pills. They say her depression caused it." Leonard gripped the opposite end of the plywood, and together the two men lifted it to the roof. "Nobody's mentioned her death because of work day. Elder Simmons is going to make the announcement this evening."

Cara staggered back against the far side of the wood. Penelope gone? *Dead?*

Biggs hoisted a sheet of metal roofing. "Are you serious? No one told her she wasn't paralyzed? Did she know she still carried the baby?"

"Nope. The doctor shot her with something to keep her numb from the waist down. They lied to her about the baby. Told her she lost it in the fall." Leonard shook his head.

Biggs propped the sheet against the wall and sneaked a look around. He lowered his voice. "Lewis was tired of her. Called her a nagging wife. I think he wanted to move on. Because he's one of Elder Simmons's favorites, uh, certain things were put into place."

Cara sank to the ground and laid her head on her knees. The moan inside her pressed against her lips, but she swallowed it back.

Penelope. I failed her.

Failed to protect her *friend.* Her earlier breakfast churned.

Stomping around these grounds would ease some of the dismay, but only a machine gun that took out the whole bunch could ease the heartache.

She lifted her head. None of those wishes would help the situation now. She needed more information. Head cocked, she peered around the stack and listened.

Leonard wiped the sweat from his face. "Yeah, Elder Simmons made plans for Kenny to get rid of her. She never knew the truth. He told the stunning Hayman woman the same batch of lies."

"Spit it out. How was he to do it?" A grimace crossed Biggs's face.

"Use a pillow to smother her, but he didn't get the chance. She played right into their hands. Did the work for them."

"He probably sobbed all night, the jerk."

"Yeah. I never did like Lewis."

At least these guys didn't appear to approve of Elder Simmons's hideous scheme. Cara swallowed but couldn't hold back the sickness. Bending over, she vomited. She pressed a hand against the stack, fighting back the weakness, and wished it would all go away. An impossibility.

Cara straightened. Her decision had just been made for her. Kenny Lewis might not want her to, but he was in for a surprise. She would stick as close to him as lamination to a picture.

❧✷❧

"What happened to Penelope?"

The drill overhead whined, stopped. Kenny, on the tall aluminum ladder, held out a hand, and Cara angled the cut piece of sheeting upward. He maneuvered the piece of roofing into place and sent her a sour glance. "What do you mean? She died last night."

"How? How did she die?"

Kenny squeezed the trigger on the drill, drowning out her voice.

She wasn't ready to give up yet. When he finished, she questioned, "How did she die?"

He jerked halfway around and snarled. "The fool killed herself."

"No!"

"Yeah, she did." Kenny gave her a sneering grin.

"Aren't you the grieving widower?" Cara snapped. "How? How did she do it? Wasn't someone watching her? Didn't anyone try to stop her?"

Probably saw and *let* it happen.

"What's to be will be."

"Rubbish."

"She wanted death or she wouldn't have overdosed."

"I don't believe you." Lied to and unloved. No wonder she'd been depressed. "How did she get hold of a full bottle of pills? Sounds like malpractice to me."

"Are you calling me or Elder Simmons a liar?" Kenny's face reddened. "Spit it out."

His accusations weren't worthy of answering. They were all liars and much worse. "Was Elder Simmons there?"

"The doctor sent for him when he realized she couldn't be saved." Kenny squeezed the drill trigger, and it whined, quit, whined again. He shook the tool. "What's the matter with this thing?"

Cara stared at the muttering man. When he lowered the drill to her by the cord, she grabbed it and set it on the ground.

"Get my heavy-duty drill on the stack of roofing."

What had Penelope gone through? Had she been so discouraged, so depressed, that killing herself seemed the only way? Yes, being fed those lies had pushed her over the edge. How could they cause her such anguish? How would he react to knowing his wicked plot against Penelope was known? She snorted. Wouldn't faze the man. He thought Elder Simmons had his back.

"Cara Hayman."

Kenny's roar penetrated her thoughts. "What?"

"Over there. Get the drill. The aluminum one." He practically danced on the ladder, rage seething from him.

The drill rested on top of the sheeting. She took her time dawdling over to it. Picking up the electric tool, she lifted a bound roll of extension cord. Another extension cord, heavier and off to the side, caught her attention. Duct tape, loosened and frayed, straggled from it. Cara fingered the exposed bare wires.

Lewis still ranted from high on the ladder. A shock might give him a jolt in the right direction. She dropped the first extension cord and picked up the second.

The cord wanted to curl, but she managed to unroll it then plugged it into the outside outlet and into the drill. With the cord dragging from it, she ran back to the ladder. Three rungs up, she held up the drill.

The ladder shook. "I can't reach it from here. Climb up and give it to me! Why are you dawdling?"

Cara gripped the drill and climbed.

"Higher."

Cara stared at the next rung, where his dusty boots rested. Sighing, she reluctantly gripped the rung between his boots. She lifted the drill, and as he bent toward her, a foot raised and settled on top of her hand.

"O-o-ow. What are you doing?" Cara grimaced and tried to pull her hand from under his foot.

He grinned down at her. "Am I stepping on your hand? Sorry about that." He twisted his foot. The pressure increased.

Sharp pain shot through her hand and up her arm. A scream built in her throat.

A cold delight glowed in Kenny's eyes and held hers as tight as a drum skin.

The hope—a devilish desire—lighting his eyes, choked off the scream inside her. Pure grit oozed through her body, down her arms, and into the paining hand. Cara clenched her teeth together and hung on. She glared at Kenny and willed her eyes to shout defiance.

Abruptly the pressure released as he scraped his boot off her hand, skinning her knuckles. She jerked her hand off the rung and grabbed for the next one even as she caught the blur of a moving boot drawing back and swinging toward her.

He was going to kick her.

She ducked as his boot slid past her head. Descending the ladder faster than a spooked cat, she wasted no time in jumping to the ground from the last two rungs. Her feet touched the ground as Kenny spit out his next complaint.

She glanced back up at him but paid no attention. His mouth grumbled, he stretched upward, positioned the screw against the metal roofing, and lifted the drill …

Wires met metal.

She saw the smoke pouring from the drill, the sparks flying, heard the hot sizzle. A loud firecracker pop rent the air. Kenny's body shook from the power of the electricity flowing through him. He appeared to bow backward, his fingers loosened their hold on the ladder, and he tumbled.

For a moment Cara stared, horrified. Was he *dead*?

Cara inched closer. Kenny's eyes fluttered open. Blood dribbled from his half-open mouth and his nostrils.

"Kenny?"

His pupil-dilated eyes focused on her.

Cara realized she couldn't resist the opportunity. "Remember Penelope? The Bible says an eye for an eye, and a tooth for a tooth."

Understanding overshadowed the pain, and Kenny struggled to speak. A grunt and a gurgle seeped from him. His body relaxed, his eyes dulled as the light dimmed.

Running footsteps sounded behind her. Loud, distressed voices shouted.

Cara straightened and stepped back. Two of the elders knelt, checked his vital signs, and shook their heads. The others gathered in a circle around the body of Kenny Lewis.

Deceased.

CHAPTER SIXTEEN

Cara fumbled with the key and finally slipped inside her home, glad she'd dropped off the girls at Cassie's before heading to the Lewises' home. Only a few minutes to get herself under control and then she'd go pick them up.

She laid her head against the door, her hands splayed on it, and shut her eyes. Kenny's death was her fault. She'd plugged in the extension cord, handed the drill to him, and watched while he reaped—her vengeance? Or God's? It didn't matter. Now she suffered a too-late moment of conscience.

All her spouting off at the mouth in his moment of death accomplished what? A small, minute piece of victory? Triumph for whom? The women? Penelope? *Herself?*

The door bracing her back, she slid to the floor and groaned. How could she be so hardhearted? Lori's eyes stared at her through her memory. Questioning. Sad. Judgmental.

Judgmental? No. Not Lori. Not her daughter. She would understand why her mother had to do what she did.

"Lori, oh, Lori." Tears escaped their boundaries and slid down her cheeks. "I miss you so much. Will I ever really live again?"

Cara pressed the palms of her hands against her temples to ease the throbbing ache.

❦

Inside the airport terminal, Professor Moore sat as far from anyone else as possible, a small duffle and briefcase at his feet, holding a book he wasn't reading. He appeared to be studying the people passing in front of him. His eyes crinkled when he caught sight of Dayne striding toward him.

"Thought you'd forgotten me." Professor Moore picked up his stuff and hefted his bag over his shoulder.

"Got carried away working on a sermon and forgot the time." Dayne held out a hand to take the duffle bag.

"No problem. I enjoyed taking in the sights."

"And I'm glad you came."

"Wouldn't miss it." The professor led the way to the parking garage. "Does Simmons know you invited me?"

"Not yet." At the car, Dayne swung the duffle into the backseat and slid open the driver's door. "No one does. You want to meet him by himself or in front of others? There's a special meeting of the elders tomorrow night."

"Hmm. I think a face-to-face would be best."

"Fine. We'll see him in the morning."

Twenty minutes later, Dayne pulled into his driveway. "Anything special you want to do this evening?"

"Let's relax. Have a quiet evening. Catch up on news. You've got something planned."

"Invited someone over I want you to meet. He's one of the ones I've been working on, hoping to see a change."

Professor Moore rubbed his hands together enthusiastically. "Have you?"

"Not sure." Dayne grabbed the duffle and slammed the back door. "I'm anxious to see what you think."

"Good. You have juice on hand?"

The professor's present health drink included several juices he'd researched. "Do you think I'd ask you here without a good selection?" Dayne prodded.

Thirty minutes later, Professor Moore headed straight for the door of Dayne's home. When the two men settled in Dayne's study, feet propped up, glasses of Professor Moore's concoction in hand, he lifted his glass and swirled the dark liquid.

"I saw Nicole the other day."

The image of the vibrant redhead smiled at Dayne.

"She asked about you. When she heard I was coming here, she sent her love."

"She knows I can't—I'm not interested." Dayne frowned.

"Because of this other woman?" Professor Moore's face sobered. Dayne ignored the probing glance the professor laid on him.

"You know, under Nicole's mask of bravado and confidence is a tender heart. I think she really does care for you."

Their one date—the conversations over the phone—swirled inside him. Nicole was fun and attractive, yet smart, and would make some man a great companion.

Just not him.

❦❧

A knock sounded at the door, and the professor sent Dayne a questioning look.

Dayne checked his watch. "Should be him. Sit tight."

When he returned, he motioned toward a chair. "Professor, this is Levi Schrader. Levi, my college professor."

"You've got company?" Levi stopped at the doorway. "I'll come back some other time."

"Nonsense. I want you to know the prof. Stay awhile."

Levi's brow furrowed.

"Good to meet you." Professor Moore rose and approached Levi, a hand extended. "Dayne's spoken of you quite a bit."

"Has he?" A quick glance at Dayne. "Did you hear Brother Lewis fell off a ladder late this morning?"

"No. What happened?" Shock rippled through Dayne. "Penelope—"

"Yeah, and now Lewis. Looks like the faulty extension cord he used must have shocked the life right out of him. Some of the others said they saw him fall."

Dayne thought about the couple—Penelope's straightforwardness and often-sharp tongue and Kenny's sly innuendoes, his eye for other women. What a mess. What a waste.

"You can't reach them all, Dayne," Professor Moore chided gently. To Levi, he said, "What do you do, Levi?"

As they talked, Dayne sensed the tension between the two men. But Professor Moore's experience in putting men at ease stood in good stead. When Levi's shoulders relaxed back into the chair, Dayne wasn't the least surprised. The sudden grin on Levi's face at one of the prof's jokes eased the atmosphere even more.

Professor Moore reclined his chair. "How are you enjoying Dayne's sermons?" The hole in the toe of one sock mocked his dignity. The man always managed to hide his favorite worn-out socks from his wife. If only she could see him now.

"Fine job he's doing." Levi took a sip of his juice. A puzzled look crossed his features. "Can't say I really understand where he's coming from. But he knows how to talk."

Curiosity flared in the professor's eyes. His profession was kicking into gear. "What does he say that's interesting?"

Levi shook his head, and a teasing smile crossed his lips when he looked at Dayne. "He keeps talking about God's forgiveness through his son. Can't figure out how someone dying can supposedly make one ready for heaven. I've read the Bible, the story of Jesus, the man dying on the cross. But wasn't that a simple story? A parable, as our old pastor used to say?"

"Simple, yes, but not a parable." The professor rubbed a hand through his thinning hair. "One word is what we found our belief upon. Faith."

"Faith?"

"Faith. We believe God is, and he has a perfect plan: Jesus."

"But the Bible tells men to work out their own salvation."

"True." Touching his fingertips together, the professor smiled.

"What is the truth? Isn't that why God uses men—certain men—to show us the way?" Levi demanded.

"Of course. We're ambassadors." Professor Moore nodded. "Another man in ancient days declared the same words, "'What is truth?'"

Dayne took a hearty drink of his juice. What was going on? Normally, the professor relished a good debate and more times than not, came out claiming victory. Yet his mild-mannered responses to Levi's almost belligerent ones seemed out of character.

"Who?" The interest in Levi's voice reeked with skepticism.

"Pontius Pilate."

"The biblical ruler? If rulers don't have the truth, what can mere people do?"

"Ah, the place where faith comes into play. If we have not faith, we have not salvation." Professor Moore's eyes twinkled.

"Faith in Jesus' death would save us?" Like a light switched on, Levi's sudden comprehension was bright and welcome.

"Exactly."

Once again, the professor surprised Dayne. Instead of pushing his ideas, he kept quiet, eyeing Levi.

After a moment, Levi raised his head. "One word, huh? Faith. I'll study on your explanation some more."

Professor Moore changed the subject. "Tell me, who's next in line if something happens to Elder Simmons?"

"I've never given the matter a thought." Levi shrugged.

"You? You're still young, but you're old enough by now to have learned a few lessons in life. Sensible and strong. Level-headed."

"What makes you think Elder Simmons is going anywhere?" Levi asked.

Instead of answering the question, Professor Moore asked another one. "Do you approve of Elder Simmons's rules?"

Levi picked up his drink. "Are you suggesting I criticize Elder Simmons?"

"Do you want to?" Professor Moore tossed back.

"You sound like a psychologist. What type of professor are you?"

The professor and Dayne exchanged glances. Was it time? Could they trust Levi? Fill him in on the real reason Professor Moore traveled here?

"So you're in total harmony with Elder Simmons's decisions?"

"I didn't say that." Levi went to the window and stared into the darkness.

Minutes passed.

A sigh escaped Levi's lips. "For a long time, I've been troubled about some of the off-the-wall decisions Elder Simmons thrusts on us."

Dayne opened his mouth, but the professor glanced at him, head shaking.

"Such as?"

"Such as lowering the age of the girls to be broken in and now this sudden interest of his for even younger girls." The words came out as if dragged.

"This bothers you?"

"Yeah." Shame rode his features like a bronco refusing to be tamed. His voice was low and gravelly. "I don't want another wife. I love Jodie."

The rumors Dayne heard said the same thing. He'd wondered if Levi would divorce Jodie for another woman. Now he knew. "Levi, you don't have to take another wife. Stand your ground."

"Easy to say, but that's not how we work here. You know our rules, Dayne."

"No one should be pushed into doing what they don't want to do."

"I don't know."

Professor Moore spoke up. "One thing I've learned in life is to give myself time to know which way to go. If I'm in doubt, I wait. No one, nothing, pushes me into an action until I'm clear on what I need to do."

"Great wisdom," Levi agreed and started for the door. "But I'm not sure it would work in my case. I will say that you've given me several things to think about tonight."

"Great. Stretching our brain into new areas is always a good thing. I'm glad to meet you."

Dayne followed the elder to the door. When Professor slipped up behind him, Dayne murmured, "Think we influenced him any?"

"I think the man is more convinced than he's letting on. He knows the risks and is weighing the consequences of his decisions." Professor

Moore stared after the receding taillights of the SUV. "What he decides in the next few days could affect the whole group."

❧❦❧

Early the next morning, Cara kissed both girls good-bye and waved as they climbed on the group's school bus. She drew in a trembling breath. She couldn't bear this burden alone. Dayne would help, whether with comfort and encouragement or wisdom on how to stop the elders.

With two hours left on her allotted time for the month, she could afford to spend one of them. Her lips pursed as she thought about women like Ruby Simmons, who no doubt never ran out of allotted time. Women who conformed to the group's rules, who never questioned Elder Simmons's orders, who looked the other way when their husbands' wandering eyes and lustful hearts left wives at home alone many nights.

She'd never cared how often Donald left. But she certainly would not go through such a marriage again.

The forest path, cool and green, beckoned. Cara took it, hoping to avoid prying eyes and be able to conserve her precious hour. When she emerged from the woods, she eyed the parsonage. Dayne's car still parked in the driveway, hinting at his presence inside, but she saw no sign of life. Had she come too early?

If she approached the parsonage, she'd hear some telling sound to let her know whether he'd awakened yet. She crept nearer, listened, wavered. Faint murmurings penetrated the walls.

Her throat went dry as a thought struck her. Did he have a woman—a girl—in his house? She turned to run, and the door flung open, banging. A voice preceded the person out the door.

"Never thought I'd see the day when—"

The man obviously saw her because he stopped all action. He was a tall man. Well-built for an elderly gentleman but kind of handsome in a worn-out way. His mop of thinning, white hair stood on end, tousled from the night. Although pajama bottoms adorned legs extended from the robe wrapped around his body, it didn't lessen the dignity he wore like a kingly crown.

"What have we here? A sprite grown to human proportions?" Twinkles of kindliness rapidly replaced the curiosity shining from his eyes.

Cara's lips tilted upward at his nonsense.

"Well, if this isn't an early-morning pleasure for these worn-out eyes. God must have known I needed an unexpected treat today."

"Or he's punishing you," Cara teased back. He was a slim, jolly St. Nick, pulling the laughter out of her when she didn't want to participate.

He threw back his head, the laughter bellowing from him, and Cara unwillingly laughed too. When he'd subsided into chuckles, he extended a hand. "I'm Dayne's friend, William Moore. And who might you be?"

Cara let him take her hand, but she didn't want him searching, probing, asking questions she had no desire to answer.

"I'm—I'm a friend, out walking. Thought I'd stop by. I didn't know Reverend MacFarland had a visitor. I'll come back some other time." She didn't give him time to object but hurried off. At the corner of the garage, Cara looked back.

Dayne stood beside the professor. She scurried around the corner but paused to peek back at the two men.

"Hey, why did you run out on me? You didn't finish wiping the dishes." Dayne punched the professor in the shoulder. "Were you talking to someone, Prof?"

"I believe it was your young lady." A degree of worry laced the certainty in the professor's voice.

"How would you know? You've never met her."

A chuckle. "Her eyes. Anyone who ever saw those eyes would never forget them."

"But I've never told you their color."

"No, but you told me a person could get lost gazing into them." The professor's voice carried a hint of firmness. "She's carrying a burden. A burden so heavy, she's going down."

"What do you mean?" Anxiety edged Dayne's voice.

Silence. Cara almost ran on to the woods. She didn't want to hear this, hear herself discussed as if she was a piece of merchandise. But anchored in place, unable to move, the desire to hear outweighed the dismay holding her body in place. After a moment, the professor spoke again.

"I think she wants to be rescued."

Cara placed a hand over her heart. Who was this old man? How did he know?

CHAPTER SEVENTEEN

The chance to meet Elder Simmons didn't materialize the first morning, after all. After Cara left, a phone call instructed Dayne on the funeral arrangements for the Lewises. At eleven, he left his study and found the professor in the kitchen, putting together a casserole containing several unusual-looking ingredients.

"What's cooking?" Dayne teased. "Looks like some inedible items."

Professor Moore waved a wooden spoon at him. A large, whitish glob splattered the countertop. "Don't knock it until you've tried it. Heard you on the phone. I take it our planned meeting is off this morning."

"Don't see how we can make it work."

"Fine. I think tonight would be best after all. Confront him in front of the other elders. Put pressure on him. Enough to do the trick, but still let him save some face." Professor licked a finger. "Hmm. Good."

Dayne cast a doubtful glance at the concoction.

"Mind if I borrow the car if you're not using it this afternoon?"

"Go ahead. I'll be busy finishing the Lewises' funeral message."

"Think they'll cancel the meeting in lieu of these deaths?" The professor wiped his hands on a dishcloth.

"Nothing stops their monthly meetings. Besides, the funerals won't be for another two days."

"I'll see you this evening, then."

❧❦❧

The tomb-quiet halls sent chills up Dayne's spine as he and the professor walked the length of the darkened corridor. When they descended the church basement steps, Elder Simmons's voice floated toward them. They stepped onto the floor, and he stopped abruptly. Heads turned like robots shifting to eye their enemies.

Dayne strode toward them, nodding. Josh Denuit gave him a huge grin. Levi inclined his head, his eyes curious. A few others held interest. The other twenty-plus stared, varied expressions playing across their features. Curiosity. Hostility. Blandness.

He threaded his way past several of the elders to two empty seats, aware the prof was right behind him, and sat down. "Sorry to be late, Elder Simmons. Don't let us interrupt."

Elder Simmons cleared his throat. "Reverend MacFarland, it's good to see you here. But you know outsiders are not allowed."

"I understand. I invited my friend to come for a special reason." As if his explanation would pass muster in the senior elder's eyes.

The head elder's gaze shifted. "Do I know you?"

"You should." The professor's grin gave him away. He loved confrontations.

Mouth open, the elder seemed ready to ask the obvious question. He turned back to Dayne, his eyes narrowed. "What is the reason, Reverend?"

Dayne rose to his feet. He returned their looks, going from face to face, measuring their probable responses and hoping for the results he craved. At last he spoke. "I'm troubled tonight, knowing God is not pleased at the actions among us. We need to consider some definite changes."

He'd thrown the gauntlet. How would Elder Simmons react?

Not so well, if his face was anything to go on.

Elder Simmons lost any semblance of friendliness. He glared at Dayne, his mouth twisted into a sour moue, his nostrils flared. "A change? A change how? God appointed me your leader. He's not spoken to me about any change."

"No? Professor Moore has some information pertinent to us. I think you'll find it vital to our well-being and worth listening to."

"God did not give you authority to rule over us, Reverend. You are to feed our souls, give God's word to us."

"I believe warning us of possible detrimental ways is part of it."

"You will take the authority from your leader?"

"If God wants me to bring truth to you, I'm willing."

"Brother, you are pushing the extremities of your profession."

Professor Moore edged his way into the aisle then ambled to the front of the room. "May I speak, Simmons?"

He gave the elder no chance to refuse. "Most of you don't know, but I'm one of Dayne's professors from seminary classes. I'm also his friend, and we've discussed your beliefs. I believe you're on the edge of trouble. I've recently located a similar group the authorities invaded and shut down."

Murmurs rippled around the room.

Elder Simmons's stiff body made an excellent statue. "What are you saying? Are you accusing us of something you hatched in your own mind, Professor?"

The professor turned his head to stare at Elder Simmons. "No accusations. Once the cult was shut down, many of the men were charged of molesting the young girls in their group."

Shock reverberated around the room. Would these men listen? Or caught up in Elder Simmons's corrupt teaching, would they ignore the professor's words because laxity and lust served them better?

"We do not molest our girls. We love them dearly and do our best to prepare them for their future." Elder Simmons's sanctimonious response didn't faze the crowd.

"Is that right?" The smile left the professor's face. "I'm afraid the law of our land will look at your—preparation—quite differently."

"And why would the law take a look at us? We've not done anything to attract unwanted attention." The words spewed from Elder Simmons's mouth. The desire to strike the professor gleamed in his eyes.

"You think they don't know you are a separate-acting group? You've appointed your own sheriff and are a small country within yourself, but they've noticed. Your actions mirror the Missouri group."

Josh Denuit jumped to his feet. "I say we listen to what the professor has to say. I've been bothered by the lowering of the girls' ages."

The group of elders broke out into a rumbling mass of mutters.

Elder Simmons thrust a contemptuous glance Josh's way, but the young man paid no attention.He raised his voice. "Let's hear more of what he has to say."

"He's right."

"Let's hear the professor out."

"You're out of line, Brother Denuit." Elder Simmons lifted a hand to still the voices.

"I'd like to say something, Elder Simmons." Levi rose as if unsure of his leader's reaction.

The elder relaxed. "Certainly, Brother Schrader."

"You all know me. I'm one of you." For a moment the man's shoulders sagged. "I'm sure Josh and I aren't the only ones troubled by some of the—the changing rules lately, and in my opinion, for the worse. We can go forward only if what we do, what we believe, is for the good of us all, even our women and children. When we lose respect for each other, we will crumble."

The ridiculous urge to cheer swept over Dayne.

Again Elder Simmons lifted his arms and signaled for quiet. He assumed a quiet facade, but Dayne sensed the anger seething inside the man.

When the group's attention focused on him, Elder Simmons spoke. "Standing here, I perceive some of you think you want change. You are allowing an outsider, a blasphemer, to corrupt your minds."

"Is it so wrong for us to question, to discuss this?" Josh hollered.

"If you're questioning what God commands, who's ordained to be your leader, then, yes, you're wrong."

Levi rose slowly to his feet again. "Elder Simmons, I'm not one to speak frivolously. I think we all respect you as our leader. But I, for one, want to hear what Professor Moore has to say. If he has news to prevent us from gaining the outside world's attention, I think we should hear it. I should hope you'd understand and agree."

Heads swiveled back to their leader. Elder Simmons's face, sweat-beaded, directed an irate glare at first one, then another.

"I have heard more than enough from this heretic, and I'm warning you, we'll have trouble if we listen to this man." Elder Simmons bellowed out the prophetic warning.

"You refuse to listen to those troubled about the lowering of the girls' ages?" Professor Moore pressed.

"I'm in charge here, and I say there will be no change."

"According to the custom of any group, the majority rules, not one dictator. Are you afraid to have a vote, Simmons?" Professor Moore taunted.

"No, I'm not afraid. But in the past I've never been questioned—"

"Put it to vote!" someone shouted.

Heads nodded approval.

Fat hands propped onto his hips as the senior elder eyed the group. "If the group's will is to vote, so be it. Brother Tobert, get us some ballots."

As his second-in-command hastened to obey, Elder Simmons pasted a smirk onto his face. "We'll excuse you, Reverend, and your friend."

Dayne shook his head. "I'm part of this group. I'd like to stay for the vote. Professor, if you don't mind?" He couldn't vote, not being an elder, but he could make sure everything was done fairly.

The professor nodded, but he addressed Elder Simmons. "One more thing. Remember Elias."

Elder Simmons's face blanched. He still stared at the professor, but the blustery self-assurance and the rage melted away. The muscles in the man's neck constricted as he swallowed. He tried to speak but no words escaped.

One of Professor Moore's bushy brows arched. "You do remember him, don't you, Simmons? He's held at Attica today. His fondness for—"

"That's enough," Elder Simmons gasped. "You've said enough.

Leave us now."

The professor made no move to leave for another moment, but like a stalking lion holding its victim in its mesmerizing glare, he held the elder's. When he broke away, he sauntered toward the doorway, but tossed back one word. "Remember."

Dayne swiveled to take in Elder Simmons's reaction, but the elder recovered. The bluster was back. The pompous I-can-do-no-wrong air encircled him like smoke.

"Let me assure you, my brothers, I will not lead you into trouble. God chose me to be your leader, and I seek only your good and God's will for us. We are a unique group. We know we have God's approval. Vote."

If God's approval was on this group, we'd have no need for the vote. Dayne almost spoke the words aloud but refrained. No need to push his luck.

No one spoke as Angus Tobert passed the ballots in his slow, methodical way. Even Elder Simmons stood in silence, arms crossed, heavy legs spread, as if daring anyone to disturb him. One look at the leader's disgruntled face, and the timid ones would scurry to side with him.

When Angus began gathering the ballots, Dayne stood to his feet. "I'd like to help count the votes."

The pressed lips didn't bode well for Dayne's future as minister to the Children of Righteous Cain. "I see no reason why Brother Tobert can't get along without help."

"*Roberts Rules of Order* declares two tellers as customary. I'm requesting permission to be appointed."

"You're insisting? Very well. Count the votes." Elder Simmons swung away and stomped to the desk, where he busied himself.

Dayne and Tobert took their time counting the votes, rechecked the ballots, and scribbled the results onto a piece of paper. Striding across the room, Dayne approached Elder Simmons and passed the paper to him without speaking.

Elder Simmons stared down at the results. His jaws tightened. His fists clenched. "I suppose you're satisfied."

"Why should I be?" Dayne asked.

"You've got a good thing going here. I'd think twice before ruining your chances of a future with us." Elder Simmons snorted.

"What makes you think I haven't thought long and hard about my ministry here?" Defusing the elder's ire might be a good thing.

The elders quieted as Elder Simmons prepared to speak, his glare at the others contemptuous.

Picking out the traitors in the midst?

"You have spoken. For now, we will put the lowering of the girls' age on hold. Now if you'll excuse me, I'm going to commune with God."

As Elder Simmons stomped from the room, the rest broke into loud conversation. Dayne bent to pick up the paper Elder Simmons had tossed to the floor. Six votes had been against lowering the girls' age. Three had been blank. The rest had supported Elder Simmons' wishes. He'd had the majority on his side.

What had caused the man to make the announcement as he had? Conscience? Distress that the vote hadn't been unanimous?

Or the seemingly threat-like conversation the professor tossed at Elder Simmons right before he'd left the room? What was behind the conversation? What did both men know that the rest didn't? Something so sinister, so real to Elder Simmons that his apprehension held him captive from going against the threat?

Or was the rage simmering inside him due to the small following of the elders he'd lost?

CHAPTER EIGHTEEN

"Who's Elias?" Dayne steered the car away from the sanctuary and toward his home.

"Must I answer all your questions before I can get mine answered?" the professor said good-naturedly.

"Yep," Dayne agreed. Prof enjoyed the sparring as much as he did. "I'm young and impatient."

Professor Moore snorted. "Elias is Ruby Simmons's brother."

"And?"

"He ran a similar religious group in North Dakota. When the place was raided, he was arrested and convicted for molesting underage girls. Simmons knows it. I wanted him to keep the fact in mind."

"How do you know it?"

"I've followed the North Dakota group for several years now. Only recently did I realize Elias and Ruby Simmons were family." The professor cracked the window and drew in a deep breath. "This country air is good for the physical."

Professor Moore's plan clicked.

"I see. You wanted Simmons to weigh the consequences. That's why he didn't tell the truth to the other elders tonight about the vote. He needs time to sort out your threat."

"Now we're getting somewhere. Tell me, what was the vote? You don't seem too distressed."

"The vote was six against lowering the age, three blank, the majority favoring Elder Simmons's wishes."

The professor straightened in his seat. "What?"

"When Elder Simmons announced the vote, he said the lowering of the girls' age would be put on hold. He wanted them to think they'd voted that way. But why did he? Did you scare him?"

"He's too brazen to scare easily." The professor shook his head. "Saving face would be more his line."

"You think?"

"If he can ride out this storm you've stirred up until things smooth out, and if he can bring you around—or get rid of you, whichever works—he'll heap condemnation on the whole group of elders. Their remorse will be so great, nothing he says in the future will ever be questioned. He's planning ahead."

"Do you really think he wants to get rid of me?"

The dashboard's eerie blue-green light shone on the professor's face, morphing him into an overgrown alien. The professor cast him an amused look. "Things are not going the way he planned for you. You're not the patsy he thought you'd be when he brought you here. He'll definitely want to rein you in."

"How can he do it?"

"I think he'll try to discredit you."

"I hardly see how. I've not given him any ammunition to pull such a stunt."

"You don't need facts. Rumors, lies, even half-truths can do the trick." The professor fumbled in his pocket and finally pulled out a piece of paper. "Perhaps this will prove Simmons doesn't have your best interests at heart."

Dayne tossed a curious look at the paper and chided. "What do you have? Were you snooping while we were voting?"

"I wouldn't call it snooping when he leaves papers lying right out in the open for anyone to see."

"Elder Simmons's office?"

"Where else?"

"What does it say?"

"It's a list. Cara Hayman's name's on it." The professor ran a finger down the paper. "Have you given him anything he can use?"

"No. A couple visits at her house—girls present. I rescued her when they scared her that night in the basement. What can he get out of those meager events?"

"You might be surprised." The professor tapped the paper. "He listed a few comments. I believe they're things you've spoken, probably during sermons—things he's noted you believe and are promoting in the group. A couple of times—dates included—when you two have disagreed."

"What can I do?"

"We'll counteract his discredit actions—if he goes that route."

"How?"

"Didn't you mention one time that the women meet a couple times a month for various activities?"

"The second and fourth Thursdays of the month."

Grim determination steeled the old man's voice. "We'll see them tomorrow. They need their eyes opened."

He's in his element. "What good will talking to them do?"

"Remains to be seen, my boy."

❧❧❧

Ruby Simmons gripped the podium stand in front of the group of thirty-some women. Her voice carried around the room—firm, confident, and strident. But she kept the women's attention, Cara couldn't deny.

Or it could be the subject she was broaching.

"Our dear Elder Simmons wishes us to give our best to seeing Brother Lewis has a respectable and memorable funeral. We will need to work together to make this a success. I know I can count on you to help me."

Kathy Raymond, sitting in the chair behind Ruby, clapped. The rest sat as statues.

"We'll need all of you to bring in at least two dishes of food and drinks for the after meal. I've prepared a list of those I want to decorate our sanctuary and the dining area. I've appointed six of you to serve as greeters. Tiffany Kisser will take charge. I'll choose the suit Brother Lewis will wear, which, as you know, the elders always finance. I've personally chosen Sister Raymond to act as my assistant. If you have any questions, please see her."

What about Penelope?

"Have you forgotten Penelope Lewis?" a man's voice interrupted.

Cara twisted in her seat. Dayne and William Moore leaned against a back wall. She glanced back at Ruby in time to see the frown, the nose tilt upward, the lips press together. Ah, one unhappy woman and as surprised as Cara was.

"I beg your pardon?" Ruby gritted out between two clenched jaws.

Dayne indicated the professor. "This is my friend, Professor Moore."

The professor lifted a hand as if to touch the brim of an imaginary hat. "Have you talked to your brother, Elias, lately?"

The woman's face blanched, but she didn't back down. "I'm sorry, but we need to finish our business here. If you have something to say, go speak to my husband. Please leave, pastor, and take your friend. We have work to do."

"I thought I'd speak a few words of encouragement to you and the others, Sister Ruby." Dayne didn't give her time to refuse, but headed to the front of the room. "You don't mind, do you?"

Cara's mouth twitched. What could Ruby say? If she refused the preacher, wouldn't it look as if she feared what he might say?

"He stops by every other month or so and talks to us for about five minutes," Mary Ann whispered.

That's what she got for avoiding all the meetings. If she'd come more often, she'd have heard Dayne talk long before now.

"Good morning, ladies." Dayne smiled, and Cara almost forgot to concentrate on his words. "God asked me to give you something special this morning, 'Be strong, and of a good courage, be not afraid, neither be thou dismayed: for the Lord thy God is with thee whithersoever thou goest.'"

With Jodie's hand clutched in one hand and Mary Ann's in the other, she drank in his words. Be strong? Like Dayne? He was the strongest person she knew. Could she ever have that kind of strength, that kind of belief?

"God loves you. Simple. Nothing complicated. No matter where you go, what you do throughout your days, you can rest in the knowledge God is with you. He loves *you*. Your salvation is through God."

A hand raised, and when Dayne pointed at the woman, she asked, "But we've been taught our salvation comes through our husbands. Without his leadership and guidance, we have no hope. Isn't that right?"

"The scriptures say, 'If any man serve me, let him follow me.' Jesus is speaking of himself. He makes it clear."

Kathy elbowed Ruby Simmons, and the two edged closer to Dayne. "Reverend MacFarland, you are undermining our basic beliefs. Brother Cain would rise up and condemn you."

"I'm not worried about offending Brother Cain as much as our God," he rebutted her rebuke.

"Professor Moore, my friend, is here today to give us information you'll want to hear."

Ruby Simmons folded her arms. "I don't think—"

"Yes, Sister Simmons, indeed we do." Dayne's eyes twinkled at Cara, the corners crinkling.

"All of you need to learn about the latest developments of a case I've been studying." The professor spoke while walking up the side of the room. "I've followed different religious groups through the years, so I have extensive experience. The last group I studied closed and the children were taken away from their families because of their unusual and cruel abuse."

"Abuse?" Ruby's eyes narrowed. "We care for our people."

Rumbling, disturbed conversation erupted across the room. Cara's heart rate sped up.

Someone called out, "What are you saying, Professor Moore?"

"What does this have to do with us?" Ruby Simmons demanded.

The professor addressed the first woman's question. "Do you want your children taken from you? As mothers, you love them and want what's best for them. In lieu of that conclusion, it's your obligation to think intelligently about some of the recent decisions being made in your group."

Stunned silence.

"What are you doing?" Kathy screeched the question, her face as red as a tomato. "How dare you?"

Ruby Simmons shook her head at the woman, but Kathy paid no attention.

"Elder Simmons will hear about this nonsense."

"He's already heard, and I think he's assessing the whole situation." The professor beamed at the women as if he shared the best news in the world. "The elders voted last night, and the whole lowering of ages for the girls has been put on hold."

For a moment, no one else spoke, and then Mary Ann choked out a loud sob and flung her arms around Cara. Like a row of dominoes, one by one, the women vented their emotions, tears dripping, hugs abundant.

Jodie grabbed Mary Ann for a joyful hug.

She'd not dreamed this result would come about because of her request to him for help. Cara wanted to fling her arms around him and thank him. Not a good idea. Ruby would report any forward actions to her husband. She'd get her thanks in to Dayne later.

When the sobs and laughter subsided, Mary Ann raised her hand. "Will this mean other changes in the future for our group, Professor?"

"Possibly. At least, it's a step forward, sister." Professor Moore held up a hand. "Any opinions about your girls marrying at fifteen and sixteen?"

"I'd like to keep my children with me as long as I can, Professor Moore," Mary Ann offered.

"Me, too," another woman called. "Why, they're still babies."

"I never did like it. My girl cried all night before she was married at sixteen," a middle-aged woman said.

One petite snip of a girl, bouncing a baby on her knee, spoke up, her lip trembling. "I've never been very brave, but I cried for days before—before I was broken in. It was the scariest time of my life. One day I ran around with my sisters, and the next day I experienced adulthood."

Not a sound disturbed the confession, but several of the women lifted hands to wipe at their eyes.

"I'm shocked, and Elder Simmons will be very displeased at this emotional stupidity." Kathy Raymond blared the disharmonious reproof. She'd be the first to tell on them all. "Speak up, Ruby. Tell them. Those who stand for the truth, come forward."

Tiffany Kisser jumped to her feet and ran to the front. Two other women hurried forward.

Cara sprang to her feet. "I think our girls should be given the chance to decide for themselves what they want. Why force them to marry if they want more schooling? Some of them will never marry."

"Miss Independent herself speaks. I'll have no part of this disloyalty."

The women standing beside Kathy laughed. Kathy Raymond meant for Cara to hear her sarcastic remark, but Cara ignored her. Dayne's presence, and the professor's, and the women's sudden shift in agreement were marvelous boons to her courage.

"Our girls should be allowed to express their choices, their desires. Why should they keep them locked inside, afraid to open up?"

"You've all gone crazy," Kathy screamed as she strutted toward the two men, her friends stomping along behind her. "Now see what you've done. You've opened a can you can't reseal. How are we ever to fix this?"

Professor Moore's kindly eyes showed sorrow and pity for the narrow-minded woman. "Fix it? Who wants to fix it? This is a start toward repair of dastardly deeds seething in this group for generations. We don't want to fix this. We want it to rip wide open."

"Elder Simmons will hear about this," Kathy threatened.

"Must I remind you that not only were the children removed from the homes, but men and women were jailed? Forcing children and women to have sex is illegal in the United States."

The women hovering behind Kathy shrank back. Kathy's mouth dropped open and cowardice shoved aside the hate blazing from her eyes.

Exhilaration bubbled up inside Cara. Ignoring any thoughts of a later retribution, she let the strange elation inside her bubble out and clapped her hands. Startled glances swung her way, but as one, the women picked up on the clapping until all but a few cheered the professor from the sheer freedom of expressing their emotions.

Ruby Simmons had withdrawn to one side of the room and now

remained strangely quiet. Cara looked at her. One hand covered Ruby's mouth, and her eyes bore into the young girl who'd spoken earlier. But Ruby's eyes—moist and oddly soft—touched Cara's heart.

Tears filled her own eyes as Cara sank to her seat. Was this the change for good Dayne wanted—the one she longed for? Would it last or would Elder Simmons and wicked people like Kathy Raymond knock it on its head before it could even stand upright?

The women's faces held a sudden breath of life, their eyes filled with hope.

No. Regardless of what Kathy or even Elder Simmons tried, these women sensed and embraced this new thought. They wouldn't forget. Not any time soon.

CHAPTER NINETEEN

Penelope's brief, heartbreaking funeral still carried a shred of warmth in its memory. The women rallied and in simple ways gave Penelope a beautiful send-off. Cara's heart thrilled. Colorful spring flowers, handwritten notes and poems, and someone found a lovely blue dress to soften the woman's sharp features.

Dayne did a superb job speaking and, thankfully, favored Penelope as much as the despicable Kenny …

The sound of a smooth-running vehicle, probably an up-to-date one, didn't register at first until it pulled up beside her, and then she recognized the truck. Travis and Dustin Martin, sons of one of the older elders. She lifted a hand to wave, but the truck screeched to a halt, and both doors flung open.

What did these two mischief-makers want? She gave them a tentative smile.

Stopping in front of her, and still smiling, the youngest said, "Get in the truck, Caralynne."

"What?"

Their faces registered the unspoken intent, and she frowned as disappointment threaded its way through her body. More evidence of the corruptness in the men. Too bad. They didn't need to stoop to rape. "Did Elder Simmons send you to get me? If he wants to see me, I'll drive myself. Why would I go with you?"

"Because if you don't, we'll have to put you in the truck, and we might not be easy on you."

"Do I get to know why?" What were these two up to? Nothing good, for sure. This section of road was abandoned. Only the woods beckoned a friendly finger. She knew them far better than most people.

If she ran fast enough, she might have a chance.

She wouldn't. Both men were thin and looked strong and in condition. But she wouldn't go like a dumb sheep. If they wanted a fight, she'd give them one.

"Should we tell her?" Travis strutted around her.

Cara wondered who he was trying to impress—herself or his brother. He'd be better off working on his brother. Nothing he did would ever convince her of his self-esteem.

"Dustin and I overheard our dad and Brother Tobert talking. Isn't that right, brother?"

"Sure is," Dustin agreed.

Dustin might be the quiet one, the one who let Travis do the talking, but Cara could see the hint of intelligence—even cruelty—in his eyes.

She tensed. Her heart pounded like a sledge hammer

"Thing of it is," Travis went on, "Dad and ole Angus didn't have much good to say about you. In fact, they were quite put out."

Both men held their grins, and creepy shivers ran up her back.

"They said you were the cause of all the bad things happening right now. Getting our women all riled up, thinking they can pressure the men into what they want. Bringing in outsiders with threats and weird ideas." The young man shook his head, his blond hair waving, a mock frown of disapproval edging his lips. "Bad. Bad."

"I didn't ask Professor Moore here." Who was behind these guys' plans? Their dad and Angus or Elder Simmons? Or maybe these two broncos devised the stupid plan on their own. Whatever, she was treading through mud here.

Thank goodness the girls were still in school.

Dustin snickered, but Travis sneered and leaned forward. "You're wrong. See, Dad asked us to keep an eye on your house. We saw Elder Denuit and his wife at your house. Now tell me, why would they both stop in one day? Wouldn't be because their girl received a summons, you think?"

Worse than she thought.

"Dustin followed you to Reverend MacFarland's house. Gave us a few minutes of diversion, wondering what a widow like you—good-looking though you are—was doing at a man's house who'd never taken a wife yet."

Panic almost sent her running, but Dustin's eyes stopped her. His left hand slapped against his left thigh, a steady, dull rhythm of menace. He'd read her mind. Cara tried to stall the shakes.

"We realized you were using your pretty self to coax the reverend to help the Denuit girl."

Dustin didn't touch her but his presence threatened and unnerved her.

"Enough talking, Travis. Get the rope out of the truck." If Cara's heart could touch the bottoms of her feet, it did in that moment. If Dustin had gone for the rope, she might have had a chance. Travis, filled with his own self-importance, would have been slow to react when she took off. Dustin, on the other hand, relished the thought of stopping any reaction from her.

Travis reached the truck, and Dustin turned to yell at his brother. It was now or never. Cara ran. Fear nipped like a pit bull at her feet, and she picked them up as if her body had no weight. She could hear his easy breathing just steps behind her, almost tickling her neck, the faint sounds of his feet skimming the ground. Dustin's hands grazed her shoulders, slipped off, and he slammed into her. She would have hit the ground, but his arms slipped around her and jerked her back against his chest, forcing her to become one body with him as they propelled forward in a slowing trot.

She sagged, but he held her up. His lips pressed against her ear, and he chuckled, not one bit winded. "Good try, Caralynne."

When Travis approached her and dangled the rope in front of her eyes, she kicked him hard.

He yelped and jumped back. Instant anger flickered in his eyes, and he raised a hand to strike her. Dustin grabbed it.

"No abuse," he snapped. "I'll hold her. Tie her feet first."

No abuse, and they were going to …

Travis bound the rope, jerking it tight, but at a word from Dustin, loosened the cord to allow her to shuffle. Her hands were next, and Travis took her arm to lead her to the truck.

Cara wanted to scream and bite, but wasting energy wouldn't help, and besides, she needed to think, to form a viable plan.

A small, white car zoomed around the curve in the road, and both men tensed. Cara held her breath. Few outsiders traveled on their narrow private roads, only those seeking the services of the group's carpenters or seamstresses.

The car whooshed by, destroying her wish for a speedy rescue. Richard Melton's frown assured her she'd get no help from him.

They loaded her in the middle of the front seat and fastened her seat belt. Travis patted her arm. "Don't want any harm to come to you."

Thanks for nothing. Cara ignored him. *God, I'm going to try you one more time. Will you please send help? Dayne or somebody with sense?*

She angled her body so she could see out the rearview mirror. A car lingered far behind them, and Cara closed her eyes. Although she tried, her sense of direction twisted into an undecipherable maze. Dustin took so many roads she lost all possible hints of where they were headed. When they finally entered a clearing where a mid-sized cabin sat, the bile rose in her throat.

Dustin parked. Travis swung open his door and jumped out. Cara, her hands sweating, begged,

"Dustin, please don't do this."

He looked down into her pleading eyes for a second. He swung open his own door and looked across her to speak to Travis. "Go easy."

Travis did. A person would have thought she was being invited for lunch, only Cara knew better. At the door, Dustin inserted a key into the lock, and the metallic click rattled in the clear air.

The door screeched open, a long, high-pitched scream of wood against metal. The dank, stale air smacked Cara in the face, and she wanted to gag.

As politely as if escorting her to dinner, Travis guided her to one of the two chairs. Dustin unlocked and raised a window. "You bring the drinks?"

"Yep." Travis eyed Cara. "I'll get them. Loosen us right up. You need to relax, Cara?"

"I want to go home. The girls—" No need to remind these two of her girls. No need to bring her babies to their attention.

"Leave her alone," Dustin growled.

"Ah, Dustin, don't be a grump. I was only having fun." He stomped back outside, and the sound faded away.

Dustin swung to her, his gaze roving over her face and body, his good-looking features serious.

Cara swallowed. The too-strong cologne wafting from him, but worse, the man smell, the sweat, the heat permeating the air around him sickened her. Fear, stark and gripping, clutched at her, squeezed her breath, tore at her senses. She shoved her body as far back into the cushion as she could.

She stared up into his eyes. Dead eyes. Eyes showing no hint of the thought processes spinning in his brain.

He stroked her cheek. "You're hot, Caralynne Hayman." His whisper barely reached her ears.

Cara cringed at the phrase. Not in these circumstances. Not from this man who surely had nothing but evil in his plans.

Travis's boots clattered on the porch floor just as the quiet rumble of a car engine filled the air.

"Who is it?" Dustin snapped.

Travis shrugged, and the two edged back to the doorway.

Cara twisted to get a glimpse of the vehicle and gaped at the sight of Richard Melton's car pulling alongside the pickup. When he approached, Travis raised a hand. "You come to join the party?"

If words would wither these men—if she could quail the shaking inside her—she'd be glad to shower plenty of them on these two.

Richard stepped onto the bottom step and thrust his hands into his pockets. His gaze passed the two men and rested on her. "Nope. Not why I'm here."

Not for anything admirable, for sure. Cara clenched her numb fingers.

Travis's face creased in puzzlement, so they'd not expected him. Dustin's remained as still a granite rock.

"Passed you both back along the road." Richard spoke to the two young men but gave her a sneering grin.

Cara debated the value of spitting at him.

"Caught us a beauty here." Travis snorted.

"Yeah, you have. Problem is, if you've got in mind what I think, I'm going to stop you."

What? Cara thought she might pass out from sheer astonishment. Richard wanted her? Could anything be more disgusting? From the frying pan into the fire.

"What do you mean, Elder Melton?" Dustin asked, his forehead creased, manners kicking in.

Richard actually looked abashed, and Cara wanted to add her snort of scorn to Travis's ones of laughter.

"I'm taking over." Richard propped his hands on his skinny hips. "Afraid it means, fellas, that I'm taking Cara back."

"We had orders."

"Orders?"

"Yeah, Elder Hayman gave us specific instructions." Travis strutted across the porch and back.

The room tilted and swirled in dizzying circles. Emery, the man she despised.

"Where is he? Why bring her here?" Richard's voice shook, but not with emotion for her. Had to be a show of bravado. Or cowardice.

Travis smirked, and even Dustin's face twitched as if he wanted to laugh.

"What do you think? He wanted a rendezvous with her." Travis smoothed his chin and eyed Cara. "Wants to mark his territory, I'd say."

"If any teaching's done right now, I'm going to claim the privilege. You two will have to get your fun somewhere else, and so will Brother Hayman."

Pompous idiot.

"Did Elder Simmons send you?" Disbelief narrowed the boy's eyes.

For a second, action and noise suspended, then Richard burst out, "Why else would I be here?"

A lie. That tick beneath Richard's eye betrayed him. But why else would he show up? Not because he cared anything about her. She swung her head to take in the young men's reactions.

"Help him get Caralynne into his car." Travis slanted a glance at his brother, and it brooked no argument. "He's an elder."

So they'd either not seen the tick—detected the lying—or else they respected him as an elder and were afraid to go against what he demanded. She couldn't see as her situation had improved.

Travis took her arm and led her back across the lot to Richard's car. He flung open the back door, stooped, and picked her up as if she was a small child. He maneuvered her through the doorframe and tossed her lightly on the seat. An eye closed in an elaborate wink. "Next time."

Cara struggled to a sitting position after he slammed the door and walked away, but Richard was in the car and backing around in minutes.

"You jerk. How can you do this? No wonder Abby dislikes you."

The rearview mirror reflected his sober eyes. "She doesn't dislike me."

He spun down the road, whipped around a curve, and swerved to miss a truck speeding left of center. He groaned.

"What?"

"That was Emery Hayman, for your information. Coming to collect you. You should be thanking me." Richard slapped at a bug buzzing around his head.

Cara twisted. The truck was a blur of distant color. Was it really Emery, or was Richard pulling her leg? As much as she despised Richard, Emery was lower than a worm in her book. Meant to be stomped on ...

"I don't believe you. Are you sure you don't have your own agenda?"

"Because of you, I'm probably going to be in more trouble than I can get out of. In fact, I don't know why I bothered. I'd rather not be within a hundred miles of you."

Really? "I'm in trouble because of the likes of you and Emery Hayman."

"Don't classify me with him. He fancies you—"

"You have no shame. With a lovely wife like Abby, how can you even consider another woman?"

"I'm not—"

"You're a small man, Richard Melton. I've always known it and despised you."

His shoulders rotated as if trying to loosen tense muscles. "If you'd lis—"

Cara's emotions climbed the mountain of her self and peaked. His disgusting habit of hitting Abby—even if they were cuffs that didn't bruise her skin—angered her. "Let me go or else."

The rearview mirror reflected his darkened eyes. She could imagine what the rest of his face looked like.

"Or else what?"

Good question. "Or else Reverend MacFarland will hear about this."

"And I should care?" The car accelerated.

"You're disgust—"

He swung around, one arm flung onto the back of the seat, the other gripping the steering wheel, knuckles white. Sweat beaded his forehead. "Shut up. I'm trying to do what's right, so lay off."

"Kidnapping me is the right thing?"

"Shut up!" His jaw clenched as he slapped the wheel. His shoulders heaved. "No wonder Elder Simmons despises you."

"As if I've done something to him."

"You've got a smart mouth someone needs to discipline."

The right tires ran off the road, and Cara cringed. Gravel spun. Richard jerked the wheel to the left, and Cara slammed against the door. She braced herself as the car spun across the road, whipping her backward and forward.

Richard fought the wheel, tapped the brakes. Released them. Tap. Release. The car settled into a straight line.

Cara flopped against the back of the seat as she struggled to slow her breathing. "Ignorant pig."

Richard's grip tightened even more on the wheel. His eyes flashed to hers in the mirror again. "You keep that up, and I'm going to regret this."

"I already do." Cara drew in another calming breath. "Can't you see abusing women and children is wrong? Horrid and demeaning?"

"Women need to be under subjection. That is biblical."

"Abuse is not right."

"I've had enough of you. You don't know anything about what or why I'm doing what I'm doing."

Cara wanted to argue the point, but given his whole body looked like a tornado about to tear into her, she kept her lips pressed together.

Silence thickened the air and threatened to suffocate her. Her head pounded. What could he really want? Chances were they didn't include a party. She pressed her forehead against the window, closed her eyes, and wished her imagination wasn't quite so vivid.

She didn't dare jump, but when he stopped, could she scramble out quickly enough to get away?

He pulled into his driveway. How could the man? Would he take her in front of his wife? His major concern was in impressing the senior elder who'd always done everything but show contempt for the man.

Halfway to the house, Richard gave her a shove. "Move it."

Cara stumbled and glared at him.

Abby was at the door, shock in her eyes at the sight of Cara tied up. "Richard, what is going on?"

"Move back. Let us in." Richard flapped a hand at his wife.

Shuffling backward, Abby stopped midway to point at Cara. "Why is she tied up?" Distress edged her voice.

Pity for her friend overrode the dread. She didn't doubt she could give Richard a hard time, but who knew whether she'd have the chance. No matter how strong or determined a person might be, ropes binding feet and hands always proved a hindrance.

Richard slammed the door. He motioned Cara into the living room and angled her toward a chair in the corner.

He took his wife's hands. "I'm trying to do the right thing here."

Abby shook her head. "I don't understand."

"Haven't I been treating you better?"

"Yes." Abby searched his face. Then more firmly, she added, "I think you have."

"Can't you trust me?"

Was the man pleading? Why on earth would he be desperate? He had the upper hand.

Abby gave him a nod, but wariness still lurked in her eyes. "You're not planning on hurting her, are you?"

Richard gave no answer, only advanced toward Cara, and she drew back.

But instead of stopping in front of her, he swerved, took a seat on the sofa, and scrubbed at his sweating face.

"Richard, what—?" Abby followed him like a well-trained puppy.

"Are you going to sit by and let him do this, Abby?"

Running a hand over his head, Richard paced to the window. His hand shook as he wiped again at the sweat on his forehead. "Shut up or I'll gag you."

"What's the matter with you?" Abby's confused eyes stared at her husband. "Answer me."

"Stay out of it."

Tears pooled in Abby's eyes and dribbled down her cheeks. "I thought—I thought things were going to be different between us."

The man stared at his wife, his eyes wild, his breath gasps of tension. "Abby, I didn't mean it."

She walked over to the playpen, placed a hand on her baby's head, and stroked his hair, her shoulders moving in silent sobs.

He went to her and touched her arm. "I'm sorry. I didn't mean to hurt you."

"Don't touch me." Abby shrugged off his hand. "You're lying again. You never keep your promises."

He stepped closer. "I haven't broken my promise."

"How can I believe that? How can I believe you?" Her eyes were red and tearful, but she refused to look at him.

He gripped her arms and whispered, "I love you, Abby. I'll never go back on the promise I made you."

The couple stared at each other before Abby melted against him. Richard wrapped his arms around her.

Cara's head spun. Was she in an Alice in Wonderland world? Living a nightmare? Fatigued to the point of delusions?

Richard pulled away, and his hands slid to Abby's shoulders. She lifted a hand and smoothed away a tear on his cheek. Her voice held a soft tinge of wonder. "You really are sincere, aren't you?"

"Yeah." Richard's throat contracted as he swallowed.

Her head tilted a fraction toward Cara. "What about her?"

Her husband drew in a deep breath. "I don't know."

"What do you mean? Why did you bring her here?" Abby's sudden frown spread across her forehead.

Cara wouldn't mind knowing the answer either.

"Remember those discussions the reverend and I have been having? I'm trying to change." Richard clomped across the room. "I put myself on the line as an elder to rescue her, but now I don't know what to do with her."

"Rescue—?"

Richard wasn't going to hurt her? He'd meant to save her from the Martin boys? She eyed the skinny man. She'd despised him for so long. Despised his jokes, his constant kissing up to Elder Simmons, his bullying of Abby. Cara swallowed. It was hard to look at the man as her rescuer, her savior.

"Why?" she demanded.

"Why, what?" Richard stopped his pacing to glare at her.

"Why did you rescue me?"

A slow flush crawled up his neck. "I'm wondering that myself."

She *had* transfigured into an Alice in Wonderland. Her new world was not fun. Only confusing and weird. And scary.

CHAPTER TWENTY

Moonlight shrouded Dayne's tabernacle office with a gentle glow. He sat in the semi-dark, arms resting on the top of his big wooden desk. Headlights swept across the building. They flashed by the room, but Dayne didn't move. Whoever had just arrived wouldn't have any idea he was here.

Two doors slammed, one after the other. Two figures met in front of their cars. One motioned, and they headed toward the tabernacle.

Dayne cocked his head and listened. Sabre growled, and Dayne laid a hand on the big dog's head. The heavy front door whooshed open, and the sound of voices boomed down the hallway and through his half-open office door. Raucous voices. Argumentative voices. Owners who didn't suspect anyone was around.

He half-stood, paused when his ear caught a name, and settled back into his chair. He winced when it gave its customary squeak of protest.

"Caralynne Hayman's a problem. Someone has to do something about her." The rat-a-tat words spat out of a female mouth. Shrill. Spiteful. "I want you to bring her to me."

Who was this woman?

"Why me? I don't want any part of this." The whiny, half-determined male voice came from right outside his door. With one hand on Sabre's head, he trod softly to the door and peered through the crack.

"Don't tell me you haven't done this type of thing before."

Whoever this lady was, she was a very angry person. Scornful and pushy.

"You didn't hear the reverend threaten me. I'm not going anywhere near Caralynne's house, Kathy."

A coward's stubbornness.

He recognized the man's voice, had heard it recently. One with a bad association.

The names clicked in his mind. Marshall Biggs and his sister, Kathy Raymond. Were these two mischief-makers working together on their own, or had Elder Simmons given them permission to move against Cara? More trouble. He squelched back the desire to groan.

"You don't have to worry about him. Elder Simmons has his number."

Hmm. Elder Simmons didn't trust him. Wise man.

Silence. Dayne took the moment to step quietly to the door and peek into the hallway. The dim nightlights held back the darkness.

Biggs showed a sudden rush of cockiness. "Why'd we have to come here? You couldn't have asked me at your house?"

"You know very well Edward would have a fit. He can't see anything beyond his nose. Work is all he can think about."

"He makes more money than most of us. You growling about that?"

"Of course not. Don't be stupid." Kathy crossed her arms and eyed her brother. "Richard has her."

"What?"

"The idiot must have forgotten Elder Simmons had Cara followed."

"He did?"

Exasperation exploded into her voice. "You didn't know? You're an elder. How do you think you'll ever rise in the group if you don't pay attention? I've told you and told—"

"Put a lid on it, Kath. You know I won't ever be part of Elder Simmons's inner circle."

"It's your own fault." Kathy's sniff rivaled the best. "Idiot."

"Are you calling me an idiot?" Outrage billowed from Biggs's voice in waves. "I'm not the one full of crazy schemes."

Get on with it. What did Kathy want her brother to do? Dayne gritted his teeth and wished the two would quit their fussing and reveal what evil plans they'd cooked up.

"If you won't help me, I'll find someone who will." Kathy poked her bony finger into Biggs's chest.

He backed away, hurrying, stumbling. "Good. You're on your own. I'm done being your errand boy. If you want Caralynne, find someone else to follow your instructions."

"I won't rest until she's placed in The House," she screamed after her brother.

A second later the huge door moaned, creaked, slammed.

Dayne peeked through the crack. Kathy faced the front door, her lips pressed thin, arms crossed over her flat chest.

"Worthless man," she muttered. "Better off to do it myself."

It was too much to resist. "Do what, Sister Raymond?"

If he'd stuck a gun into her ribs, he couldn't have scared her any more. The woman jumped and screeched her fright, loud and piercing.

"Easy. Easy. It's me, Dayne MacFarland." He forced back a chuckle.

"What are you doing here?" Her nostrils flared as she huffed in and out and backed up against the wall.

Shame ripped through Dayne. He should have kept quiet. Scaring women—even a woman like Kathy Raymond—wasn't his thing. "I'm sorry. I heard voices—"

"Can't a woman talk to her brother in privacy?" she huffed.

"I heard you mention Cara Hayman. Is she having trouble?" Dayne peered at the woman and hoped to catch her off-guard.

Kathy's eyes narrowed, her shoulders hunched even higher. Another huff punctuated her words. "Her? She's a whore."

"Sister Raymond." Dayne struggled to keep the dislike from his voice. If she'd been a man, she wouldn't be standing. He unclenched his fingers long enough to grip her arm. "What are you planning?"

He'd heard about cackles, but the noise erupting from her throat brought the word to life. "Do? What the elders should have done a long time ago. Bring her down off the pedestal she's placed herself upon."

"What pedestal? The woman only wants to be left alone in peace to raise her children," Dayne snapped.

"Is that why every man in the group lusts after her?"

"If they do, it's because of their own—"

"No, Cara Hayman flaunts herself. Delights in the attention." She stuck a finger under his nose. "I see the way she holds herself aloof from everyone else. She knows it drives men crazy."

He'd have to agree with Biggs: Kathy Raymond was the crazy person here. Stark, raving, lunatic mad. Could he say anything to make a difference in her sick way of thinking?

Her hollow cheeks were as red as two ripe cherries. Fanaticism lit her eyes with an unhealthy glow.

"Why do you hate her so?"

"Hate her? I despise her. Loathe her." She drew back and pasted a sneer on her lips. "I'd like nothing more than to see her locked in the stocks and beaten within an inch of her life."

Dayne was sure his heart sank clear to his feet. As if Cara didn't have enough to worry about, women like Kathy had to get into the act. Well, not on his life.

"Leave her alone."

"What? What did you say to me?" Her tone spoke loud and clear: he'd injured her feelings. She stepped close, half a foot from him, tilting her nose to point toward his.

Dayne wasn't about to let her intimidate him. He lessened the distance by two more inches. "I said, leave Cara alone. She's done nothing to you, except in your own jealous imaginings, and I won't have you persecuting her because of your lack of emotional stability."

He couldn't make the words any plainer. If she had any sense at all, she'd get the message. Shock flickered. Understanding flared in her eyes. But he wasn't about to back down. He shook her arm.

"I mean what I say."

She jerked from his grip and backed down the hallway until she bumped into the exterior door. Her hands fumbled with the bar, and the door whooshed open again. Throwing a last look backward, she fled.

What a mess.

The far-off blast from his cell phone interrupted his thoughts. He hurried back to his office and snatched up the phone.

"Reverend MacFarland," the low voice practically whispered. "I've got Cara."

❧❧❧

"Does she have to stay tied up?" Abby asked.

"Yes." Richard shrugged. "If we were followed, they're liable to pop in here checking."

"The Martins?" Cara butted in. What if someone else had followed them? Someone worse than the Martin boys. Someone like Emery Hayman. Gigantic moths fluttered inside Cara's stomach. She'd been frightened of the Martins. But Emery—what had Lori gone through if Cara was so terrified? The moths beat their wings faster.

"Don't have the foggiest. What I do know is this: if it was the Martins, they'll run straight to their father, who'll run straight to Brother Tobert. Who will make sure Elder Simmons hears about our misdeeds tonight." Richard's shoulders hunched. "If Elder Simmons does hear about it, prepare for an invasion. He didn't order the Martins to kidnap you, but he won't like my interference either."

Cara's nerves quivered. Richard was right.

"If it was Emery, God help us all."

The tree line bordering the other side of the road yielded no evidence of his presence, yet Cara could feel him there. "He'd already be pounding down your door if he'd followed us. Untie me."

Richard shook his head. "I'm in deep now. I've gotta keep up the pretense of stealing you away from those Martins for my own plans, or I'm dead."

Cara opened her mouth to slash at him. His cowardice sickened her.

"Wait." Richard checked out the window again.

"My girls," Cara moaned. "They'll be on their way home from school."

Beads of sweat dotted Richard's forehead, and he swiped at them, spraying the vicinity. "Listen."

Cara tilted her head. Even the baby quieted, as if some sense urged him to silence.

A car. Driving slowly, its engine purring smoothly. Richard peeked around the curtain as a dark blue car crept past.

"Whose?" Cara whispered

"I don't know." Richard lowered his voice. "They're watching, either by car or in the woods."

Abby whispered, "How can you know that?"

Richard flashed his wife a half-annoyed glance. "I may not be well-liked, but I'm not dumb. I know when I sense something's wrong."

"Please, Richard, at least let me loose so I can defend myself," Cara pleaded.

Once again Richard stared at her. He pulled out his cell phone and punched in a number. "Reverend MacFarland, I've got Cara."

CHAPTER TWENTY-ONE

Dayne swerved into Cara's driveway. Now to pick up the girls and get them out of here. He wasn't about to take no for an answer again. Cara must listen now. She was in too much danger. Richard hadn't given him many details, only that he'd rescued Cara.

At the house door, he knocked lightly and called out. "Leila, Lacey, it's Reverend MacFarland. Are you inside?"

No giggles. No teasing answer.

Weren't they home yet? When he'd dropped by the school, their teacher assured him Cassie had picked them up and would drop them off at four. Dayne shoved back his sleeve and glared at his wristwatch. They should have been home fifteen minutes ago. Taking the steps two at a time, he wracked his brain. Had Cassie stopped for food?

At the bottom, he ran to the back of the house and shoved open the door. No point in calling out. He thrust his head in and checked out the kitchen. Signs of girlish attempts at sandwich-making lay on the table. That put a cap on his previous hope.

Heart thumping, he checked every room. Back at the door, he remembered the picnic spot. He couldn't believe the girls would disobey their mother and go there without permission, but it didn't matter. He'd have to make sure.

Dayne ran the whole way, panic building at every step. The closer he got, the more he strained his ears, hoping to hear some little-girl laughter. Hoping their happy squeals would spill into the air.

He burst onto the meadow and swept a glance around. No toys. No shoes lying around. To give himself a measure of relief, he made sure the pool held no small bodies.

He picked up his speed until he'd lengthened his stride into a mile-eating trot.

He burst onto Cara's property, praying the girls would be at their swing, playing in a mud hole, tearing the house down. He really didn't care, as long as they were safe and at home.

No sign of the girls or Cassie. Where were they? He ran a hand through his hair. Frustration and the lunch he'd eaten earlier churned together. There was no way he could see Cara without Leila and Lacey. She'd go out of her mind, fretting over them.

Think. Had to be a logical explanation here if he was smart enough to figure it out. They wouldn't have vanished into thin air. He was almost positive they wouldn't have taken off anywhere else. Cara had trained them well. He could call Cassie. Perhaps she'd taken them home. But why would she do that without Cara's knowledge? According to Richard, Cara had wanted them with her.

He couldn't bear to think of the alternative. If Elder Simmons picked them up—or even one of his henchmen—God help them. God help him. He'd never live with himself. And Cara would die from the grief.

He couldn't think about her.

He had no other choice. He'd have to approach Elder Simmons.

❧✦❧

The sound of tires crunching gravel. The faint squeaky sound of a loose belt. The quiet purr of an engine. Cara swallowed back the frustration. If only Richard would untie her. Why he thought her being bound would improve the situation was beyond her. "Who is it? Go check."

The man ran from the room. Cara strained forward. Low voices. Mumbles.

Cara inserted every ounce of pleading she could in her request. "Abby, please."

Abby stopped rocking and hugged her baby closer. She walked to the child's swing.

"If Emery's here, I'm done. Isn't that so?"

Slowly, Abby placed her baby in it, turned, and dropped to her knees in front of Cara. She buried her face in her hands. "You know I can't go against Richard. I don't want to make him angry."

Arguing with Abby would get her nowhere.

A high-pitched voice from the other room demanded answers.

"Who is that?" Cara whispered.

Cara's nerves tightened as footsteps echoed from the hallway. Richard reappeared, and behind him, Ruby Simmons.

She pushed past Richard until she stood in the middle of the room, staring down at Cara.

"Why do you have her tied up?"

"I—I—"

"Never mind. Untie her. Now."

Richard dug for his knife from his pants pocket. He stooped and sawed at the ropes binding her arms and legs. Cara shook away the stiffness from her limbs. Although they hadn't been tight enough to hinder circulation, it still felt good to be free.

"Are you all right?" The skin across Ruby's cheeks was drawn tight, the pucker between her brows marked and heavy, defying her usual look of attractiveness.

Ruby sounded sincere, but there had been few instances when Cara trusted anyone in the group, least of all the woman married to the senior elder and self-appointed leader of the Righteous Ones.

"I'm fine—now."

Richard rushed over to Cara. "Get back."

"What?"

"I said, 'Get back.' Do you want someone to see you?"

"I have to go home. I can't stay here forever." Cara edged away from the window but continued to study the dark outlines outside. "What's all the hoopla, anyway? The Martin boys kidnapped me—"

Ruby came to life and confronted Richard. "I didn't hear that."

Face pale, Richard didn't back down. He gave a shrug. "I saw them on the side of the road with Cara, figured they were up to mischief, and I followed them. At the hunting cabin, they admitted Emery bribed them into kidnapping Cara. He was afraid something would stop their marriage."

"Richard." Abby's whisper barely floated across the room. "How wonderful of you."

Richard's neck grew a dull red.

"We don't have time for sentiment." Ruby sniffed.

"How did you find out Cara was here?" Richard asked.

Ruby waved a hand as if knocking his question aside. "Never mind. We've got work to do." She squinted at Richard, and Cara realized the woman was narrow-sighted. "What's your plan?"

"I don't have a plan. Didn't think too far ahead."

"Excuse me."

The quiet words were almost ignored. Abby sat beside the cradle again, rocking gently, her face stiff and determined. Her bottom lip trembled, and she sucked in a breath as if to steel herself.

Ruby stared at her. "What? Speak up, Sister Melton."

Abby straightened her shoulders. "I think—I think you should tell us how you found out about—about this. How do we know we can trust you and that you won't cause Cara and us more trouble?"

Ruby's mouth dropped for a second but snapped closed an instant later. "You're impertinent. Would I be here if I didn't want to help?"

Abby taking a stand? It was hard to believe, but she was right. They needed to know what side Ruby Simmons was on. "She's right. We need some proof you really want to help." Cara crossed her arms.

Ruby sank to the sofa.

Figuring out an answer? Cara doubted Ruby's authority had ever been questioned.

Finally the head elder's wife looked up. "I suppose you all have a right to be skeptical of my intentions."

To put it mildly. Cara disciplined her lips.

"I overheard our executive committee discussing Cara."

"You were eavesdropping?" Abby asked, wonder in her voice.

"Of course not." Scorn as thick as syrup laced Ruby's words. She softened her tone. "At least, not much. I was checking some records in the next room. I'm sure Brother Simmons forgot about me."

Cara sank onto the sofa beside the woman. "What happened?"

Ruby fidgeted as if realizing once she spoke her next words, there was no turning back. Or something else? "Don't get me wrong. I think you flaunt yourself too much, Caralynne Hayman. You're a temptress, stubborn and insubordinate and unruly."

Gulp. Cara gave her a feeble nod. Not that she agreed.

"But I can't forget the young girl who spoke up at our women's meeting the reverend and his friend crashed. Her story brought back all my uncertainties when the same thing happened to me. The fear and helplessness. I was only fifteen. Her words got to me. I saw again how our girls feel."

A good explanation for the stricken look on her face that night.

"I've learned to forget, accept, and keep quiet through the years. It was the best way to get through."

"And Elder Simmons?"

"Elder Hayman was pressuring them to forget the agreement to give you extra time. He wants you now."

Cara fell against the back of the sofa as if she'd been shoved. The heaviness hovered, pressing, pressing, pressing until she thought she couldn't breathe. Her glance flickered around the room, searching for the lifeline she needed to keep from being pulled once again into the sinkhole of despair. It rested on Ruby. Was that pity in the woman's eyes?

She didn't want pity, especially Ruby's. The woman might have changed—to a degree—but Cara couldn't forget her past actions and attitude. "Tell me their answer."

"They agreed. Gave Emery permission to have you now."

"That's not fair. Elder Simmons gave me an extra month. Why couldn't they have told me about this?"

"I don't know." Ruby shook her head.

Cara's mind skipped from thought to thought, the others' voices a background hum.

Ruby had never answered Abby's question. How had she known

Cara was here? At Richard and Abby's house?

She broke into the excited conversation. "Before we go any further, I think you need to be up front with us."

"What do you mean?"

Had the woman's eyes narrowed?

"How did you know I was right here?"

Ruby's fingers interlocked. "I heard Elder Martin tell Elder Hayman his boys were still following you. They reported you here."

"I told you someone followed us," Richard added. "I told you."

Would Emery really kidnap her and force her into an early marriage? Yes.

Over her dead body.

Yet the thought of death did nothing to comfort her. Who would care for her girls? They'd be forced into a horrible life. They'd have no one who loved them. Now they were fairly protected. Now they had her.

Her only option was escape. She should have listened to Dayne when he wanted to relocate her. But she'd been determined to wreak havoc on the men, and she wanted that insurance money.

Had she stalled too long?

Her imagination zipped into action, seeing Emery's sly eyes piercing the walls to mock her. Winking. Smirking. Watching until she stepped outside.

No, that wasn't right. If he was here, he had enough confidence to stomp his way right inside, claiming her and ignoring any feeble protests from the Meltons or even Ruby Simmons.

She had to get away from here. She'd talk to Elder Simmons and plead her cause. Insist he keep his original agreement, which would give her enough time to finish what she needed to do. If that didn't work, she'd leave for good.

She wouldn't trust Ruby Simmons. Not even Richard or Abby. Although she loved her friend dearly, she was dominated by the orders of the group and her husband far too much. Nope, she couldn't take the chance someone would coerce her plan out of Abby.

But how could she get out of here without their knowledge?

Cara focused on the people in the room, who tossed ideas back and forward as if saving her was their greatest desire. "I think I ought to leave in the morning. Early, before anyone is up and about."

Would they believe her? To her excited emotions, it sounded like a foolish action.

Richard looked at Ruby as if he would trust her with his life.

Ha, Richard. It's too early to trust her. She could be the trap that will snap on our freedom—mine, at least.

"You could be right." Ruby laid a forefinger across her lips. "Emery's a late sleeper, so you could be gone if he does come here."

"What about us?" Abby asked.

"What do you mean?" Cara asked.

"If Brother Simmons finds out we helped you, Cara, although I want to, what will he do?"

Ruby waved away Abby's worry. "Make sure he doesn't realize. Richard, you'll have to do some smooth talking to appear like you took her from the Martins to get her to my husband. Can you do that?"

"I think so."

Doubtful. No one believed anything Richard Melton ever said, which reassured her she needed to get away without their knowledge. She wasn't about to stick around any longer than she was forced to.

"My girls. Where are they?"

"Reverend MacFarland is supposed to pick them up."

"But he should have been here by now."

"Busy with other stuff to do. Don't you trust the minister?" Richard stretched but he eyed her as if to see her reaction. "I'm hungry, Abby. How about a snack?"

Cara's stomach rolled. The doubts were jiggling inside her like Mexican jumping beans.

His wife jumped to her feet. "I'll get it. Sister Simmons, will you stay?"

"No. I've got to get back. I don't want Elder Simmons wondering where I am." Ruby headed to the door, and Abby followed her, chatting in her soft voice.

"Richard, thanks." Gruff, but at least halfway sincere. She cleared her throat.

"Thanks?" He had no idea what she was talking about. But she owed him that much anyhow. Dislike him or not.

"Thanks for rescuing me today."

For a moment, a trace of shyness flickered across Richard's face. Cara would never have expected to see any deep emotion in the man. Certainly not anything as simple as bashfulness.

"No problem. I did what I thought I ought."

Abby entered the room, a tray filled with sandwiches and a pot of coffee in her hands. "Are you hungry, Cara?"

"No, thanks." She couldn't eat, fear for her girls robbing her appetite.

Richard hurried to open a card table, and the Meltons settled at it.

Cara checked and rechecked the clock and the waning light outside. Would they never get done eating? Cara willed them to hurry. How could they eat and talk as if nothing was happening?

Dayne, where are you? Why hadn't he at least called? Had he had an accident? Something was wrong.

Cara drew up her legs, wrapped her arms around them, and laid her head on her knees. *Hurry, hurry, hurry.* As much as she loved Abby, she would scream if these two didn't leave her alone soon.

It seemed hours before Richard left the room, but the wall clock revealed it'd been twenty minutes. Abby gathered the plates, piled everything on the tray, and carried it all to the kitchen. Fifteen minutes later, she returned with sheets and a pillow in her arms.

"I'm sorry, Cara, but you'll have to sleep on the sofa."

At last. "Fine. No problem." *Go to bed, Abby.*

"Richard has to get up early for work. Sorry." Abby brushed back a strand of hair. "Is there anything else I can get you?"

"Could I use your phone to call Reverend MacFarland? I want to check on my girls."

She glanced up the stairs and sighed. "I think it'll be all right. Leave it on the stand when you're finished. Goodnight." Abby picked up her baby and went out, her footsteps tapping the stairs as she climbed.

Cara tapped the number, and Dayne's voicemail picked up.

She bit back the moan. Where was he? Had she made a mistake to trust him?

The sofa was made up, the sheets inviting and cool. Cara lay down, staring in the dark at the ceiling. Murmurs and rustles from upstairs floated into the room.

Flopping to her side, Cara sighed. She'd never be able to nap, not even for a few minutes, but she closed her eyes to rest them. If she could doze for an hour or so and still be out of here by midnight, all the better. She'd grab her girls—wherever they were—and get away before anyone knew what she planned.

Her fingers touched the snapshot of her girls she'd tucked under the pillow. She imagined Leila and Lacy smiling at her, curled up beside her, listening as she read one of their favorite books.

Her body relaxed, and Cara drifted off.

After what seemed like minutes, she struggled out of a deep sleep.

The hand that covered her mouth and nose smelled of strong, brisk cologne. Definitely not Leila or Lacey's clean, childish scent. Her eyes popped open, and she stared in the dark at the hawkish figure bent over her.

She tried to scream, and the smallest sound came from the figure. He was laughing at her. Cara flung up a hand, scratched a long streak down his hairy arm, and lifted her legs to kick out at him. The man grunted when she connected.

"Lie still, you wildcat."

She knew the man's hissing voice, and her heart didn't stop at her stomach but sank clear to her feet. She didn't give herself time to think about it. She groaned as loudly as she could, kicked, squirmed and fought, fear for herself pouring the adrenaline into her body.

He slammed down on top of her, knocking her breath away. She grabbed his arm and struggled to pull in air around the hand smothering her.

"Are you gonna go quiet?"

She resisted, struggling.

Two fingers pinched her nose, and Cara's strength weakened.

"Give in, you wretch." He tightened his grip.

Cara nodded, and he snorted.

"As if I'd trust you. I'm going to make sure you go quiet, sweetheart."

The crack on her skull flittered as a microsecond bit of pain, and Cara tumbled into the land of darkness.

CHAPTER TWENTY-TWO

The throbbing pain kicked like a cantankerous tethered mule determined to get free of a rope. Cara whimpered and groaned at the exploding gun inside her head. Memory teased and pranced, fading in and out.

The Martin boys' good-looking faces convoluted together.

Richard's eyes stared at her through a rearview mirror.

Ruby Simmons's voice ordered, "Cut her loose."

The demonic laughter in her ear. The dark form …

Cara went still as her memory synchronized with the recent events. Emery Hayman breaking into the Meltons' home. Standing over her. His strong, sickening cologne smothering her. His sly words and sinister laugh. And the crack on her head.

She remembered scratching and clawing at his face, remembered kicking. She hoped she'd hurt him good. Injured him beyond repair. Cara tried to grin but realized she couldn't. The gigantic pain in her head overpowered the ache in her jaws from the rag binding her mouth.

She wiggled her arms, her feet. He must be really scared she'd escape if he trussed her like a stuffed turkey ready for the oven. Cara forced her muscles to relax. No need to fight a battle she couldn't win. She'd save her strength for any future chance.

Cara shut her eyes, intending to drift off to sleep, but flipped them open again. Where was she? What time was it?

Daylight. So morning had come.

Another thought hit her, and she fought the panic surging inside. Where were her girls? Were they home wondering where she was? Or was Dayne protecting them? The image of her daughters under Emery's supervision taunted her. Was he even now mistreating them?

The dark depression was like a cumbersome cloak, threatening to pull her into unconsciousness. It was too much. She couldn't bear it. Her breath tightened and came in gasps through her nose. The weight on her chest pressed down, the bile rose to her throat.

Convulsively Cara swallowed, forcing the lump down, down, down. She couldn't vomit now. She'd choke to death. She squeezed her eyes shut and willed her body to relax.

As if some well-loved person had walked into the room, a calmness permeated the air. Cara clung to the impression.

Her right leg jerked. A cramp gripped her calf, but she threw all her mental juices into soothing her screaming body.

Loosen those muscles in your legs and feet.

Slowly. Slowly.

Way to go. Good.

Now unclench your hands.

One finger at a time.

Roll those shoulders.

A badly maneuvered roll.

Not bad, Cara, not bad.

Saying it didn't make it so.

A maniacal grin pulled at her cheeks.

Calm down. Concentrate. Now your mind. Relax-x-x. Blank everything out. You've got to forget the bad stuff. Forget what could be happening.

All she could do for the girls now was to survive. She had to trust Dayne had them.

God, if you really do exist, take care of my babies. Please.

❧❦❧

There was a light knock, the doorknob rattled, and the door cracked open. A pale-faced woman looked in, and when she saw Cara awake, she whispered, "Are you hungry?"

Felicia?

The door flew open wider, and the woman stepped inside. She hurried to Cara's side, set the tray on the bedside table, and fumbled with the cloth binding Cara's mouth until it fell away.

"What are you doing here? I thought you'd gone to your parents."

The woman's eyes grew moist.

"What's wrong?" Cara whispered. "What is this place?"

Felicia scooped up the napkin covering the tray and folded it neatly. She lifted the half-filled bowl of chicken soup and dipped a spoon into it. "Please eat. This is really good."

She put the spoon to Cara's lips, but Cara shook her head. "Felicia, I want some answers. Tell me now."

Felicia set down the bowl and rested her hands on her lap as she stared at Cara. "Don't you know?"

Cara shook her head.

"We all heard the rumors, the whispers." Felicia smoothed her wrinkled skirt. "Like me. I heard, shivered, and secretly laughed at the stories. I never once thought I'd live here."

Was she crazy or had Felicia gone mad? "I don't understand." The strange glint in her friend's eyes frightened her. "What?"

"This is The House. The place that doesn't exist."

The place that had scared the bejeebies out of all of them, even though they'd laughed and joked and kidded each other about it. And wondered if it was truth or rumor. Privately dreaded the thought one of them could be sent here.

And here she was. At The House.

❧❧❧

Dayne approached the Simmonses' house and frowned. He searched the windows and noted the two open ones on the second floor. The awful moaning sounds seemed to be coming from them. He knocked lightly, and the moaning stopped. What on earth?

No one answered the door. No one called out. Dayne knocked again and twisted the knob. Unlocked. He stepped inside. The living room was empty and disturbed. Sofa cushions lay scattered onto the floor. Various ornament items on the coffee table lay strewn across the table, out of place and turned on their sides. Dayne frowned. What had happened here?

"Elder Simmons?"

No answer. He glanced into the study. Empty. He paused at the kitchen door. Other than a few dishes collected in the sink and a couple half-empty boxes of animal crackers, nothing seemed wrong. For good measure, he checked each of the other rooms with the same results.

"Simmons?" he called out louder.

"Rev-erend MacFar-land?" The tentative words were shaky and weak.

"Elder Simmons? Ruby? Where are you?"

A groan. "U-p here."

Upstairs. He took them two at a time, checked the first door, then the second. The third door stood open, and he peeked inside.

Ruby lay on the floor. Her eyes were the only part of her moving. One side of her face was bruised and swollen, her clothes ripped, the flesh beneath torn and bleeding.

Dragging a quilt from the foot of the bed, he dropped to his knees and spread it gently over the woman. "What happened?"

"S-immons."

"Your husband?"

A slight nod. A groan.

He had to get this straight. "He did this? Why?"

Her tongue flicked out and tried to moisten her lips.

"Never mind. Let me get you on the bed. I'll get you a drink and call the doctor."

"No-o."

"No? A friend?"

"Y-es."

Dayne bent, slid his hands beneath her. "You okay? No broken bones?"

A shake of the head. "I d-don't think so."

He lifted, and as gently as he could, laid her on the bed. "Let me get you that drink."

Dayne left the room in search of a phone. He wanted to get to the bottom of this, but making Ruby comfortable was priority.

And where was Elder Simmons?

❧❧❧

"Why am I here? Did Emery Hayman bring me?" Cara asked.

"I think so. I didn't see you when you arrived, but some of the other women said he and Elder Simmons did."

"Why are you here?"

"I don't know." Felicia's lips puckered, and she licked at them. "I did everything they wanted me to."

"Do you think the elders placed you here because of Mike's death?"

"I didn't tell."

Cara eyed Felicia. Tiny worry lines spiked out from around her eyes. Whatever she'd gone through hadn't been easy for her. Cara's heart ached that she hadn't checked on her disappearance better.

"Didn't tell what, Felicia?"

"That we killed Mike."

A gigantic hand punched Cara's chest. She'd wanted him dead. Did that make her a murderer? "We didn't kill Mike. It was an accident."

The bowl rattled onto the table. Felicia wrapped her arms around her waist and rocked. "No, it wasn't. I shouldn't have provoked him. I caused his death."

"You were the most wonderful wife a man could ask for. Don't you dare put yourself down like this. Mike was crazy."

The other woman straightened. Fire spat from her eyes. "He was not. I loved him. He was a saint."

Felicia's eyes were haunted, and the apparition that peered back at her gripped Cara with bony fingers. Felicia had lost it. The trauma had been too much for her delicate state.

"Okay, but please don't fret."

Felicia's blaze of anger faded. A small smile curled her lips. "You need to eat."

"Could you untie me, Felicia? I could eat so much easier."

And escape.

Felicia dropped her voice lower. "Oh, no, I can't. That would be bad, and I'd get punished. They specifically said not to untie you."

The rush of disappointment brought a lump to her throat. It wasn't going to be as easy as she'd hoped when she'd first seen Felicia peeking around the doorpost. "They say that to scare you. What can they do once I'm free? Anyhow, I need some exercise. You could untie me, let me walk around in here. Tie me up again before anyone comes."

Would she believe her? Trust her? A twinge of guilt at using her friend pinged at her heart, but now wasn't the time to worry. There was too much at risk. If she couldn't get free, she'd become a victim too and unable to rescue Felicia and the other women.

"I can't—"

Time for desperate measures. "Felicia, listen to me. Where's your son? Do you want me to help you get him back? Get you out of here?"

The answer radiated in those pain-filled eyes.

"You've got to do your part." Cara drew in a breath. "Untie me. Now."

Confusion, understanding, and resolution flickered across Felicia's face. Her hands fluttered toward Cara.

Cara shifted so Felicia could easily get to her bonds.

The door slammed open, and a plain woman, arms crossed, her shabby clothes straining to cover her ample curves, leaned in. "What are you doing, Felicia?"

Felicia jumped to her feet. "Nothing."

A groan built up in Cara's throat. Great. Felicia looked so guilty the other woman would have no problem pinpointing her lie. Cara pasted as bland an expression as she could onto her face.

"You should have finished feeding her twenty minutes ago." The woman eyed them as if they were specimens pinned onto a scientist's board.

"Yes, Linda. She's not very hungry. I had to—to coax her to eat." Felicia twisted her fingers together. "She's exhausted and it's very hard for her to eat tied up."

Linda's lips pursed, and she bent to peer into the soup bowl. "Doesn't look like she's eaten a bite."

Felicia opened her mouth as if to object.

The woman swung around to look at Cara. "Not good enough for you, huh?"

"That's not—" Cara said.

Her sneer was an object of perfected disbelief. "You think you're a notch above the rest of us." She leaned over Cara. "Better get those thoughts right out of your head, 'cause you're in for some grand times, if what Emery has to say comes true."

She walked to the door and gave Felicia—standing as silently as a frozen animal—a rough jerk of the head. "Out. You've got other work to do. If she doesn't want to eat tonight, she'll be hungry enough in the morning to appreciate breakfast."

Felicia hurried to gather the tray, and without looking at Cara, fled the room. Linda gripped the doorknob and said, "I could care less about what happens to *you*. But if you want to see your friend again, don't put any troublemaking thoughts into her head."

More hours of being tied up. If she didn't get loose soon, she wouldn't be able to move once the ropes were off.

❧❧

The nurse's shocked expression—though she said nothing—convinced Dayne that Ruby's injuries were serious. She held Ruby's wrist, taking her pulse.

His boiling anger eased. Dayne slipped out of the room to give them some privacy. Ten minutes later, the nurse appeared in the hallway and said, "Don't be long. She needs to rest."

He approached the bed, and Ruby's eyes fluttered open. "Sit," she whispered.

He settled into the chair close to the bed. "Can you tell me what happened, Ruby?"

"Yes. I want to."

"You said Elder Simmons did this. Why?" As much as he loathed the senior elder, he'd thought the two had a good relationship.

Her rueful glance slid across his face. "Because I acted out of bounds." She lifted a hand, winced, and let it drop back to the bed. "I overheard Elder Simmons, his executive committee, and Emery Hayman. Emery wanted them to wave their promise of an extra month to Cara. They agreed."

"But what's his hurry? They've already ordered the marriage."

"Elder Simmons had her followed. He knows she's hard to handle. I think they're afraid of what she might do."

Exasperation exploded inside him. "Like what? She's a wonderful mother and good person. All she wants is to be left alone."

"Unfortunately, you know that wish won't happen. Emery has had his eye on her for a long time. If she hadn't been his brother's wife, I'm afraid he would have taken her long ago."

"Is she still at Richard and Abby's? Emery hasn't gone there, has he?"

Ruby tried to move. A moan escaped her lips. "She was at their house earlier. I think she was going to try to leave in the morning. Early. Before anyone was about."

"He hasn't found her yet."

"Richard thought Emery followed him after he rescued Cara from the Martin boys."

What a nightmare. "When did this happen?"

"Those boys were ordered—probably by Emery—to take Cara to their remote cabin where the men stay when they hunt. Richard happened to see them, followed, and claimed her for himself. They didn't know any better and let her go. Emery probably spit nails when he found out she was gone."

No doubt. And if he hadn't already, Emery would locate her quickly. Dayne had dawdled too long already. Time to go. "She will never marry

Emery Hayman."

What would Emery do to get what he wanted?

"Thanks for the information. I need to get going. The sooner I pick her up, the better." Dayne patted Ruby's hand.

Ruby gripped his hand, surprising strength in her squeeze. "Don't be too sure. Emery has a hold over her."

Dayne frowned. He didn't like the slyness in her eyes.

"He has Cara's girls."

CHAPTER TWENTY-THREE

Cara slid her lids open. Something had wakened her. The wind or the creaking of an old house protesting the actions inside its structure?

The dark was total. No moon, no stars twinkled friendly beams. A faint breeze stirred through the cracked-open window and kept the room from stuffiness.

The room seemed vacant, and Cara stared wildly, hoping to identify anything out of place, anything that shouldn't be there. In her mind, she could see the old dresser in the corner. By the door, a pine wood stand and a stone lamp. The mirror above it was large and cracked in one corner and faced the only window in the room.

She strained to listen as the granddaddy of all shivers crept up her back. Was Emery even now creeping closer?

There. A creak. Another one. Cara held her breath, hoping it wasn't true. Surely God in his heaven wouldn't …

The doorknob rattled, and the door opened. Softly. Slowly. A faint, flickering light—like a candle—from the hallway, barely silhouetted the opening. A pause. Cara sucked in a breath.

Fingers curled around the edge of the door. A body edged through the doorway, and in the person's other hand, a knife glinted.

❧❧

Dayne drove away from the Meltons', his helplessness mounding like an erupting volcano. Where was Cara? These two had no clue. They'd simply thought she'd gotten away during the night. But the mussed cover, the pillow halfway across the room, and most of all, the picture she'd left behind told a different tale to him. She wouldn't have left a mess like that, and surely not the picture of her girls. He touched the pocket where the picture lay.

Someone—Elder Simmons or Emery—had kidnapped her again. Could they force her, even blackmail her into another unwanted marriage? It was a terrible mess.

He drove aimlessly. He'd failed to protect her girls. Granted, he hadn't known about the mess until after the fact. Still, he should have prevented this whole fiasco. He'd failed to protect Cara as he'd promised.

Dayne slapped the steering wheel and groaned. Glancing at his wristwatch, he realized he'd been driving an hour, going nowhere, no destination in mind. Another whole day gone, and he had no idea …

Marshall Biggs.

Dayne slammed his brakes as the name struck him like a hammer. *Are you trying to tell me something, Lord?*

The man was a hunter. Surely he'd have an idea of any out-of-the-way place where Cara and her girls could have been taken. It was worth a shot.

Dayne made a U-turn and headed back toward the Biggs home. If the guy gave even a hint he knew something, he'd beat the truth out of him. Dayne tried to pray. Begged for strength to tamp down the savageness raging inside him. If God didn't help him now, he was sunk.

❧❧❧

Cara lifted her head to follow the person's progress. The woman—she wore a dress—crept nearer. The light from outside the room outlined the figure but gave Cara no clue as to who it was.

"Cara?" The one-word question was a feathery whisper.

Felicia.

The woman retrieved the candle from the hallway and set it on the dresser. She turned to Cara, the knife still clutched in her left hand.

Her body as limp as a wet washcloth, Cara asked, "What are you doing here, Felicia? Why do you have a knife?"

"Shh." She laid a finger over her lips. "I'm going to cut you loose for a while. But you've got to promise me you won't try to escape."

She couldn't make that promise.

Felicia waved the knife. "I doubt you could anyhow. They let the dogs loose at night, and they're vicious. I tried once and almost got my arm chewed off."

Cara closed her eyes, defeat beating a steady drum. Was she never to get a break? "What will we do in the morning? They'll know someone let me loose."

"I brought rope. I'll tie you up again." Felicia brandished the knife then sawed at the rope. "Stay quiet now."

The tension eased as the rope loosened, and as the last strand let go, Cara pulled her arm down from over her head. The blood pounded in her limb, tingling from the sudden circulation.

Felicia tiptoed quietly to the other side of the bed.

"Where's Linda?"

"Asleep. I made sure."

"Who is she? She was terribly unfriendly."

"Not really. That's her way. Once you know her, she does everything she can to make things here—well, acceptable."

When her left hand was free, Cara sat up in the bed. "My legs now, Felicia."

"Linda's in charge of all the women here."

"Head whor—" Cara winced at her slip of the tongue. How could she?

"You don't understand, Cara. None of us want to be here, but Elder Simmons and the elders ordained it. For one reason or another, God has placed us here."

"Nonsense. God didn't do this." Cara flung a hand out in a wide sweep. "He doesn't want you here. He wants you, your son, and your parents together as a happy family."

Felicia's forehead puckered. "We're not whores. That's what you meant, wasn't it?" She shook her head. "No, we're not. We serve God by serving our elders. We've got assurance of heaven because we're obedient."

Should she argue the point? Felicia had obviously been brainwashed. "Where's your son?"

"One of the mothers in our group is training him. I'm not fit to raise him." Her eyes were blank again. She glanced down at the knife lying on her lap. "Perhaps in time, when I've learned to be more obedient, I may get him back. Elder Simmons said."

Her friend's eerie imitation of Elder Simmons's voice spooked Cara. Felicia rocked gently, her vacant eyes staring out the window, her thumb absently rubbing across the blade of the knife.

Cara swallowed the lump climbing up her throat and blinked to keep back the tears. How could those evil men do this to Felicia? Fighting her husband and seeing his horrible death would have been enough to send a woman over the edge. She needed comfort, not punishment. To take her adorable baby away and place her here to serve any and all men who wanted her—unspeakable.

Her friend needed a lot of things, but right now all Cara could offer her was a heartfelt hug. She eyed her friend, scooted close, and enfolded her within her arms. "Thank you, dear friend, for untying me. I'll never take freedom for granted again."

"I knew you'd appreciate it."

Cara pulled back. "Let's walk to the window. Will anyone be outside to see us?"

"I don't think so."

They both shoved the stubborn window as high up as it would go, and Cara leaned out. Felicia's soft giggle floated to her. Cara reached behind her and pulled her friend toward the window. "If we had wings, we could fly away from all this."

"I'd be a swallow."

Cara bumped her friend's shoulder. "Not me. I'd want to soar. I'd be an eagle."

"How like you." Felicia hung out the window until her feet left the floor.

Cara grabbed her arm. "Careful, or you'll get the chance to fly without the wings."

Reluctantly, Felicia squirmed back inside. "Wouldn't be much fun, would it?"

"Where do you suppose the dogs are?" The ground below seemed a long way down, deserted, eerie. Shadows flickered from the outside nightlights.

"Who knows?"

"If we had some nice meat to toss at them, we could get past them. Do you think you could get some?"

"I don't know." Doubt tightened Felicia's voice. "I could try."

"Now?"

"What if Linda hears me?"

Would she make irreversible trouble for Felicia in pushing her? The images of her daughters' faces swelled in her mind. She had to risk it.

"Tell her you're hungry or I am."

"No. Won't work. We're not allowed to eat whenever we want. Meals are on a strict regimen." Felicia wrapped arms around her body. "She'll know in the morning."

"She will?"

"The kitchen help will report the theft to her."

"Do you all have certain jobs?"

"We work in the mornings. Afternoons are our leisure time. Nighttime is—"

"Will you get the meat?"

"I can't. I can't. Not right now." Felicia backed against the door. "I don't want to risk worse punishment."

A retort pushed at her lips. Cara wanted to lash at her friend. Not fair. Felicia had a reason to be fearful. She'd lost her baby. At least Cara still had hers.

She hoped.

❧❧❧

The door opened, and Marshall Biggs gaped at Dayne, but Dayne didn't give him a chance to react to his late-night presence. He pushed forward and grabbed the man by his shirt front. "Where is she?"

"Who? What are you doing, Reverend?" Marshall tried to pull Dayne's hands from his T-shirt.

Wasn't going to happen. Not till he got some answers. "I want to know where they've taken Cara."

Marshall slid a glance at the stairs to the right. "Shh. The kids and Darlene will hear you."

Dayne shook the fistful of shirt in his hand, jarring the man enough to stagger him. "Tell me."

"Is she gone?"

The question sounded sincere. "Don't act stupid, or you'll really upset me."

Marshall raised a hand. "Honest. I don't know a thing."

"Do you want me to talk louder? In here? So the kids can hear what a thug their father is?"

The man shook his head.

"Let's step outside and get some answers." Dayne pulled him out the door and kicked it shut with a satisfying bang. "Now you can either tell me something, or I'll drag you around in my car until you think of some reasonable explanation."

"What do you want me to say?" Marshall whined. "Elder Simmons doesn't confide in me. If Cara is gone, he would have been the one to give the order. You'd do better to go to one of the inner-core elders or to him."

Not another dead end. "Okay, tell me this. Where could they have hidden her?"

Marshall shrugged, halted. "Did you check at The House?"

"What is The House?"

Marshall's mouth twisted into a smirk. "You don't know?"

Would the Lord forgive him if he wiped off the man's smirk? Probably, but he might also want him to apologize to Biggs. Best to hold onto his patience. "I wouldn't ask otherwise."

"Our resident whore house. The place Elder Simmons and the Inner Core send all the women who fail for one reason or another."

Dayne let go of the other man's shirt. Why hadn't he heard of this place? Had Elder Simmons kept it from him on purpose, knowing he'd oppose the whole idea? "But why? They've planned to marry her off to Emery Hayman."

"To scare her? Hide her from you? Who knows why Elder Simmons does what he does?" Marshall eyed Dayne. "I know I've done some things you don't like. But I'm not totally against those things you've been preaching. Between us, I think Elder Simmons is out of control. Needs reining in."

So. Here was another possible recruit. Or was his failure to achieve the Inner Core sanctum causing the man to speak out of bitterness?

Time would tell.

❧❧❧

Cara and Felicia knelt by the windowsill, whispering. The air cooled, and the clouds rolled across the sky, threatening rain. Cara refused to think about the next hour or so when Felicia would insist on tying her again. Yield to bondage when Emery would come for her soon? How could she?

Why *hadn't* someone come for her? Where was Dayne? She'd thought for sure he'd be here to rescue her. Only one answer: he didn't know where she was. No one did.

Cara stared down at the bare ground, the gigantic rocks scattered around. She'd rather take her chance with the ground and the dogs as be with Emery. What would it be like to fall? Three stories up, could she survive a jump? No, she'd end up with a broken leg, which would effectively prevent her from running from her worst enemy.

"You can't get away, you know."

Cara jumped at the toneless voice coming from Felicia.

An outside light barely reflected Felicia's soft mouth drawn down into a grimace. She gave a half-shrug. "I know what you're thinking because I've been in your shoes. When I first came here, I wanted out so badly, I contemplated jumping. Imagined all kinds of ways to escape."

How could anyone survive so much horrible abuse? Felicia's thin face and peaked features had aged her. She seemed to hover between despair and acceptance. Between life and a fantasy world. Would Cara herself become the same?

Cre-e-ak.

The drawn-out sound screeched through her body. Cara tilted her head, listening, and turned to face the door. From the corner of her eyes, she saw Felicia standing, one hand at her mouth, no doubt holding back a scream.

"Easy," Cara whispered. "This old house might be shifting."

Or not.

Thick, suffocating silence.

Was that a scuffing sound?

Cara gripped Felicia's hand and shrank back against the windowsill. Felicia moaned, and Cara tightened her grip. "Shh."

Linda? Or someone much worse?

"Can we lock the door?"

"No locks." Felicia's voice trembled. She pulled on her hand until Cara let go. Scurrying across the floor, she pressed her back against the corner, hands splayed on the wall. She slid to the floor and wrapped her arms around her knees, eyes wide, lips clamped together as if to hold back her sobs.

No help from her. Cara faced the door again, swallowed, and tiptoed across the room to press her ear against the door. Was that heavy breathing on the other side? The person could be catching their breath from climbing three flights of stairs. Or were they listening for noises from Cara's room?

Cara laid a hand on the doorknob, felt it move, and spread her fingers as if the knob had burned her, but too late. The door flung open, and she back-pedaled, tripped, and landed on her backside. She gasped for her knocked-out breath and stared up at the man who stared down at her.

One thing for certain. She'd startled Emery Hayman as much as he'd startled her. And he recovered quicker.

He stepped into the room. Cara sat up, prepared to scuttle backward. He took another step closer and snarled, "What are you doing untied?"

As if she'd tell him. Cara slid a sideways glance at her friend shrinking against the wall. As long as Felicia remained quiet, perhaps she, at least, could come out of this unscathed. Cara tensed and bent her legs, preparing to rise. He shuffled forward, dropped to his knees, and captured her arms. "I've never done it on the floor before," he growled in a low, raspy voice.

Cara sneered back and opened her mouth to retort, her heart pounding.

"At least not for a long time." His breath assaulted her nose, fanned her cheeks, tickled her neck. Way too close.

"And not for a long time to come either." Cara squirmed as far away as she could get.

"You're mine. We're going to be married in the morning."

"Never." Cara shook her head, all the vehemence she could muster in it. "Never, never, never. I'll die first."

"When I get through with you tonight, you'll have second thoughts." Emery's hand lifted, stroked her cheek, slid down …

Cara sucked in her body, trying, trying, trying to get away from the big hand. She jerked her hands he still held above her head, hoping to free one, to scratch, pluck out an eye, or tear off an ear.

"I hate you. How can you do this, you devil?"

"I don't need your love, Caralynne." His lips changed into a mocking smile. "Nope. Don't need that. I want to awaken all the passion simmering inside that man-maddening body of yours. Make it mine."

Stop him. Scream. Beg … Get away.

"I want you to beg for more, implore me never to stop."

The black tornado raging in her mind loomed closer.

He stared down at her, saying nothing but freezing her mind, his snake-eyes hypnotizing her with an unseen power.

The tornado tunneled through her body, incinerating her bones, cooking her mind into mush. Weakness descended onto her and seeped into every pore. She allowed her eyes to close, allowed her mind to drift into dark blankness where she didn't have to think.

Go away, mind, body, far away. It's not happening. He's not here. You're in a world of intense darkness. The bad will be gone soon.

Her mind closed down, her life oozed closer to the storm pulling and whirling her into its vortex.

Cara!

The devouring heat cooled, her mind jelled into one thought.

Dayne. Dayne was here.

Cara moved her head, moved her lips, her fingers tingling as life flowed into them again.

Hold on. I'm coming.

Life rushed into her body, a raging torrent. Her eyes opened. Emery's head bowed over her. Her skin crawled at the sight of both his hands touching her ...

Both hands.

Hers were free. She lifted her head and sank her teeth into the arm in front of her face. The nauseating sweetish smell of his cologne and the sweaty body odor wafting from him sent her already-queasy stomach into a rolling mass of bile. But she held on, sank her teeth as tightly onto his forearm as she could, ignoring the hairs and smells. The roar of outrage blasted from him, and he jerked away, giving her the moment of freedom she needed. She rolled away, jumped to her feet, and ran for the door.

He'd catch her. Easy escape was too much to hope for. But she got her hand on the stone lamp and swung at him, glancing the blow off his head. He staggered and raised a hand to rub his head.

Cara tossed the remnant aside and backed to the window. If nothing else, she would jump. Death was better than Emery.

Leila. Lacey.

No, she couldn't die.

Felicia still sat in the flickering candle-lit corner, the woman's eyes as vacant as they'd been minutes ago. Her silent rocking did nothing to reassure Cara.

What to use for a weapon? Nothing. The room was as bare as a newborn baby's rear end.

Felicia's knife.

Emery rubbed his head then looked up and grinned. "I love a good fight. Especially with a woman. You'd think she'd know she'd lose, wouldn't you?" He shook his head. "But nope. Every time you get a feisty one, she fights like she's going to win."

The knife lay on the bed. Could she grab it before he got to her? She had to make the attempt. She slid forward, lunged, and grabbed it. Stabbing desperately, she hoped she'd hit a vital spot.

She jabbed again, and the knife sliced deep into his hand as he grabbed for her wrist. "That's for Lori, you beast."

He didn't even wince. His fingers dug into her skin, cutting off any feeling. She struggled, and he increased the pressure like a vise that refused to be defeated until, at last, she released the knife. It clattered and slid across the wood floor in a circling pattern.

With a cry of outrage he flung her away. She landed hard against the window frame, rattling the glass.

The outside ledge, just a little under twelve inches wide, lay behind her. The rain peppered it now, soaking the wood, turning it into a slippery slide that promised anything but safety. Would it hold her?

Of course it would. She ran to the window, leaned backward and out, and gripped the window frame halfway up, preparing to draw her legs out. The rain slapped her on the back of the head.

A loud curse burst from Emery's mouth. "What are you doing, you fool?" He rushed across the room and clutched for her ankles. His fingers slid across her bare feet, and she kicked out.

She scrambled onto the ledge and slowly straightened, her head dizzy, the ground below floating toward her. Emery lunged out the window and grabbed for her legs, caught one, and tugged. Cara dug her fingernails into the rough siding, pressing against the wall of the house, holding on.

"Get in here before I let you fall," he hissed.

"Do it."

He jerked her leg forward, and Cara screamed, tottering on the edge.

She was going over. Then his strength pulled her back, back, back. Cara fell against the wall, gasping. For a moment, his grip loosened, and her mind registered the plant hook protruding from the wall.

In a single motion, Cara wrapped her fingers in a death grip around it and kicked away Emery's hold.

Perhaps he thought the near-fall business had scared her enough to draw her back inside. Or maybe he was so caught up in the drama he didn't realize his grasp had loosened. Whatever the reason, in yet another kick, she was free and moving out of reach.

Too late he threw himself further out the window and missed her by inches. He cursed. "If I have to come after you …"

He let the threat hang, but when she refused to respond, he threw his leg onto the ledge.

Cara shrank from the thought of both their weights on it. Would it hold?

He crawled out, the perpetual sickening grin still plastered on his face. "Where you going now?"

Cara forced herself not to think about the ground too far below and fixed her attention on the man instead. He started to shift his weight from one knee to the other to stand.

He was off balance, or it wouldn't have happened. A look of surprise rolled across his face as he tottered then pitched backward. He threw himself forward but it was too late. His legs slid off, and his hands clawed at the ledge, seeking a life-saving grip.

Two small hands—Felicia's—gripped an iron clothes rod and slammed it onto his hands.

The rain dotted Cara's face, blinding her, but for a second his gaze held hers. The next, he lost his grip and disappeared.

Felicia waved a hand. "Get in here before you fall."

Cara scooted back to the window and scrambled in as Felicia backed up. Cara whipped around to look for him. No thud. No body on the ground. Where was Emery?

She stretched out into the rain.

"What?" Felicia cocked her head.

"He's not down there."

"You probably can't see him for the ledge." Felicia rubbed her bare arms. "I wonder why Linda didn't come when you screamed."

"Unconcerned."

A hand slapped the edge of the ledge and sent Cara's heart into overdrive. She jumped and cracked her head on the window. Emery's head rose into view, his eyes orbs of determination. "Thought I was a goner, didn't you? This fancy Cornish trim saved my life."

Too bad.

"Give me a hand. I twisted my shoulder."

Cara answered before she thought. "And have you pull me over? No, thanks."

He grunted. "Why would I do that? I have plans for you. And your girls."

Anger surged through her, blinding her, consuming her. She wanted to push him back. Watch him fall.

He must have read her expression. "Kidding. Give me a hand."

"That is not funny." Could she believe him? "Promise you'll leave me alone, and I'll help you."

"Can't do it, sweetheart. Gotta make sure you get to heaven." He swung one leg up. "I have an obligation to my dear departed brother. And to God."

The urge to scream at him, hurl ugly epithets at him was overwhelming, but she swallowed it back and started to pull down the window. "Promise. I don't want to ever see you again." She slapped his hand.

Quick as a snake's strike, Emery latched onto her wrist, and even though he already was half way up, his heavy weight jerked her part way out the window.

"Cara, no. Don't trust him," Felicia pleaded.

Emery increased the pressure on her wrist. "Either help me or we'll go down together. Romantic thought."

Cara shrank from the craziness lurking in his eyes, at the evil grin pasted on his lips. "Let me go." She drew back her left arm and put all the strength she had in the punch that landed on his nose.

Surprise registered first in his eyes even as the blood poured from his nose, and the hand gripping the ledge slid. He let go of her wrist and grabbed at the rain-soaked board. Emery's leg dangled off the ledge. His fingers contracted, grasping, digging—and found nothing to stop his slow slide.

Cara stared wide-eyed as he sank lower and lower until only his fingers pinched at the ledge. At the last second as his fingers disappeared, he yelled, "You'll never find them now."

For an instant the quicksand comment threatened to suck her deep into an ever-widening hole. He did have them. Hidden where she'd never find them.

Cara started to grasp his hand, to keep him from falling, to discover where he'd taken them.

Her hand clapped onto the empty ledge. Rain soaked her already-drenched hair as his body fell.

Somewhere behind her, Felicia screamed over and over, and Cara was sure her voice joined Felicia's. She stared as Emery floundered in the air, his arms and legs kicking as if trying to fly. The bedroom door slammed open, and Dayne's voice called out, seemingly from a distance. "Cara!"

Too late.

Emery's body slammed onto the ground below, the sound echoing upward. Cara lay across the windowsill, wet and cold, all emotions wrung from her heart.

CHAPTER TWENTY-FOUR

Cara hung out the window, the bottom of one foot cocked up, the tiny tattooed eye glaring at him from the wrist she held behind her back. Her clothes were drenched and clung to her slim body, and her hair, darkened from the rain, hung in rivulets across her shoulders. She lay as if her first thought had been to … as if she were … jumping? Dayne's throat contracted, and he croaked out her name again, "Cara!"

She didn't turn, didn't move, didn't acknowledge she'd heard him. Dayne tossed his flashlight onto the bed and rushed across the room. He lifted her and drew her back into the room. Her eyes were wide open and unseeing, her body limp and cold as he supported her.

His heart pounded with such intensity he wondered if he was having a heart attack.

Only then did he see Felicia. He snapped, "I need to lay her down."

Dayne settled Cara's body onto the bed and lifted her hand to check her pulse. Weak.

He pressed his forehead on her limp hand and mentally shot a prayer heavenward. "What happened to her?"

"Emery. He was here trying to rape her. She fought back."

Lifting his head, he said, "Did he hurt her?"

"He didn't rape her, if that's what you're asking."

"I'm taking her out of here."

"She's in no shape to move."

"I can't take a chance on leaving her."

"I won't let anyone get to her."

Dayne grimaced. "I hardly think you'd stand a chance against a couple of Elder Simmons's men."

"Probably not. But I've got this." Felicia pointed at the knife lying on the floor in the middle of the room.

Could he trust this fragile woman? She looked willing to use it. Dayne said, "I'm calling a doctor. Can you find some dry clothes for her?

Dayne left the room in time to run into a big woman barreling down the hallway.

"What are you doing here?" she bellowed.

Who was this woman? He tilted his head, but he wasn't going to be cowed by her or anyone else. "Reverend MacFarland, ma'am. I'm here to see about Cara Hayman."

The woman's eyes contracted. Was deceit glittering from behind her pupils?

"Who called you?" Her question was an accusation.

"God." Dayne wanted to chuckle.

"Funny. Did Emery send you?"

"No."

"Let me pass. Those two are making mischief. I'm going to get to the bottom of this." She pushed against him, trying to force her way.

He gripped her arm. "No, you're not. No one is to go near Cara's room. Do you understand?"

Her shoulders reared back, stiff, unyielding. Her lips were a thin, red line as if to defy him. But he didn't flinch, didn't back down, and the defiance ebbed away. "Fine. Cara Hayman is more bother than she's worth." She tossed the words over her shoulder as she rushed away.

A matter of opinion. Dayne hoped she wouldn't double back. Meanwhile ...

He maneuvered down the hallway, studying each of the other five shut doors. As he descended the stairs he paused at the bottom. The woman held a telephone receiver in her hand.

"You need to get here and see what's going on. I can't find Felicia. Some man is here—says he's Reverend MacFarland—and forbids me to enter the Hayman woman's room. Emery promised he'd stop by and pick up—"

The woman paused.

"I thought you said—"

Another pause.

The woman cleared her throat. "All right. Whatever you say."

She banged down the receiver, grumbling, and swept him with a sour look. "Elder Simmons says for all of you to stay put till he gets here."

Dayne couldn't resist teasing her. "Really?"

The woman stomped away.

❧❀❧

Dayne tapped lightly, and Felicia called from inside. He pushed open the door. "How is she?"

"She's sleeping, I think."

The dagger in Dayne's heart twisted another inch. What would he say when her beautiful eyes questioned him about her girls? "Elder Simmons is on his way over."

Felicia's eyes were wide and frightened. "What are we going to do?"

"Talk to him." It would be a fight. If Elder Simmons agreed on Cara being here, he wouldn't want to let her go. Dayne wasn't about to budge, even if he had to call in outside authorities. Was he doing the right thing? Once he spoke, there was no going back. All chances to redeem anyone in this group would be gone.

Cara moaned, and Dayne glanced at her wan figure. "Where did Emery go?"

"His body's on the ground below the window." Felicia pointed outside.

"What are you talking about, Felicia?" Dayne asked.

"Emery Hayman. He fell out the window."

"Are you making this up?"

"Of course not." Felicia frowned. "What gave you such an idea?"

Dayne picked up his flashlight, moved to the window, and shone the light on the ground below. "How on earth did he fall?"

"Cara climbed out on that ledge. He went after her and slid off. At the last minute, I think—I think Cara decided to help him even though I warned her not to." Felicia shook her head and patted the blanket that covered Cara. No emotion played across her features now.

What on earth had Cara gone through?

❧❧

The taillights of the group's doctor's vehicle, carrying Emery's body, faded in the distance. Blood from Emery's body stained the huge rock beside Dayne. Two big dogs sat on their haunches, eyeing Dayne.

Elder Simmons, who'd spun onto the grounds minutes before the doctor arrived, grunted. "Fool."

"What do you mean?"

"Pulling a stunt like that. What did he think he was doing?" Elder Simmons shook his head solemnly. "The man was irrational. What a waste."

"He was more than irrational. He tried to rape Cara Hayman."

Elder Simmons rocked back on his heels. "What are you doing here?"

Dayne slid a look at Elder Simmons. The man had shed his cordiality. Seething anger bled from every pore. "What do you mean?"

"What do you think I mean? How did you find out Cara was here?"

A soft answer turns away anger. Could he defuse Elder Simmons's wrath? "Partly guesswork. I suppose you could say God led me here."

Elder Simmons snorted. "If I find out someone's been talking when they shouldn't have …"

"Did you order Cara to be brought here?"

"No, I did not."

That sounded like the truth. "Who did?"

Several puffing breaths hissed between Elder Simmons's lips.

"Was it Brother Hayman?"

"I gave him permission last night to marry Cara this morning."

Could he pierce the man with a dagger-stare to make him tell the truth? "And what did Cara say about this?"

To give the man credit, he did shuffle his feet as if suddenly ill at ease. "I didn't want her told, knowing how she felt."

"You know." Dayne bit off the words. "And yet you still insisted she marry a man she despises? What possible happiness can come from a marriage built on a relationship of hate?"

Elder Simmons's chest swelled. "We're not purporting happiness. I want only to assure Sister Hayman and her girls of heaven's wonders."

God, help me. Dayne clamped his lips shut to hold back a retort. "She despised her brother-in-law. How could you force her into such a relationship?"

"Brother Hayman coveted her. He's wanted her for years."

"That certainly doesn't make your decision right."

Elder Simmons patted the flower sticking from his shirt pocket. "Son, I know you have a soft spot for Sister Hayman. She's a beautiful, passionate woman but with an ancestry of corruptness. She has a level you know nothing about. I've observed her for a long time. Willful. Defiant. Scheming. Uninterested in our traditions."

Cara's little-girl face flashed into his mind. Those sad, sad eyes, silently imploring his parents for love. Willful? What this man called willful, Dayne defined as independent. What was ascribed to Cara as defiance, he preferred to label determination. And she wouldn't suffer fools willingly. Activities she'd see as hypocritical, she'd shun.

No, Cara wasn't any of those things Elder Simmons described. She was, though, a strong, determined woman who exercised her mind.

Someone the group could not condone.

Elder Simmons bellowed on, but Dayne paid him no mind. He was beyond caring about his senior elder's opinion. Cara was, and would always be, the most wonderful woman in the world.

When he could get a word in, he said, "I'm taking her home."

"I don't think so." The senior elder nodded at someone behind Dayne, and he turned. Five men stood as if guarding the door to The House. Five guns pointed at him.

❦

The silence was prevalent when Cara opened her eyes. Felicia sat in the chair beside the bed, dozing, the soft bedside lamp casting a glow on her friend's face. By the strain riding Felicia's features, she was the one who needed to be in bed resting.

Where was she? Nothing seemed familiar, and yet—

Her memory returned in a rush. Emery Hayman. Forcing his way into the room. Forcing his way on her. Emery on the ledge. Falling. Flailing. Slamming onto the ground.

Was he dead?

She had to know. Cara shoved back the covers and tiptoed across the room. She pushed up the window and peered below. The rain had softened to a light drizzle, and the moon peeked in and out of the clouds scattered across the dark sky. She looked down.

No body. And no chance to find out if Emery had hidden her girls.

Cara sank back against the wall. Had she dreamed it all? No, why would Felicia be in here? Why was she untied?

A sudden thought stirred her to action. Could she get out? Now? She hated to leave Felicia, but she had no choice. She could get around better without her tagging along. She'd come back for her when she'd assured herself of her daughters' safety. She kissed her fingers and flung the kiss toward Felicia.

"Cara?"

Cara stopped dead.

"You can't go out. Elder Simmons is downstairs."

Cara whispered, "What's he doing here?"

"I don't know. He and Dayne were down there—" Felicia tilted her head toward the window—"a while ago, talking."

"Dayne was here?" The flutter in her chest meant something, but what? Why couldn't she remember him here? "What did he do?"

"Carried you from the window to the bed."

"I think I remember leaning out the window in the pouring rain." Cara lifted a hand to her hair.

"I probably looked like a drowned rat."

"Pretty much. I don't think he noticed. He was too worried."

"About me?"

"Who else?"

"*Why* was he here?" Cara plopped onto the bed.

Fluttering her lashes, Felicia drawled, "I think he came for you."

CHAPTER TWENTY-FIVE

Elder Simmons's mouth writhed in a smile that widened his fat face. Why, then, did his eyes deliver a different message?

"Nothing personal, Reverend. We have your good at heart." Elder Simmons actually smacked his lips. "You are not the man for Cara Hayman."

Surely something more concrete would be forthcoming.

"I don't want all the money and interest we've invested in you to go to ruin. So we've made some decisions."

The men's faces showed determination, their eyes rabid with loyalty. They would use *guns* to keep him away from Cara? He indicated the men. "Why are the armed men here?"

"With all the subterfuge, we want to make sure all's in order."

Subterfuge? What on earth was he talking about?

Elder Simmons threw an arm about Dayne's shoulders and walked him off a few paces from the others. "God didn't ordain me to lead this group for nothing. I'm his vessel. He gives me the plans, and I carry them out. They've worked. When we stay within these rules, all goes well. Order. Happiness. Satisfied families."

Stuff Elder Simmons had touted before. Dayne grew up with the brainwashing. Did the man think Dayne was an idiot? Repeat the basic doctrine enough, and he would hunker down and accept? Dayne shrugged off the arm lying heavy on his shoulders.

"I've made my decision." Elder Simmons frowned at him, his lips a hard line, eyes narrowed into slits in the fleshy face. "You will abide by it."

"What is your decision?"

"Two things: you accept our suggestion of marriage and stick to your duty: give our people the spiritual leadership they should have."

"I haven't heard any complaints." No need to address the marriage issue. No way would he consider any of their suggestions.

"Your messages are fine." Elder Simmons waved his words away. "Although they push the extremities of our beliefs, I've found little fault yet."

Yet?

"No. No. We have a fine preacher." Elder Simmons slapped Dayne on the shoulder. "You've been a good investment, Reverend. We're pleased."

Was that supposed to make him happy?

"We want you to be happy, and marrying will help achieve that goal."

"Your choice or mine?" That could have been left unsaid, but too late now. "Your second decision?"

His leader's face sobered. "You leave Sister Hayman's welfare up to your leaders. You have to trust we want the best for her. Given proper handling, she will come around. She'll learn our way is best."

At what cost?

"Tell me, what have you decided for her future now that Emery Hayman is gone?"

"She will remain here. That will give us time to look for another husband for her."

"Why can't she live in her own home? She'd at least have a measure of peace."

Elder Simmons's head shook before Dayne finished talking. "We've tried that, but unfortunately, for a woman like her, too much freedom gives Sister Hayman a sense she can do whatever she wants. She must be brought under control."

"If I don't agree?"

The lines sharpened in Elder Simmons's face. "There won't be any ifs."

"I can't agree, Elder Simmons." Dayne lowered his voice and hoped the man would be reasonable.

No such thing.

"You have no choice." Elder Simmons mocked Dayne's own tone.

"I think I do." Dayne drew in a long breath. Time to show his colors. "I won't be a part of certain conditions any longer, sir."

"Meaning?"

"Meaning, the young girls' marriages sicken me. Meaning, this House business."

"You are blaspheming our beliefs, Reverend."

"Ours?" Dayne shook his head. Might as well lay his convictions on the line. "No, not mine. *Yours. You've* held this group of people captive for years. *Your* perverted words and actions have deceived. *You've* led them far from true Biblical principles."

The elder's lips curled, but into nothing pleasant. Words spewed from his mouth in a rush of spittle that sprayed Dayne's face. "You. What do you know? You've betrayed me. I sent you away in good faith, trusting you would stay true to our beliefs and me."

Dayne unclenched fingers tightened into a fist and drew in a sharp breath. He softened his tone. "Sir, I can't help what my heart tells me is truth. Do you think I wanted to go against what I grew up believing? I fought as hard as you are now. Professor Moore showed me—"

"Bah! Moore and his foolish ideas. Coming here thinking he can ruin what I've built." Elder Simmons struck out at an offending branch that dared brush against him. "I won't have my work destroyed by him."

Exactly what needed done.

Elder Simmons flapped an arm in his direction then settled himself on two spread feet, arms crossed. "Or you either, for that matter. I built up this work. I selected you as our next minister. I urged the funding for your schooling when others balked. I paved the way for you—"

"Paved?"

Elder Simmons looked nonplussed at the interruption. Or was it something else totally different? "Got rid of any hindrances so you could follow the directives God gave me for you."

He didn't seem so pompously angry right now. But his explanation clanged off-key. "What hindrances? Why should there be any?"

For a second, Elder Simmons stared at him. Licked his lips. Tapped nervous fingers together. "Never mind. It's enough for you to know I overcame them all. For you. Now are you going to stand with me?"

He couldn't pledge his allegiance to this man. "I'd like to take Cara home."

Raw emotion clouded the other man's eyes. Resignation that Dayne wouldn't change his mind about Cara? That something would have to be done … about him?

❧❧❧

Dayne's thumb caressed Cara's picture. The horizon outside showed streaks of color to herald another day. Promising what? "I had to show my hand."

"I was afraid you'd have to. Simmons is pressured, not only from you, but from the whole group of elders. Give in to a few demands or show a front of strength? He's on the verge of ruin and is fighting for all he's worth," Professor Moore said, his voice coming loud and clear through the phone.

"He says he didn't kidnap Cara. Blamed it on Emery Hayman."

"Don't know the man, but if he did what you said he did to Cara's oldest, I wouldn't put anything past him."

"Why drag Cara into this mess right now?"

"If he can make it work, it's a way to strengthen his leadership. Bring the most rebellious woman in the group to heel, and the men will rally around more fervently than ever. They will see his supposed directives from God are good and right."

"How do you know this stuff?"

"Don't forget, I've majored in cults for years and especially honed in on Elder Simmons's family. I know how their minds work."

"I wish I didn't."

"It'll be over shortly. I hope to have the rest of what I need within hours. If I can obtain the last part of my investigation, we'll be ready to move on The Righteous Ones. We're talking total disbandment, at the least."

Good news, so why did he still feel as if he were floundering? "I'm not sure what to do about Cara's girls. No one will confess to having them. Should I call in the cops?"

"Someone knows, and I have no doubt Elder Simmons is at the helm. No one would make a move against them without his orders."

Dayne groaned. How could he ever face Cara again? "Emery Hayman told Cara he hid them."

"Maybe. But you can be sure Elder Simmons knows where they are. He's behind everything. I'm also pretty sure he won't harm them. Not yet. He's facing too many iffy situations to risk harming those girls."

"I can't sit by and do nothing."

"What about the men who seem favorable to your teaching? Would they help look for them?"

"Could be worth a shot. I'll check as soon as we hang up." Dayne paused. "Simmons said something this morning that caught my attention."

"Hmm?" Interest perked up the prof's voice.

"Not actually what he said, but a lack of clarification. Kind of an impression that there was a meaning behind his words."

"Such as?"

Was he being paranoid? "Something pertaining to my past. He said he took care of all the opposition to my training as a minister."

"What opposition?"

A crash pounded through the phone. Dayne hoped it wasn't one of the professor's wife's treasures. "I'd love to know the answer."

"Did your father oppose Elder Simmons's wishes?"

Past questions nibbled at his mind. "I don't know. *I* complained, but Dad didn't tell me he argued with Simmons about my career. Never pushed me into anything. Told me I'd have to make my own choices. I'm the one who was responsible for what I did in life, and not to let anyone ever talk me into—"

The thought struck him as forcefully as if a baseball had smacked into his forehead. He *had* been talked into ministry. After his father's sudden death, Elder Simmons insisted ministry was Dayne's supposed calling. God revealed it to Elder Simmons in a vision, and reluctantly,

Dayne had given in like some kind of puppet. Rebelling, frustrated, and angry, but obedient.

Until the professor rescued him.

"So you don't remember any arguments between your father and Elder Simmons over you?"

"Only what I took for healthy debates. My dad was quite a thinker and loved nothing more than debating his favorite topic at the time. Of course, whenever Elder Simmons paid a visit, mom ran me out of the house anytime she caught me hovering at Dad's study door." Dayne swept a hand through his hair. "Dad was troubled for several months before he passed away, though. I remember I asked him over and over what bothered him, but he wouldn't say. He just gave me a strained smile and waved away my questions."

"Don't let it bother you. Until you can learn more, concentrate on finding Cara's daughters and getting her out of the group. I'll work from this end, gathering all the weapons we can possibly use against your leader."

Dayne set his cell on his desk in slow motion, his mind still on Elder Simmons and the possibility waving a yellow caution sign in his mind.

The late nights when Dad came home from the elders' meetings, dragging his feet.

Dad's haggard morning face. His mom, sober, standing over the stove, casting worried glances at Dad.

The loud voices coming from the study, where Dad and Elder Simmons secluded themselves night after night.

Were these meetings the reason Dad suffered a heart attack?

Dayne walked into his bedroom and opened the closet door. On the top shelf was a box. Lifting it down, he placed it on the bed and stared at the square piece of cardboard. He'd never had a reason to open it. Never had a desire after his parents' passing. He lifted the lid and set it aside.

Could something inside this small box hint at the events happening when his father died? His dad had been the writer, the journalist, but he'd been through many of his dad's journals and found nothing.

He leafed through the papers, searching each one, and finally lifted his father's death certificate. He scanned the document. Heart failure. Nothing surprising there.

Flipping it over, he saw the small strip of paper someone—his mother probably—had taped to the back. He unfolded it and read:

I suspect my husband's death was premature. He was pushed to an early death—intentionally. I know it, but can't prove it. I can see the facts in the man's eyes. The satisfaction, the triumph.

What was his mother talking about? And the man—who was he? Was she trying to say this man caused his father's death?

Slowly he pulled a thin book from the stack on his end table and ignored the others toppling haphazardly. The sight of the worn blue cover warmed his heart. He opened the book.

Flipping to the final entry, he pressed the spine and reread the last lines.

I have failed my family miserably. I don't know how I could have done more, but in my heart, I realize how wrong I've been. I should have guided them better. Now … I don't know.

Worst of all is Caralynne. Our little girl. How could I have done this to her?

Dayne's heart lurched. The entry had troubled him the first time he'd read the inscription, but now, in light of his mother's message, it was frightening. What was his father writing about? This line about Cara sounded ominous. What had he done to her? She'd never given any indication his father had mistreated her. He'd never, ever seen signs of it.

Unless …

His mind froze. Dad adored Cara. Made excuses for her no matter what kind of trouble she got into. Not like Dayne, who had to be accountable for every misdeed. His dad loved him. He never doubted it. But his father hadn't suffered any out-of-bounds foolishness from him either. He glanced down at the words his father penned.

I must get them out before it's too late.

Was this second thoughts about membership in The Children of Righteous Cain? Worse, had Elder Simmons seen his father's doubt?

What had Simmons meant about the funding? His father—he was sure—laid back more than enough money to cover any schooling or training Dayne would have wanted.

It was compulsory for any savings or insurance to revert to the group's account if a man died and only the wife and younger children survived. But at the time of Dad's death, Dayne had been a young man bordering on adulthood. Elder Simmons should have consulted with him before taking over his father's accounts.

The sudden memory of Elder Simmons talking to his mother, her set features, her body shrinking from the man and his words, could have been the precipice that drew the life out of his mother.

Simmons confiscated the majority of the MacFarland funds to keep him in line. The sudden truth hit him with clarity.

"I've delegated enough finances for a good start once you return."

The words blazed as if on fire. He never before thought about where the money came from, but as sure as he was sitting here at his father's scarred desk, Dayne's suspicions were correct. If only he had the answers to all his questions and some way to prove them.

But for now he'd have to push this away. Focusing on Cara and her daughters was priority now.

Dayne slipped into his car and headed to Levi's house. If anyone could help him, Levi would be the person.

The door opened almost immediately. Levi's rugged good looks broke into a weary smile. "Come on in, Reverend. What brings you here this early in the day?"

"I'm after answers." Dayne took the seat Levi indicated.

"Not sure I'm your man." Levi crossed his legs. He looked up when Jodie peeked into the room, her brows raised in question. "Do you still have some fresh lemonade?"

Jodie nodded and disappeared.

"What do you want to know?"

"Someone kidnapped Cara Hayman and took her to The House."

Levi rubbed a hand over his face. "I've been gone the last three days, but before I left, I heard Emery Hayman was badgering Elder Simmons for Cara."

"Elder Simmons said the same."

"I think he was afraid the longer he gave her, the more set she'd be to fight the marriage."

"Can you blame her?"

"No, Dayne, I don't. Most of the elders know you have your eye on her." Levi leaned forward as if he wanted to get his point across more forcefully. "You realize, don't you, Elder Simmons will never permit you to marry her?"

"I don't need his permission to marry whom I will."

"You are the minister in our group." Levi sat back. "In a sense, you're second in command. If you don't keep our orders, why should the others?"

"I can't—"

"I'm serious. Elder Simmons is rabid about this. For some reason, he despises Cara. I think he would—"

Dayne's heart stilled.

"—would have her killed before he'd let the star of his plans marry her." Levi sat forward. "Ever since I can remember, he's been obsessed with Cara."

"Why Cara?"

Why not Cara?

You're mine. Remember.

Elder Simmons's words, whispered from the past, floated to the top of his memory. The image of a younger Simmons stalking from his father's den, angry. Glancing down at Cara, who sat on the floor waiting with Dayne for his father to emerge from his study.

"All I know are rumors from my teenage years, understand?" Levi crossed his long legs.

Dayne refocused on Levi.

"For a brief spell, Simmons courted another woman. Was wild about her. But when she rejected him and refused to join our group, it was too late. He'd already given Cara to Donald Hayman." Levi's eyes focused on the past. "Probably an act Simmons regretted ever since."

"I still don't understand why he'd give Cara to Emery Hayman if he was so infatuated with her."

"You know Cara." Levi grinned. "No one has ever conquered that independent streak in her. She despises Elder Simmons, although to give her credit, she's never flaunted it."

"But he knows, and whatever affection he carried for her changed to hate quickly."

"I think so."

He'd been a fool to think he could outwit Simmons. Those guns back at The House convinced him they would have shot him down. Simmons left nothing to chance.

"I've got to get her to safety."

Levi pursed his lips. "Has Simmons posted a guard?"

"Armed."

"Worse than I thought. He's really serious about this." Levi shook his head.

"On top of that, someone picked up her girls before I could get to them."

"Definitely Simmons."

"According to Felicia, Emery's last words were, 'You'll never find them now.' He must have hidden them."

Jodie walked in but stopped at his words. "Someone took her girls?"

"I thought perhaps you might know who'd be the most likely to have them."

Levi shook his head. "I don't, but Elder Simmons called a special meeting tonight."

"Because of Hayman?"

"I suppose so." Levi rubbed a hand across his face. "There are rumors floating around. I know for a fact Simmons filed a report after Kenny's death."

"With our area sheriff? That's normal procedure."

"Yes, but it's on record."

"What is?"

"Rumor has it he accused Cara of causing Kenny's death and has our sheriff sniffing around, asking questions."

"Nonsense."

"I don't know, Dayne. Someone supposedly saw something suspicious and reported it to Elder Simmons. Again, this part is rumor, but I *imagine* we'll be discussing it too."

"Great. As if she doesn't have enough to worry about. Simmons is determined to destroy her."

"What on earth possessed Emery to behave so crazily? He already had the promise of marrying her."

"Are you sure Elder Simmons wasn't in on it, encouraging Emery to push her?"

"I can't think of a reason benefiting him. It would be out of character. He's not the type to pull suspenseful acts. He's more methodical."

"Unless he was afraid of what Cara would do, and to force her into another marriage, he gave his permission to Emery. When that didn't work, he ordered the girls taken." The longer he talked, the more hideous it sounded.

"I can see him thinking that." Levi took a long drink of his lemonade and wiped his mouth.

Dayne rose. "I'll keep digging until I get some answers."

"Have you talked to Ruby?"

Dayne swung around to face Jodie. "Not since I found her. Did you know Simmons beat her?"

Jodie grimaced. "I heard. I'm not sure how much you can trust her."

"Those bruises were real. You think she deliberately misled me?"

"I believe *you*." The look she gave him echoed his own sense that his words were silly. "How does any woman know what her husband's up to? I don't care what Emery said. If Cara's girls are gone, Simmons is behind it. She can give you some ideas where to look."

"By the way, how on earth did Emery fall?"

Dayne looked at his friend. "He fell out of a third-story window after trying to rape Cara."

"Good." The word was a whisper, but Jodie's face blazed her

satisfaction at the news.

"Jodie, don't." Levi sent her a reproving glance.

"I know I shouldn't, but I can't help how I feel. I despised him for what he did to Lori. She was the sweetest kid."

"It was never proved—"

"Everyone knew." Jodie shrugged.

He should quote scriptures of admonition. Rebuke their words and give them advice, but Dayne couldn't rake up the enthusiasm. Sometimes people asked for what they got, and Dayne kind of wondered if God agreed when it came to Emery Hayman.

CHAPTER TWENTY-SIX

No one bothered to bring any food around. Finally, Felicia said, "I'll check the kitchen and try to grab us a sandwich or a couple boiled eggs."

"Are you sure you should? I'm not very hungry." Cara frowned. She'd been so afraid last night. "I think we should stay together."

"I'm going." Felicia tugged at the dresser they'd shoved against door. Cara rushed to help.

"Please be careful. I don't trust Elder Simmons or the woman who's over this place." She gripped her friend's arm. "What if they're hoping we come out so they can whisk you away … or something worse?"

Felicia gave her a small smile that was absolutely no reassurance. "They won't bother me."

What? Had Felicia forgotten her part in this whole episode? She skimmed Felicia's eyes and sighed. Vacant again. Reality forgotten while lost in a world of denial. Cara stepped back. "I love you."

If Felicia heard, she gave no indication. She gave a last tug at the dresser and squeezed through the crack. The door shut behind her slender figure.

Two hours later, Cara paced. This was so stupid. Dayne was gone. Why didn't she walk out? Who would stop her? Linda? Elder Simmons?

But when she opened the door, a man at the end of the hallway looked her way and straightened. Cara slammed the door shut, her heart pounding.

Was that why Felicia hadn't returned? Had they whisked her away to put more pressure on Cara? What did they think she was going to do?

The bed creaked when Cara sat on the edge. Something was wrong. She tiptoed to the door and checked the hallway again. The same guy still lounged at the end, only now he squatted on the floor and seemed not to hear her door opening. The narrow stairs looked alluring. Could he be distracted?

Cara headed to the window, whirled, and returned to the door, thinking, thinking, thinking. She peeked into the corridor. Two doors down, she caught a glimpse of a woman she'd never seen. A hand lifted, a forefinger laid across red lips, and a bright blue eye closed in a slow wink. Cara tilted her head. Was the woman signaling her? Offering—help?

The woman withdrew, not looking at her again. Her door shut, and Cara followed suit but remained by the door, peeking through the barest of cracks.

Seconds later, the sound of female arguing reached her ears. Cautious at first, then louder. Something crashed against a wall. A loud shriek pierced the thin walls, and Cara heard the hurrying footsteps from the man down the hall. His pounding on the woman's door exploded into the air.

Silence, as if the women ceased their arguing. Someone from inside the room shrieked out a defensive comment.

"Open this door now." The man gave the door another knock.

It opened a little, and the man shoved his way inside. Cara could hear their loud voices as he remonstrated with whomever was inside.

She slipped out her door and flew down the hall. The strident voices followed her. She ran down the stairs and nearly tripped over her feet backpedaling as Linda entered the foyer on the first floor. When she walked straight through into the next room, Cara hurried to the front door and caught sight of the men loitering on the front porch. Guards? Cara scurried through room after room. A door beckoned to her, and she ran to it and peeked out. Good. No sign of anyone.

Outside, the woods at the edge of the property called, and Cara wasted no time getting to it. She peered back at the three-story, rambling house and nearly passed out at the sight of a hand fluttering at one of the top windows. Calling her back?

No. It was the woman who'd given her the opportunity to escape. For a second, Cara's eyes misted. She rubbed away the moisture and waved energetically.

"I'll be back," Cara whispered before trotting off. "If I can at all, I'll be back to save you too."

But right now she had to find her girls.

❧❧

Cara stayed on the path through the woods. No one would be on the trails this time of the day, yet she kept her mind on the surroundings. If the Martins or someone worse were around, she wanted plenty of time to hatch a plan before they spotted her.

Her first stop would be at Dayne's. If he had the girls safe and sound—if Emery lied about taking them, fine. She'd head for home and dare any of the elders to touch her. Whether her confidence was strong enough to keep her here permanently was a question to be answered later.

If Dayne didn't have them—perish the thought—her first priority would be to check out the hidden places she'd created at her own home—the secret, hidden nooks she'd drilled into her girls' minds.

No one would catch her unprepared again. Vigilance and alertness would save them. She'd been stupid, parading along the main highway where she was an open target for idiots like the Martins. She might be no match for their physical strength, but she'd bet her wits against theirs any day.

Dayne was right. She needed to leave the group while she still could. The events boomeranging in her life prompted her decision. Yet the ugly revenge she wanted to heap on these men hissed at her. Nipped at her ankles. She wanted it as much as ever, but she had to rein in the desire. She couldn't endanger her daughters any longer.

Cara swiped at her forehead. There was something peaceful and safe about the woods. Yet behind it, her subconscious pelted her to remember something. Her head pounded. Shadowy figures from her numerous nightmares pranced in her mind.

Eyes.

Haunted.

Blank.

Glaring.

Tears built behind her eyelids, and she blinked them back.

Not now. No time.

Cara quickened her pace. She loved to run. Had run all her life. But running the miles to Dayne's house was beginning to drain the energy left in her body. Lack of food and the strain of the last three days increased her fatigue.

No matter. Cara bit her lip and pushed herself harder.

❧❧❧❧

Was he too late to help Cara? To find her girls?

Fifteen minutes later, he sat inside his home. As if he was in an icehouse, his heart numb, he stared at the bowl of cereal he hurriedly prepared, telling himself to eat.

His mind wouldn't allow even a shred of comfort. The images of Leila's shy smile and Lacy's wide-eyed innocence blocked his every move. How could he shovel in food when they might be hungry?

Truth be told, he seriously doubted it. Not one of the elders had ever been known to withhold food from his children or wife. They might beat their wives into submission to gain heaven, force their families into obedience, but food was provided in abundance.

Dayne dumped the soggy cereal into the disposal and ran water over the bowl. He started to slip the bowl into the dishwasher when a whisper caught his attention.

Was he going mad?

He set the bowl down gently.

"Dayne."

The whisper floated on the air, tentative and soft and pleading.

He opened the back door a crack.

Cara's strained face looked up at him. Tiny drops of sweat dotted her face. Her chest rose and fell, harder than usual. Had she run all the way from The House?

"Cara. How did you get away?"

She collapsed onto a kitchen bar stool. "Where are the girls?"

"Let's get you a drink first." Dayne opened the fridge.

"Where are the girls, Dayne?" Cara slapped a hand onto the countertop. "Do you have them or not?"

Dayne took the stool beside her. "No, I don't—"

"Where are they? Where are they?"

"Shh. I don't know. When I—"

"Does that stupid Simmons have them?" Cara's eyes were wild. Her fingers dug into his arm.

"I don't know. I've questioned everyone, but no one will tell me anything."

Cara burst into sobs. "Richard said you'd have them. He told you to pick them up." Her head jerked up, and she slammed a fist into his chest. "Why don't you have them?"

He grunted but made no move to stop her. His throat clogged up as the tears stung his eyes. He swallowed the silly lump.

"How could you? How could you lose them? I trusted you." Cara collapsed against his arm and sobbed. "My babies. Where are you?"

Dayne drew her closer, patting her back and mouthing soothing words.

Her body shuddered, and Cara drew in a long breath. Dayne pushed a napkin into her hand. She straightened and mumbled behind the napkin, "I'm sorry. I know this mess isn't your fault."

"It's okay." He kept his voice soft and low. "You have a right to be worried sick. I'm sick myself."

She propped her forehead on her fist and moaned. "How could he? How could he take my girls?"

"What are you talking about? Do you know who has the girls?"

"He said he had them, and I'd never find them." Cara bent over and wrapped her arms around herself. "I think I'm going to throw up."

Dayne jumped up and led her to the bathroom, handed her a wet cloth, and quietly shut the door.

He listened outside the door to Cara's moans and dry heaves. The woman would have to eat, whether she wanted to or not, or she'd be so weak she'd pass out again. Dayne headed for the kitchen. He had no broth, but he'd bake a potato and try to get some of his electrolyte performance drink down her.

Minutes later, he heard the bathroom door open. She wobbled into the room, her face white and wan, her hair damp. "I hope you don't mind. I used your comb and tried to clean up."

Dayne waved a hand. "Fine. Now come and take a few bites of this potato."

"I can't. Thanks, but no."

"If you don't eat, you're going to collapse, and what good will that do?"

Cara twirled the stool until she could settle on it again. She eyed the potato.

"You don't have to eat a lot. A small bite to see how you do," Dayne coaxed.

With a trembling hand, she picked up the fork and dug into the potato. "You always bullied me." Her tone was light, but Cara didn't laugh, and neither did he.

"Seems to me I remember a girl who ordered me around as if I were her servant."

"Why don't I remember that?" Cara's lips nibbled a tiny bit, then she sobered. "This is good."

"We'll find them. I know we will."

She lifted the fork and slid another minuscule piece into her mouth. Her eyes questioned him.

"Professor Moore and I think they have them for a hold over you."

She chewed but said nothing. Methodically she lifted another forkful of potato to her mouth.

"What did you mean when you said *he* said you'd never find them? Who's *he*?"

"Emery. Right before he fell, he said he had them, and if I didn't help him, I'd never know where they were." Her voice was toneless. She lifted her glass and sipped at the blue-colored drink.

Dayne shook his head. "That doesn't make sense. Why would he take them when he'd already been given permission to marry you? He didn't need a hold over you. He had you. If his lust hadn't overcome his senses, he would have had what he wanted."

A spark of energy re-lit her body. "You don't think he took them?"

"I'm not positive, but it sure doesn't make sense."

"Who? Elder Simmons?"

A big accusation to make, but he was the more logical choice. Jodie was right. Few of the elders would move on a scheme like this without his direct order. Besides, what purpose would it serve any of them? To carry out a kidnapping against children because of a grudge or jealousy and know you could face Elder Simmons's wrath—well, it didn't sound plausible.

"I have no proof."

Her fingers clamped around his wrist. "But what do you think? Feel, Dayne? Is he the one?"

His heart lifted heavenward, seeking wisdom. "I think so."

Cara jumped to her feet. "If he has touched them, I will kill him."

❧⤫❧

He should have known better than to tell her before the proof was in hand. She'd been a hot-tempered child. Obviously, she hadn't shed the trait.

"Calm down. We can't make accusations without knowing what we're doing."

"I know what I'm doing. Allowing him to harm my girls is not in my plans." Cara crossed her arms and eyed him, her bullheadedness coming out strong and plain.

"He's been pretty busy with you—"

"I didn't ask to be bothered."

"As I was going to say, and with me."

A pause.

"*You?*"

"Yep. I've been rebelling."

"You? The reverend?"

"Of course. I know what rebellion is." Dayne held back a laugh at her expression.

"Saint Dayne?"

"Saint Dayne? You call me that?"

"Not often. Just when you won't go along with any of my plans. And I don't say it aloud—only in my head."

He scowled at her. "For two cents, I'd—"

"What? Tell on me? I don't think so." She sighed. "What am I going to do?"

"Finish your potato and let me think a minute."

Something nagged at his memory. Something about one of his stops.

Dayne tapped his fingers, his mind running through the list of people he'd talked to, and in his mind's eye, Ruby Simmons's name jumped out at him. He snapped his fingers. "Got it."

"What?"

"When I was at Ruby Simmons's house after I found her beat up, everything seemed off."

"How?"

"Wouldn't you say both Elder Simmons and Ruby are fastidious people?"

Cara shrugged. "Never think about them any more than I have to."

"They are. Trust me."

"What does trust have to do with getting my girls back?"

"Hold on while I run this through my brain." He thought about the scene. "Their house wasn't its usual immaculate place. Cushions from the sofa were disturbed, and in the kitchen were two bowls. I wasn't close enough to see, but they were the colored plastic ones, some kind of childish emblem on them."

Cara's dawning look of understanding confirmed his own suspicion.

"And I didn't realize it until now, but the crowning clue was—"

"What?"

"Boxes of animal crackers sitting on top of the counter, as plain as the cute nose on your face."

"They have no grandchildren, so why all the mess? He has them in his home, doesn't he?" Cara shrieked. "Ruby put on a real convincing act at the Meltons', trying to make us think she'd switched sides. She's a rat."

"I was so wrapped up in her injuries, I ignored my gut. Ignored the strange glints in her eyes. She even tried to make me think Emery had taken Leila and Lacy."

"Trying to cover up for Elder Simmons?"

"What else?"

"Let's go get them."

"And what if I'm wrong?"

"Isn't it worth the risk?" Her big eyes filled. "I should never have let this happen."

"Don't blame yourself."

"I do." She straightened and sucked in a breath. "Do you have a plan?"

"We'll go after them and do a lot of praying."

"You pray. I'll fight." Cara shoved away the food.

He took her hand and smoothed it. "Let's give it a bit."

"You stay. I can't sit here and do nothing. I'm going over there." She pulled away.

"I didn't say stay here. We'll confront Ruby first and do a bit of spying if she doesn't cough up."

"On Elder Simmons?"

"And his loyal wife."

For the first time that afternoon, Cara's face split with a smile. "Let's go."

The drive didn't take twenty minutes, and only Ruby's small blue car sat in the driveway.

The door opened and Ruby's face, still swollen, appeared. Shock flashed in her eyes, but she was too experienced to let it last. Smiling, she invited them inside.

"How did you get—how are you, Sister Hayman?" She poured cups of tea, lifted hers, and sipped. Her cautious eyes peered at them over the rim.

"I'm fine." Cara sat forward. "We think your husband has my girls."

Her mouth fell open, and the cup fell from Ruby's hand, splashing her skirt and tumbling to the carpeted floor. She gasped and rubbed at her clothes.

Dayne jumped up and handed her his napkin. "Are you all right?"

"I'm fine. I drink my tea lukewarm, you know." She looked up.

"Does your husband have my girls?" Cara's eyes blazed.

Ruby paid her no mind. "Why come to me, Reverend? Elder Simmons doesn't confide in me."

Cara snorted and opened her mouth. Probably for one of those scathing rebukes she was so talented at. Time to intercept.

"You are his wife. I'd think you'd have access to inside knowledge." Dayne took a drink of his tea and barely held back a grimace. Way too sweet and weak.

"Me? Look at me. Does this look like I'm on his good side right now?" Ruby chuckled. "Hardly. You'd do better to talk to him or one of the other elders. Try Brother Schrader."

Was the whole group in a conspiracy to send him in circles?

"He's lying." Cara's accusation was loud and angry.

"Your husband denies any knowledge of the girls."

Ruby shook her head, her lips thinned into two scarlet lines. "I can't help you. I wish I could, but I know nothing of what goes on in the meetings."

Cara jumped to her feet. "Any woman knows what her husband's up to."

"Cara." Dayne tried in vain to stop her rant.

"Did you know everything about Donald, Cara?" Ruby cocked her head back to look up at Cara.

"Maybe not. But I knew when he was up to no good—which was most of the time."

"Cara, please."

She threw him an angry grimace but paced to the door and stared down the hallway.

"You heard about Emery's request for his marriage to Caralynne." Dayne fought to keep the accusation from his voice.

"Yes. I did." Ruby placed a hand over his. "But Emery came to the house. Elder Tobert and a couple of the other elders happened to be here. It was an accident that I overheard anything. It will never happen again."

Trying to convince her of something she wouldn't or couldn't admit was a waste of time. He'd be better off doing more productive things.

"So you have no idea where they could be?"

"I'm sorry."

"I don't believe you. Where are my girls? You have them."

He'd known Cara long enough to recognize the glint in her eyes. She was preparing to battle. But she didn't know the one thing he did.

"Cara, no. Sister Ruby's given us her answer." He deepened his voice to gain her attention. When she looked at him, he stared at her, silently signaling his demand. Shut up. Then he turned back to Sister Ruby. "You will let me know if you hear anything that would help Cara find her girls?"

"Of course. You know I will." She led him to the door. "Please keep me informed."

Dayne followed Cara as she stomped to his car. He started it but didn't shift into drive. "What?"

"She's lying."

"I think so."

"I know so."

"Not enough to go on." Dayne shook his head.

"It is for me." Cara flopped back in the seat. "I think she knows where they are."

"I do too, but here's what I heard. Simmons has a private area somewhere, either in his house or on his grounds. No one knows anything about it or even if it's true. Do you understand what I'm saying?"

"Yes. If they have the girls, we'll not find them."

"Exactly. Our best bet is to watch the house. Ruby won't physically abuse them."

"No, but Elder Simmons would, and if she will lie to cover up his deeds, then I don't trust her either."

"Give me something to prove you know she's lying."

Cara tossed her hair away from her face as she dangled a pearl barrette in front of him. "How about this?"

CHAPTER TWENTY-SEVEN

Dayne pulled off on a side road, and they walked the rest of the way back to the Simmons's. Cara headed for some thick shrubbery and crawled beneath it. She stretched out on her stomach, and Dayne followed suit.

"Why are we skulking around?"

"To make sure he doesn't move them." He brushed a fluttering branch out of his face. "If he really has them."

"He has them." Cara's confidence was reassuring.

"Where did you find the barrette?"

"Bathroom. Remember when I asked where it was?" Cara smoothed her fingers across the barrette, remembering a little girl who'd loved wearing it. "It was on the floor behind the toilet. Leila loved this and begged to wear it every chance she got."

"They've been there."

"Yes." She tightened her fingers around the barrette.

A second later, Dayne's hand lay across hers. Cool. Calm. Reassuring. "I'm with you on this. You're not alone."

They were quiet for several minutes.

Dayne asked, "You said Emery wanted you to help him. I saw you hanging out the window as if you tried to help him."

She shook her hair until it fell over one side of her face. Hiding her emotions? "What did you see?"

"You were trying to save him."

"You can't know what I was doing or thinking."

"He threatened, scared, and disrespected you, yet when I burst through the door, you had your arm outstretched. You, lighter than a feather, trying to hold onto a man almost twice your weight."

She stared at the house.

Both garage doors remained closed. No curtains moved.

"What if he's in there now?"

"He's not. I happen to know he called a special meeting tonight for his inner core."

"And you weren't invited?"

"Huh. I'm afraid I won't ever be in that elect group."

A column of ants marched in single file. Going where?

"You could be, you know, if you'd do what he wants."

Her words were quiet, uncondemning, curious.

"Do you think?" Dayne rolled onto his side. Her beautiful face, lined with worry, was so close he could have stroked her cheeks. "I came back to make a change. In my enthusiasm, I ignorantly believed I'd make a difference. Show everyone a better way."

"You have. Look at Richard."

"Yeah. Look at him."

"Well, he did save me, and he really loves Abby," Cara offered.

"I have a suspicion that's what caused the change. I opened his eyes to the fact he was going to lose her if he didn't show her some love more often."

"Hmmm. You think that's all?"

He could hear the teasing in her voice.

"What about Levi? He's starting to wonder about a lot of things."

"Because he doesn't want to take another wife?" Dayne laid a twig on the ground in front of an ant.

"Why are you doing this?" Cara drew a circle in the dirt.

"Doing what?"

"All this—this negative talking? It's so unlike you."

"I'm facing reality. I can't make a difference if people don't want change."

"I think Levi and Richard and Josh and a few of the others are adjusting because they like what you're saying. Makes sense."

"You don't say?"

"I do." She picked up the ant trying to cross her circle and set the insect inside. "Makes more sense than Elder Simmons and the stuff he spits out."

"You've talked me out of feeling sorry for myself."

Cara bumped his shoulder. "Silly."

Evening was slipping in, and Dayne loved the quiet. Loved having Cara here beside him. Hated the worry she felt for her daughters. "What about you?"

"What about me?"

"Have I influenced you to change?"

"Do I need to?"

"Quit answering my questions with a question."

"You mean spiritually?" Cara flicked away a bug crawling on her arm. "I'm not much into spiritual things, Dayne. God and I don't seem to mix. He hasn't done much for me, and I doubt if anything I've done meets with his approval."

"I don't like to think of you with an attitude."

"You'd probably be better off not to think of me at all. You've heard Elder Simmons. I'm a load of trouble."

"Nonsense. I won't believe it." Nothing she could say would ever make him think about her negatively. Sure, she'd gone through a lot of bad stuff. But her life could change for the better. If she let him, he'd make sure it did.

"I didn't want to save Emery, you know." She looked at him and saw the doubt in his eyes. "It's true. I hated the man. The only reason I reached for him—and mind you, at the last minute only—was because he said he'd hidden my girls where I couldn't find them."

"But—"

"No buts, Dayne. I told you before I'm no saint."

"Who of us is? We're all sinners, Cara. We all need to be forgiven."

A flash, a reflection, registered across the road and vanished. A lamp switched on? A curtain moving?

Dayne squinted and wished he'd brought the binoculars from his car. Was a face peering out?

A small red car pulled up and parked.

"Cassie," Cara whispered.

The front door swung open. Ruby appeared to be checking the immediate area before motioning for the woman to enter.

For a tense minute, Cara's fingers dug into his arm. Dayne covered her hand with his and wished he could make all this go away.

Seconds later, the door opened again, and Cassie reappeared. She ushered the two small girls in front of her.

Cara rose to her knees, but Dayne stopped her. "Not yet, Cara. Look."

From around the house marched a man carrying a gun.

"Let's see what we can do once Cassie has them at her house."

"I hate this. I want to jerk them away and never let anyone touch them again."

"I know."

Cassie spoke to Ruby. Too bad her voice didn't reach them.

"Let's go," Cara scooted backward. "I don't want to lose sight of her."

Dayne followed her, but once they headed toward his car, she caught his hand. "I'm getting my girls tonight. I don't care about anything else."

She was right. What perimeters would have to be pushed remained to be seen.

❧❦❧

They arrived at Cassie's house as she and the girls exited the car. Dayne parked where they couldn't be spotted but pulled out a set of binoculars from his dash and handed them to Cara.

Cara raised the glasses to her eyes and tensed. Her girls' small bodies trudged up the walk. Lacy dragged a stuffed animal in one hand, a half-deflated balloon tied to the toy.

Leila held to her sister's other hand, but the ten-year-old's shoulders drooped as if she was too weary to walk. Cassie placed a hand on each girl's back and urged them on.

Cara handed the glasses to Dayne and gripped the car door handle.

"Hold on." Dayne placed a hand on her arm.

She jerked, but Dayne didn't let go. Instead, he pointed.

"What?" Her patience had worn thin. "I'm tired of this."

"So am I." Dayne's voice grew softer. Some hidden tone overrode his words.

Grabbing the glasses, she raised them.

Cassie and her girls were climbing the porch steps. Lacy jerked her hand from Cassie's and plopped onto the bottom step. Even at Cassie's obvious coaxing, the little girl refused to budge.

Tears pricked Cara's lids. She swallowed, holding back the sob. "If you don't tell me in the next fifteen seconds why we're stalling, I'm out of here."

"Look over by the woods."

At first Cara could make out nothing in the fading daylight. The waning sunlight reflected off—

A gun?

"Dayne." She clutched his hand, panic building inside her. "Are they going to *shoot* my babies?"

"I don't think so."

The grim reply sent shivers up her arm. "That's not a good enough answer."

"The guns are for you."

"Guns? There's more than one?" Cara sank lower into her seat. "Why do they hate me so much?"

"I count three men, and I'm sure more are around back. Circling the house, no doubt, to keep you from them." Dayne shook his head. "You haven't made it easy for the group to love you, Cara."

"Are you condemning me?" Hurt seared her heart. Criticism from others was one thing. Condemnation from Dayne was another.

"You know better, but it is the truth."

"What are we going to do? I hope you're not going to say we have to wait."

"I am." He raised a hand. "Just until dark."

"What?"

"We'll storm the fort." Dayne smoothed back a stray bit of hair straggling in her eyes. "Cara, I want you to promise me once we get your girls, you'll take them and get out. You can't afford to stay any longer."

"I know." He was right. Letting the hurt and anger and her plans go was a must.

She stared at the woods where some of the group's men hovered, and she realized it wasn't enough. Not for Felicia and the other women still stuck at The House. Not for Leila and Lacy, and definitely not for Lori. No matter how many men suffered, it'd never be enough.

❦

Cara thought the sunset never more beautiful than tonight. Too bad the beauty had to be over such an ugly scene. Blind men, led by a self-centered man, perverted in their thinking, trying to keep her from her girls. She looked at Dayne as he slipped up beside her. "Ready?"

He didn't answer.

"What now?"

"One of the men has stationed himself on the back porch." Dayne ran a hand over his chin.

"You can see the others."

Cara slammed a fist against the tree trunk and winced. "You promised we'd storm the fort. If you'll distract them, I'll get in."

"Cara, come on. You're not thinking."

For the first time she could ever remember, she felt anger at Dayne. *His* kids weren't being kept from him. What did *he* have to fret about?

But lines edged his mouth. His brows drew down in a worried frown, and more telling—his eyes radiated loving concern.

How could she doubt him? Hadn't he stood beside her, believed in her when she didn't deserve such trust? She could at least hear what he wanted to say.

"What then?"

"As much as I hate to suggest it, let's hold off the storming business for a while longer." He shot an apologetic glance at her. "I believe Cassie will care for Leila and Lacy. Don't you?"

"Yes. But she's no match for Elder Simmons if he decides to send them elsewhere."

"I know, and she's probably following orders now. Perhaps not willingly, but knowing she's the best choice to care for your girls. Thank God someone like Kathy Raymond doesn't have them."

Cara's heart lurched.

"They think this will put you back in their hands. You can't let them succeed, Cara."

"And if I don't surrender? Then what? They'll never let the girls go until I do." Agony ripped at her heart.

"I think you're right. But we have one thing up our sleeves that they don't know."

Cara eyed the best friend in her life. "What's that?"

"They don't realize we know where they've hidden—or think they've hidden your girls."

"As far as we know."

"Right. So as long as they think they've got the upper hand, and we're running scared, they're not apt to move them again."

"So, we do what?"

"We'll head to your house and scout out the area. If it's clear, you can pack enough clothes for you and the girls for a few days. I'll call the prof again to see how soon he can get here." Dayne blew out a soft breath. "I'm afraid this has gone further than I figured. We're going to have to bring in the cops. I've got a trusted friend who's in the state patrol."

Would things get even messier? What if his trusted friend was in with Elder Simmons and the rest? Not good. "I think we should handle this ourselves."

"Maybe. But this ball has grown way out of proportion. We can't take a chance on that."

"I'm scared, Dayne."

"I know you are. So am I."

Scared for her girls. Scared for Cara. Those gun-toting men under Elder Simmons's thumb looked as if they meant business. Who knew what they'd do to follow his orders? If something happened to him, then what would Cara and her girls do?

"Something deeper's going on than I can put my finger on." Some flicker of memory teased the edges of his mind. Faces, angry ones, scared ones. Elder Simmons, his father, men he didn't recognize. Faces ran together and blurred the hint from years before. Something forgotten. "Cara, can you remember anything from our past?"

"Lots of things."

"Don't be flippant. I'm serious."

"Like what?" She searched his face.

"Something that would ultimately have caused this."

For a second, her face whitened.

"What?"

"It's nothing. A nightmare I've had for years. Silly."

"Could be important."

Cara shook her head. "It comes in different ways. Sometimes I can see the man's face clearly in the dream, but when I awaken, it's gone. I can't remember anything. Other times, he takes on the form of other people and animals. It's really weird. Most times I push it out of my mind."

Nothing of help there. Who didn't have nightmares at times?

"Let's head to your place and grab those clothes."

"Dayne, will they be all right? I can't believe I'm walking off and leaving them."

"Cassie won't let anyone hurt them. We'll be gone an hour, at the most. When we come back, we're going in after them."

Her beautiful face radiated happiness and was worth the answer he'd given her. Whether they could accomplish his promise was another story.

❧❧

Fifty-five minutes later, Dayne's mouth pressed against Cara's ear. "Go softly. No noise."

A nervous giggle feathered its way up her back.

With a warning squeeze of her arm, Dayne shushed her. "Shh. Careful."

She whispered, teasing yet serious. "Let's take them out, one by one." "Cara."

The caressing reproof sent another smile to her lips. "I'll be good, but you have to admit it's tempting." She'd love the chance to crack a couple of skulls.

"I should have left you in the car."

As if he could.

He crawled forward a few feet and crouched again. No sign they'd been seen. It was late. The men were tired, no doubt, and careless. The lights inside the house were all on the left side, close to the driveway. Obviously the men figured that if someone made a move, they'd be ready by congregating at the obvious spot. Three of them hovered together, talking in low tones. The other man, at the corner of the house, talked on a phone.

Dayne kept his crouch and trotted toward a large bush, and a second later, Cara joined him. They were about fifteen feet from the nearest window.

He pulled her close and whispered, "Let's give it a few minutes to see if we've been spotted. I'll go first, and if nothing happens, you can follow."

"Right."

"We'll check the windows on this side and see if any of them are unlocked. Does she have a door here too?"

"No, only the front and the one in the back."

"Okay, we'll have to see if they're being guarded."

"If that idea doesn't work, I've got one."

"What?"

She could sense his frown, his jumpiness, his readiness to shoot down a foolhardy suggestion.

"I've got a key."

"You've got a key to her house?" Incredulity raised Dayne's voice, and it was Cara's turn to shush him. "Why didn't you say so?"

"I loved the thought of Saint Dayne breaking into a house." Cara wiggled her shoulders. "Are you ready?"

Still no sign of detection, and Dayne straightened. No sounds. No movement. The grounds could have been deserted, had he not known better. "Let's head for the back door. Give me the key."

Cara held her breath as Dayne sprinted to the corner of the house. Thirty seconds later, she followed him. He peeked around the corner and gave her a gentle shove. "All's clear. Let's go."

Cautiously they edged their way toward the back door and stepped onto the small landing. They paused while Dayne inserted the key. The small click seemed as loud as a firecracker in the quiet, but no forms stirred, no guns exploded into action.

Dayne twisted the knob, and the door slid open. He motioned, and Cara passed him into the ill-lit sunroom. When Dayne joined her, he whispered, "We've got to be careful now so we don't startle Cassie and alert the guards outside."

"I know my way. Follow me."

They tiptoed down the hallway and paused to peer into the living room. No sign of Cassie. Had she gone to bed so soon? Cara frowned in the semi-dark.

"Bed."

This didn't feel right. Cassie was a night owl. Where was she?

She edged down the hallway another five feet and stopped dead.

A faint sound penetrated the walls.

Someone was in this room. Cassie? Her girls? She tried to remember which room Cassie used. She reached for the knob, but Dayne's hand was pushing it open ... slowly.

A garbled noise. Was Cassie talking in her sleep? The hinges squeaked.

Her nerves screamed. She barely whispered the word, "Cassie?"

Her fingers clutched Dayne's shirt. From the corner of her eyes, she caught a movement, then she felt Dayne shift. His arm moved, the muscles beneath his shirt tightened as he flicked on the flashlight he held.

Cara slapped a hand to her mouth to hold back the scream. She shuddered and for a second she closed her eyes.

Dayne tore away from her frantic grip, and Cara followed him to the chair where Cassie sat bound and gagged, her head back, her eyes lolling back in their sockets.

"Is she—" Cara plucked at Dayne's shirt again.

His fingers pressed at Cassie's neck. "I think she's fainted. Get some water."

"The girls?"

"We'll check in a second."

Cassie's eyes fluttered open, her mouth opened as if trying to speak, and slowly her lids dropped.

Cara ran for a glass of water and wet cloth.

CHAPTER TWENTY-EIGHT

Cara panted, but not from being out of breath. Her heart yearned for her girls, and when she passed the end bedroom, she pressed the palm of a hand on the door. What had they gone through? The image of Leila's brown eyes flashed into her mind. Her daughter's recent fear of her mother's desertion caused Cara to wince.

For a second, she pressed against the door, imagining her girls' soft breathing. Leila and Lacy were safe now. No one would get to them.

Back in Cassie's room, Cara thrust the glass of water in Dayne's hand. She bent over her babysitter and dabbed at her cheeks and forehead. "Come on, Cassie, wake up."

Cassie moaned.

"Cassie?"

The woman's eyes fluttered open. "Cara?"

Cara knelt in front of the woman, took her hand, and smoothed the red mark where the ropes had chaffed Cassie's wrist.

"I wanted to call you."

"They wouldn't let you, would they?" Dayne knelt beside Cara.

Cassie shook her head and sipped at the water Dayne held to her lips. "They made—made me so angry."

"Take a minute to rest." Dayne held out the glass again.

They couldn't have much time before someone checked on Cassie and the girls. Cara wanted to urge her babysitter to hurry, but Cassie needed to regain her strength.

"I'm okay now. Let me talk."

Dayne patted her hand. "Go ahead. Why did they tie you up?"

"Because I threatened to call you and let you know the girls were here."

"I can't believe they didn't take them away from you and put them somewhere else." Cara settled on the floor and crossed her legs.

"They made me promise not to call you." Cassie half-grinned. "But they caught me on the phone as I was dialing."

"Did they hurt you?" Cara asked.

"They slapped me around. Being tied up was the worst. I'm glad I already put the girls in bed."

"They're safe?" Cara's heart thumped.

"For now." Cassie tossed back her hair. "They'd get to them only if they made sure I was dead, Cara."

"Why did they call you to pick them up from Ruby? They surely know you'd call Cara." Dayne asked.

"I got the idea Lacy wouldn't quit crying. It was either call someone familiar or have a sick child on their hands." Cassie took another sip of water. "Sister Simmons called and wanted me to take them. Gave me orders not to call you. Said her husband would be in touch in a few hours."

"Which means Elder Simmons would come pick them up." Cara wanted to throttle Ruby. "How could she?"

"I know. I didn't trust her, so when she excused herself to go get the girls, I sneaked down the hall and listened. She called her husband and told him you suspected the girls were with them. She also let him know she'd called me."

Cara bit her lip. "I knew we couldn't trust her."

"It gets worse, Cara." Cassie wiped her eyes. "I listened at the top of the basement stairs when Ruby slipped downstairs. She threatened the girls. Told them if they didn't go quietly and quit their crying, they'd be shipped off and would never see you again. It nearly broke my heart to hear Lacy's whimpering."

"Shipped off? What was she talking about?" Anger rushed through her like molten lava and blinded Cara. Weakness melted her bones and left her exhausted. Cara wanted to pound something, anything, to vent, to wreak the same kind of havoc ravaging her heart.

"You know what I told you about Simmons's secret room. She could have been talking about that." Dayne's grip on her hand and Cassie's pats penetrated the blackness of her mind.

"Or something worse." He could have meant send them away where she'd never find them. Cara shook her head. "I'm okay. I need to check on the girls."

"We've got them now." Dayne squeezed her hand.

Cara met his gaze. "Yes. We do."

"They're all right, I think." Tears filled Cassie's eyes.

The one person she'd trusted with her girls had risked a lot to keep them safe. She owed her.

"Thank you, Cassie. You've always been wonderful."

Dayne rose. "Go ahead, Cara. We'll be right behind you."

Cara headed to the door. She paused outside the room and savored the anticipation of wrapping her arms around her daughters. She twisted the knob and pushed the door open. Cassie had obviously left a low-wattage lamp on, for she spotted their small silhouettes curled up together in one twin-sized bed.

Swiping a hand across her eyes, she tiptoed across the room and knelt beside the bed. Cassie must have given them baths. Hair damp and sweet-smelling, bodies still warm from the clean water, their sheets were rumpled as if they'd slept restlessly.

No toys, no objects of affection lay close to Leila, but someone— Cassie or Leila—had made sure Lacy had enough to keep her secure: the almost-flat balloon, a half-eaten apple, the stuffed rabbit, and a fuzzy blanket with a parade of funny characters dancing across it.

"Leila."

Her daughter didn't move.

"Leila." Cara touched her shoulder.

"Cass-ie?" Leila turned on her side.

"It's Mommy. Shh."

Leila sat up and squealed. "Mommy." She threw her arms around her mother, her relief at Cara's presence evident in the tight hug. She swallowed back a sob.

"I'm so sorry, baby."

"Sister Simmons was mean to us." Leila rubbed her face against her mother's chest. "She said—she said if we cried, she'd send us off."

It was a good thing Ruby Simmons wasn't here. The angry words almost came out, but she forced them back. Instead she patted and soothed and hugged her distraught daughter. "You cry all you want, sweetheart."

Lacy whimpered, and without letting go of Leila, Cara smoothed her youngest's hair from her face. Lacy cried out and flung herself away, raising her voice in sleepy terror, knocking the stuffed animal toward Cara. "No. I don't wanna go. I want my mommy."

She scrambled after Lacy, dragging Leila after her. "Lacy, baby, mommy's here now. Wake up, darling."

Dayne appeared in the doorway. "We need to get out of here, Cara. There's some movement outside."

"You think they heard the girls?" How could they not have?

"I'll get Cassie. She's grabbing a few things to take."

"Right." Cara bent over Lacy and covered her mouth lightly with a hand. "Lacy. Wake up."

Lacy squirmed then opened her eyes. "Mommy?"

"Whisper, sweetheart."

The child wrapped her arms around Cara's neck and closed her eyes again. Cara scooped up her youngest daughter and reached to pull Leila close to her side.

"Well, if this isn't the coziest scene I've seen in a long time."

At the door, two men watched her.

❧❧❧

The tall, heavyset man stared at her, his dark eyes rattlesnake-mean and sinister. He wouldn't be easily fooled. His pudgy, short friend looked as if he'd never done a day's work in his life. A braggart he might be, but no fighter.

Aggressiveness would be the only thing to save her. She wondered where Dayne had disappeared. Had he heard the men coming in time to hide? She hoped so.

Cara pushed Leila behind her onto the floor and lowered Lacy into her sister's arms. "Stay still, Leila."

Lacy let out a screech and lifted her arms. "No. I don't want Leila to hold me."

"Be quiet, Lacy. Now." She moved closer to the men, hoping to keep their attention off her girls.

The men watched her as if waiting on her next move. She couldn't remember ever seeing them before. "What do you want?"

The second one snorted. "Think we've got what we want."

The man in front dug an elbow in the other's arm. "Shut up. You know what Elder Simmons said."

"I'm not going anywhere with you."

The first man slapped her across the cheek. "Just came in to check on the noise."

Cara staggered against the bed and pressed a hand on Leila's head when the girl whimpered. "Quiet, Leila. Stay still."

A figure, darker than the hallway, edged toward the room. If Dayne had plans to get them out of here, she needed to do her part. She'd better keep these men's minds focused on her. She allowed her lips to curl. "Coward."

The first man raised his hand again, but the second one nudged him. "Elder Simmons."

First man grimaced. "Yeah. I got it. You come on quietly if you think much of them girls."

Heat rolled through her. "Don't you dare touch them."

The tight-lipped smile he gave her was no assurance. "Come along. We'll leave Cassie here to watch them as long as you behave. That's Simmons's orders once we've got you."

"Where are we going?"

"Where else? Elder Simmons wants to see you."

Dayne, behind the men, raised a hand. The second man half-turned, and Cara frantically spoke. "I don't know if I can trust you."

"You don't have any choice." He leered at her daughters, and Cara moved to shield them from his view. As she took two small steps toward him, he grabbed her arm.

Lacy took that minute to scream. "I don't want you to leave, Mommy."

✀❧✀

Dayne raised a lamp base to bring it down over the first man's head, but the man ducked then jabbed at Dayne's stomach. Dayne grunted but rebounded with a punch to his cheek, sending the guy staggering back.

Catching his breath, Dayne waited then waded in with another swing with his left hand at the guy's right cheek. This time the guy stepped back and let his head go with the punch. The blow glanced off his cheek.

The guy had done some fighting. Dayne was no professional, although he'd joined the boxing team at college for a year. Short as the time was, it'd given him enough training to take care of himself.

This guy had either done some extensive training or he'd been a short-term natural boxer. Either way, this battle might be more than Dayne could handle.

But he had to win.

With renewed vigor, he sent a series of jabs to the first man's abdomen.

First Man's chin lowered toward his chest as he gasped. His body weaved and then he sank to his knees and tumbled to the floor.

Cara stood over him with the shards of a vase still in her hands. Her startled eyes went from the collapsed man to Dayne.

Behind her stood Cassie, holding a broom.

"How did you get the drop on him?" Dayne tilted his head toward the second man.

"He's a wimp." Cara's eyes lit with the reflected lamplight. "He was so absorbed with admiring the fighting between his friend and you, he forgot we were there. Cassie used her broom to swat him repeated times, and I used the jump rope to tie him up when he girlishly begged for mercy. A piece of cake to subdue him. Teamwork."

"Good work." Dayne knelt, grabbed both arms, and twisted the lamp cord around the first guy's hands. When the man mumbled and

❦ 301 ❧

moved his head, Cara pulled a scarf off the dresser and wound it around his mouth.

"Get the girls. Let's get out of here, now. There are three more of them around somewhere. If they heard him, they'll be in here to investigate." Dayne edged to the window and peeked out.

"Right." She pulled Leila to her feet and cradled Lacy in her arms.

"Get him, Mommy. Don't leave him." Her little girl pointed at the stuffed animal.

Cara scooped up the toy and stuffed it into her daughter's grasping hands.

At the doorway, Dayne reached for Lacy.

Lacy clung to Cara and whined, but Cara patted her back. "Shh. Let Dayne carry you, sweetheart. Mommy's right behind you." She pushed Leila toward Cassie.

Dayne started to speak as Cara headed back into the room. Whatever. Obviously, she needed to get in a few last words, and letting her get it done was the quickest way to get them all out of here and to safety.

❧❦❧

Cara checked to make sure the others weren't nearby.

"Don't you come near me or my girls again."

The man mumbled behind the gag, and one eye closed in a slow wink.

She wanted to slap him, but she didn't have the time. "You'd better hope I don't see you first if you ever come near my girls again."

She didn't give him time to react.

In the laundry room, she caught up.

Cara ignored the questioning look Dayne shot her and squatted beside Leila. "We have to be really quiet, sweetheart, so the men outside won't hear us. Okay?"

"Lacy will cry."

"I'll keep her quiet. You follow as closely to Cassie as you can. I'll be right behind you."

"Promise?"

She put all she had into the smile she gave Leila. "I promise."

"Ready?" Dayne shifted Lacy to his left arm. "Cara, you and Cassie head for the nearest tree. We'll circle back around to my car after we're away."

"I think you should follow Leila since you're carrying Lacy. Let me bring up the rear. If need be, I can distract the other two men."

"Absolutely not. I've got her shielded with my body, but if you insist, you can carry her. I'm last."

"Fine. Have it your way." Cara opened the door a crack and peered out. "I don't see any signs of movement. Cassie?"

Her friend nodded.

There was a shout from the bedroom. "They're getting away."

Dayne touched Cassie's arm. "Let's go."

"We need a distraction. I'll lead them away."

"No, Cara. Stay on our planned course. After we're in the woods, you and Cassie can take the girls on to the car. I'll distract them."

Cassie took Leila's hand, hurried across the porch, and trotted toward the woods. Cara followed, Dayne on her heels.

The wood line was only feet away when one of the men shouted, "Eddie, get over here. Come on."

A bullet blasted over their heads.

"Go, Dayne, get them to safety. I'll meet you at the car in a few minutes." Cara ignored his protest and veered away. She slid behind a tree and clung to it, gasping, trying to still her pounding heart.

Two more blasts tore into the tops of the trees. Warning shots. If they'd wanted to shoot them, they would have done the misdeed while Cara and the rest were out in the open.

"Hurry up. Get a flashlight. The kids will slow them down." One of the men ran up, and the first guy motioned for him to keep it. "You come with me. Stewart, head north. Ben, check on the guys in the house."

Cara peered around the trunk. They could no longer see her—or the others. The men appeared to argue, so Cara fled to the next tree in line, shuffling her feet.

"I hear them."

"Someone's trying to be quiet. We've got them now. Come on."

She deliberately kicked a branch to make a satisfying crack, and she moaned out loud. Turning, she headed the opposite direction from Dayne's car, creating enough sounds to keep the men following. Only when she was sure she'd developed the lead on them did she veer away, taking a path to lead her back to her friends.

Bumbling idiots. If Elder Simmons wanted her, why not send trained men? Men who were familiar with these surroundings?

A cloud covered the moon, but Cara wasn't worried. Her sense of direction was great. She slowed and wanted to hum in delight but repressed the desire. She'd do a Snoopy dance when she and her daughters were safely away from this bunch of insane men. She should have known better …

Big arms slipped around her. A hand covered her mouth, and lips pressed against her ear. "The next time you pull a trick like that, I'm going to shoot you myself."

CHAPTER TWENTY-NINE

Cara slammed a fist into Dayne's chest and whispered, "You nearly gave me a heart attack. Why are you sneaking up on me?"

"Come on, we'll talk while we walk." He gripped her upper arm and pulled her along. "A satisfying payback for scaring me to death."

"I knew what I was doing. They weren't going to shoot me. Elder Simmons wants them to bring me to him. I knew that." In spite of her rambling logic, her heart leaped at the thought of Dayne anxious for her. "Where's Cassie and the girls? Are you sure they're all right?"

"Of course, I'm sure. Do you think I'd leave them if I wasn't?"

Dayne's voice held a tell-tale edge. She'd pushed him too far. As a child, she'd backed off.

Now, her womanly curiosity wanted to test these strange waters. Check out the parameters of Dayne's feelings.

She eyed the dark figure who walked beside her.

He took her hand and linked his fingers through hers. "Don't ever do that again." His voice shook, and Cara realized he'd been scared for her.

Her heart warmed. Her fingers tingled from his touch. His hand almost covered hers, and despite trying to hold back the attraction, she loved his firm grip. His manly strength. The assurance within her that his hand had never done an evil deed. She allowed the contentment to flow inside her body. If only life could be so peaceful.

Dayne's car sat ahead, and he held her back from rushing forward. "Hold up a second. Let's make sure all's well before we go tearing over there."

She waited, shifting on her feet, while he surveyed the area. When Dayne let her go, she flew to the car.

Cassie sat in the back, Lacy's head cradled on her lap, Leila's head propped on her shoulder.

"They're good."

Dayne shut the door behind Cara after she slid into the front passenger seat. He hurried around to the driver's side and once seated, he turned the ignition key. The car ground over, almost drowning out the sound of his phone ringing.

An alarm rang along Cara's nerves. Who would be calling Dayne this time of the night? She cast him a sharp glance.

He checked the number. "Elder Simmons."

"Calling to see if you know where I am." Cara forced her voice to stay calm, but her heart beat like a tom-tom. Was Elder Simmons or his men out there now? Paranoia pounded on the doors of the car. The phone rang again. "Are you going to answer?"

"Should I?" Dayne's smile held a hard edge. "We shouldn't let Elder Simmons know where we are or what we're doing."

"I'm not sure it's possible to avoid it. Seems he has his spies everywhere." Cara shivered.

He patted her hand and checked his cell again. "He's left a message."

Dayne lifted his cell and listened, his face sobering. Bad news.

"What is it?"

In slow motion, Dayne slipped his cell into a pocket and tapped the fingers of his left hand on the steering wheel. At last he spoke. "He said all the roads are closed. He wants us to turn ourselves in."

"He said that? As if we're criminals running from the law?" Cara shook her head as the fright of being chased swept over her then vanished. She hissed, "Why is he doing this?"

You're mine. From a distance the words played in her mind. Surreal. Frightening.

Dayne drew in a breath. His left eyebrow edged up. "The only thing I can think of is that he can't stand for you to scorn his rule. Your independence drives him nuts."

"Could be."

"But I don't think so." Dayne started the car and drove out onto the highway. "He's unreasonable toward you. Almost as if he's afraid of you."

"What?" Cara laughed. "Are you kidding?"

But Dayne was right. His hatred was beyond reasonable. There had to be a deeper motive, and sometimes she felt she was on the verge of knowing. But the knowledge was as elusive as a flittering butterfly.

Lacy whimpered, and Cara turned to check on her. Leila's eyes popped open, and she smiled sleepily at her mother.

Cara said, "Leila, where did Lacy get the old toy?"

Leila's face twisted into a scornful expression. "They don't have any new toys."

"Who, precious?"

Leila cast her a sleepy glance then rubbed her head on Cassie's shoulder, no doubt trying for a more comfortable spot. "The Simmonses. Elder Simmons gave it to Lacy so she'd quit crying."

Had he used it for bribery? To shut up her rowdy daughter? Cara reached into the back and took the worn animal from Lacy. She propped it on her knees and felt her body shrink from the toy.

The raggedy thing sucked Cara's inner self into a dark, dark room. A room of horror and death. People. A woman and a man.

A man.

Her head pounded, and she swayed. Her hand lifted to press trembling fingers to her temple.

A little girl. Clutching—

Her body shook.

Terror.

Flight.

And the unbearable longing for a lost toy swarmed over her like a horde of angry bees. Tears dribbled down Cara's cheeks, and she blinked.

"We can get rid of it if it bothers you," Dayne said.

"No. It's okay." But was it? Why did this dilapidated thing take her back—back to where she didn't want to go? Why did it frighten her, and at the same time, make her feel secure?

She replaced it where Lacy would see it when she awakened. She smiled at Cassie but spoke to Dayne. "How are we to elude Simmons?"

"I've got an idea." He retrieved his phone again and texted a message. In seconds there was a reply, and when he'd read the message, he shoved the phone in his pocket.

She'd endangered him enough. "I think I can get around these guards Elder Simmons has posted."

There went his left brow again.

"What's that supposed to mean?"

Careful, or she'd never talk him into this.

"Leila, Lacy, and I can get around the guards by going on foot. I know my way through these woods."

"Am I to fold my hands and twiddle my thumbs while you're beating off wild creatures and dodging Elder Simmons's goons?"

"Don't be silly. Listen to me. Once I'm out of the way, Elder Simmons won't be so gung-ho about you. I'm the one he's after."

Dayne looked as if he was about ready to explode. "That's the craziest thing I've ever heard from you, and believe me, I've heard about every scheme going."

Real sincerity was called for if she wanted his cooperation. "Please, Dayne, I'm sure this is the only way I'm going to get out—alive. Cassie, side with me."

That was dirty. To play on his emotions, his concern for her. How else? He wasn't going to give in otherwise.

"No."

The single word from his lips said it all. He wouldn't budge.

Cassie laughed softly. "Don't get me into this argument. I think you need to listen to Pastor MacFarland."

"Thanks, Cass, for nothing." Joking or not, Cara really wished she'd had Cassie's support.

The worry lay heavy on Dayne. Cara almost wilted under the strained look on his face. She looked away and stiffened her resolve. "Dayne."

"Won't do any good to use that tone."

The tone had always worked. Way back when. All the times she'd badgered and coaxed and threatened him to get what she wanted. And he'd given in. Had the coaxing done the trick? Maybe another emotion she'd been too blind to see overrode his usual caution. Maybe love for the contrary little girl his parents raised pulled on his heart strings and persuaded him to give in?

She eyed him. "The more people who try this, the more the chance we'll get caught."

"Not with me along."

He was more stubborn than one of Mike Farmer's old mules. "Okay. Okay. You win. Happy?"

His sour expression told her different. "Nope. Let's go."

"Where?"

"I'm going to see some people."

"Who?"

"Can't you wait and see?"

Cara allowed her lips to tip up and mocked his earlier word. "Nope."

"Too bad," he said, and Cara sat back, for once content to let Dayne have his way. It was enough for this moment that her girls were safe and Dayne was willing to sacrifice his career for their safety.

When twenty minutes later he pulled into the Schrader's driveway, Cara sat up. "Dayne?"

"I want to talk to Levi and get the temperature of the group after their meeting last night. I'll be right back."

Dayne walked up the sidewalk, knocked on the door, and disappeared inside the house. Five minutes later, he approached her side of the car.

She rolled down the window.

"Come on inside. You've got to see this."

"The girls? Cassie?"

"They can come too."

Levi met them at the door. "Come on in."

Cara paused at the doorway to the Schrader's great room. Many of the couples gathered were her friends. Some she didn't know. Children lay sleeping, scattered on the floor beside their parents. She faced Dayne and Levi. "What's going on?"

"Relax, Cara. These people are our friends."

Were they? Dayne might trust them, and though she did count Jodie and Mary Ann and Abby as friends, she wasn't at all convinced about the others. And what was Marshall Biggs doing here?

"I'm not sure about this."

Jodie led Cara upstairs to put the girls to bed. "Please stay. Levi and I both want to help you."

"How did they get here? I didn't see their cars."

"Hid them and walked the rest of the way." Jodie preened as if she'd arranged everything the way she wanted.

Cara tucked blankets around her girls snuggled in the painted pink beds. "What's Marshall doing here?"

"I know what you're thinking." Jodie watched her motherly actions from the door. "But Levi questioned Marshall and his wife intensely before he allowed him to join us tonight. Levi really believes Marshall's eyes are open."

"He is Kathy Raymond's brother."

"He doesn't think like her." Jodie folded her arms. "He's sick of her badgering, her constant harping at him. Give him a chance, Cara. As much as I love you, you are very opinionated."

Ouch. But that was Jodie. She didn't hold back her own opinions.

"I don't trust him, but if you and Levi do, I'll try to keep a check on my tongue."

Jodie motioned to her girls. "They'll be fine here. Let's head downstairs."

"Why is everyone here?"

"To make plans." Jodie slipped an arm around Cara and drew her along the hallway. She gave Cara one of her I-know-what's-going-on-and-you-don't looks. "We want to strike out on our own. Leave the Children of Righteous Cain."

Cara stopped dead. "Are you serious?"

"Very. Levi and I have been secretly talking about this for a long time. When Josh and Mary Ann dropped in one day, they hinted others were becoming dissatisfied too." She shrugged. "Levi called a meeting."

"Why doesn't Dayne know about this?"

"We weren't sure if we would compromise your escape by calling him. Now that you're here, we can discuss the best way to handle it."

"Let's go."

Jodie linked arms with Cara. "Dayne's professor is here."

"I didn't see him."

"You will." Jodie tugged on her arm. "Come on."

When the two women walked into the great room, Professor Moore called to Cara. "Ah, the lady who has the backbone of a giant."

All eyes focused on Cara, and her cheeks warmed at the attention. "Hello, Professor."

He held out a hand, and Cara slipped hers within it. The professor pulled her close. "Stand here beside me while we begin our discussion, will you?"

For what purpose, Cara had no idea, but if this jolly older man wanted her support, he had it. She nodded.

"Good. We're ready."

The murmurs quieted. Bodies relaxed back into their seats. Each person concentrated on the tall, thin man, his air of kindliness inviting confidence.

"Some of you might wonder why I'm here tonight. One of my interests—let's say, obsessions—has been the study of cults." He held up a hand as if to still objections. "I know. Members seldom realize or acknowledge their involvement."

Dayne sat on the other end of the hearth. "I think you should go back even further. Tell them what you confided in me."

"If you wish." He drew in a breath. "What hooked me on the study was the fact that my parents were caught up in a cult when I was a baby. Fortunately, they got out in time. Unfortunately, the experience soured them completely against any kind of religion but had the opposite effect on me. I experimented with many religions but finally found my way. After that, all of my research was to help those caught in cults."

"So you consider our group a cult?" Josh's face scrunched up as if resisting offense at the professor's words.

"I can't call it anything else, Josh."

"Well, since we're being honest here tonight, I'll say that I always wondered what the matter was. I never came away from any of the services inspired." Josh looked at Dayne. "Until you came back, Dayne."

"Back on track here." Professor Moore patted Cara's hand. "We're here tonight to straighten out the abuse going on now and to make sure Cara and her girls are protected. Sometime back I ran across the Stark family, Ruby Simmons's family. Their practices date back further than I've been able to trace. They are the current leaders in developing cult groups across our country."

"When did Simmons come into the cult, Professor Moore?"

"From what I've deduced, Leroy Simmons was the black sheep of his family. Rich, wild, and into one scheme after another. His mother doted on him. His father was a tyrant who doted on only one person. Himself. Simmons got into one scrape too many, and his father cut him out of his inheritance. Without money, he was limited in his activities, but it didn't take him long to locate a girl who had money. He wasted her money, and when she got fed up with him and his abuse, she left him."

"You can prove this?" Levi asked.

"If his aging father is to be believed, I can. I've several witnesses who are ready to talk to the authorities."

"Sad." Levi shook his head.

"Right about now, the facts become fuzzy. I can't find many details about the next few years of his life. The next documented event I located was the start of the Children of Righteous Cain, a branch-off of the Stark group."

"Wow, sounds like a lot of work," Mary Ann said, her blue eyes round.

Heads nodded. Murmurs echoed around the room.

"I don't call it work when you love what you do," the professor said and chuckled. "Are you tired, Cara? Let's sit here on the hearth."

Cara settled between Dayne and the professor but propped her chin on her fist so she could watch the professor and take in his words.

"It was difficult to get many details about the Righteous Ones. From the outside, members appeared normal, hard-working people. Eventually rumors began. Women with beat-up faces and broken bones. Bruised bodies and worse. There were very few who would talk."

So carefully hidden from prying eyes beyond their bounds. So no one would guess, would interfere. A way of life no woman inside the group would betray.

"Finally, though, I found someone who got out. That happens very seldom, from what I understand. She went into great detail about the activities and beliefs of the CORCs."

"Corks?" Dayne asked.

"C-O-R-Cs. An acronym I gave the Children of Righteous Cain. Leroy was a charismatic influence on enough families that he started out big, and it kept rolling, increasing in membership until finally, early in the nineties, it leveled off." Professor Moore shook the papers in his hand. "In spite of the role of leadership and the satisfaction he gained, Leroy's appetite for women didn't fade."

Cara felt the familiar rumblings, recognized the loathing seething in her body. She rubbed her stomach.

The professor must have sensed her disturbance because he glanced at her. "You all right?"

"Yes."

"Good. Because we're going to band together to make sure you're safe. Simmons can go only so far."

Cara shook her head. "I think he goes as far as he wants to get what he wants."

"I know, my dear. But no man is all-powerful. We will put a stop to his actions." His faded eyes peered down at her.

She just hoped he could carry through on his promise.

The professor picked up where he'd left off. "He had several narrow escapes with the law in questionable circumstances involving other women. But never was convicted due to excellent alibis from your community police."

Levi jumped to his feet. "I can't see this. I'm no dummy, Professor. Surely I would have known some of this stuff."

"Perhaps, yes. But his escapades were presented to you in an entirely different way. In such a way they were reasonable to your sensible mind."

"None of this matters unless you have proof," Levi said.

"I have proof, Levi, at least enough to give the authorities a start in their investigation. They are on alert for my call. Do any of you remember a woman called Rita Davenport?"

"Yes." The word was out before Cara could stop herself.

Heads nodded.

"So all of you remember her? She's the one who got out." The professor eyed the group. "I won't go into details, but she heard of my research and contacted me. She is more than ready to testify against Simmons."

The professor pulled from his jacket pocket a paper. "This should be the final nail in his coffin."

"What do you have?" Levi asked.

The men stiffened. Eyes showed the eagerness, the expectation inside the listeners.

"Proof that one Leroy Simmons is indeed the Leroy Davis, accused pedophile, who has eluded the law for years."

Levi shook his head. The other men looked stunned.

Cara smirked. She'd always known he was wicked.

"You're sure we can't settle this amiably?" Levi asked.

"I'm positive it's not going to happen. Simmons will do anything to squelch what he calls rebellion."

Levi's back was to the group. His image reflected in the darkened window pane. "Let's make our decision. What should we do?"

"Let me finish one thing. All along, since Dayne brought me into this to help, I've wondered why Simmons has such a fixation on Cara."

"Me, too," Jodie murmured.

"And it came to me. Cara either knows something of which he's afraid or has something he wants."

Was it true? "What could I know or have, Professor? I can't think of anything. This makes it sound as if I've brought this trouble on myself."

"Not at all. Nevertheless, it's the only reasonable explanation." The professor gave her a benevolent smile. "Children have been known to repress unpleasant and terrifying memories."

He started to lift his glass of juice but replaced it. "Dayne, didn't you tell me once that after she joined your family, she never spoke of her early years?"

"That's right."

"I'm wondering if something happened so horrific, her young self couldn't accept it and unconsciously blocked it from her memory."

All of a sudden, the room was too warm. Sweat dampened her skin. Cara stared at the professor, but her mind shrunk back from the door she didn't want to open.

"What do you think it could be?" Dayne frowned.

The professor studied Cara's face, a hint of a smile curving his lips. "I don't know. I figure her memory will return in time."

"When?" she gasped out.

"I don't know, Cara. But you'll know."

CHAPTER THIRTY

Cara and Dayne slipped outside after the last of those gathered quietly took their leave, then they strolled along the Schraders' extensive brick patio. Subdued lighting along the borders pushed back the darkness.

The full moon was high in the sky. Stars glittered far above.

"Were you surprised to see Professor Moore here?"

"No. He was ready to return as soon as I called. His evidence will do a lot to help our cause."

"I don't know. Elder Simmons is used to having his way. I can't see him giving all this up without a stronger fight."

"You're right, but at least we have more ammunition to fight him."

Elder Simmons's face lurked in the depths of her mind. She wished it didn't, that she couldn't visualize it. But his features were there—stuck like a parasite that had attached itself and refused to die. She shuddered. Would Professor Moore's plan work, or would Elder Simmons weasel out of any accusations? What effect would a paltry handful have against their leader and all the elders still standing for the cult's beliefs? She didn't want Professor Moore's plan to fail, to have to take matters in her own hands again.

Dayne slipped an arm around her shoulders and pulled her close for an instant. "Try not to worry. I trust Professor Moore. If anyone can resolve this, he can."

"I trust him too." But that didn't change the fact Elder Simmons was sly and smart. A lethal combination when used for self-centered activities, and she definitely didn't trust Simmons. "But I'm scared. I have this awful feeling that no matter where we hide, Elder Simmons will find us. We—I can't escape."

"I won't let him get to you. I promise. If the group's plan works, we'll be home free this time tomorrow." He lifted her hand. "Cara, when all this is over, I want to—I want us to—" He stopped and looked at her.

"What are you trying to say, Dayne?" Dared she hope? *Don't be silly*, she scolded herself. Dayne deserved better than her.

"Now if this isn't a cozy scene."

Words straight from a living hell. The round figure half-hid at the edge of the shadows. She might not have seen him had he not moved and the glint off the object in his hand flashed for a second.

A gun.

Pointed at her? Or worse, at Dayne? Did Elder Simmons intend to shoot Dayne? Her heart hardened. She couldn't let him do it. She had to keep the man's focus on her.

Before she could speak, Dayne asked, "What do you want, Simmons?"

Simmons? When had he stopped referring to the leader as Elder?

"You've ruined my plans." The gun wavered an inch to the right.

Cara's breath caught. "Let him go. You want me, don't you?"

The gun jerked toward her as he said, "You've got that right."

Dayne edged away from her, and the gun jerked to the right again.

"Stand still." Elder Simmons drew in several raspy breaths as if he'd been running. "Problem is, you started the ball rolling. You couldn't come back and do your job, could you? Stuck your nose into my affairs."

"The welfare of the people is my business."

His protest had no effect on Simmons.

"My group. My people. I'm the one who fostered the concept and promoted it." Simmons's voice deepened to a snarl. "Moore thinks he's pulled a fast one, calling in the cops."

Where were they? It'd be nice if they'd show up about now.

"What do you mean?" Dayne cleared his throat.

"Fortunately, I had the foresight to prepare a way of escape in the unlikely event I'd need it. Happened to be in the basement when the county sheriff pulled in my driveway. Ruby called out the warning, and I was gone before he ever stepped foot inside the house."

"And you left Ruby to face the music? How do you know she didn't blurt out all your despicable actions?" Disgust at the selfish brute's attitude sharpened Cara's voice.

He chuckled. "She knows better. I'll be back to take care of her if she opens her mouth."

"Coward." The word was out before she could stop herself.

The moonlight played across his face, and the self-righteous emotion pasted on his features said it all. "That's not true. What would she do if something happened to me? I'm her ticket to heaven."

Cara didn't bother to stop the snort.

If his eyes had been swords, they'd have pierced her heart. "Your trouble is you refuse to see the obvious. If you'd been more submissive, your husband wouldn't have died."

Typical for him to blame her.

"If you'd taught your daughter better—"

"Shut up. Don't even breathe her name."

"You should have been the one who died."

"Why on earth do you hate her?" Dayne demanded.

"You wouldn't take up for her so much if you knew what she'd done."

The taunt sent the blood pounding in her head. What had she done that was so awful? Something so bad, the action would force Dayne to hate her.

"She killed your father."

"What? You're delusional."

Dayne's croaking comment was only a background noise to the whirlwind inside her. Was the missing puzzle piece about to be revealed? Why she always felt as if something was lacking in her life? Had she killed Dayne's father and didn't remember?

Dayne still protested. Trying to convince Simmons, or himself? Her mind spun backward into the past, remembering the sweet, quiet couple who'd been the only parents she'd ever known. They never once raised their voices, and as far as she remembered, she never defiantly disobeyed their direct orders. Danced around a few, but one look from Mr. MacFarland's eyes had been enough to halt her inclination to disobedience.

How could she have killed the father figure in her life?

She hadn't.

"I did not kill your father."

"You don't have to tell me that, dearest."

"If it hadn't been for her, your father wouldn't have driven a wedge in our friendship."

"You're spouting the most ridiculous stuff I've ever heard." Dayne sounded as scornful as she felt.

"The man insisted on taking in an orphan no one wanted. The only proper place would have been—"

"Enough, Simmons. My father loved Cara as a daughter."

"And I loved him."

"Are you sure there wasn't—something more vile going on between them?" His smirk was as dirty as his words.

The hateful words sank in. Horror like slimy, green gel dropped over her. Simmons was abominable.

"What a filthy thing to say." Dayne's fists were clenched.

"Never!" Cara stomped the ground.

"Why did he get into such a rage when questioned about his motives? A rage precipitating the heart attack that took his life. He had no reason to be so angry if he was sinless."

"You pushed him." Dayne edged closer to the taunting man. As if a light flickered on, Dayne's voice rose. "You used his medical condition. Figured if you pushed hard enough, his heart would act up, didn't you?"

"Was it my fault he insisted on being so stubborn?"

Dayne took a few steps closer.

"Stay where you are." The gun inched higher.

"Did you hope you'd get rid of your problem—my father? I'd like to—"

"You'd like to do what?" Simmons waved his gun. "He was unreasonable when it came to her. I couldn't let him get away with it. Had my own God-given plans for her."

"And me?"

"We needed a new minister. You fit the bill. Besides, my idea got you away from Cara long enough I could place her where I wanted her."

"It didn't matter what my father—your friend—wanted? What Cara and I wanted?"

"All that mattered was that she be where I could keep an eye on her. I had to make sure she kept her mouth shut—"

"Why?" She felt more confused than ever. What did she know that he feared?

"It's over, Simmons. Why not get out of here before the cops get to you?"

"I've got my plans made."

Dayne tilted his head as if listening. "I thought I heard sirens minutes ago."

Why hadn't she heard them? She listened but heard nothing but the normal creaks and croaks of nightlife.

He held out a hand and beckoned to Simmons. "Come on, give me the gun."

"Not before she gets what's coming to her."

"Simm—" Dayne started to speak, but he must have seen—or sensed—a movement from Simmons. With a cry of warning, he leaped in front of Cara. The explosion drowned the rest of his words.

It was a movie. Had to be, because this couldn't be happening in real life.

Dayne's strong, young body jerked. He began falling. He swayed first, and he dropped to his knees. At last, he toppled over, and he turned his head slowly.

Cara stared at him, not wanting to believe what her mind was screaming. But Dayne lay so still, not moving, not speaking. Was he dead?

"Dayne. Dayne." She fell to her knees.

Bending over him, she touched his white, bloodless face. The moans poured out of her, and she kissed his eyes, his nose, his mouth. "Don't, Dayne. Please wake up. You can't leave me now. Not now. I love you. I've always loved you and no one else."

She sobbed, hysteria building inside her. The anger. The desire to kill the man who'd taken everything exploded inside her.

Elder Simmons did this. He killed Dayne because he wanted to make her suffer. She twisted on her knees to stare at him, and a shadow fell on her face. She looked up. "You—you did this."

"Something extra for you I planned. Do you think killing you is enough? No, I want you to suffer to the fullest." Elder Simmons bent toward her, his eyes cold. "I'm enjoying the show. Relishing the suffering you feel."

Before she could speak, he gripped her neck. "You've ruined my life, you trouble-making whore—"

As if he'd slammed a ball bat into her head, her mind whirled back, back, back. The image of a younger Leroy Simmons's hands around her mother's neck, the words he'd spit at her mother filled her mind. The nightmare was no longer a dream, but a real memory. A vivid, horrible part of her. "It was you. You killed my mother."

"And I'm going to kill you now, you—you—"

No. I won't let you succeed. Not after all these years. I won't let you …

She struggled to breathe, to pull in the air her lungs begged for, but the pressure on her neck increased. She clawed at the big hands choking the life from her. Tried to scratch, dig, injure, but her limbs refused to obey.

A deep abyss pulled her into its darkness.

❧❦

Cara fought the hands holding her still. "No-o-o."

"You're all right. Lie still, miss—"

It wasn't all right. Nothing would ever be right again.

The person spoke in a clipped voice to someone else. "He was strangling her."

"Let me talk to her." Someone squatted in front of Cara and took her hand. "Mrs. Hayman, we have Elder Simmons in custody. Can you talk? Can you tell me why he tried to kill you?"

She didn't want to talk about it, especially to these two men, kind though they sounded. Dayne was the only one who'd understand. Why were they wasting time here on her when Dayne was dead?

"Dayne—" she flicked open her eyes and tried to whisper, but her words were a croak.

"What did she say?" the one standing asked.

The squatting figure shrugged. "Here comes the EMS."

Minutes later, the EMS personnel loaded her onto a stretcher. The spot where Dayne had lain drew her attention like a magnet. A sob tore from her sore throat at the sight of the blood smeared on the porch. She squeezed her eyes shut. So much blood. How could anyone live after losing that much? The world whirled faster.

The loud voices penetrated her grief, and Cara slowly opened her eyes.

Elder Simmons, hands behind his back, was being led away, two deputies on either side of him. He twisted his head, and his gray eyes radiated a message. *I'm not done yet.*

A shiver coursed its way through her body and iced every inch. He'd won, and even the sight of him in handcuffs didn't give her any satisfaction.

Not when the thought of Dayne dead suffocated all other emotions from her.

CHAPTER THIRTY-ONE

Six months later

The courtroom was a hive of activity.

Cara sat beside her suave, handsome lawyer and twisted her fingers together. She drew in a deep breath, trying to calm her nervousness.

Mr. Bates lowered his voice and whispered from behind his hand. "Don't worry. It'll come out all right. The judge wouldn't dare go against public sentiment."

Wouldn't he? Cara eyed the august figure seated in the front of the room.

The judge had not smiled, not once. Not when dozens of people testified for her. Not when he and Attorney Bates exchanged jokes. If she wasn't mistaken, she'd caught a frown or two from the man. She was sure he didn't approve of her.

But she didn't blame him. She wasn't too fond of herself either.

She heard Jodie clear her throat behind her and smiled. Her friends had supported her even after hearing her case, and attended every day. So where were they today? Her day of judgment?

She cast a quick glance behind her. No one but Jodie. Cara tried to squash the disappointment threatening to engulf her.

Surely Dayne could have come. Today of all days. His recovery—instead of his death as she'd supposed that awful night—had been a miracle.

I'll see you in prison.

Even behind prison bars, Elder Simmons had done his best to destroy her. Being charged for the negligent deaths of Kenny and Emery was the ultimate slap of hate. One that had given her a miserable six months.

Now, today, it was almost over. Whether the head elder won this last battle was about to be seen.

So where was Dayne? His support through this had been one of the best things in her life.

"Mrs. Hayman."

Cara froze as the judge spoke, and Attorney Bates took her arm. He practically dragged her from her seat.

"Stiffen those knees," he whispered, then he straightened his tie as he directed his attention toward the judge, who peered at them from over his glasses.

"Mrs. Hayman, I hope you appreciate the support you've been shown." The judge's mouth drew down even lower. "I've taken five days to deliberate, and I must say, I'm not inclined to be lenient."

Her fingers gripped the table in front of her, and she swallowed. Her stomach rumbled, and Cara wanted to wrap her arms around the offending part of her body. If she didn't get out of here soon, she was sure she'd spray vomit all over the austere judge's courtroom.

He pierced her with a look as if daring her to do it. "I've heard testimonies from numerous people appearing on your behalf and read written submissions from others supporting you. I've heard expert witness from Dr. Professor Moore. After spending some time reviewing these testimonies and submissions, and taking into account the unique circumstances of the specific facts of your case, I've made my decision. Along with the months of jail time you've already served, I'm sentencing you to two hundred hours of community service."

The judge picked up some papers and shuffled them before his dark gaze fastened on her again.

"Because of the undue stress in the circumstances you've been under and the recommendations on your behalf, I'm deviating from the normal sentencing guidelines issued by the state commission on sentencing. Do you understand what I'm saying, Mrs. Hayman?"

An elbow poked into her ribs.

The black-robed judge leaned forward and stared straight at her.

Cara nodded. "Yes, your honor. Thank you."

Judge Williams reached for his gavel and pounded it once. Attorney Bates took her arm and led Cara out of the courtroom.

She sank onto the bench across the hallway and closed her eyes. It was over. Papers still needed to be filled out, and plans needed to be completed. But she was free. Free. Elder Simmons was in jail, awaiting trial. Some of his cohorts had escaped capture, but many of his top men were sitting behind bars. With her testimony, and those of the members who'd agreed, the district attorney promised her she had nothing to fear from Simmons for a long time. And the insurance agent assured her Donald's money would come to her. The fund would tide her and the girls over until she could get a job.

Her heart thumped with the anticipation. Dayne urged her to go back to school—and she might. But her first priority was the girls and their comfort. She'd work all hours to give them everything. Cassie had indicated her willingness to move into their home for a short time, and between them, one of them should always be available for the girls. She allowed herself a small smile.

"She looks pretty self-satisfied, doesn't she?"

The words sank in slowly. Her cheeks warmed. How could she sit here in a public place and daydream? A smiling Dayne and her attorney walked up to her.

At the teasing light in Dayne's eyes, the heat deepened in her cheeks. She smiled. "You caught me. I couldn't resist sitting here enjoying my thoughts."

"And a very pretty picture you make. Doesn't she?" Dayne stroked his chin as if making a decision.

Attorney Bates beamed at her. "I'll say."

Cara liked him from day one. He'd been friendly and understanding, flirty but business-like and capable when needed. Cara was sure his fluency swayed the court on her behalf. "Thank you, Mr. Bates."

He inclined his head. "My privilege. I've gained so much attention from this case, my name will be a household word. By the way, if you're interested in an office job, I'll have an opening in a month. Stop by and fill out an application."

"I have no training—"

"Hey, what are you trying to do? Take my best girl?" Dayne protested. "You're going to make us late."

Bates flapped a hand at Dayne and headed down the hallway. He tossed back his comment. "Go on with you. I know you've got—uh, things to take care of."

"What did you mean, make us late?" Cara asked.

Dayne helped her to her feet, tucked her hand on his arm, and strolled away. "We're supposed to meet some people in a few minutes."

"I wanted to take the girls out for ice cream."

"Cassie will bring them."

"Where?" Cara glanced at Dayne and was struck by the look on his face. He was hiding something from her. She tapped his arm. "What's going on?"

His frantic expression deepened. Desperately, he took her hand and led her behind one of the big pillars supporting the porch roof of the courthouse.

Dayne's obvious disturbance tugged at her heart. "What's the matter? It's not a big deal. If you want to meet some of the others, fine, as long as Leila and Lacy are there."

He held both her hands, and now, he lifted and kissed them. "Cara."

The one word sent her heart into a full marathon race. "What?"

"Will you—?" He loosed one hand, led her to his car, and helped her into the passenger seat.

"Come with me."

"I don't have much choice." Cara giggled. "What's going on?"

"You'll see." He shut the door and refused to say any more for several miles. At last he pulled over to the side of the road. He propped an arm along the back of the seat. "Remember what you said when Simmons shot me?"

If he kept bringing up these—uh, way-too-personal subjects, she *would* have a heart attack. Her heart began its thudding again as if it'd sneaked off into an African jungle. Why did he insist on bringing up words said in a moment of stress? "I was afraid you were dead."

"Your fear didn't make you say what you said." Dayne lifted a lock of her hair, sifted fingers through it, and let it drop back to her shoulder.

"I wasn't aware you could hear me." Cara held back the shiver at his touch.

"I heard every word."

She lowered her head. It wouldn't do for him to read what was written on her heart. He'd never said what she had spoken that night.

When she refused to answer, he squeezed her fingers and prompted. "Are you telling me they were untrue? You didn't mean it?"

"Yes. I mean, no, I'm not telling you anything."

"Say it."

She tried to turn away, but he wouldn't let her go.

"I want to hear you say those words again." His voice deepened into a husky murmur.

The glint in his gorgeous eyes was too intense. She couldn't hold out against its compelling demand. She eased her gaze away from his.

"Look at me."

"I'd rather not."

His voice softened to a seductive whisper. "What are you afraid of?"

She looked up. "I'm not afraid of anything." Her heart flip-flopped out of control.

"C-a-r-a."

His breathy, drawn-out voice was her undoing. How could she refuse what he wanted? Why should she when she wanted it with all her heart? Had never wanted anything more?

She drew in a long breath. "I—I—"

His lips, his tone, his words coaxed. "Tell me."

"I love you," she whispered.

His breath released. "Ah." He drew her close into his arms. Pressed her head against his chest. "Will you marry me?"

She pulled out of his arms. Was he serious? Another glance at his face assured her he'd never been more so.

"Will you? Right now?"

"Now?"

He drew her back against his chest. "They're all waiting at the park for us. Cassie has a dress for you, and the girls will be your attendants. They've been bursting with excitement, trying to keep it secret from you, and hoping you'd say yes."

"No wonder they were hyper this morning. I didn't have time to think about it, or I'd have suspected something was up."

"Nothing wrong, sweetheart." He kissed her gently. "Only the best thing in my life will happen if you say yes."

His kiss, his touch, his being filled her with love and warmth and security. Yet the old demon of doubt and fear nudged her, demanded acknowledgement. "I'm afraid, Dayne. What if …"

"What if what, dearest?" He lifted her hand again and twined his fingers with hers. "Not afraid of me, are you? I'd never do anything to hurt you."

"I know you wouldn't. It's—" She bit her lip. "What if I can't do it? I despised Donald. It did something to me, and I swore I'd never marry again. I do love you and want to be the kind of wife you need, but what if I can't? What if I'm not capable of loving someone with a long-lasting love?"

"Love can't be rated on how you perform. It's an emotion admitting the faults in the other person, but loving him or her so much they don't matter."

"You're not worried—"

"Not in the least. Now I might be getting a tad bit anxious about being late for our own wedding."

Was he trying to be funny? "Well, if you would have told me ahead of time."

"Your mind was full without adding to it."

"I'm a criminal. Won't my record bother you?" Worry tugged at her heart.

"Nope."

His one word lifted the world off her shoulders. Hadn't he proved his love when he'd stepped in front of her and taken a bullet? His manly gentleness had always been the main trait that attracted her to him.

And his looks. And the way he said her name, weakening her knees. She loved his hands and …

She shook her head. She couldn't name them all.

One of Dayne's brows lifted, and the tiniest of wrinkles appeared between them. "You're saying no?"

"No. I'm saying yes. Yes, Dayne. Yes. Yes. Yes." She laid her head on his shoulder as the unfamiliar emotion choked her. "If you're sure …"

Dayne started the engine again and headed into the park. "Good." He pointed at Cassie running toward them, Leila and Lacy following like a kite tail in their colorful dresses.

Cara grabbed his arm and stroked the spot on his chest where the bullet had gone in. "You haven't said you love me."

He swung open his door. "You know I do."

There was no more time. Cassie yanked open her door and pulled her from the vehicle. The girls each took a hand, and the three of them ushered her toward the stone building. Inside, Cassie helped her into a beautiful yet simple shimmering blue gown. Cassie twisted Cara's hair into curls at the top of her head, pinned silvery flowers into it, and thrust a huge bouquet of lilies and roses into her hands.

"Mommy, you're boo-tee-ful." With one finger, Lacy touched her arm. Cara hugged her and pulled Leila to her side. "Cassie, did you have to turn these two into beauties? They will be the beauties today, and everyone will forget I'm here."

They giggled and pressed against her, mussing the front of their frocks. She looked at Cassie over their heads. "Where did this stuff come from?"

Cassie knelt to retie the ribbon at Lacy's waist. "Dayne bought the flowers. I used my savings for your dress and the girls." She pointed a finger at Cara, her eyes twinkling. "You owe me. Again."

"What if I'd said no?"

A shrug lifted one shoulder. "The store has an excellent return policy." She adjusted the slender watch on her wrist. "Time to go."

At the doorway, Cassie stopped them and tilted her head. As the sweet, high tones of a flute filled the air with "Bridal Chorus," she thrust open the double doors and gave Leila a gentle nudge.

Cara stared at her preteen daughter as she walked slowly, carefully down the path to the decorated gazebo. One of the neighborhood ministers stood erect, waiting. How beautiful her daughter was in the pale sage dress, the pearl barrette Cara's mother had given her years ago, shining like a crown in her dark hair. What a wonderful future lay before her.

Lacy, her pale purple hair ribbons shimmering against her blonde hair, started down the path and smiled at everyone. Each petal dropped from her childish hand and floated to the ground in graceful motion. With her daughter five steps down the pathway, Cara spotted the tattered bunny dangling over one arm. Somehow Lacy had sneaked the stuffed animal into the wedding. But who cared? Cara's heart swelled with love for her girls.

The music danced into its triumphant crescendo, riding the air waves as if a billowy cloud, then gradually, softly melted into the ending.

In the silence, the strong, vibrant tones of a man's voice poured into the air, stirring her mind and cajoling a response from her.

Sabre hunkered on his rear feet at the gazebo beside Dayne. Like a best man, big white bow tie around his neck and a wide doggy grin on his long face, he looked every bit the regal animal he was. The image of a friendly dog caressing her tear-soaked cheek years ago eased from her memory. A dog and a boy. Her rescuers from an evil man bent on destroying a child who'd witnessed her mother's murder.

Dayne, tall and wonderful, sang the old, old song. From his heart to hers. His arms outstretched, and his voice soared as if he wanted the world to hear what he sang.

"I love you truly …"

She didn't need the small urging from Cassie. Her feet moved of their own accord, straight toward Dayne and his outstretched arms.

He sang, his voice drenched with pathos about a life of sorrow and tears. A life again filled with dreams her presence had brought.

His voice lured her closer, and if she hadn't been aware of all their smiling friends, she would have forgotten all about any kind of decorum and run to those welcoming arms.

"I love you truly …"

Her heart thumped in time to his singing.

The long years of sorrow and doubt and fear were gone because of a love that had survived years—lying dormant—waiting for this time.

He captured her hands and drew her close for a kiss. Before she closed her eyes, she saw Leila's wide grin and Lacy's small form jumping up and down. Sabre's long nose pointed upward, his doggy mouth opened, and howls blended with Lacy's shrieks.

She paid close attention to the minister as he coached them on their vows. Her voice was low and shook as she repeated them. Wonder filled her at the solemnity of the moment, the awesomeness of Dayne and her girls and her friends' love today a wonderful feeling. Dayne's voice rang with truth as he stared deep into her eyes, the love in them shining straight to her heart while he repeated their vows.

The minister pronounced them man and wife, and everyone gathered around the gazebo to reach for one of the many balloons floating above the roof. Dayne untied the biggest one and gently placed it into her hands.

"This is for Lori."

He'd not forgotten her oldest daughter. Tears pricked at her lids as she stroked the helium-filled pink balloon, white ribbons streaming from it. Pink, Lori's favorite color. Cara lifted her hand. Her eyes closed as she whispered, "I'll always love you, Lori, my daughter. Always."

With shaking fingers, she let it go. The balloon soared toward heaven. In perfect timing, dozens of other balloons, released by eager hands, followed Lori's balloon. They drifted upward, higher and still higher, right between the canopy of trees until becoming a speck in the blue sky.

Dayne placed another balloon in her hand, and his clasped hers. It was a blue and silver one, decorated with their names and the words, 'Just married.'

When they unclasped their hands in unison, Cara caught a glimpse of the small printed words at the very bottom of the balloon. "And so we begin a new life together … in Christ."

An idea expanded within her mind. That's why Dayne acted the way he did, why Levi and Jodie, Mary Ann and Josh, Abby, and even Richard, and the others, were drawn to Dayne and his words and ministry. It wasn't Dayne. It was God through Dayne.

We're all sinners, Cara. We all have to be forgiven … His words from months ago rang strong and true in her heart. For one minute, Cara wanted to clutch at the octopus-like emotions that had driven her so long, and then consciously, mentally—willingly—she unleashed her grip. The hurt and lust for revenge dissipated, and like the balloons flying above their heads, disappeared.

Cara leaned into her husband and stared at him in awe. Her perfect husband needed to be forgiven, had been forgiven. Could she be?

The gasps of ahs drew her attention back to their released balloon. The sun caught the silver on the simple balloon and morphed it into a blazing star. For a long moment, it shone in the air, a testament of their love. With a sudden explosion, the balloon disappeared.

For the first time she could ever remember, a faith bloomed inside her.

God *was* here, and he loved her.

The End.

Made in the USA
Lexington, KY
21 October 2013